The BLUE CORD

a semi-autobiographical novel

Laurel Duran

DuirSoul Books

Santa Fe, New Mexico

The BLUE CORD

a semi-autobiographical novel

by Laurel Duran

Published by:
DuirSoul Books
Post Office Box 22596
Santa Fe, NM 87502-2596 U.S.A.

Copyright © 1995 by Laurel Duran
Writers' Guild West reg. #: 591855
10 9 8 7 6 5 4 3 2 1
Printed in the United States of America

Duran, Laurel.
  The blue cord; a semi-autobiographical novel / Laurel Duran
--1st ed.--Santa Fe, NM : DuirSoul Books, 1995.
      p.   cm.

ISBN   0-9646909-0-X

   1. Spine -- Wounds and injuries -- Rehabilitation -- Fiction.
   2. Near-death experience -- fiction.   3. Life change
   events -- Fiction. I. Title.

813.54 - dc20

The quote on page iv is from Volume 1, page 338, of A Course in Miracles, Copyright © 1975, Reprinted by permission of the Foundation for Inner Peace, Inc. PO Box 598, Mill Valley, CA. 94942.
      "A Prayer To The Mother Earth" on page 17, Copyright © 1995 by Catherine H. McNeil.

Library of Congress card number 95-92113

Acknowledgments

I wish to express my deepest gratitude to the medical and therapeutic touch healers who helped me during the most difficult time of my life.

My family's unerring support during my recovery years carried me through. Ma, Ricky, Dian, Ken, Matt, Les, Anne, Campbell, and Nene, I love you. Thank you, Dee, for selflessly lending me your healing spirit when I most needed it.

The following souls lent priceless moral support and editorial input, and "held the form" during The BLUE CORD's gestation years: Melinda Arnold, Daulat Dipshan Aurnash, JoAnn Baldinger, Bruce and Deborah Barton, Sally Fisher, Constanze Frank, Renie Haiduk, Michael Hall, Kathleen Hurley and Theodore Dobson, Patrick McNamara, Cathy McNeil, Maisie, Vance Masci, Mary Beth Peters, Dan Poynter, Dorsey Ray, Kenneth Ring, Richard Stang, John Thorndike, and friends of Bill W. worldwide. Thank you all for helping me give birth to The BLUE CORD.

To doctor Bernie Siegel, special appreciation for holding my hand in 1987 and literally passing your courageous strength directly to me as 400 of us sang "Amazing Grace." Along with Robert O. Becker and Gary Selden, Barbara Ann Brennan, Deepak Chopra, Clarissa Pinkola Estes, Louise Hay, Nelson Mandela, and Oprah Winfrey, you continue to encourage me to keep the windows of my soul open.

Thank you, dear reader, for investing your energy in The BLUE CORD.

Copy editing: Jo Ann Baldinger
Typography: Marcie Pottern
Cover design: Laurel Duran and Anne Farrell
Cover photos:
    Laurel in halo: Dawn E. Evans
    Laurel jumping: Renie Haiduk of Santa Fe, and Anne Farrell

For my mother, Mary Baldauf,

whose limitless love has been my rock of Gibraltar.

If you bring forth what is within you, what you bring forth will save you.

If you do not bring forth what is within you, what you do not bring forth will destroy you.

- Jesus, The Gnostic Bible

Your task is not to seek for love, but merely to seek and find all of the barriers within yourself that you have built against it.

Heaven waits silently, and your creations are holding out their hands to help you cross and welcome them. For it is they you seek.

- A Course in Miracles

The kingdom of heaven is within you.

- Jesus, The King James Bible

- 1 -

August 18, 1994

Soft golden light filtered through the tall grass surrounding Cedar Pond where twelve firemen, good and true, practiced underwater rescue. Steam arose from warm bodies sealed in scuba skins as they re-entered the earth's atmosphere from the deep. Thick summer morning air was already crossing the cool-to-hot-and-humid threshhold familiar to these Massachusetts men of many generations. Some already stood on shore, arms crossed, quietly awaiting their turn to step up in the "awards" procession.

"Thank you for saving my life." Mora's clear petal voice rang out like a magic carpet set with gifts. She offered each man a handshake and a homemade cookie, allowing her green-brown eyes to rest in theirs as her tears fell. The men's eyes opened wider as they absorbed the sight of her standing strong and tall before them with feet planted firmly on the ground. Her long dark hair and pink and white checked dress blew full in a sudden gust like flags waving her declaration of independence.

"Not many people ever come back to tell us how they are. In fact, this is the first time I've ever seen anyone hurt as bad as you make such a miraculous recovery and come back to show us we did some good!" The man facing Mora spoke earnestly while the others nodded in agreement.

"It really means a lot to us to see you like this, Miss Donovan," said another fireman. He released his crossed arms to wipe his eyes, quickly shifted his weight, and returned to the safety of folded arms. His words brought forth another volley of agreement.

"I wanted you to see for yourselves that your work is needed in this world," Mora said. "If it weren't for the care you took moving me out there on the highway four years ago" - Mora raised her arm and pointed toward the road visible in the distance - "I wouldn't be able to help other people with massage therapy today. I wanted to give you a gift from my heart and hands. That's why I made the cookies. There's a lot of gratitude and love baked into them." Mora let the empty cookie bag fall to the ground. "And I wouldn't be able to do this." Carefully she rolled her head around in an imperfect 360 degree circle. Then, raising her arms skyward, she sang out "Look! I'm free!"

The men's applause sent joyful energy pulsing up and down Mora's spine. Through her tears she saw the cord of bright blue light encased in gold descend from above, encircling and rejoining them with the heavens.

Many people believe that we're all connected in some way, that there are no accidents or coincidences. Some say that each soul lives many different bodily cycles or lifetimes, and that any relationships left incomplete or unforgiven in one lifetime are destined for completion in a lifetime to follow.

Some say there is an energy field known to connect souls together the instant they have forgiven their shared pasts.

If you've ever experienced it, you know. If you haven't yet, you will. Someday, and probably many times over, you will know the greatest joy a human being can experience in this world is to be hooked up to The BLUE CORD.

This is the story of one woman's path to forgiveness.

August 17, 1990

Mora paced her office over and over, checking the clock at each cycle. With every other stride she released a hot exhalation. Finally she decided to leave. She walked out into the hallway and plastered a big smile across her mouth before passing through the aerobics class. It was crowded with students she knew.

"Hi, Mora," came from a few women in between panting breaths.

"Hey Judy, don't forget to breathe," Mora answered lightly and quickly exited the building. Once in the parking lot she let the plastic smile slide off her face. She got into her car quickly, rolled down the windows, and sped away. "Oh God, I feel like shit!" she shouted. "What am I going to do?"

She drove through the town and into the next one, gripping and wringing the steering wheel. "Sixty fucking days! Just sixty fucking days without alcohol! How am I going to do this, God? Is this what life is now?" she shouted and burst into tears. The shrillness of her own voice tasted like vinegar and bad air.

Mora pulled up to the light at Cross Junction in Duffin. Other open-windowed traffic gathered around as she forced tears back behind a flat face. Her eyes landed on the 300-year-old granite road marker and she read the inscription aloud: "Boston 100 miles East. Whitelaw 15 miles West."

*   *   *

Mora sat waiting, fidgeting with her purse. One by one people filed in and took seats in the circle. The only chairs in the fluorescent lit, basement Sunday School classroom were multi-colored plastic, fit for second graders' bodies.

Anticipating the evening meeting was what she hung on to all day. Here she was safe for at least an hour, or longer if she stayed to talk. It was terrifying to imagine another night alone. Now, every night she was alone. The thought brought more tears to her swollen eyes. She held them back and they burned her contracted throat. *I wish I could scream.*

With every sober day and night that had somehow piled up for 60 days, Mora's failing soul bled deeper. She had found this lifesaver, these meetings, the day after she had drunk a fifth of Scotch and puked herself past dry heaves. She'd stood looking at a strange woman's worn, puffy, prematurely aged face in the bathroom mirror. "Who are you?" she asked the face. "Whoever you are, you're not who I started out to be."

That was the night, the final stop on the ride to living hell. She went to the phone just as the sun came up and dialed the only truth-telling friend she knew. "I'm an alcoholic and I can't stop drinking," she confessed.

"There are meetings," her friend said. "Go to a meeting and get help from other alcoholics."

So she did. All she had to handle now was life.

*   *   *

Every Monday night Mora came to this basement room, and others like it on other nights. By now she knew she could let the crisp seams of control begin to fall open as soon as she heard the beginning words.

"I'd like to start the meeting now. I'm May and I'm an alco-holic." Mora collapsed her mind into the long-awaited phrase and let out a heavy sigh. At her first meeting she had been drawn to May, the bright-eyed woman dressed in white who seemed to rest on a cloud of peace. Mora had found a safe haven in the empty chair beside her unknowing guardian angel. The older woman's sincere kindness temporarily pasted up a space in Mora's hollow insides.

"God, grant me the serenity to accept the things I cannot change, the courage to change the things I can, and the wisdom to know the difference." Everyone in the room said the words except Mora, who couldn't remember them. She listened, trying desperately to be fixed by their meaning.

"Does anyone have an urgent need to speak, or to suggest a

topic for discussion tonight?" May put forth the question.

"May I speak?" Mora asked.

"Yes Mora, go ahead." May nodded gently.

When Mora recognized a space had been made for her, the dam of tears broke. "I can't hold on any longer. My life is pure hell." Although it was difficult to continue without sobbing, she needed them to know, so she pushed on. "Today I sat in my office, in an empty building, and I just screamed. It came out so loud it hurt my ears. I hate my life!" She dropped her head and tried to hide her hot, puffy, red face in her hands. "I hate myself." The room was absolutely still and silent except for her sobs. "My husband doesn't want me any more. The divorce will be legal in a few days. The only thing we agree on is that it's all my fault."

If Mora had looked up she would have seen the compassionate faces trying to help her lay down her burdens. But she could barely swim through the waves of emotion to get to solid ground.

"I feel like a total failure. I own a health club with 22 employees. There isn't any money for me to pay myself and I don't have enough to meet the payroll next week. My husband was supporting me." She laughed bitterly. "Isn't *that* wonderful. A drunk health club owner breathing Scotch fumes over aerobics students!" Again she sobbed. "I've piled so many burdens on myself to try and fill in this empty, raw, pained place deep inside. It's as if all my life I've begged the world to love me back, but it's useless. I've tried everything. I don't know where to turn. I've worked 60 hours a week for years to get away from home and I *still* can't make any money. I try and try, I give everything I have, but I just can't do it anymore!" She covered her face with her hands. "I'm dying inside." Finally the words were out.

"I'm Jack and I'm an alcoholic." A man's voice called through Mora's veil.

"Hi, Jack," everyone answered. He spoke directly to her.

"Mora, I'm real glad you're here tonight. I've been sober a while now and sometimes I forget how bad it was in the beginning. But honey, I've got to tell you, if you look around the room right now you'll see that I'm not the only one who's been exactly where you've been, to hell and back. And we feel for you. Believe me, we do."

Mora looked around the room and saw that he was right. Some faces were sad, some eyes were filled with tears, some people nodded, but each one radiated compassion. If there was one thing she recognized, it was compassion.

"Maybe your higher power is throwing you a rope right now and saying 'Here. Tie a knot and hang on, no matter what. Trust Me. I'm with you always,'" Jack continued. "I'd stake my life on one thing right now and it's this: if you keep coming, if you keep asking God or whoever your higher power is to help you when you feel desperate about anything, I guarantee He will come to your aid. He'll help you no matter what and your life will get better. Just don't give up on yourself, okay?"

Mora lifted her head and looked directly at him. "Okay." She wiped her face with her sleeve. "I'll try. Thanks for letting me say all this." She looked at all the kind faces in the room. "If it weren't for all of you I really would be alone."

The rest of the meeting evolved into a moral support session for Mora. It was odd, she thought, that in her life's darkest time she, the big giver of support, was receiving such support. Rather, they were offering it. Letting it pass through the walls around her heart was still difficult. She was amazed that exposing her deeply hidden secret brought relief rather than punishment. One truth exposed led to another. Many of these people came from divorces, financial ruin, legal troubles and much worse. Yet they had lived to tell of it. They'd say "You remind me of myself and when I reach out to help you, it helps me too." Those who were long-time sober were clearly calmer, laughed at little things, and easily offered kindness to others. So Mora did what they told her to do. She stopped fighting. She surrendered.

After the meeting, a woman named Margaret handed her a business card. "Call me if you get into trouble," she said, turning to leave.

Panicked, Mora reached out to touch Margaret's arm. "I don't have a sponsor yet. Would you be my sponsor?"

"Well, I can be a temporary sponsor, until you find someone permanent. I have a few other women I'm sponsoring. But sure."

Margaret nodded as if convincing herself she could handle another newcomer. "I'll help you out for the time being."

Mora said "I'm afraid to be alone with myself. What if I can't sleep?" Again she touched Margaret's sleeve but this time her frightened fingers closed ever so lightly around the older woman's arm.

"Then get down on your knees." Margaret's response was instant. "Wherever you are, whatever you're doing or trying to get done, if desperation hits you, get down on your knees. It's the surrender position." She flashed a smile. "Then call on your higher power, God, if that's who or what your higher power is, and ask for help. Expect help. It will come. Just ask, then let go. " Margaret looked toward the door. "I've got to go now. You'll be all right. But call me if you need help. Just don't drink — and get to a meeting tomorrow, okay?" Smiling, she turned and left.

Mora slowly walked out into the humid August darkness. "All I need to do is walk over to my car, get in, drive home, put on my nightgown, talk to God and go to bed. I think I can do it." She whispered her plan of immediate action to an empty parking lot. "Okay," she said as she fumbled through her purse for keys, "I'm getting into my car now." She'd heard at a meeting that if you're alone and you tell yourself what it is you are doing right at a desperate moment, it helps you get through it. "I'm sitting in my car and now I'm going to start my car." She turned the key, started the car and put it into first gear. With each passing second of words spoken outloud, her terror subsided. She headed for home.

Images arose on Mora's mind screen as she drove through the quiet town. She imagined herself in her old living room with Carl. The clear mental pictures drew perspiration from flesh that had suddenly grown hot. They wouldn't dissolve. Her grip on the steering wheel tightened as sweat slid between it and her hands. Sitting face to face with her ex-husband to offer amends was a prospect she did not relish. But the need to make amends had clearly surfaced. As the feeling in her gut grew stronger, the pictures took on a bitter flavor of urgency. "I have to go and apologize now," she declared. "Something could happen to me and I'd always regret it if I never apologized face to face." The endless sorrowful tears began to flow once more as she headed for Carl's house.

She pulled into the edge of his driveway and prayed he hadn't heard her car. Trembling, she sat and stared through the lighted living room window. He was home alone. "God, please do this for me. Please put truthful words in my mouth, help me keep a clean apology. I can't do this alone," Mora heard herself say. "I have to do this now because I could die tomorrow for all I know. I have to tell him before it's too late that I'm truly sorry for the damage I did." She fought back tears. "Don't let me trip on myself, God. Help me change what I can and give up the rest." It was the best she could do to mimic the Serenity Prayer. Taking a deep breath she got out of the car, walked quickly to the screened front door, and rang the bell.

Carl came to the door. When he saw her, he stepped back. "Yeah?" he demanded.

"Hi, Carl. I hope I'm not disturbing you too much but may I talk to you for just a minute? I have something really important to tell you." Mora's forehead fell into its familiar, doubtful, double fold as she awaited his reply.

Carl curled up and turned down one corner of his mouth. "Yeah, I guess so." He opened the screen door.

Mora entered quickly and sat down on the couch. She looked up hopefully at Carl who stood several feet away with arms folded on his chest.

"Can you sit down, too? I mean, so I can tell you face to face?" she asked, her hands clasped tightly on her lap.

"I guess so." Carl shrugged and sat down across from her. Slumping into the thick couch, he maintained his crossed-arm shield. "Okay, what do you have to tell me?"

She recognized his anger but willed herself to speak no matter how he responded. Fidgeting with her cold hands one last time, she held them together tightly for warmth, took a deep breath and let her shoulders drop into neutral on the exhale. "Carl, I quit drinking two months ago. I'm an alcoholic." She leaned foreward. "Did you know that about me?"

"No." he replied without expression.

"I've been going to meetings for recovering alcoholics, and part of what you do is make amends for the trouble you caused while you were drinking. . . while I was drinking. So that's why I came over now." Mora's voice began to waver. She lifted her head higher, stretching out her throat in an effort to get the words out. "I've started to see how much of my behavior during our marriage was affected by my drinking. So many memories of being drunk and miserable have been coming back to me." Her voice cracked. "I want to tell you I'm sorry. For all the bad things I did to you, how angry and impatient I was with you when I was drunk, for the affair. I was so desperate for your love and I tried to force you into noticing me. It was the worst thing I could have done." Her throat stung, wanting to burst and release the well of sorrowful shame stored within. "I've been feeling this deep, old pain coming up from inside me now that the booze is gone. It feels like I'm 15 all over again, only worse. As if I have no choice but to pick up the pain where I left it when my father went away. I know that an apology isn't going to fix anything but. . ."

"True," Carl interrupted.

"But I *am* very sorry." She could no longer hold back tears and said her words through them anyway. "I was driving home from a meeting tonight and something inside told me I had to apologize before it was too late. That's why I came here now." Dropping her head and covering her face in her hands, Mora let herself cry for just a moment. Then she raised her head and seized control of her voice. "I don't expect you to forgive me now, but. . ."

"That's good," Carl interrupted again, barely disguising his anger.

"But I just had to tell you I'm sorry. That's all." Mora absently wiped her wet face on a sleeve. She vacillated between looking down at her hands and up at Carl with undying hope. When she lasered through the veil of his glasses, searching for him as she had done for seven years, she finally recognized that he was already gone. This time she accepted it and let go.

"Do you want me to know anything, Carl?"

"Nope. It's all been said." He stayed steady as a stone.

"Okay." Mora nodded. "Then I guess I'll go now." She rose slowly from the couch and walked toward the door, then turned to face him. "I hope your future is happy, Carl," she said quietly, looking directly into his blue eyes. "And I'll always love you. Goodbye."

The last word barely left enough breath for her to hold back an explosion of collected grief as she ran out into the dismal darkness. Once in her car, the wail flew out her throat and propelled her flight forward into the night.

Inside the house, Carl heard her cry. He remained motionless long after she drove away. Only when he was sure he was alone did he allow the veil before his eyes to drop safely, where no one could see.

*   *   *

Mora's thoughts were focused on surviving the flood of now. Instinctively, she drove to a secluded spot in the woods where she could let herself go. She'd never make it home otherwise. Pulling over she got out and fell to the ground in a heap, broken open at the heart.

"Oh God! Please help me!" she cried. She lay curled in a fetal position and cried until the waves subsided, until sorrow was mostly gone out, and only a stream trickled. Then she drove home.

In a protective cloud of numbness Mora climbed the stairs to her tiny apartment where Frankie, her female cat, was waiting. "Hi pussa." Leaning over she lifted Frankie and drew the purring soft body to her face. "You love me, don't you?" she asked. Her request for love from her only companion in the world brought forth more tears. Frankie struggled to get free. "I guess I have to let you go, too," Mora said.

She got ready for bed. Just before climbing in, she knelt on the floor and bowed her head. "God, please help me live through this." She cried the night's final tears and imagined them rising up on a plate toward heaven, to God. "Thank you for keeping me sober today. Please help me sleep in peace. Give me the courage to live."

After a few moments of quiet Mora turned off the light and climbed into bed. And in the still, indigo darkness the gentle sound of copper windchimes sprinkled their song outside her bedroom window, lulling her into deep sleep.

- 2 -

Dreaming. . .

Traveling. . .

her spirit moves fast and weightless over land. . . dreaming. All is the color of midnight ocean. . . deep indigo blue. . . .

It's past sundown and the windows of the packed church in Salem, Massachusetts are brightly lit from within. She flies in from the top, through the steeple, but nobody can see her. She knows all that is happening, what each one is thinking and feeling.

The congregation is holding meeting and everyone is upset, anxious, angry. The air is thick with fear. Standing at the front of the church facing the congregation are two women, a man and the minister. The minister seems to be the magnet, sucking in everyone's attention and intensifying their fear. He steps up to the pulpit and rings a bell loud and strong. Accustomed to wearing angry accusation, his face slips into deep, familiar lines. He relishes the role.

"Silence brethren! Silence!" he bellows, barely masking contempt. "We may no longer delay! As we gather now, the heathen women bring the devil's evil curse upon our good Colony!" He pauses purposefully, planning every sound and silence to evoke emotion from the congregation. Then, turning toward the three seated behind him, and with a smooth, calculated wave of his arm, he says "Sister Josephine, we call upon thee now to reveal thy witnessing of Abigail Fenn and Hortense Coopersmith's sacrilegous deeds!"

The congregation hushes as the middle-aged woman approaches the pulpit. She is severe and controlled, her steely cold eyes issuing foreboding strength. Taller, broader, and more sturdily built than most women, she is not to be taken lightly. Before she begins speaking, she raises her head slightly above eye level with the congregation. Looking down her long bony nose she spits out her words like venom, "I have seen them!" Then, lowering her voice to an ominous hiss she continues: "They knew not I gazed upon their vicious doings, but as I stand before God, the eternal witness unto truth. . ." She raises both arms heavenward. "I have laid witness to their demon rituals and false idol worship, and I stand to tell thee of it!"

A booming thunderclap suddenly shakes the church, electrifying the crowd. Better emphasis could not have been planned by mortal minds united for attack. Just as the eyes of sister Josephine and the minister lock and flash agreement, a hard rain begins to fall on the roof. The congregation is suddenly abuzz.

"It is the word of God speaking to us!" says a wild-eyed man now standing at his seat, facing the congregation. Fearful energy gains momentum among the people as they nod and mutter their agreement. The minister rings his bell again. He shouts above the voices, the rain, and thunder.

"Silence! Silence!" He waits for them to return control to him. "Sister Josephine, pray, tell us precisely what thou hast borne witness to."

"Good brothers and sisters of our Lord God and Savior," sister Josephine begins, "what I have to tell thee may burn your ears so accustomed to sounds of a righteous and holy life, but I must tell thee the truth of what mine ears heard and mine eyes gazed upon, else be burned in eternal damnation for withholding witness." She pauses and takes a deep breath.

"On the eve of Thursday last, from behind the part-opened window of the Robertson hearth, on Bradbury road, I witnessed Abigail Fenn lay her hands tainted with the devil's poison upon the crippled leg of the Robertson boy. A boy whom God rightfully saw fit to punish for the misdeeds of his soul. It was God who deemed the will to walk be taken from the boy. And she, the devil woman, spake evil words, made motion to evil things over his leg and alongside of Hortense Coopersmith they each closed their eyes shut, spake their devil words, and," she gasps deeply before continuing, "as God is my witness, I say to thee, the boy arose from his bed and walked straightaway!"

The crowd roars suddenly in response and the sound swells up into the ceiling rafters. "It's the devil I tell ye!" shouts sister Josephine. "I witnessed it by my own God given sight!"

"Burn the witches, I say!" shouts a man. "Ayes" echo loudly throughout the sea of vigorously nodding heads.

As if now satisfied with an assumed-guilty-and-executed verdict, the minister half-heartedly states, "We must submit action to a trial. It is the law of the land, however clear and true the evidence against the witches." He has resumed his position at the pulpit.

The spirit hovering above senses a strong source of disagreement in the midst of the congregation. There is a single person in panic who emanates an urgent need to leave. The spirit then sees the face of a man utterly lost in distress, with his wife beside him looking to him with equal worry. His urgency is not caused by fear for his own safety but for that of another. He wants to move quickly toward something, someone outside.

"Brother Fenn," says the minister, as if he also has become aware of the man's urge to leave. "We the good congregation of Salem church recognize that the woman Abigail was made thy sister by God. But surely we have proved beyond any doubt, that thine own flesh and blood has laid waste her soul as the devil's handmaid! Surely thou would not deny the voice of thine only God who speaks through the pious voices of thy brethren herein gathered. Surely not!" He smiles righteously as he sweeps a raised hand across the congregation. Contempt-filled faces are turned toward the man named Brother Fenn.

"Tribunal, what say thee now?" The minister asks as he turns to face the three behind him. Sister Josephine glances toward the man and woman seated beside her. Silver-haired, bespectacled elder Thomas and his wife nod their agreement. The minister quickly turns back to the congregation. "And what sayst thou, good people of Salem congregation? In the name of our Lord God I seek thy wise guidance: shall we dispatch our appointed deputies, twelve men good and true, to seek, find and retrieve this night, the women named Abigail Fenn and Hortense Coopersmith? Those representing agreement signify now by speaking 'aye'!"

A great din of "ayes" blasts the air at the same moment brother Fenn and his wife quickly stand and exit. A shiver of foreboding cold runs through the hovering spirit.

In a much quieter, smug voice the minister says "Anyone opposed to the good people's decision, represent thy opposition now by speaking 'nay'." Silence descends upon the crowd as many turn to see the two empty chairs.

"May God's will be done!" bellows the minister.

Doom's voice, having sounded below, gathers heat and rises up into the ceiling, shaking the rafters. Quickly goes the spirit, brushed up and out into the night. Howling wind replaces the death knell voice as the spirit moves faster and faster, through silver-lined crisp-cold clouds, over farms and fields, crossing the face of a bright white full moon.

The sound of women's voices, chanting soft and graceful, reaches the spirit's awareness as she draws closer and closer.

A circle of twelve women moves slowly clockwise. They chant together gently, sweetly, silver moonlight guiding their steps.

"Neesa, Neesa, Neesa
Neesa, Neesa, Neesa,
Neesa, Neesa, Neesa.
Gaiweo. Gaiweo."

It is a chant of Native American origin, sung to the full moon they call grandmother. They are women of many shades of skin, some elders, one or two in their teens sprinkled among most who are full-blossomed women. The spirit discerns a shared intention of benevolence.

A young woman in the center stirs the brew in a large cauldron over flame. Deeply aromatic steam arises from the pot and permeates the brisk autumn air, quickly evaporating. The aroma touches a distant but always known memory of the hovering spirit: she recognizes its meaning as benevolent. Without any noticeable cue, the women cease chanting and their forward procession halts easily with one unified step. They turn to face the center of their circle. The cauldron keeper, a 16-year-old named Rene, has creamy brown skin and long, thick, dark hair crowned with a wildflower wreath. She shows the strength of her smooth, firm arm muscles as she stirs. Her voice cuts the silence with conviction. "Nettle, Burdock, Blessed Thistle, Hops, Mistletoe and Comfrey. Thy unified spirit reaches within us to heal and strengthen our vessels. We thank thee now for thy gracious gifts."

All thirteen women respond in unison: "Blessed be."

The twelve women resume their movement, this time circling counter-clockwise. One by one each steps forward to the cauldron, takes the ladle from Rene, inhales the steam deeply and slowly sips. When Rene is the last to partake, they all stand quietly in place. Then, again without any discernable signal, they sit upon the ground and each woman places her hands together for prayer, fingertips heavenward.

The one named Hortense, or Hattie, occupies a position of guidance among them. Her good and fair counsel is respected, yet she holds no air of superiority. Hattie opens her hands, palms facing up, and says, "We offer our intentions of benevolence forth into this sacred surround unto thee, Great Spirit of Earth, our Mother. We seek thy most olden wisdom to guide our earthly functions, our visions, our hands' work, our thinkings, and our hearts that only greatest good may be served for all."

"Blessed Be," respond the thirteen.

Next, Abigail, a strong, dark-haired, dark-eyed, young woman, opens her hands palms up and says: "Spirit of Mother, upon whose lap we rest our bodies now, thy humble servant asks thy assistance in these and all ways: My brother asks thy light to guide his leadership in our troubled colony. The force opposing his every turn becomes too great this day for him to bear alone. With no importance to what may befall me, we ask thy especial guidance over him for greater good. For the woman Ruth upon whose person I lay these hands, we ask thee to send benevolent light upon her hard-breathing chest. I ask thy blessing upon these herbs," (she turns to retrieve herbs from the ground beside her and continues) "black cohosh and blue cohosh to mend her broken-hearted loss of child from within. We graciously thank thee for thy healing work upon the leg of Adam Robertson, returning the walking will to his young body. I seek thy eternal guidance in my hands' work and upon all my days that remain."

"Blessed Be," respond the thirteen women.

A woman seated beside Abigail recites an ancient Druid prayer in Gaelic:

"Go bhfaighimid neart an cruthu o brollach ar mhathair
thorthuil agus go mbeimid cosuil leis an cailis
an soitheach a d'iomparodh cumhacht do gra cneasu."

English translation:
"May we draw from the bosom of our fruitful Mother,
the life force of creation, that we may be as the chalice,
a vessel to carry the power of thy healing love."

"Blessed Be," respond the thirteen women.
 A dark-skinned woman sitting beside Abigail begins to speak: "Mamon, to way we know, take dese hons ta bring fore de babe. . ." She is interrupted by the pounding vibration of horses' hooves in the ground beneath them. Startled, the women look around at each other. Suddenly a strong cold wind blows up Salisbury Plain and extinguishes the cauldron fire. As the hooves grow louder, the women turn in the direction of the man approaching on horseback. He leads two riderless steeds behind him. Ezekiel Fenn dismounts before bringing his horse to a full stop, then runs toward the women now standing close together.
 "Abby, Hattie, they come for thee! The tribunal has issued call for the posse comitatus to come for thee now. I bring you horses. Thee must both make haste toward the Berkshires. Sister Deborah MacWain of Whitelaw shall keep thee safe the days and nights required, but thee must make haste!"
 Rene makes her way quickly through the women and wraps her arms around Abby pleading: "Mama, Mama, please! Take me with thee!" She sobs and holds her mother's body tightly, burying her face in her mother's soft chest. Abby embraces her daughter and for the last time inhales the bittersweet fragrant marking of hair and wildflowers, engraving it forever upon her memory. When Rene's sobbing subsides Abby gently holds her daughter at arms' length and says: "Child, I shall always be with thee. My love goes with thee wherever thou goest. Know this for all time." Rene cries and embraces her mother once again, but only for a moment. Then she drops her arms, steps back wiping tears from her face, and says to her mother: "My love goes with thee wherever thou goest." A woman quickly steps forward and slides an arm around Rene's waist. She is sister Faith Blanchette, and she says to Abby, "I shall care for thy child as my own. In the name of God, as I am called Faith, I shall live to witness thy reunion. Peace be with thee always, Abigail."
 The thirteen women stand motionless and silent for a moment, as if communicating a prayer of understanding. They know this is their final

moment in this life together. Nods are quickly and quietly exchanged. Soft, sad smiles cross the faces of some, while others' open faces glisten in moonlight with silent tears. Then the thirteen hold together in a unified embrace.

As Abby and Hattie take the reins of the two horses from Ezekiel's hand, he says "I shall accompany thee as far as the Postal Road in Duffin, whereupon I shall be assured of thy safe passage to Whitelaw."

Hattie steps closer to see the man in moonlight, looks into his worried eyes and says, "No, Ezekiel. We must carry our chosen fate alone. This is not of thy doing. Thy family needs thee." She gives his arm a gentle squeeze. "With all my heart, I thank thee for thy blessed courage!"

Abby steps up quickly to her brother, holding the rein in one hand. She embraces him intensely as silent tears fall down his cheeks. Looking deep into his eyes, she says "Thee shall live in my heart for all time, brother."

First thunder, then a bright, white-blue blast of lightning slams across the night sky, and it begins to rain.

The two women ride fiercely, their long capes slapping wet behind them. As the rain intensifies, their clothing now soaked and the road deep in mud, their pace slows. Then, just as they approach the outskirts of Duffin Farms along the Postal Road, the faint sound of horses' hooves reaches their ears. Their efforts to increase speed are futile. Fate seems to pull them back.

Behind Abby, Hattie's horse stumbles on a tree fallen across the road. Hattie falls and the horse lands on her leg. She screams in pain and Abby turns back, dismounting instantly. Through the pounding rain and her own pain Hattie yells "Go! Leave me! My leg is broke, they come upon us and I accept my end here. Save thine own precious life! Go!"

Crying, Abby shouts "No!" and moves quickly to lift Abby's upper body out of the mud. It is all she can do. "I stay with thee, my beloved friend. We shall accept our fate together."

They hold each other's gaze, mindless of the cold pouring rain and the intensifying pounding vibration of horses' hooves. Abby reaches for Hattie's hand, and with closed eyes brings it to her lips and kisses it.

Awareness of the riders' arrival first reaches the women's ears then their eyes. They are now surrounded by twelve men.

"Seize the witches!" shouts the one in charge, a solid, thick man with blue eyes and steel gray hair. Immediately four men grab hold of the

grounded women, who offer no resistance.

"It's too wet for a burn!" Shaking his head, the chief looks from one man's face to the other. "No sense carting the heathens back alive. Our work is done when they're dead! I say we string them up here and now 'til their necks is broke." He scouts the men's faces for dissent and finds none. "There!" he shouts pointing to a solid tree nearby. "Bring the rope!" As the four men drag the women over, Hattie cries out in pain. Their hands are tied behind them with wet handkerchiefs, they are thrown in clumsy haste onto the backs of the horses, and the nooses are thrown over their heads. Just as the leader slaps the horses' rumps, Abby yells with her last breath of life: "May thee forgive thine own souls!"

Their limp bodies swing from the tree. Just below their feet is a granite road marker that reads: "Boston 100 miles East. Whitelaw 15 miles West."

August 18, 1990

At 6 A.M. the sound of the radio shook Mora out of a heavy sleep. "God! What was I dreaming? It was horrible!" she told Frankie, dragging herself to the floor. On her knees she began the new day as she ended the old: "God, please help me stay sober today. And help me with everything. I really need it." She stood up and dressed for her first aerobics class of the day at Teknet Corporation. Winning the contract for Fitness & More had been a major achievement for Mora at one time. But now it offered only superficial satisfaction along with the ever-present demand to "look happy" in front of students. What make-up could not mask of her puffy face and red eyes, her acting ability would at least distract.

And so Mora began another day pumping out an hour of super-motivating aerobics instruction because she had committed to it. What little satisfaction she received came from these students, and for that she was grateful. Her adrenalin pumped to a peak, she bid students farewell as they departed to shower before work. Then she headed for the seclusion of the walk-in storage closet, sat down in the corner and let the tears fall. "God, please help me. Please," she whispered.

"Ah-hmm." A woman's voice came from the other side of the slightly opened door.

"Oh, Hope. Hi. I was just. . ." Mora halted the lie dead center. "What the hell. I was crying," she said.

Hope pushed the door open, squatted near Mora, leaned her broad back against the wall, and said good-naturedly, "Well, I can see that. May I help? I came back to see if you were okay because you seemed troubled in class today."

Mora searched Hope's clear hazel eyes and rosy face for signs of disapproval and found none. "Really? You mean it shows?" She dropped her head into her hands and cried, "I'm terrible."

"Do you want to tell me about it?"

Mora remembered Jack's words at last night's meeting about God throwing her a rope and telling her to tie a knot and hang on. Hope was offering her a rope and she needed help.

"I quit drinking two months ago. I've got a problem with booze. I'm getting a divorce Friday, and Fitness & More is a financial mess. Aside from that, I'm fine."

"Oh, is that all!" Hope laughed kindly and Mora burst into tears again.

"Oh, I'm sorry. I've always got my foot in my mouth."

"It's so hard to put on a strong and cheerful front when my nerves are exposed raw. I feel like a hopeless hunk of shit, a total failure, and I can't handle it anymore," Mora said. "I feel trapped with nowhere to turn. Every direction I look in I see a big sign that says 'Mora is a worthless failure.' I can't find a solution and this closet feels pretty safe right now."

"Look. Ever since you first came here and brought in your fitness crew I've been really impressed with you. I've thought 'Hot damn! A businesswoman with a lot of spunk, a lot of heart. Here's proof you can have a heart in business.' Everybody here loves this program. You have obviously trained the instructors well because the locker room talk is the same: 'Those folks from Fitness & More have spirit.' And you're at the bottom of it all. We've never had this kind of uninhibited, crazy, energetic, enthusiastic fun sweating before, and right here sandwiched between floors of office cubicles!"

These last words sparked a fresh flow of tears from Mora.

"Thanks, Hope, but kind words don't hack it anymore. I've been saying 'Look at me, world! Notice me! Tell me I'm good so I'll know it too.' I just can't find anything valuable in me anymore. Positive feedback is wasted on me." Mora's crying subsided and she kept her eyes glued to the floor in front of her.

"I know the pain of a broken relationship can be excruciating." Hope nodded sympathetically. "How long were you married?"

"Seven years. Don't you have to go to work? It's almost 8:00, isn't it?"

"Fortunately, my job doesn't come with an actual schedule, but if your question means you want me to leave, I can do that."

Mora looked up at her. "Oh no, I just don't want to get you into trouble, that's all. I appreciate having someone to talk to about this, even though I'm supposed to be your super-peppy, up-energy, positive thinking, fitness instructor!" Mora finally got a smile out of herself.

"Actually, I've been trying to get myself into trouble for years but so far nothing's worked. Management, and I use the term loosely, is pretty weird themselves and quite tolerant of the well-known, shall we say, uniqueness inherent in designer minds. As far as your being super up-energy, well, even in the midst of your entire life being a disaster area from what you say, you still manage to make a semi-joke of it now. That takes balls."

"It's brass ovaries." Mora said, glad for the distraction. "Back in my radical feminist college days I had a friend who called it brass ovaries. Actually, in these days of talking to your body, brass isn't such a good thing to be made of, is it?"

Hope let out a rich laugh. "Ah yes, this conversation is much more interesting than the piece I've been working on for the last couple of days. There's no mention of human reproductive organs anywhere in it that I can find. But I'm not finished yet."

Mora laughed too. "My ex, or I should say my soon-to-be-ex-husband is a Teknet designer too. Maybe you know him? His name is Carl Fischer."

"No, I don't recognize the name, but he must need design modifications for divorcing you."

"I don't blame him. I did a lot of wild things drunk. I scared him. But he was so distant, and like a Virgo elephant he doesn't easily forgive and forget."

"Not all of us Virgos are unforgiving."

Mora shot a wounded, sideways look at Hope. "You mean you don't all keep a detailed mental list of other people's mistakes?"

They sat in silence for a long moment. Finally Mora heaved a shoulder-slumping sigh. "Well, I guess I'd better get back to work. I have places to go, classes to teach and clients to massage. " Moving slowly to get up, Mora gave Hope time to move away from the doorway where she squatted. "Thanks for being my friend, Hope," she said, once they were standing. "You have no idea how grateful I am, really, you have no idea." Mora shook her head gently and tears began to well up in her eyes again. "Jeez, I cry so much these days, every day." She looked away to hide the tears and wiped her face with her hand.

Tentatively, Hope asked "May I tell you just one more thing?"

"Sure."

"I've known people, people very close to me, who never spent a sober day in their adult lives and died of alcoholism. I want to say that I admire the courage it takes to face your drinking problem and admit you need help." Hope's eyes began to well up and her voice took on a light tremor. "You're doing what they could never do, and I'm proud to know you. I'd like to be your friend."

Mora's tears returned as she said, "I could use a friend right about now." She opened her arms and the two women sealed their pact with a gentle bear hug.

"Now maybe I can handle life until I get to a meeting tonight. Thanks again."

Hope reached into her purse, pulled out a business card and wrote on it. "Here's my number at work if you want to talk. I'm putting my home phone number on the back. Call me any time."

Mora drove back to her office. Colleen, the part-time secretary, wore her usual genuinely happy smile as Mora entered.

"I can tell you've been singing spontaneously again, haven't you Colleen? Come on, fess up, you're having another wonderful day, aren't you?"

Colleen's eyes sparkled. "I am feeling quite good today as a matter of fact. How are you this morning?"

"Colleen, what planet are you from? How is it possible that no one I know, including myself, has ever seen you unhappy? How did I find you? Do you know how glad I am you work here? None of these questions require an answer." It relieved Mora's tension to make her steadfast employee laugh. She would hold off the dreaded plunges she knew lay ahead as long as she could. Yet in her mind's eye she could see shadows already racing around the corner to meet her. She sighed deeply as the corners of her mouth drooped along with her mood: it was that quick.

"I'll be in the back doing payroll." Mora gathered up what she needed. Every two weeks for the last six months she had faced this job unwillingly. How could it be that she always had just exactly enough money to pay all the employees but none for herself? It was hopeless. And now that she'd gotten the corporate fitness contracts, she felt as if she were on a high-speed treadmill. Money came in and went out immediately and that was that. The only way to get off would be if somehow the plug got pulled, neat, clean, and swift. But how could that possibly happen without upsetting everybody?

"I can't figure it out." She spoke to herself aloud, sitting at the massage table that doubled as her private office desk. Looking at the final, barely-three-figure balance, she rubbed her forehead, dropped her heavy head into both hands, and cried. "I can't do this, God. This is impossible."

After she repaired her puffy face, Mora gathered up the books and went back to Colleen's desk.

"Have you got any deposit for me?" she asked.

"Right here, ma'am."

"I'm going to run this to the bank and I'll be back sometime this afternoon. Just lock up when you leave, okay?"

"Sure enough," Colleen said in her musical voice. "I'll see you on Thursday."

- 3 -

The dark gray, swollen belly of sky hung low later that afternoon. News of the impending hurricane came over Mora's car radio but she paid little attention. Then it started to rain.

Traffic was mild as she headed east on the Old Postal Road. She played the traffic game with automatic dexterity. Meanwhile a thin thread of thought sailed out and up the silver cord of light that had suddenly appeared from the sky. In an instant she cried out: "GOD! Help me! Stay with me!"

The crash was painless, catching her unaware from behind. In the instant of neck snapping, her head, arms and legs dropped completely limp and lifeless. In that single flash Mora's physical sight was gone, as were all bodily sensations. At last! She found herself relieved, so easily occupying a greyish world between worlds, devoid of good or evil. That fast. And without any more suffering she was gone from her body.

The car kept moving, her dead, limp body still behind the wheel, in 45-mile-an-hour traffic. Her unlimited thoughts contained everything and knew exactly all that had just occurred from where she was, from this perfectly peaceful place of complete mindfulness. Her neck had broken instantly, and in that same instant she exited her usual judgemental world and effortlessly entered the endless universe. She knew exactly everything that was wrong with her body, every cell that was suddenly out of place. Yet all was well and in place! With perfect calm she understood. *Oh yes, the car carrying my body is still moving. It'll need another impact to stop.* Sure enough, the second impact came. No trouble. Just another crash from behind.

Perfectly it shoved her car into a smashed can. Motion halted and silence prevailed. No longer occupying her body, she was aware of everything but bodily sensations.

"Is this death?" Mora asked the all-knowing inside herself, which felt like God but was much, much bigger than any God she'd ever been told about.

"*If this were your chosen time of death you would know because people you've known would be here to meet you,*" came the answer from God living inside herself.

"I'm not finished being Mora yet. I'm not ready for death now. But my body is REALLY badly damaged. I'm paralyzed." She conversed back and forth inside with her God-Self, even though she already knew the answers to her own questions.

"The fact is, I'm still alive. So I'll LIVE!"

At that moment Mora was lifted open and filled with brilliant bliss, Light that illuminated, in an instant, the perfection in everything. The only name by which this Light is known is the Love of God. She was in heaven.

"Oh. . . JOY! Everywhere! It's all *perfect!* I *am* loved. . . . Carl *does* love me, he always did. I was only mistaken. . . . It was only a tiny mistake for me to believe I was worthless. Oh, God, You really *do* love me completely!"

"*Of course, Mora. I have been with you always and loved you always. Never for one instant has it been otherwise. Your original knowing of everything is now merely uncovered.*"

Mora breathed the tender, pure beauty of endless innocence that enveloped her. There was nothing else. "Oh yes! What joy this is, dear God! I am completely FULL. . . . Nothing but Your Love exists. I was just mistaken in my thinking, wasn't I, in thinking You saw me as bad. Even though I was twice raped, twice aborted, I can see now that I've been innocent all along. You never took Your Love away from me. But oh. . . ." A single, brief whisper of regret floated through her. "I've wasted so much of my life striving for narrow perfection, crying for Your forgiveness when I never even *needed* it. I was already there. You never condemned me the way the nuns and priests told me You did. Feeling guilty was my only mistake. My only regret. . . to have wasted a single moment believing You didn't love me anymore!"

Joy that life on earth had never glimpsed filled her and she *knew* that all earthly fear was unfounded. The illusory burdens of the strange world she left behind disappeared in less than a breath. In an instant transformed, her mind, her spirit, her soul filled with the Light of Pure Love.

"Everyone I have known really *does* love me! I can see them all now." A bittersweet edge surrounded her years of life past.

The reply came ever so gently. *"My beloved Mora, you'll always know this love. From now on, you'll remember it's the only thing that's real. This is your gift, this marker upon your interrupted life. You have helped many people and you will help many more by your willingness to accept forgiveness for yourself. You will go on with My Love as the only tool you will ever need. You can build anything on My Love."*

"God, you're completely with me now. I have Your undivided attention but so does everyone else. Only You could do that! You're so far beyond what they tell us You are on earth. They try to frighten us, telling us we're damned if we don't fear You. They tell us you're vengeful, and none of it's true! It's as if everything is already perfectly done with Your Love throughout, yet we souls on earth still need to figure out how to consciously apply Your Love."

"Yes. You live to use your free will until you use it only to love everything and everyone with your free will, just as I do toward you. Your soul's work in human life is not yet finished as Mora. Therefore you have chosen to return and finish. This time you will use your free will to find me in everything."

Yes, God! I can see now. I want to go back." Mora's awareness outshone the risk before her. "How can my paralyzed body have more power than Your limitless everything? I can see that it's a wisp of a thought, a tiny speck of dust compared to the All contained in Your Love. I'm going back to my life. I want to share this. I want to use it. I want to go on living!"

"Now you know for all eternity that I will never leave you. Now you have remembered again that nothing is impossible through My Love. Simply remember that My Love is in everything you experience. Use this

understanding in every apparent struggle, in every circumstance of seem-
ing lovelessness. Hold My Love first in your mind. There is nothing else.
You will see how perfect it is to be without harm, either giving or receiving
it. Receive this love, Mora, and I will always keep you free.

"*Although you understand everything now, when you return to your*
life on earth, you will not recall exactly how your life will unfold, how these
truths will be revealed in time. Trust that I will always guide you."

"Oh yes, God. I'm so completely grateful for this bliss, this
remembering! My heart is full!" Mora began to make hasty, waver-
ing steps back and forth, almost into body then back into blissful
union. "Just stay with me always! Can you keep this undivided
attention on me for the rest of my life God, just like now? Will I
always know I'm your beloved child as I am now?"

If God could laugh, Mora heard it. "*Of course. All you need do is*
remember this feeling. My love will always comfort you."

"Just stay with me, God. Stay with me. . . . "

*   *   *

"What's your name? What day is it? Come on! What's your
name? What day is it? Chief, she's coming back. Hallelujah, we've
got her!" The sound of men's cheering voices reached Mora's ears.

She understood the EMT's frantic questions and thought *Stay*
with me, God, but answered "I'm Mora Donovan. It's Tuesday." Her
eyes opened and she saw her hands flat and limp in her lap. *I'll just*
get out of the car, she thought and attempted the action, but nothing
happened. *How strange. . . I'm disconnected from my body's circuits* she
realized, terror shocking her mind. "God! Help me!" she vaguely
heard her own voice struggle to utter. *Look at those limp hands and*
legs. They could be mine but they seem miles away. How strange this is. . . .
None of my body is real! Where I just came from is real! It would be horrible
if it were true that I'm paralyzed. . . . But I AM!

Her head remained dropped motionless, and she might have
dwelt upon the gravity of this last thought were it not for the noisy
urgency of activity around her.

"Mora, can you hear me?"

"Yes," She answered, but when she tried to inhale, her ribcage
locked. "I can't breathe. . . my chest is squeezed!" Mora panicked

when she understood her own words.

"Okay! Oxygen!" the man yelled over his shoulder. "We're going to give you oxygen, okay?" He quickly fitted the mask over her mouth and nose and she began to breathe easier. Still, her eyes dropped down and she saw her poor, sweet lap.

"Mora, we're going to get you out of there real fast. We've got the jaws of life cutting you out!"

She could hear the sounds of heavy equipment cutting, metal screeching and tearing metal.

"Stay with us, Mora. Are you still with us?" The voice of the same EMT asked, strong and urgent.

"Yes. Hurry." Mora began to cry. Her ribs felt like iron barrel rings clamped tight against fragile breath. But pain? This discomfort was stranger than she'd ever known: not really feeling, too shocked to register. What happened? She could see hundreds of pieces of broken glass everywhere, including on her body. But she felt nothing.

"Mora, just hang on, okay? We're going to slide a back board under you, and without changing your position, we're going to get you out of the car, okay?"

"I can't move! I can't feel anything!" Upon hearing her own words, the meaning slowly registered in her brain and made her cry.

"Okay Mora. Stay with us. We've got you!"

She could sense several men around her. Her physical sensation was limited to an experience of her body's weight, density rather than any real feeling. Everything else of her body was gone. Oh, the heavy gravity of earthly life!

The EMTs very carefully slid the body board between her and the car seat, then gingerly removed her from the wreckage.

Mora's awareness slowly began to return to the world. Yet, after where she'd just visited, it was difficult to completely believe in the physical world's reality. Peripherally she could see a large crowd gathered 100 yards away in a parking lot.

"What happened? What are those people doing?" She asked the EMTs.

"You just had a bad car wreck. Those people are watching you. They want to know you're still alive."

While the men lifted her out into the world and began carrying her fully horizontal, Mora remembered. And as the warm, misty rain fell from the pale gray-white sky gently onto her face, she called on God's love again. This time she was inside her body. *I feel You again now God.* She thought, looking up at the endless sky of heaven where God lived. *Thank You for staying with me. . . I feel your undivided attention on me. I'm still important to you, aren't I?* She already knew the answer.

Inside herself she heard the happy reply. *Yes. Always. I will carry you.*

Mora's frightened tears turned to peaceful, grateful tears. She knew she was paralyzed, that she might never move again. But the joy of knowing what she now knew could not be erased by anything of the earth. Now, as she looked into the eyes of the EMT walking guard over her, she said "Thank you for saving my life. Thank you!"

He looked down at her, their eyes met and with surprise in his voice he answered "We're just glad you made it! We're gunna take you to Drayton Community Hospital now. They're standing ready to take care of you. Hang on and we'll get you some help."

Mora's grateful heart overflowed with tears. As the rains fell harder, her gratitude began to mix with terror of the life to come. *God! This is horrible!* she thought, suddenly drawn into the believability of sirens complete with the absence of physical feeling. She was helpless to shield her face from the rain falling on it. *There's nothing I can do but let go. Just let go and let You take care of me, God. If I can't move, I'll just have to trust these good people to help me now. All I can do is trust You'll work through them.* The instant Mora surrendered her mind to trust God, the bright glow of love refilled her.

"It's so kind of you to help me," she said to the EMT climbing into the ambulance with her. "It's love you give in what you do." Now she knew it was too important a thing to keep to herself.

"Thanks." He smiled, surprised and embarrassed. "People don't usually say things like that after. . . I mean when they've just. . . uhh. . . at a time like this."

Mora's heart filled to overflow knowing it was love that had saved her life and love would take care of her from now on. Sirens hailed her voyage into the unknown.

*   *   *

Traffic had been backed up for over an hour. Commuters on their way home from work began to collect, especially in the Eastbound lanes behind the seven-vehicle pile-up. Three police cars, two ambulances, a firetruck and scores of personnel worked the scene. The newspaper delivery van was first in line behind the flattened sardine can that used to be Mora's car. Its driver, a shaking young man with a mildly bleeding cut on his forehead, was being questioned by two policemen. "Are you willing to submit to a sobriety test?" one asked.

"I din' do nothin'." The man wiped blood from his forehead. "I was just drivin'. It's a fucking hurricane! It's not my fault!"

The policeman sighed. "You have the right to remain silent. . ."

*   *   *

After the ambulance departed the crowd in the parking lot of Cross Junction Restaurant gradually dispersed. As fire chief Arnold stood roadside surveying the clean-up, EMT McDonnel approached him.

"And what a mess we have here," McDonnel said. Arnold's only response was a long nod.

"Again," added McDonnel.

"Yeah. Same general location. Two crashes. Two women. Two broken necks. Too weird." Arnold shook his head slowly without taking his eyes off the scene before him.

"Yeah," answered McDonnel. "And did you get a load of *that*?"

"Huh?" Still in deep thought, the firechief looked at McDonnel to see him pointing up at the street sign.

"With all due respect to the injured, maybe we oughta recommend the town fathers change the name of the road over here."

The two men stared and read the sign: Breakneck Hill Road. Just beneath it was the pre-Revolutionary War granite road marker which read: "Boston 100 miles East. Whitelaw 15 miles West".

*   *   *

Three long lines of bumper-to-bumper traffic were backed up over Whitelaw's three hills. In one of these cars was Mora's younger brother David, an environmental engineer headed home after a long day. With his radio tuned to a local Christian station, David allowed his mind to relax.

"We have a special bulletin for those of you headed Eastbound right now on Route ll, and for all of our listeners who have a moment for prayer. There are delays of at least one hour in the Duffin area of the Old Postal Road, Route ll due to a multiple-car accident, in which there has apparently been at least one critically injured person. Police and emergency workers are at the scene now. We'd like to take a moment right now to send out a prayer for those involved in this serious car crash."

The announcement grabbed David's attention just as he noticed the sight far ahead. He listened intently:

"Lord, we ask You to watch and keep in your divine care, all those injured in this accident. We pause together and join our faithful hearts in silent prayer."

David shut off his idling engine and pulled the brake before closing his eyes to pray.

"In the name of God we thank all of you listeners for your prayers. Now, we'd like to play a song of gratitude. . . ."

From the middle of the Lexington Hill incline David could see the rescue and towing vehicles leaving the crash site as surrounding traffic slowly filed through. He started his car and began to inch forward. Within minutes he drove past the scene.

"Father God, I ask you in Jesus' name to save and keep the life well of whoever has been injured. Thank You, Father." As he glanced quickly at the scene to his left, a chord of uncanny familiarity was struck within him and chills ran up his spine. David prayed hard all the way home.

- 4 -

The swift entry of three EMTs and their stretchered patient cleared a path to the emergency examining room. Doctor Anwar, the neurosurgeon on call, received Mora immediately. His voice was as smooth and calm as his touch beneath her neck.

"Can you feel my hands on you?" He spoke with a Middle-East accent.

"No." Mora began to cry again. "But I hurt now." She heard her words entering the atmosphere at a speed as slow as her thoughts.

"Yes, we're going to give you something now. Nurse?" The doctor nodded to an assisting nurse who quickly administered the injection. Removing the oxygen mask from Mora's face he asked, "Is your breathing easier?"

"Yes." Mora could not release the words any faster than this labored pace. "But my chest feels squeezed."

The doctor nodded. "I'm going to have x-rays and a CAT scan taken now." His gentle voice soothed Mora as the pain medication began to dull the discomfort. She was quickly wheeled into emergency x-ray.

With the body board still beneath her, two nurses slid her onto a long tray and electronically glided her into a long cylinder. Helpless, she listened to the low-pitched buzz and stared at the ceiling inside the tube. Panic knocked and nearly took hold. She closed her eyes and remembered her private peace on the highway. How much time had passed since then? She had no grasp of the world's reference point of time. It didn't matter anymore. "God, please help me," she prayed in a quiet whisper, not wanting to disturb the machine.

Now maybe Carl will forgive me, she thought. *And this is a good reason not to have to work. I can't even move! Nobody will ask why.* Only the barest glimpse of this reality sunk in. *Oh God! I'm paralyzed. Help me!*

"Is there anyone we can call to let them know what happened to you?" A kind woman's face framed in a white cap looked down on Mora as they wheeled her into the examining room.

"My husband. . .ex-husband. Carl." It took so long for her to say what she needed.

"What's his telephone number?"

"Uh. . ." Mora struggled to draw the information from her memory. "It's uh. . . 772-6781. Tell him. . . call my business. Tell them."

The nurse rushed off and returned quickly with doctor Anwar, a solidly built man whose creamy-brown, polished face was framed in silver waves. Another nurse cut Mora's tights and leotards from her body. Mora searched the doctor's face intently for a read-out of her condition, but he gave nothing away. He wore a dark-green silk suit jacket and a pale green silk bow tie that was the exact color of his eyes. Like bright desert oases, his eyes assured her she was in the best of hands.

"Did I take you away from a dinner party, doctor?" Mora asked.

The two nurses looked at each other and laughed. "Doctor Anwar always dresses like that," said the one cleaning blood off Mora's face.

Embarrassed, the doctor glanced at them and then at Mora before directing his concentration on the x-rays. "Your neck is broken, Mora." He refocused his eyes on hers. "Cervical vertebra 5 is completely shattered and there is a great deal of bleeding and swelling around your spinal cord." The utter calm with which he spoke held Mora's panic at bay. "What I am going to do now is place what's called a halo on your head. It's a support device to keep your neck and head absolutely stable. We will need to allow time to pass before we can determine exactly what we must do. Do you understand?"

Mora began to cry again. "Oh, no! Am I going to be paralyzed for the rest of my life?" Terror spread across her contorted forehead.

Doctor Anwar looked directly into Mora's eyes. "I cannot discern the present condition of your spinal cord due to inflammation and bleeding. Our first task will be to reduce the inflammation and wait patiently. It is extremely important that your neck remain absolutely still. Then we shall see. Until you have stabilized, we must hope and pray for the best. Do you understand all I have said, Mora?"

She held his eyes, searching them with expanded vision that took in his face, his head, and the field of white light around him. "Yes. I can see God in you, doctor," she said in a shaking voice. "I trust you."

The completely clear vote of confidence from one in such dire circumstances was met by the doctor's surprise. The nurses' eyes lit up with recognition.

"Thank you." Doctor Anwar gracefully bowed his head and raised it again. "If you will excuse me, I shall return in a moment." He left Mora with the nurses.

"You're lucky you got doctor Anwar," said one of them. "He's the best neurosurgeon anywhere. When he does something, he never has to go back and repair it. His reputation is impeccable." As she finished cleaning Mora's face the other nurse set about chopping off clumped lengths of tangled, blood-matted hair. Then she shaved and prepped four circular patches on Mora's head.

When he returned, the doctor injected novocaine into Mora's forehead while she concentrated on his serene eyes. He placed the metal band around her crown and drove the four metal connecting screws directly into her skull.

"Where are you from, doctor?" Although her skull was numb, Mora directed her attention away from the doctor's barbaric work, and focused on his beauty.

The doctor shot her a quick glance and returned to his task. "Harvard. I received my training from Harvard."

"No. I mean where did you come from before you came to the United States?"

"Paris."

"No." Although her speech was slow she persisted in lifting his veil of mystery. "I mean, in what country were you born?"

"Kuwait," he answered, staring even more intently at what he was doing.

"I'm glad you're here now. Thank you for helping me."

With the fourth screw in place, the metal halo was secured to Mora's head like a gravity-bound crown. The nurses wheeled her toward Intensive Care, where she promptly fell asleep.

"She's an odd one, isn't she?" said one to the other as they were met by two ICU nurses. "Wearing a halo, telling doctor Anwar she sees God in his eyes. . .makes me think of an angel." Barely disturbing their patient, they lifted her smoothly onto the high, narrow bed in the tiny, glass-walled room. The ER nurses left and the ICU nurses hooked Mora up to vital sign wall monitors. Next, doctor Anwar attached traction wall pulleys to her head pins with precise tension. Strung to the wall, her neck and head were immovable. Two I.V.s were hooked up: liquid glucose for food in one arm, an anti-inflammatory in the other. A catheter was inserted to remove body fluids and oxygen assisted breathing. She lay on an electric air mattress that simulated movement beneath her, keeping her circulation going. Finally, at 8:00 P.M., Mora was officially listed in critical condition at Drayton Community Hospital.

Time lost meaning. Drifting in and out of merciful, drugged sleep, Mora sometimes opened her eyes to throbbing horror. It couldn't be real, she thought. Crying and crying, until she couldn't breathe, nurses helped her blow her nose, and she fell back to sleep. There was no place else to go.

Late in the afternoon of the following day, Mora opened her eyes to see doctor Anwar standing bedside studying her chart, a nurse at his side. His kind smile contrasted with serious, sharp eyes. Dressed in a dusty rose silk bow tie and a burgundy silk jacket, he asked, "How are you feeling today, Mora?"

"Oh. . . " Mora moaned. "Where am I?" she answered, mentally working to command her body to move. When it didn't she burst into tears.

"Now, Mora," the nurse chided, "doctor Anwar is here to help you. Don't cry. You're in the ICU at Drayton Hospital and you were brought here last night."

"What do you mean? Where am I?" Mora's mind processed the information with the sluggishness of a 1955 computer, and she cried louder. "What happened to me?" At last, she had awakened to a nightmare.

"You were in a car crash yesterday, Mora," the doctor said. "Your neck was broken and you're in the Intensive Care Unit of Drayton Hospital. I am doctor Anwar and you are in good care now."

"I'm paralyzed, right?" Mora locked her eyes on his.

"Now, Mora. . ." The nurse was cut short by the doctor.

"You have lost movement, yes. But we do not know the exact condition of your spinal cord at this time. We must be patient." His steady eyes offered comfort to her terror-filled eyes. "We are giving you anti-inflammatory medication so that the swelling will reduce sufficiently for us to discern the extent of damage. Do you under-stand?"

"Yes." Mora's eyes filled with tears.

"Now I would like to determine what, if any, sensitivity you presently have." He retrieved a long, sterile, straight pin from the tray, moved toward the foot of the bed, and gently raised the covers. "Tell me if you can feel any of these pin touches."

He began pricking her skin, first one spot, then another, and another, glancing at her face to see if she registered any response.

"Are you doing it yet?" Mora's frightened eyes held onto the ceiling.

"Yes," he answered, continuing to pin-prick her skin. "Do you feel anything yet?"

"No." Mora closed her eyes and cried. "I can't feel anything!"

"It's okay, Mora." Finally dropping her efficiency mode, the nurse stood on the opposite side of the bed and tenderly touched Mora's numb arm.

"Oww!" Mora cried out. "It hurts. It feels awful!"

"Ah, you have some sensation here." The doctor had worked his way up to her torso. "Good. Here you are hypersensitive but at least there is feeling on some dermatones."

"Am I ever going to move again, doctor?"

"Only time will tell, but you must not abandon hope. The future is unknown and full of possibility."

Mora drank in his strong, gentle energy. She answered him with a heavy blink, then instantly fell asleep.

Doctor Anwar left the room and the nurse caught up with him. "Doctor, Mora's family is here and wants to have a word with you. Do you have a moment?"

"Certainly. Where are they?"

Just as the nurse was about to respond, a petite, blue-eyed, silver-blonde-haired woman approached.

"Excuse me, are you doctor Anwar?"

"Yes, I am."

Extending her right hand, the woman said, "I'm Ellen Donovan, Mora's mother." As they shook hands, Ellen tried to smile.

"How do you do, Mrs. Donovan? I am very pleased to meet you."

Observing the handshaking scene from the waiting room, Carl got up and came toward them. Mora's brother David remained asleep on the couch.

"Do you mind if I eavesdrop?" Carl nervously glanced at Ellen before extending a limp hand to the doctor. "I'm Mora's almost-ex-husband, Carl."

"Yes, of course. I'm pleased to meet you, Mister. . ." Doctor Anwar shook Carl's hand.

"Fischer. Carl Fischer. Pleased to meet you, too."

"Would you both like to know of Mora's present condition?" Doctor Anwar's straightforward approach redirected the tension between Carl and Ellen.

"Yes, please doctor."

"As you may know, Mora's neck was broken yesterday in a car crash. The x-rays have indicated that cervical vertebrae 5 was completely shattered." The doctor delivered the information matter-of-factly. "I am very pleased that her family is with her, helping her through this trying time. She's been through a terrific ordeal."

"She's always been a courageous survivor," Ellen said simply.

"Yes, I can see her strength." Doctor Anwar nodded gravely, his hands clasped in front of him. "Now, I would like to tell you what our tentative plan of treatment shall be." He explained what he had done so far, and where he intended to go. "The fact that she cannot move at all indicates that there is, minimally, damage to the spinal cord. Within the next three to ten days, depending on how rapidly the swelling reduces, it may be necessary for me to perform a surgical fusion of C5 and C6. In other words, I would connect cervical vertebrae 5 and 6 together, restabilizing them, without restricting her spinal cord or spinal nerves. All we can do now is wait, and pray that all proceeds well." He waited for understanding to register in the two faces before continuing. "When you see her, you may be alarmed by the imposing appearance of the halo now connected to her skull. Its purpose is to completely stabilize her head and neck. Do you have any questions?" Again he paused and looked directly into each one's eyes.

"Is it dangerous doctor, I mean the surgery?" Ellen's face tightened with anguish. "Is there any risk of further damage being done?"

The doctor paused momentarily, deliberately choosing each word. "There is always risk involved in any surgery. However, if we proceed cautiously, taking measures to minimize risk, there is every reason to believe it will be a success."

"What about her spinal cord?" Carl's face uncharacteristically revealed distress. "Is it possible it's been cut? Could she be permanently paralyzed?"

After a moment's thought, the doctor responded gravely. "We will not know the full extent of the damage or its potential to heal until we actually enter the area surgically. However, as a sign of hope, the fact that she has some slight sensation on several dermatones leads me to believe the best is possible. Only God can provide truthful answers to our questions." He smiled and looked from one to the other. "Please be assured that this is a fine hospital and Mora is receiving very good care. If you have no further questions just now, I shall be on my way." He nodded at them. "Good day, Mrs. Donovan, Mr. Fischer."

Carl and Ellen remained standing in the hallway, neither one knowing exactly what to do next. Carl shrugged and planted his hands safely in his jeans pockets while he stared at the floor. Ellen sighed exasperated as she searched the contents of her purse.

Mustering all his nerve, Carl broke the silence. "Ellen, I know you may not feel very friendly toward me right about now."

Ellen barely listened as she wrestled with her purse.

"Even though Mora and I are getting a divorce, I care about her very deeply." Carl's voice quavered with emotion. He cleared his throat. "If you need a place to stay while you're here, the spare bedroom in the house is empty. You're welcome to stay if you want to."

Ellen stopped rummaging. Turning to face Carl, she allowed her armor to fall. "Well actually, that would help. I haven't arranged for a hotel room yet." She took another few seconds to decide. "Okay, I accept. Thank you." Carl smiled and released a heavy sigh of relief. Then Ellen made her way back to the waiting room chair beside her sleeping son David, and Carl followed behind.

Teknet Corporation Files: entry 19-AUG-1990
FROM: ALPHA::Fischer
TO: Aerobics Students Info Line
SUBJ: Mora Donovan

    Mora Donovan was involved in a 7 vehicle crash this
past   Tuesday, 8/18 at 3:35 pm in Duffin on Rt. 11. Her
name may be familiar because she is in charge of the fitness program at Duffin/Teknet, as well as the owner of
Fitness & More. She was driving along eastbound on Rt 11
when a pickup and a truck going westbound "bumped" into
each other. The pickup swerved out of control into the
driver's side of Mora's car. Then 4 other vehicles crashed
on top in the pouring rain. The Duffin Fire Department
EMTs cut her out of her totally smashed car with the "jaws
of life" and took her to Drayton Hospital. She is now in
intensive care. She has a cervical fracture of C5 and
will probably have to have a fusion in a week or 10 days.
She has already had some feeling in certain areas of her
body (skin zones called "dermatones") so the doctor is
hoping that her spinal cord has been damaged rather than
cut. She is being made as comfortable as possible, considering the fact that she is mostly paralyzed. Her thoughts
seem surprisingly coherent.
    She asked me to forward this message to everyone and
anyone who cares, and she asks that you pray for her and
send her only positive, healing thoughts. They aren't

allowing any visitors in the ICU except for immediate
family. I'll keep you posted regarding progress.

Mora and I broke up a while ago, but we still care
very deeply for each other. Her brother, sister, and
mother are also here to take care of her.

This distressing occurrence has made me realize how
much I take for granted in life. . . all the things Mora
can't do now, like walk outside and feel the wind or
watch the clouds. I feel more thankful for these things
now. This is the first time I've ever been close to
somebody in the hospital with a serious injury. It's
very sad to see someone so full of energy one day, then
unable to move the next. Well, that's about all I know
right now. Just send her your love. She really needs it
now. Thanks.

  - CF
            ....

The ceiling tiles had little tiny holes. God was in each one.
Hours were seconds were days were all the same. Time stood still, or
crept along like a tiny caterpillar finding its way in the new world, or
rushed past like water down a drain. It didn't matter now. Mora
could move only her facial muscles, her voice, and her thoughts, so
she worked with those.

Every two or three hours a nurse came in and turned her to a
slightly different angle in order to avoid bedsores. With her skull
screwed to a halo and the halo screwed to wall pulleys, Mora's range
of movement was limited to the realm of imagination. And she had
plenty of time to imagine what the tiny holes in the ceiling tiles
contained.

Since the blissful moment of her death, Mora had an endless
well from which to retrieve comfort. All physical sensations except for
pain were nonexistent, and "feeling" took on a much deeper meaning
than she had ever known. A world within the world, it was quiet, simple, pure, and still. When she just let it all be, it was beautiful. Nothing

would ever look the same to her again. Her new awareness of life's true value had freed her, even while her body remained paralyzed. The physical world seemed almost insignificant. Mora smiled to herself, lying still on the electric burping air mattress, her eyes riveted to the endless world inside one little hole in the ceiling tile.

"God, I know You're with me now," she almost whispered. "I can feel You fill up the room. Hold me, God?" Mora closed her eyes and felt herself embraced warmly. Out poured grateful tears, sorrowful tears, spilling down her temples and into her ears, while she remembered a voice from a recovering alcoholics meeting: "Give your troubles to God. Then let go, because they've been solved." Behind her closed eyes Mora imagined her tears falling onto a silver platter, which she sailed up to God. *Thank you for my life, God*, she dreamed. *Please help me.*

It was a strangely beautiful and impossible place Mora inhabited. Grace was her constant companion, the sword with which she cut away the treacherous, fast-growing vines of terror that were so ready to root. And after each internal fear-against-faith battle she slept deeply. Never in her life had she known with such clarity that she was not alone, that God was with her and taking care of everything. Second after second, hour after hour, she remembered her body's condition, cried for its pitiful nature, prayed to be made well, then surrendered the outcome to God. Over and over and over this was her life now, her full-time, waking occupation. In between she slept, entering and exiting the underworld of mind and spirit, the unfathomable ocean of dreams and imagination. From the moment of death onward, what she needed to remain in the world was not generated by rational mind but seemed instead to be birthed by a bigger plan for her soul's voyage.

The first signs of life returning to her body came as pain. Everywhere there was miserable discomfort with nowhere to move, not even the slightest twist or turn. Forced to wait, her normal impatience brought her to tears and tears brought her to call "Nurse!" for a noseblow. It was hard to breathe after crying, but she had to cry. There was no stopping the truth from coming up.

"Nurse!"

A flash of crisp white blew into Mora's room. It was the I-mean-business, sharp-edged nurse on day duty.

"Nurse, I'm so thirsty," Mora labored through words.

"Now you know full well we can't give you anything to drink. And I can't keep coming over here swabbing your mouth." She screwed up her tight-lipped face. "I've got other patients besides you, you know." She grabbed a sweet lemon swab and stood over Mora. "Come on now, open up. This is what you wanted and I haven't got all day."

Mora began to cry, softly at first then all out, as a child would.

"What's the matter with you now? My goodness, you're such a crybaby, aren't you?" The nurse leaned her elbows on the side rail and grimaced.

"Go away! I don't like you." Mora heard her own raw voice scratch. "I want somebody nice to take care of me." In pain, groggy, and thirsty, she still knew what was what, and so did the wall monitors. Her blood pressure and heart rate took off.

"Settle down!" Miffed, the nurse shuffled tray utensils.

"You're mean! You don't know how it feels!" Mora wailed.

"Shhhh!" the nurse hissed. "You'll disturb the other patients!" She looked around for anyone within earshot, then leaned forward and whispered hotly a few inches from Mora's face. "Just because you want something doesn't mean you're going to get it. Huh. . . . You're behaving like a spoiled brat! Now settle down."

"Help!" Mora yelled, using what she had: a voice. Another nurse rushed into the room as the vital sign monitors fluttered higher.

"What's the matter here?" The new nurse asked.

"Mora's just having a bad. . ."

"I want another nurse. This one's a bitch. Please, is there someone kind who can help me?" Mora's wild eyes pleaded with the new nurse. "I'm in pain, I can't move. . ." Hearing her own words, Mora fell back into crying.

The new nurse leaned over Mora. "There, there now. Judy, I'll stay with Mora." She watched as Judy left the room in a huff.

Mora pleaded on behalf of the helpless child inside herself. "That woman doesn't understand how hard it is. Everybody else is kind, except for her. Can somebody else be my nurse? Can you?"

"I'll talk to her. Just relax now, okay? Everything's going to be all right. Here, let me help." The nurse swabbed her mouth. "Let's see if we can give you a turn. Would you like that?" The wall monitors began to calm and the frightened child relaxed into a 15 degree torso turn.

"Could you put my right hand down on the bed? Being moved is so painful, but staying in the same position for a long time is worse. I need my arms and hands moved separately." Each vocalization of her own helplessness brought sorrow's terrible tightness to Mora's throat. "Thank you for being kind. It makes life bearable. Could you lift my left arm and lay it on my side?" She sighed her frustration. "I hate asking people to move me. I'm so tired of it."

The nurse smiled. "Don't let it get you. You just get some rest and I'll talk to Judy. She really is a good nurse."

"But she's mean. Isn't compassion part of nursing?" For an instant, Mora was absolutely lucid.

*   *   *

"Hello? Can we come in?"

Mora heard the familiar voice of comfort from just outside the curtained glass door. "Mommy, is that you?"

Ellen Donovan entered with her youngest daughter, Claire, a pretty, blonde, blue-eyed young woman who resembled vanilla to Mora's chocolate coloring. Ellen's son, David, a tall, gentle young man with Claire's coloring, followed behind.

"Mommy!" Mora reached out with her voice and eyes. "Oh. . . what happened to me. . . I can't move."

Ellen's eyes filled but she held back her tears, her voice quavering as the outlet. "Mora honey, it's okay. We'll stay with you. It'll be all right." She stepped over to her daughter's bedside, but hesitated to touch her.

"Mommy, would you hold my hand?" Mora wanted her mother's cure-all care. Being one of six children to a goal-achieving woman had left unfilled comfort gaps in Mora's past, and in her childlike state of helplessness, she was instantly transported back. "Mommy, you never had time for me when I was little." She burst into tears.

Ellen gingerly grasped Mora's puffy, limp hand. "It's all right, honey. I'm with you now," she said softly.

"How did you find out?"

David moved next to Ellen and whispered, "Carl called me last night and I called Ma and Claire."

Claire walked to the opposite side of the bed. Wearing the Donovan worry face, she whispered, "We left Florida on the first flight this morning. David's been here since last night. Are you. . . is there anything we can do?"

"I wish you could make me better. I wish this never happened. It's awful." The desperate words left Mora's mouth so slowly. There was nothing else to do but breathe: take it in, let it out, another few seconds gone by.

"David." Mora's tears returned as she caught sight of her brother. His kind blue eyes lit a candle for her. She was ready to tell them all about the thing that happened. "Do you want to know what happened to me?"

"Doctor Anwar told us about your neck being —" Claire began.

"No, no," Mora interrupted with slow words. "I mean, something happened to me."

"What do you mean?" Ellen asked.

"I died." Mora answered, her eyes glazing right through them to somewhere beyond. "I died and I met God. I met Love. They're the same. It was the most beautiful. . ."

The three listened silent and still.

"And you know what I found out about Carl?" Mora's voice cracked, her emotions leaking through. "He really does love me. I never really knew. It's okay. The divorce. Everything's okay. And everybody. Now I know I'm really loved." She stopped talking to allow the truth to permeate the air they inhaled. "I can't say true words to express all that it was. It was everything. Everything is perfect. Love is the only thing that's real. That's all there is. The rest is nothing."

Mother and sister looked down at Mora, awestruck. It was incomprehensible to them that someone with a broken body could be thinking about love. The words' significance didn't quite sink in. But David understood. His pale face dropped its shell of fatigue and rushed with rosy color. He smiled recognition.

"I still feel it now. All I need to do is remember and it comes back," Mora continued. "Oh." She closed her eyes and sighed heavily. "But my body. It hurts. And I can't do anything with it." She opened her eyes and looked at them through tears. "I'm afraid. What if it never comes back?"

No one had an answer.

"It's so strange." Mora's mood shifted on a breath. "I feel like Scrooge waking up on Christmas morning saying, 'It's not too late! I've got another chance.'" She began to cry again. "Thank you for coming to help me. Mommy, David, Claire, I really love you."

Ellen remembered her daughter as a child, those same big brown eyes craving attention, attention Ellen had not always been able to give. "Whatever happens Mora, we'll help you. We're together now and we'll stick by you. Okay?" Ellen tilted her head closer to her daughter, tenderly squeezing her hand once more. She'd said the precious words but didn't really know what to do to activate them. Here was something she hadn't a clue about how to achieve.

"Okay." Mora closed her eyes.

"Mora, are you awake?" David's gentle baritone drew her attention back.

"Huh?"

"Mora, may I ask my minister to come in to see you? We want to pray for you. Would you like that?"

"Yes. . ." She barely spoke with eyes still closed as a mild smile touched her lips. "I'd like that."

*   *   *

Awake, asleep, diving deep. . . dark indigo-blue and silver mist-wrapped images. . . diving down in where she remembers. . . something, voices she's heard before. Their combined signatures engraved forever on her heart, locked long and buried deep beneath oceans of memory. But now, it's not the same.

"Lord, we pray for our sister Mora lying here now without use of her body. We ask you now to heal her broken neck."

David. . . his voice. . . her brother still, as he once was. . . the same soul she's always loved . . . he's come to her aid. . . again.

She doesn't want to open her body's eyes now. Something draws her down deeper. . . "Ezekiel. . ." Risk her fear she must if she wants to remember.

"Ezekiel. I'm still alive. . . they didn't kill me." Behind closed eyes Mora looks through the deep sea of memory, grasping for something.

"She's dreaming. We'll keep praying." This voice belongs to someone else. Long, long ago. . . it once meant harm. . .

"No!" Mora cried out from the deep. She sees him now and remembers. . .

The church is packed full. . .

"Tribunal, what say thee now?" The exact same voice booms in echo. *"Let God's will be done!"*

"No!" Mora's own scream yanked her out of the memory. Her eyes shot open. "Huhhhhhh. . . what?"

"It's okay, Mora. You're all right now." David's clear, bright blue eyes met hers like a rope thrown out and caught on storming waves. "Reverend Keyes is here. We've come to pray over you. Remember?"

Mora saw the man standing on the other side of the bed. Her eyes widened as a strange sensation made a full circuit up and down her body, beneath her flesh. Their eyes locked for an eternal instant.

"Here," John Keyes said, breaking the curious, shared spell, "let me come around to the other side so you don't have to strain to see me." She watched the man softly step around the bed and take his place beside her brother. "There. Is that better now?" His voice was kind and he let her look into his eyes. Apparently he had no intention of fleeing, and somehow Mora understood that a window of hope had just flown open. His eyes were unmistakably familiar. As if hearing her intuition speak the recollection, he squinted and refocused his eyes on hers. "I feel like I've met you before. I know you. . . ." His face displayed momentary puzzlement.

She understood he was there now to help. The true time was

now and that was all that mattered. He was there to stay, to help her, and he meant it.

"Mora," David said, "would you like us to pray over you?"

"Yes, I would." She answered hopefully, feeling closer to God than she had since their reunion in death. "Could you both put your hands on me, please?"

"Of course." The two men answered almost in unison. John Keyes smiled firmly and moved closer to the brother and sister.

"I want to tell you something first." Mora spoke clearly. "Even though I don't hold the same religious beliefs you do, I know that love is still love and it all comes from God. When you lay your hands on my body to pray for me, I know it's love that comes from God. And I want it. . ." Mora's voice wavered and her eyes brimmed with tears. "I want love to help me."

"Mora," John's eyes filled like two pools reflecting hers. "You have a courageous spirit and I believe God has marked you. I am so very moved by your strength, I can't say. . ." He looked down at his hands, trying to hide the stream of emotion, then back to David. "Let's pray now."

David moved closer and gently placed one hand on Mora's crown, extending the other to his friend beside him. John rested a calm hand on Mora's palm and the three were connected.

"Lord God," David closed his eyes and supplicated in his deeply sweet tone. "We call Your Name so that You will be with us now. In Your Name we ask for Mora's healing, that her neck now be completely and fully healed. We place our trust in your infinite power and we thank You, God."

"Thank You, Lord God." John rejoined with closed eyes. "Use our hearts and hands as Your instruments for Mora's healing. We are united here together and we ask You to extend Your perfect repair to Mora's body now. We accept that it's already done. Thank You, God."

"I feel something like electricity shooting through me!" Mora cried out from behind closed eyes. "God, I know You are the only One who can fix my body. Please! I don't know what You do or how You do it, but please heal me." Tears blended joy with desire. "Thank

You, God, for preserving my life. Thank you for giving me back my life and for the love shared among us now." Without understanding why, Mora felt compelled to say the next words out loud. "Thank you God for healing whatever past we three shared. Thank you for joining us together. . . again." The spoken words sent surges of delicious joyful electricity, through hand to heart to head to ground to hand and all the way back down and around. And again, over and over until John's words marked the circuit even stronger. "I feel chills, too. Can you feel it, David?" Tears fell from John's closed eyes.

"Yes!" David chuckled and was first to open his eyes, then John, then Mora. As sure as a sunrise, each one saw the cord of brilliant blue light wrapped in gold encircle them and join them together.

- 6 -

Two days had passed since Mora's surgery. She wove in and out of consciousness, in pain but out of danger. On the third morning she opened her eyes to a different, larger room filled with sunlight and was greeted by the sight of her mother's blue eyes. "Wake and shine, brown-eyed girl," Ellen called melodically from the bedside chair where she held Mora's hand. "You made it."

"What. . . where am I?" Mora asked, still hovering beneath the veil of anesthesia.

"You had a spinal fusion, let's see, three days ago, and doctor Anwar says you've done very well. You're doing so well, in fact, that you're out of the ICU in a nice new room by yourself, and I'm so glad to see you awake."

"I already had the surgery? It's over?" Mora asked incredulously.

"Yes, it's over. You made it and doctor Anwar says it looks good. Very hopeful."

"Can I talk to him? I need to know what happened. Could you get him, Ma?"

"Sure honey. I'll go out to the nurse's station and see if he's around. I'll be right back." Ellen got up and left Mora alone to greet the new world with sobs.

"What is it?" Gentle words came from a nurse standing over Mora. "Are you frightened, hon?"

Mora opened her groggy eyes to answer. "Oh, when is this going to end? I feel awful!"

"You know, I'd be worried about you if you didn't feel that way after what you've been through." The nurse smiled serenely.

"You've really had a rough time of it, haven't you? I'm Kathleen. It's nice to meet you, Mora. And I'm going to take your vital signs." The nurse glided through taking blood pressure, pulse, and temperature in seconds.

Ellen returned with another nurse.

"Good morning, Mora. Today's the day we sit you up." Nurse number two was suddenly positioned on the opposite side of the bed from her colleague.

"Wait, wait, wait, wait a minute. Ma, where's doctor Anwar?" Panic fluttered in Mora's throat.

"He wants us to get you sitting up today," announced the second nurse in a louder voice as if Mora's surgery had resulted in hearing loss.

"Wait a minute! Ma. . ."

"They said he'll be here sometime this morning. Nurse, I think you should wait a minute." Ellen quickly interpreted her daughter's words.

Kathleen turned to face her worried patient. "Doctor Anwar wants us to sit you up because it's time to get you going again. They used to keep post-surgery patients still for a long time but now they know you must move as soon as you can."

"Okay. But I can't yet," Mora declared flatly.

"Doctor Anwar suggested we at least try today." Kathleen left the door open for a choice.

"How would we do it? I want to know ahead of time." Mora needed to feel her own way into physical security.

"First, we slowly raise the head of the bed. Then, if all goes well, Debra and I are going to carefully ease you up into a sitting position. How does that sound?"

"Impossible." It had been two weeks since the crash. The world had crumbled around her, and safety consisted of lying supine, her head attached to wall pulleys, her body fully supported by a bed. Mora was terrified by the prospect of altering her plane of gravity. Her newly-fused neck felt completely incapable of providing support. She also had five extra pounds of metal attatched to her upper body. *How the hell,* she thought, *will I ever be able to sit up?* She lay there pushing out hot, angry, panicked breaths while the two nurses and her mother waited.

"So. Let's give it a shot, hey?" Debra suggested, moving toward the bed control.

"Wait a minute!" Mora growled. "Please come and put your hands on me now so I know you're there." She would not allow them to do it without her full agreement.

Kathleen put her hands on Mora's left arm and hand.

"Should I do anything?" Ellen asked, looking at each of the two nurses.

"Just stay here, Ma, in case." It was one thing to surrender to death, but a totally different matter to sit up after surgery.

Debra pushed the button, the bed engaged, and the head rose several degrees.

"Okay stop." Mora snapped and held her breath to wait for settlement.

"Aghhhh. . . I feel dizzy. Wait." Mora started to cry. "I feel sick. I can't do it."

Debra exhaled a hot, impatient breath.

"Look." Mora's tears were replaced by defensiveness. "Don't push me! This is my body, and I'm inside it. I know what it feels like. I decide what happens to it. You got that?" Her anger shook off anesthesic residue. "If you don't do it the way I want, go get another nurse who will." She maintained an immovable stare at the wall straight ahead.

"Okay, Mora. Come on now." Ellen's characteristic impatience was beginning to show through. "Just relax and let's try again."

"You're doing great, Mora, and I bet you can go further," came from Kathleen who maintained a steady hold.

Closing her eyes and taking a deep breath, Mora said, "Okay, but just a little bit more."

Debra pushed the button again and Mora's upper body elevated a few more degrees.

"Stop!" Mora shouted.

"Got it," Debra responded instantly.

The three women watched and waited for the patient to adjust.

Mora flicked her eyes open and breathed a few deep breaths. "Okay. A little more."

The gears engaged and raised the bed several degrees more until she was sitting up halfway.

"Wait!" Mora snapped.

Debra's hand missed the control button and the bed continued to rise.

"Stop!" Mora shouted.

"Oh, I'm sorry!" Debra finally stopped the bed.

Mora's face drained of color and her breathing quickened.

"Are you okay?" Kathleen's voice came through. "I think we better bring her down a little." They lowered the bed a few degrees.

"I can't do it!" Mora cried. "I feel as fragile as glass. Please let me lie down again!"

Just as they returned the bed to flat, doctor Anwar came in. "What's the trouble?" His deep soft voice cut the tension in the room.

"I can't even sit up!" Her sobs crashed like waves on a concrete wall.

"That is temporary, Mora. At this moment you cannot sit up. Don't worry. You will be able to later. Isn't that so?" The doctor turned to the nurses who quickly picked up the reins.

"Of course!" Relief floated out Kathleen's words. "Hey, you gave it a good try. We'll let you rest and try again another time."

"Doctor, Mora wanted to know how the surgery went." Ellen picked up a constructive rein, too. "Could you explain it to her? I think that would give her a little encouragement."

"Of course." Doctor Anwar stood at Mora's bedside facing her, his hands held together in front of him. "First, I want to tell you that we found it necessary to fuse only C5 and C6, rather than 4, 5 and 6 as I had originally anticipated. I am quite sure of the stability of this single fusion. It was perfect. And you were fortunate in that we did not need to transfuse blood. You lost very little. Now, as to the condition of your spinal cord." He paused and looked from mother to daughter. "It was unnecessary to access it directly in order to fuse your vertebrae. In other words, I did not see the exact condition of your spinal cord, so the precise potential of all damage being recovered is unknown. Whether or not you regain all of your function, only time will tell."

Mora closed her eyes and collapsed into crying.

"Mora, as a physician it is my duty to tell you the truth. As a human being I would like to offer my personal opinion. Mora, listen to me now."

She opened her eyes and looked into doctor Anwar's familiar and deeply comforting, clear green eyes.

"I believe that you can hope for a full recovery."

Mora saw light pouring out his eyes. It was the same strength of spirit she had experienced in death. She knew that this man's hands in her life were a gift. Nothing was certain. . . nothing except the one thing in the world you could absolutely depend on: the power of love. She opened the door of her heart and let it pour in.

"And now I would like to examine you." Doctor Anwar produced his flesh-pricking pin and proceeded to find out if Mora's dermatone sensitivity had increased.

*   *   *

Deep and restful sleep drew Mora into God's comforting arms again. It was a saving grace to have both worlds in which to dwell. The realm of the spirit provided true meaning, while the other served as a laboratory for its application. When one was thoroughly taxed, her mind mercifully shifted gears. Every day was an endless trail of effortful, gravity-bound labor soaked with emotions. Her task was to bring forth the dark feelings into the light that she now knew was true. It was the only way to survive.

*   *   *

She awoke in the hour of stillness, at two or three in the afternoon when everyone else in the world seemed absorbed in normal occupations. All her life she had noticed this part of the day move onward, carrying everyone while only she stood still. She could sense but not see hospital staff passing her open door on their way to someplace important. In the past, she had always felt guilty about being still at mid-day.

But now things were different; now she had a legitimate reason to be still. It was her job not to move because she was paralyzed.

Guilt over non-productive time was gone, replaced by a measure of serenity and honest introspection. "Maybe that's what my hour of stillness was offering. I was so busy trying to get people outside me to give me what I thought I didn't have," she whispered to love. "How foolish I've been, God. Meeting You again showed me You've always been inside me, this love I've searched for." And as if God were verifying her conclusion, Kathleen and Debra waltzed into the room.

"Ready to try sitting up again?" Kathleen was full of energy. "I've got a chair here waiting for you to warm it up."

"Well, I guess I have to face it, don't I. Just go at my pace, okay?" As long as Mora had some control, she found it easier to hang on.

"Yes indeed. You're the boss." Debra wore a devilish grin that made Mora laugh.

The two nurses positioned themselves at either side of Mora. In tiny steps they raised the head of the bed and allowed Mora time to adjust. After five or six increments she was sitting up, the two nurses still holding her arms for psychological security.

"Look at me!" A smile broke across Mora's face. "I've just entered the world of the vertical people!" The three women laughed with delight. And at that exact moment Ellen walked in with Mora's eldest sister, Louise.

"Louise! What are you doing here?" Mora drank in Louise's delicate beauty. Her long, auburn-red hair complimented the hand-made, cotton, lavender and green print dress she wore.

"I came to be with you, to help if I could," Louise answered as she took in the shocking sight of Mora sitting up in bed, metal screws jutting out from her forehead, chopped hair, I.V.s in both arms, catheter hose and bag. Louise's green eyes filled with tears to see her sister's helpless state.

"What about Steven? Is Donald taking care of him?" Mora was surprised Louise could get away from her husband and son.

"Yes, and they're fine." Her face took on the Donovan expression of worry. "How are you. . . I mean, this is a terrible thing. . . how do you feel?"

"Oh, sometimes awful, most of the time happy to be alive, all mixed together. I'm so glad to see you. Thanks for coming." It didn't take much these days to trigger Mora's tears, and they slid down her cheeks. "You look so lovely. Your hair and your dress. . . I wish I could get dressed up but I can't even move." Hearing herself speak the truth brought forth sobs from Mora. Her mother and sister came closer and Louise wiped her own tears.

"Mommy called me and told me what happened. I thought 'God, Mora's had such a rough time. . . the divorce, the alcohol problem, the business. How could this happen on top of everything else?'" Louise reached out and gently touched Mora's swollen, limp hand. "And here you are. Telling me I'm beautiful." She shook her head in disbelief and struggled to hold back her tears. "Now you're already sitting up. I don't know how you've done it. But you've always been so strong. I'm just so relieved to see you alive."

It was a rare moment of affection between them. Mora had childhood memories of conspiring with Claire to mentally torture Louise. The most vivid recollection came to Mora now: Louise had been instructed to get the two younger girls into bed by 9:00 P.M. Naturally they resisted, finally manipulating her into dragging them physically up the stairs. When Louise gave up and collapsed in tears, the two girls took pity and went peacefully to bed. Louise had gone off to live on her own as soon as she reached eighteen, and Mora had always felt at least partly responsible for driving her sister out of the house.

"Do you think you'll ever forgive me for being such a bratty kid?" Mora asked Louise now, only half jokingly.

As if Louise had been reviewing that very same memory she raised her eyebrows and swept her free hand between them in peaceful absolution. "The past is gone, isn't it? Today is what we have, and I'm happy you're alive."

*   *   *

Every day Sherrie, the physical therapist, came in to move Mora's limbs. She would lift Mora's leg and rotate it around as far as it would go wherever it would go, then stretch the muscles just up to Mora's "Aghhh!" spoken limit. The procedure would be repeated on the other leg and on both arms.

"Way back a couple a weeks ago in my other life as a massage therapist I never got anywhere trying to push clients past their limit," Mora told her, "because of the contraction reaction. It's funny how people are. If you push them past where they're ready to go, get ready for resistance. One way or another. Aghhh!"

Mora appreciated Sherrie's easy tolerance. Sherrie chatted about her husband, her friends, her life. Listening empathically had always been Mora's way of worth in the world. It was an old habit to measure her own value according to how much energy she spent helping people. Now that table was wiped clean. All but the inner world of her relationship with God seemed out of reach. It was a new way for her, to live inside and draw out what she needed from there. For the rest, she was forced to let love's designated helpers feed, visit, pray over, and stretch her.

There was stiffness not only in her muscles, but also in her pride about being mother-hen to employees and customers. She had plenty of time to think about the tiny empire she'd built. The employees and friends she now wanted most weren't there; and although it was still hard to accept the fact that certain people weren't returning the attention she wanted from them, an unexpected stream of human angels came to her aid.

Carmella, for instance. She was a registered nurse and a down-to-earth, responsible mother of four who had attended aerobics classes since the day Fitness & More opened. Spotting her ease with movement and people, Mora had invited her to take the instructor training. And what refreshing humility greeted the suggestion! Had the situation been reversed Mora imagined her ego would have swelled. Mora told Carmella she needed a good instructor, so Carmella took the training and the job. Now, lying still with nothing to do but think, Mora questioned the purity of her past motivations for helping others. She marveled at Carmella's selfless helping to answer others' needs. On the day of the crash it was Carmella who volunteered to take care of the bookkeeping and the payroll so the business could stay open, and she refused extra pay after she saw the bank balance. If Mora could have shaken her head in awe of her employee, she would have. Instead, when Carmella came to the hospital to visit, all Mora could do was watch and learn, and thank her verbally. "I want to be like you when I grow up," Mora told her. Carmella just smiled, shyly lowered her eyes and said, "Yeah, but my house is a mess."

*   *   *

Then one day Hope showed up.

"Hey girl, how are you doing?" The Teknet aerobics student asked, tentatively sticking her head into the room. "May I come in?" She carried a bouquet of flowers and a bagful of get-well cards from other Tekies.

"Hope! Come in!"

"I am sent by my people on a mission of good will. But most of all I had to see you for myself. God!" Hope pushed out a hard exhale and shook her head. "I am so sorry."

"Pretty bad, huh?" When a new visitor came and first took in her shocking appearance, Mora would often cry. It was as if she saw herself from the outside and it was still a slap in the face. This time was no different.

"Oh Mora, I feel so bad for you." Hope's voice shook. "I just want to help. Is there anything I can do? Anything at all."

"Yes. Could you blow my nose for me? I think I've had about thirty crying spells so far today. They just keep coming but I'm sure as hell not going to stop them. That would be stupid. It's more fun getting my nose stuffed up and not being able to breathe and having my mouth dry up and having to pester a nurse to blow my nose and swab my mouth." Mora's laughter stopped her crying. Amazed, Hope tentatively joined in while holding a tissue to Mora's nose.

"I really want to help. . . if you want me to, that is. I know there must be things you need. I talked to Carmella today and she filled me in on what happened. Do you have any feeling, any movement? You don't have to tell me unless you want to."

"Well. . . yes. What do I say first. . . . I feel almost nothing, but it's something. Doctor Anwar, my neurosurgeon, comes in once or twice a day to stick pins in me. Most of them I can't feel but some I can and it's horrendous. He calls it hypersensitive and gets paid a lot. I call it torture and cry a lot." Mora tried levity again. "Anyway, that's my skin, dermatones. He says it's a good sign. Where there's any reaction at all there's life. The movement. . . well. . . look at this." Mora lowered her eyes to her legs. Hope's eyes followed and waited to see what would happen next. There was the slightest hint of movement of her right leg, steered by the big toe. "Maybe more tomorrow." Mora closed her eyes and broke into tears. "It's so horrible, Hope! Day after day, I don't seem to change much."

"I was here before," Hope interrupted excitedly. "I came to see you in ICU the day after the crash and you were asleep. I peeked into your room. You looked so pale and completely vulnerable, as if life wasn't all the way in you." Hope kept the words coming through a quavering voice. "You have no idea how happy I am that you're asking me to blow your nose. You're incredibly courageous and strong. I don't think I could live through what you've been through. You *are* better, I'm here to tell you. So don't give up. I believe in you. And I want to help. Okay?" Tears fell down her cheeks and she wiped them away, adding quickly, "Bossy, aren't I?"

The two women laughed and cried, one emotion finally pushing the other aside.

"Thanks Hope. I needed that. Could you blow my nose again please?" They laughed some more. "Aren't you glad you signed up for this job?"

"The pay ain't much but the benefits are terrific!"

"If you want to, pull up a chair and tell me your life story. Or anything. I'm just so glad you're here."

Hope pulled a chair bedside and settled down to reveal what was in the bag. "Would you like me to open and read these cards from fellow aerobic Tekies?"

"I'd love it." Mora sniffled. "Before you start, could you scratch my right cheek, about an inch under my eye, but not too hard?"

"Couldn't you be more specific?"

"Sure. Could you bop yourself over the head first?" Mora sighed in relief. "Oh, it feels good to laugh. Okay, read on."

*   *   *

Visiting hours officially ended at 9:00 P.M. but Hope stayed later. At around 8:45 the nurse assigned to the night shift stopped in, took vitals, cleaned Mora's "pin sites" (the screw holes in her skull), and gave an easy okay for Hope to stay late. The two friends watched a little television, talking back to everything they saw. By 10:15 Mora's eyelids were closing and Hope departed with a promise to return the next evening after work.

Alone again in the dark room Mora connected with her Constant Companion. "Thank you, God, for my life this day. Thank you for letting me meet You again and come back to another chance. Thank you for staying with me." She drifted into dreamy sleep.

*   *   *

Wind. . . rising wind. . . swirling spirals arise in hope.

She's standing, not on ground, yet supported. The wind lifts her body and carries her. "My body is so perfectly fine that I can fly!" breezes through her mind, lifting her free. . . .

Her arms are wings, spread open wide. Instantly she feels lighter and stronger than she's ever felt! Her body is graceful, weightless, and nourished by winds of joy. She flies over clouds, friendly, welcoming, billowy white and silver clouds, so safe.

Suddenly there appears a glitteringly lovely shopping mall beneath her. It's empty. . . except. . . look! All the wide glass doors are opening and friendly clerks are coming out waving at her to come down. "Come in! Come in!" they say through welcoming smiles. "It's free! You don't need to pay! Come! Pick out all the beautiful clothes, gowns, lovely dresses, shoes, hats, and accessories you desire! Come fly in! This is all here just for you!" The bright neon signs and gorgeously garbed manikins blink and smile, waving to her, inviting her into every store, empty of other customers just for her. What delight! She flies in and through the stores, drinking in all the lovely outfits but passing them by. She has so much more now! Deliciously filled she flies over it and away. . . she flies and flies, alive, strong and free!

In a half-second jolt, Mora moved her entire body; in the next half-second, the real motion yanked her awake. *Wait a second. . . I'm paralyzed. . . I CAN'T move!* Her gravity-bound mind reminded her, and her body fell back into the room, motionless once again. But not before the whole sequence registered in her consciousness. "Oh yes I can!" she argued back. Chills of delighted recognition shot up and down her spine. "You can't fool me, my brain! I saw the whole thing. I moved!" She shouted out loud into the dark room. "If I can move for a split second, I CAN MOVE!"

- 7 -

Rosy morning flooded her bright, hopeful light into the room. Mora's eyes opened to Jessie, the morning custodian, mopping her daily path across the floor. The middle-aged woman had an unintrusive tread among sleeping patients, but was transformed into a broom-carrying spiritual counselor once they were awake.

"How are you feeling this morning, Mora?"

"Oh Jessie, I feel wonderful." The excitement from last night's dream was uncontainable. "I had a dream I was flying last night, and you know what happened?"

"What?"

"I actually moved and it woke me up! Now I *know* I'm not going to stay like this."

"Hmm-hmmm, that's so fine, real fine." Jessie shook her head, smiling. "See? The Lord is helping you in all kinds of ways, sending you a dream you can grab hold of."

"You're right, Jessie." Mora's first batch of tears for the day arrived. "God is with me, boosting me every inch of the way. And I'll have you know you're a spiritual booster disguised as a sanitary technician."

"You got that right." Jessie laughed and returned to her work. "You have yourself a good day, y'hear?"

P.A. voices called doctors and rolling breakfast carts announced that the rest of the 7 A.M. hospital world was awake. Kathleen breezed in. "Ready for breakfast, my dear?"

"You mean *food*?" Mora asked in disbelief.

"Well, I know how much you crave I.V.s but today we kick the habit." Kathleen took a tray from the hallway breakfast cart. "It's about time we used this bed tray for its intended purpose instead of as a desk for opening fan mail."

"I can't believe it! *Food!* Real food! Oh my God, and I thought my dream last night was as good as life could get. Wait 'til I tell you my dream." Mora's hungry eyes consumed the contents of the tray. "Jeez, I need a drool cup!"

"Now I get to find out what kind of table manners you have. But first we're going to move this bed and sit you up." In slow stages she raised the head of the bed. Within twenty seconds they established better equilibrium than they had achieved in an hour of trauma the day before.

Mora enjoyed having Kathleen around. She extended dauntless encouragement, and eased pain and frustration with gentle teasing and listening.

"I really value your tender loving care," Mora said. Expressing appreciation had taken on more importance to Mora since her death experience.

"Thank you."

"Do you want to hear my dream?" The green flecks in Mora's brown eyes sparkled.

"I'm all ears. . . and hands."

"I dreamed I was flying over the most beautiful, sparkling shopping mall in the world. All the doors opened and store clerks called up to me, 'Come in and shop for free!'"

"That was a dream, all right," Kathleen laughed.

"I didn't even want anything because I felt so full and satisfied from flying. And I *love* to shop. It was so realistic, the physical exhilaration of flying, that I went along with it. Or I let it take me. I actually started to do it! I literally moved and the movement woke me up! Then I thought 'Hey, I can't move. I'm paralyzed.' But Kathleen. . .'" Mora halted and drew Kathleen's eyes to hers. "I watched my mind try to tell me I was still paralyzed right after I moved! So I can't completely believe this paralysis any more. I *know* I can get out of this hole."

Kathleen stopped what she was doing and looked into her patient's eyes. "You know, it doesn't matter how hope talks to you.

You use everything to help you. Hold onto that dream, and anything else that gives you a glimpse of what can happen." She narrowed her eyes, wagging a pointed finger at Mora. "And don't let anybody take hope away from you. God's the only absolute decider, no doctor, no preacher, nobody but you and God." She smiled and returned to opening and pouring milk over oatmeal. "You like milk on your mush?"

"Pretend I'm nodding my head." Mora answered quickly, hoping for more encouragement.

"You're a strong woman, Mora," Kathleen continued seriously. "I've seen lots of patients come and go and I'll tell you, you're going to do what you set your mind to. Do you want to know why?"

"Of course."

"You're in charge of your own thoughts. You know what you've got inside. You know what you want and you stay with it. And you speak up for yourself. All the nurses have noticed that."

Mora laughed. "Oh really? You mean I'm already notorious?"

"You're not the only one, though. Have you ever heard that guy across the hall?" Kathleen opened the napkin and gently tucked it into the halo vest front.

"He's hard to ignore! Is the psych ward so filled up that they had to put him down here? What's wrong with him?"

"He's a medical doctor." Kathleen leaned toward Mora and whispered. "In fact, he works in this hospital."

"You're kidding! What's his problem?"

"He had a hernia operation and boy, I'll tell you, he is the complainingest, crabbiest, most demanding patient I've *ever* seen. But you know what? When he yells the staff comes running. Everybody wants him out of here so the staff is, shall we say, highly motivated to give him what he wants. Okay, food time. Ready?"

It had been a long time since Mora had the pleasure of tasting food. She closed her eyes and savored the experience. "Oh God, this is orgasmic. Hhhhh."

"Sex'll be unbelievable if mushy oatmeal is great."

The instant the Forbidden Word was released into the atmosphere, they both willed it to evaporate. Kathleen regretted slipping on it and Mora ignored it, wanting to keep hold of what she already had: her hopeful dream and breakfast.

Mora seized the awkward moment by the horns. "I love to eat. The only reason I exercise — I mean when I used to — was so that I could eat whatever I wanted. Could you give me some of that banana too?" Mora used her eyes to point.

"Sure." Kathleen peeled and offered it. "It's pretty normal for a person getting off I.V.s to have super-sensitive taste buds. As I was saying. I've noticed, over fifteen years of nursing, that the most demanding, supposedly 'selfish' patients get released quicker, and the ones who just lie back and don't want to trouble anyone take the longest to recover. Sometimes they don't particularly recover. They seem to just go home unfinished."

"Kathleen, are you in there?" scratched a woman's voice over the wall speaker.

"Excuse me, Mora." Kathleen reached over and pushed the button. "Yes, I am. What's up?"

"207 needs *only your* assistance right away. Can you, or should I call Dora?"

Kathleen whispered to Mora, "See? That's him. Will you be okay for a minute? It won't take long."

Mora laughed. "Sure. I can amuse myself while you're gone. I learned a few tricks from being born into a big family."

Mora's moment of solitude didn't last long. Ellen and Louise glided in, dressed in lovely handmade Vogue-patterned dresses that inspired a bittersweet blend of awe and sorrow in Mora. She felt like Cinderella before the ball, woefully dressed in a raggedy hospital gown complete with matching hardware. She wished she could share the ancient Donovan female bonding ritual with her mother and sister. Worse, she had no idea how she looked these days, and was truly afraid to find out.

"Oh, you two look so beautiful. I wish I could get dressed up." She tried in vain to fight back the tears.

Ellen was quick to respond. "You will honey, don't worry." Looking down at the breakfast tray, Ellen's face lit up. "You're eating food today? How wonderful!" She started to laugh, then thought better of it. "I'm sorry honey, I'm just remembering how you've always loved to eat. It's a definite sign of improvement."

"I started this morning and oh. . . food tastes so delicious." Mora blinked long and hard. "It was as if I'd never eaten before. Ma, could you feed me some of that banana?"

"Sure." Ellen brought the fruit to Mora's open mouth. "I thought my feeding days were over. This reminds me of when you were a baby. You were the best baby when it came to eating." Finding relief in a family story, Ellen fed both daughters and herself a pinch of the past. "You always ate everything I put in front of you, those big brown eyes waiting expectantly for the next mouthful."

"Yeah, and when I got old enough to feed Claire and David I'd give them each a spoonful saying 'one for you' then refill it and eat it myself saying 'and one for me'. I never told you that, did I?" Mora opened her mouth in readiness.

"It's a wonder they didn't starve to death." Ellen played along.

Louise spoke up. "Speaking of food, I bought some cookies in what passed for a bakery in Duffin. For your visitors. I thought it would be nice."

"Louise, only you could transform a hospital room into a tea salon. May I please see them?" Mora asked while Louise and Ellen glanced at each other and laughed.

"Mora," Louise said, opening the box, "may I interest you in a cookie, or two, or three?"

"Okay, I'm back." Kathleen 's voice heralded her return. "Good morning, ladies. I see I've been replaced."

"Not a chance," Mora retorted, "watch them scatter when you do the enema thing."

"And how about a bath?" Kathleen winked and began preparing a wash tub. "That is, if you ladies don't mind my company."

"We'll just wait outside and come back when you're finished." Ellen's Irish modesty came forth.

Kathleen pulled the curtain around the bed and began the morning cleansing ritual. Mora savored feeling fresh and clean even though the bath excluded her torso beneath the vest. Nearly three weeks had passed since her hair had been washed and the nursing staff was avoiding the logistical nightmare it presented. Every day fresh patches of skin reawakened to mostly uncomfortable sensations. Roughness against her flesh hurt horribly, like tart bitters on a lacerated tongue. Kathleen dabbed around the halo vest's plastic breast and backplates to avoid jolting the screws in Mora's skull. She lifted each arm carefully and with the softest, most worn-out washcloth she could find, delicately washed Mora's arms and each swollen finger.

Meanwhile, Mora thought about why she had hesitated to mention her dream to Ellen and Louise. The reason was that she and her family, particularly her mother, saw the world differently. The etheric realms of the spirit, God, dreams, and the underworld of imagination had always been Mora's preferred dwelling places. Ellen had turned away from "the God idea" years ago, preferring to rely heavily on outcomes in the tangible world. In times of illness, medical tests, procedures, surgery, and medication carried weight. She and all of her children except Mora and David depended primarily on the dictums of the traditional medical community. David and Mora, on the other hand, believed that any and all change was possible. Mora's confirmation had come in death. It was a rare gift of comprehension that no one could take away from her.

"You're quiet." Kathleen's voice ended Mora's internal conversation.

"I was just thinking." Mora's eyes focused far beyond the sky they saw outside the windows.

"I thought I saw smoke coming out your ears. Ready for teeth?"

"Oh yes, I love having clean ultra-white teeth as sparkly bright as the metal of my halo vest." Mora grinned and Kathleen rolled her eyes.

"You know, it really takes attentiveness to detail and sensitivity to brush someone else's teeth." Mora opened her mouth to receive the paste-smeared toothbrush.

"Well, the only time I've ever been a patient in a hospital was when I had my daughter," Kathleen said, keeping sharp focus on Mora's molars. "I didn't need all this kind of care. But I figure if I did, this is how I'd want to be treated. Okay, here's a rinse."

Ellen and Louise returned ready to work out a plan. They had enlisted a group of Mora's friends to move her belongings out of her apartment over the weekend. As soon as they settled in for a conference, Mrs. Franklin, the occupational therapist, arrived with a plan of her own.

"I hope I'm not interrupting anything but I've come up with some photographs of modified halo shirts I thought you might like to see." She tentatively displayed the magazine. "According to the instructions you cut flaps here on a button-down shirt, double hem them and sew velcro onto the ends." She smiled innocently as the two fashion queens exchanged conspiring glances. Mora watched what was really going on.

Getting things done efficiently and with individual style gave the Donovan women immense satisfaction. Ellen had discouraged her girls from watching soap operas, playing bridge, and bowling because "everybody" did those things. Ellen designed clothes, built bunk-trundle beds, tore down bathroom walls, and installed mirror-and-tile vanities in their place. She designed and built brick patios and stone walls singlehandedly. And she had a particular aversion to being categorized as a suburban woman, resisting the feminine conformity of post-war America at every turn. She vociferously rejected the title "housewife" long before protest was politically correct. Ellen Donovan was slave to no one, especially Mora's traveling salesman father, who had abruptly left the family without a trace when Mora was fifteen.

The Donovan girls and their friends amused themselves for hours playing imaginative dress-up games in the basement. They pieced together stage-worthy wardrobes from cast-off clothing and pranced dreamily across the linoleum floor to the accompaniment of show tunes on the record player. Doll dishes were cut out from magazine pictures and pasted with flour and water onto cardboard. Very early in life, imagination became Mora's favorite plaything.

Being an individual with constructive, creative outlets merited paramount honor in Ellen's eyes. Whatever creations were birthed also had to be functional if they wanted to stay around. That included children. Just before she was ready was when little Mora had to clear dishes off the dinner table or, later, get a job to help support the family. "Do it anyway" wasn't appreciated at six or sixteen years of age. But at nineteen, when she had her own apartment, part-time job, and full college schedule complete with a social life, her peers asked her advice on elementary tasks like how to fold laundry and buy groceries with parents' money. Only then did Mora begin to see that her mother's independent, achieving spirit had rubbed off on her.

These memories ran through Mora's mental storage plates as Mrs. Franklin gave Ellen Donovan and her daughter Louise instructions.

"Do you sew?" Mrs. Franklin inquired guilelessly.

"Uh. . . yes," replied Ellen.

"Haven't you noticed those modified French seams?" Mora said, daring only to fantasize interrupting them with puffery. *Of course! I'll have you know that my mother has reupholstered more furniture than you've ever sat upon. In fact, in the summer of '61 she retrieved a beat up old fan-back chair from someone's trash heap, brought it home and reupholstered it with green velveteen. Someone offered her three hundred dollars for it!* Mora smiled, watched and listened.

"Well, all you need to do is take an old, slightly oversized, button-down collar shirt and. . ."

"Ma," Mora interrupted, "I have never owned a button-down shirt in my life, unless it was against my will, like when I had to wear a uniform in catholic school."

"So we'll buy some." Ellen kept her attention on Mrs. Franklin.

"But I *hate* button-down collar shirts," Mora persisted. "I hated them before, I look terrible in them, why would I want to look even worse with chopped hair and screws sticking out of my head?"

"Oh, this will just be an alternative to wearing the hospital johnnie gown," Mrs. Franklin offered. "You'll want some clothing variety for the several months you'll be in your halo."

Mora's chin dropped. "Several months? Oh, fuck." Her eyes welled up with tears.

Ellen rebounded. "Oh, I'll go out and get you some nice shirts."

"How about bright colors like turquoise and magenta?" Louise followed; but it was too late.

"I don't care! I still fucking can't move whether my shirt is red or green!" Mora shouted and sobbed.

"I know this is a terrible thing to have to go through, Mora." Mrs. Franklin came to her bedside and gently touched her arm. "You're discouraged right now, but you've made a lot of improvement. One thing leads to another. I know it's easy for others to say, but it's true. Don't let it keep you down." She gently touched Mora's shoulder, then whispered to Ellen and Louise. "I'll be downstairs in OT if you need me."

Louise averted her tearful eyes from her sister. "May I discuss this with you, Mrs. Franklin?" she whispered. When the two women left Ellen pulled a chair up to Mora's bedside.

"Mora, honey. Don't worry. No matter what happens, we'll help you through it." Ellen picked up her daughter's hand and fought back tears of her own. "I love you very much, we all do, and we'll stick by you no matter what, okay?"

"Mommy, I love you." Mora sobbed. "You're the one I really need."

Mother and daughter rested in their true, eternal bond.

                    *   *   *

It was almost eleven when a refreshed Louise returned with Kathleen.

"We have an idea," Kathleen announced. "How would you like to go for a ride in a wheelchair? See the hospital?"

"What a great idea!" Ellen said, relieved.

"Ma, wait a minute. I don't know if I can yet. What if I pass out? I've never left the room." Mora's heart pushed against her chest.

"Okay," Kathleen nodded. "We'll just try it. If you're not ready, we won't do it."

Mora sighed. "Okay."

Louise and Kathleen lifted Mora into the wheelchair, placed her swollen feet onto the footrests and her hands on the armrests, and belted her in.

"Would you like me to take you?" Louise stood in front of the chair to read her sister's face.

"Is that okay, Kathleen?" Mora asked.

"Sure. It's time to see the world."

"I'm scared." Mora's lower lip quivered. "Nobody out there has seen me yet. What if they stare at me?"

"Then you stare right back!" Kathleen growled fiercely. "Hey, if they do, you know they just don't know any better. Ignore them."

"Okay." Mora mumbled. "Let'er rip."

Louise went behind the wheelchair, grasped the handlebars, and released the brakes. "You just tell me if I'm going too fast, of if you want to change directions."

Rolling down the quiet med-surge hall, they encountered a few hospital staff who either smiled or looked past.

"Where do you want to go?" Louise asked.

"Let's go to physical therapy and surprise Sherrie."

"Physical therapy it is." Louise wheeled her into the open patient transport elevator. The doors opened to the hospital's busy, spacious, sun-drenched front entrance.

"Jeez, look at all the people," Mora whispered. "I must look like some kind of space monster."

"Do you want to keep going?" Louise asked.

"Might as well. We've come this far."

A couple with two small children approached. When the little boy caught sight of Mora he pointed, shouting, "Mommy, what happened to that man?" His mother stared at Mora in silent horror.

"I'm a girl and it's not nice to point," Mora snapped as they quickly rolled past. "I hate that."

"I can see he learned it from his mother," Louise said, steering the wheelchair into the wide doorway. "Okay, here we are."

A full-length mirror greeted Mora's eyes. "Agghhhh!" she screamed. "Turn me away!"

"Oh! Mora, I'm sorry!" Louise grabbed the handles and jerked the chair away from the mirror. "Oh, I'm so sorry. . . are you okay?" she asked, leaning over.

Mora burst into tears. The image she'd just seen flashed in her mind. "Louise. . . please turn me back. I want to see."

"Are you sure?"

"Yes. I need to see."

"Okay," Louise hesitated before changing directions. "If you're sure." She positioned Mora to face her reflection.

Mora drank in her own body's appearance. Puffy hands were limp and frail, resting where someone else had placed them. Harmless, they waited for life to return. Thin, delicate legs were spindly from atrophy, purposeless. Short, chopped hair framed the face. . . etheric, strangely beautiful, unguarded, without pretense. . . peering back at her so soft and tender, hiding nothing and showing everything. The eyes of her own soul saw the woman she was. . . completely vulnerable yet struggling with all her will to survive.

"I love you," Mora said as she gazed upon this woman, "and you're me."

- 8 -

The hour between four and five in the afternoon was a quiet one on the med-surge floor. Mora lived in a semi-private room but because she had so many visitors, the nursing staff thought it best she have it to herself. The second bed remained an illegal resting place for guests, gifts, laundry, snacks, and other homey necessities.

Alone in her room, Mora thought about the people who had sent the nearly 100 get-well cards covering the wall. Handwritten words reached over to her in bed, some from people she knew barely or not at all. She relished the surprises. One woman who worked at Teknet had sent a card: "Although we've never met," she wrote, "I know you've always encouraged others when they were down. Now you have a lot of people, including myself, praying for your recovery. Don't give up."

"I'm in your corner," was printed on a handmade card from her friend Eric, an acupuncturist and polarity practitioner she had briefly dated before the crash. These days, thoughts of romance never crossed her mind.

The flood of support from family, friends, and customers came as a complete surprise. If the crash hadn't occurred, Mora might never have known how much people cared. The veil that had kept her blind to her own worth had lifted. Heaven came back with her into the physical world.

As the Indian summer light spread an orange glow over her bed, she let her eyes rest on the quilt covering her legs. It was a gift from its creators, her friends Claudia and Paul. "We made it on the day of your surgery," Claudia had said. "See the date embroidered in the corner? Paul took the day off from work and we sewed it together.

Every stitch has *'Come on Mora, you can make it!'* sewn into it."
Another gift-bearer, Carolyn, made vegetarian sushi, brought it in on
a little Japanese plate, fed it to her with chopsticks, then gave her a
gentle head massage. Harriet, one of the aerobics instructors, fed her
a chocolate milkshake and fresh lobster meat. Her friend Ruth fed
her garden-fresh tomato slices. Mora chuckled to realize that others
noticed her love of food.

She was visited by doctor Howard, a minister who had been
her massage client, one rainy, frustrating day. All she had to offer
him was tears. He called her courageous. She asked him if she had a
choice, and he reminded her she was making it every second.

Mora marveled too, at the rare visitors who came in to tell her
their troubles. "Boy, it's terrible being in the hospital, I know," said one
acquaintance as he shook his head and looked out the window. "My
gall bladder surgery was awful. Let me tell you what they did. Oh, it
was terrible!" Astounded by his idea of a "visit," Mora barely listened;
he would have helped her more, she thought, by staying home.

It came as a surprise to Mora that receiving a steady stream of
visitors was exhausting. Although surgery's trauma and anesthesia
had worn off, remnants of people-pleasing behavior patterns lin-
gered. But as fatigue sat down beside her, she was forced to pay
attention to her own needs. Along with thinking, eating, and feeling,
sleep was her primary occupation, requiring half of the daylight
hours and fitful parts of the night. She imagined new cells were
being manufactured at a furious rate while she slept.

Earlier in the week Mora had begun to move in bed, dragging
each leg two inches toward the other. Everyone was thrilled, while
Mora was frustrated with what remained paralyzed. Her innate
body was a robust, half-human, half-horse, spirited Sagittarian patterned to live at a gallop, fired by powerful thigh muscles. Freedom
of movement had always been a strong, motivating thread running
through her. She knew the memory was *in* there. . . somewhere.

Mora saw herself at the bottom of a deep, dark, tight pit whose
cold walls kept her closed in. Far away at the top were ground, light,
and the rest of the moving world. If only she had a way up.
Sometimes she closed her eyes and saw herself yell up to the light at

the top. "Help! Would someone throw me a rope? I could get up if I had a rope to grab!" The picture always brought tears.

"God, I wish You could show me a video tape of me in five years. Me from the future showing me now how it will be. I wish I could see that."

One day someone knocked on her door, interrupting Mora's prayer.

"Hello!" An unfamiliar female voice called. "May I come in?"

"Yes."

A petite woman entered and timidly approached Mora's bed. "My name is Patty and my husband works at Teknet. He heard about you through the computer net and told me about you. I hope you don't mind that I came to show you these." She pointed to the two scars, little round dents in each side of her forehead. "I broke my neck too."

"Oh, my God! I don't believe it!"

"Oh yes, it's completely true!"

"I didn't mean I don't believe you," Mora said. "You see, I just finished asking God to show me a video of me in five years. Then you showed up! This is too amazing. . . just too amazing." Mora laughed. "Please, tell me what happened to you."

"I had a car crash like you. I was in the hospital four months and I wore the halo for six. It was awful, the waiting, not moving. But that was four years ago. I'm mostly fine now." Her smile was as placid as a still lake.

"Wow." Mora visually digested the woman's vitality, coordination and normal stature, and the two badges of courage on her forehead.

Mora knew then that there was no giving up. "If you can do it, I can do it. You have no idea how I appreciate you coming here."

Patty smiled. "If someone had come to me when I was in the hospital and showed me how I could be down the road, it would've helped. I thought it might help you."

"Thank you for giving me a real, live picture I can hold in my heart. You're a miracle and I'm going to remember you."

When Patty left, Mora was a little closer to the top of the pit.

*   *   *

At 5 P.M. Mora awakened groggy just as Carl arrived.

"Hi, Carl."

"Hi. How are you doing today? Any new developments?" He stood at her bedside with his hands in his pockets.

"May I have a hug?" Mora asked, and he obliged.

"Would you give me a kiss too?" she asked hopefully. He carefully kissed her cheek.

"Thanks, Carl. You know, I haven't told you about what I saw when I died."

"What?"

"My body's eyes didn't see this." She spoke slowly, searching for the best words. "I saw with my mind. I understood that. . ."

"Look, I don't like being talked down to," he interrupted accusingly. "I'm not stupid you know. You're still doing it to me."

Short, shallow breaths chased her words. "No, Carl." She began to cry, scrambling to explain. "I'm talking as fast as I can think. I can't talk any faster than this right now."

"Oh."

"May I tell you what I saw?"

"Yeah, sure." He shrugged.

"I know you still hold things against me from before. But when I died, I saw, or understood with my heart, that you've always loved me the best you could. And you still do." Mora labored to speak through a stinging throat, unwilling to withhold important information. "And I have always loved you. . . I still do. . . the best I could. Even if it means we go our separate ways for the rest of this life, the important thing I know now is that you *have* loved me."

"Yes, you'll always be important to me, and I've learned a lot from you."

As Mora listened, the charge dwindled, the old bondage of self-blame was going away.

"Oh, I remember what I came to tell you. I went to divorce court today and told the judge the reason you couldn't be there. He said it was a legitimate excuse." Carl smiled and blinked, waiting for Mora to laugh.

"Oh?" Mora began to feel the weight of an anvil pressing down on her chest. "What happened?"

"Congratulations. We're officially unmarried, as of today. He signed the papers so the divorce is final." Carl's smile expanded.

"Oh."

"Ahem, hmmm. . . anybody home?" Hope's cheerful, clear, voice of comfort cut the congested air.

"Come in, Hope, and meet Carl, my new ex-husband." Suddenly exhausted, Mora closed her eyes.

"Hi." Hope scanned Carl and quickly turned to Mora. "And how are you feeling this evening? Sorry I'm a little late. I had to run home first."

"I'm wiped out. It just came on me all of a sudden." Mora struggled to keep her eyes open.

A student nurse breezed into the room. "Time for pin care," she said, and quickly set up the cleaning tools. "It won't take a minute."

Mora closed her eyes and relaxed into the buffer the nurse provided. When the nurse was finished, Mora opened her eyes.

"You're a design engineer at Teknet, right?" Carl asked Hope.

"Yep." Hope answered.

"If you're interested, I can put you on the 'Mora's condition update' network. Which group are you with?"

"Thanks, but I'm already on it. Have they brought your dinner yet, Mora?"

"No, not yet. It's late." Mora dragged her words.

Carl said, "I read an interesting article the other day about how lepers gradually lose their sense of feeling on their skin and although they can still use their muscles, they can't feel things. There was one guy who grabbed a door knob that had a jagged piece of metal on it. He turned the knob and it ripped the skin off his hand but he couldn't feel it. He knew something was wrong when he saw blood pouring from his hand." Carl blinked and waited for a response.

Mora burst into tears. "Carl, why are you telling me this?"

"I thought it was interesting. And since you can't feel things in your hands, I thought you might want to know what it's like for lepers."

"Dinner!" The voice sang from the hallway. Hope quickly cleared space on the tray and received dinner at the door.

Mora sighed and closed her eyes. "I don't know if I have the energy to eat."

"Do you mind if I sit down? It's been a long day," Carl asked.

"Sure," Mora answered.

Hope squinted at Mora and began feeding preparations. "Let's see what's for dinner." She lifted the stainless steel cover to reveal baked chicken, fresh mashed potatoes, and peas. Beside the plate was a small paper cup filled with sliced strawberries. After cutting the chicken Hope began to feed Mora, sharply attentive to the amount of food on each forkful, and the timing of each swallow Mora took.

"You know, it's really hard to eat when I'm being watched. The dignity of feeding myself is gone." Mora dropped her gaze to the plate, closed her eyes and let tears escape.

Hope gently put the fork down and waited, embarrassed. After several seconds of silence she whispered, "Do you want more dinner now?" Someone else might have slunk away and quit the volunteer feeding job, but not Hope.

From behind closed eyes Mora whispered, "No."

Carl piped up, "Since you're full, can I eat your strawberries?"

Hope's jaw dropped and she turned to Carl. "You're kidding, aren't you?"

Mora chuckled, her eyes still shut.

Carl shrugged. "I hate to waste food, and since you're not hungry anymore. . ." He shrugged again.

"Carl, I'm starting to drift off; I think I need to sleep. Why don't you take the strawberries with you?"

"Okay, thanks." Carl stood up. "I'll try to make it in next week when they transfer you." He leaned over and gently kissed the top of Mora's head, then picked up the cup of strawberries and left.

- 9 -

"Congratulations!" Hope clasped Mora's hand and gently shook it the instant they were alone.

"For what?"

"Your divorce. From here, it looks like there's real cause for celebration."

They laughed, and Mora said, "Yeah?"

"Yeah. Okay, so he's an engineer. *I'm* an engineer, for heaven's sake! But let me put it this way: I wouldn't hire Carl to give sensitivity training to families of the physically challenged. May I ask you a question?"

"You just did." Mora laughed.

"Wise ass." Hope played back, then got serious. "Why did you marry him?"

Mora thought for a moment before answering. "Have you ever been in a situation where you just *knew* you *had* to do something and it wasn't the perfect forever thing but you still had to walk right into it?"

"Got it." Hope nodded.

"I really loved him and I just had to do it. Is it destiny? I don't know. Besides, he was the opposite of my father. I figured a reliable, rational, scientific guy wouldn't leave me like my flamboyantly emotional traveling salesman father did. Silly girl, huh?"

"Ah yes, the wisdom of hindsight."

"It's funny. . . lately I've been feeling how deeply I was hurt by my father's disappearance, and that I blamed myself for it. Maybe I was trying to escape my own blame. Drinking, marrying Carl, working day and night with Fitness & More, and having an affair.

Maybe they were all coverups." Mora sighed. "When I died I saw that Carl has always loved me the best way he knows how. And I'm even more convinced that we go back a long, long way."

"What do you mean?"

"I've known him before. I'm sure of it."

"You mean reincarnation?" Hope cast a sideways glance at Mora.

"Yup. The initial attraction I had toward him was uncanny. I remember lying in bed one night right after I'd met him and saying to God in the darkness, 'I'm going to marry him.' I just knew it. The power of instant attraction is a dead giveaway. I'm sure he and I had things to complete from another lifetime."

"How can you be so sure?" Hope asked, furrowing her brow.

"Everything was clear to me in my union with God. Things like time, distance, and distance in time are illusions in reality. Haven't you ever met a person and heard an alarm go off inside you? It can be attraction or repulsion or simply peaceful. You just know there's something familiar about this person. Hasn't that ever happened to you before?" Mora studied Hope's face.

"Yeah, sure I have. Hasn't everybody?"

"Where does the 'knowing' come from? When did you start knowing them? You recognize who that person really is. It's their soul you know. Their current vehicle or body is different from the last time. But it's the soul of the person you see when you look into their eyes." Mora chuckled. "That's the *one* thing the nuns taught us that was true."

"Well, I don't know," Hope said as she shifted her weight. "Does this job require a belief in reincarnation?"

Mora laughed. "Wouldn't that be job discrimination?"

"Does that mean you still want me to massage your neck and arms?"

"Do you mind if I fall asleep while you do it?" Mora asked.

"Would you mind telling me what you want me to do first?" Hope bounced back.

"Why are we answering every question with a question?"

"Does anyone really care?"

The two easily fell into laughter.

"Okay," Mora said, naturally picking up the reins of command, "pull up the chair and get yourself as comfortable as possible."

"Ready."

"First, a basic thing about massage is that any place you touch, you're changing things. With contact, you're automatically opening energy doors. The way I see it, extra cells instantly came to assist my neck when it snapped and they've been working constantly ever since. Now you become a support wire conducting my natural energy current where my connections were cut. The best part is you're sending your tender loving care through your hands into me. I'm taking it, I want it, and I intend to use every bit. That's how it works. My intention combines with yours to help me get well. I asked doctor Anwar what needs to happen for me to get my function back. He said I need to grow new spinal nerve roots. I asked him how fast that happens. He said *if* they can regrow, it's at a rate of about one millimeter every few days. Know what I said to him?"

"I can just imagine."

"I said, 'Mine grow five millimeters a *day*.' He looked at me like I had two heads."

"Well, there's yours. . . and then there's mine."

"You're absolutely right. I thought we might put our two heads together, join minds for a single purpose. I'll verbally guide you on the kinds of strokes and movements I need. Picture me as a tree. My trunk remembers being strong but I've been hit by a few trucks. Deep down inside I have all this vibrant, juicy energy that desperately wants to come back to life. I'm ready for those roots to regrow, to reach out to the tips of my leaves. A tree regrowing nerve roots is what I am. And with both of us concentrating on it, maybe we can do it. What do you think?"

"It sounds great!" Hope answered, settling into her seat. "But there's just one thing."

"What?"

"I thought spinal nerves don't regenerate."

"It depends. Don't worry about the technicalities. If you ask me, the officially accepted medical theories are full of holes. I asked doctor Anwar '*If* it were possible, what would need to happen?' and he gave me an open-ended possibility which I can use. And I might as well tell you now, just in case you haven't figured it out: if you tell me I can't, it just inspires me to defy your limitations. I'm Irish and a lot of us are like that. Who but God can say what's impossible, I mean, really?" Mora's voice elevated then dropped back down. "Look, it's what I want. I *have* to try. I want to use everything I've got available, including your loving help and both our imaginations. What harm is there?"

"You're right." Hope nodded vehemently. "I'm sold. I mean, what have we got to lose? And it's free."

"Oh, that reminds me. Do you have a portable tape player I can use? It would be so helpful to hear peaceful music, funny tapes, anything encouraging or uplifting. We could play soft music while I do the verbal visualizing and you massage me."

"Sure, I have a boom box we can use. I'll bring it in tomorrow. Are there any particular tapes you want?"

"Go down to Fitness & More and have Carmella show you the music library. Get the ocean waves tape. Anything with the ocean helps me fall into the bottomless sea of my imagination. Other than that, whatever peaceful music strikes your fancy will do." Switching gears Mora closed her eyes, inhaled deeply, and said, "Why don't you start massaging me with some gentle, easy, long strokes down my arm. That's called effleurage."

"I'm kind of nervous about hurting you." Hope attempted her first few strokes down Mora's right arm. "Is this okay? Am I doing it too hard?"

"No, that's good." Mora kept her eyes closed. "Keep doing it all around the whole arm, don't forget my shoulder, and let yourself relax and fall into it. It's okay. You're helping me."

Gradually Hope found a groove and slid into place.

After several minutes of effleurage, Mora guided the next move. "Let's plug me in now. With your left hand, gently make contact with the base of my skull."

"Plug you in. Okay, whatever that means." Hope scanned

Mora's body, hoping it would give her a clue. "What about the stitches? Won't I hurt you by touching them?"

"No, don't worry. Put your fingers next to the stitches. I want you to hook up the entire circuit of my spine, to get the energy going where it's needed. Inside knows what to do. We're pre-programmed to release blockages when they're contacted." Mora grinned, her eyes still closed. "Now slide your right hand under my sacrum."

"I'll try." With great care Hope slowly eased her hand under Mora's tail bone. "Is this okay?"

"That's fine. My skin feels dull and annoying down there, but I can feel the vibration of your touch in my bones. Now just hold it there. You've got me plugged in. I'm hooked up like an electrical cord. Your healthy circuitry is encouraging my ailing circuitry to fall in place behind you. We can picture the life energy flowing where it might not have been before. The energy is filling up all the nerve juice receptors along my spinal cord right now. It's doing repair work even as we speak."

"Funny, I don't remember the term 'nerve juice receptors' coming up in anatomy classes."

"Shhhh. . . please refrain from casting dubiosities upon our extemporaneous improvisations."

Hope held her hands steady and still for a long time until Mora broke the silence.

"Boy, are you ever steadfast. If I didn't know it before, it sure comes through your hands loud and clear. Okay, you can let go of that position. Do you need to rest?"

"No, actually I feel better than I have all day."

"It's like that. The benefit that come to me goes through you first. We both get it. Are you ready for more?"

"Yep."

"You can disconnect now and I'll show you how to drain out pain."

"Sounds good."

"I've got this hard, lumpy place in the middle of my upper arm, the origin of my brachialis muscle, on my humerus to be exact, that is in constant, throbbing pain. Could you touch it?"

"Did I ever tell you I used to be a phys ed teacher, before I was a design engineer?" Hope's sensitive fingers searched Mora's upper arm.

"No, but it sounds like a logical transition. Up a little higher."

"I used to know anatomy. Tell me if I'm in the right spot."

"There! That's it. Just put a finger in the middle of it. Can you feel it? Is it kind of lumpy? A little more pressure. Yes." Mora sighed deeply into the union of her pain and Hope's contact. "Ahhh. . . when that spot is in excruciating pain it feels like it's the miserable center of my universe. Now it's as if you're pulling the plug on the blocked energy and I'm melting all around it." Mora let her jaw drop open. All of her attention was focused on the pain's gradual exit. "What a relief."

A minute passed before Mora released a heavy sigh. "Well, I guess you can't hold that one spot all night, although I wish you could. But we've got other spots to free before I sleep. Now could you please do some petrissage, which is like kneading bread, in the same general area? Feel free to experiment a little."

"How's that?"

"Good, except could you give me a little more pressure?"

"I don't want to hurt you."

Mora put on a comic wrinkled expression. "Do you think I'd forget to tell you?"

Hope laughed. "Good point! Sometimes I forget it's you."

"Okay. Now if you would gently feel my neck. Try to get as close to my spine as you can without pulling on the stitches. Just find a spot and touch it with a tiny bit more pressure than you gave when we hooked me up. That's it. Perfect. Just hold it a few seconds." Mora sighed loudly. "My neck is in constant pain unless I focus all of my attention on it. It's strange what happens when I focus. It turns into something other than pain. It's as if I can actually see the cell reconstruction site inside and I relax, content to know my body is working very hard to rebuild me."

At 10 P.M. Mora said, "Oh, it's so late. I should let you go home. You must be exhausted after a full day of work on top of all this."

"Yeah, I should go." Hope released her hands and pushed the chair back. "I'll be back tomorrow. Do you need anything before I leave?"

"Would you ask a nurse to help me on your way out?"

"Sure." Hope leaned over Mora and kissed the top of her head.

"Thank you so much for everything, Hope. I don't know what I'd do without you."

"Sleep well, my friend."

*   *   *

```
Teknet Computer Files:   entry 08-SEP-1990
FROM: ALPHA :: FISCHER
TO:  Aerobics Students Info Line
SUBJ:  Mora Donovan
```

Mora looked much better today than the last few times I saw her. She's still in awe of the work that's ahead of her, but she seems to have a better grip on reality. Maybe she's gotten rid of all the anesthetic.

Every day she gets a little more use of her nerves. Sometimes she doesn't notice the progress herself, I guess because she feels overwhelmed with how much more there is ahead.

This week she moved her legs. It was just a little bit but everyone including Mora is very encouraged by this. They sat her in a chair for several hours. She's progressed a lot since the operation.

Almost every time I've been there at dinner time and have fed her, she's had broccoli. I wonder if she's doing that on purpose knowing how I hate broccoli (haha).

For all those who tried to visit her back in the Intensive Care "immediate family only" days, try again. Although her black friends had a hard time convincing the nurses they were cousins, now anybody can visit her.

She's off sleeping tablets and pain pills now, and they just removed the "plumbing attachments" so she can relieve herself the way the good Lord intended, which is also a thrill and a half.

This Saturday is Mora's moving day. Anybody who can help move her stuff from her apartment into a friend's barn for storage should call Hope Lester at 438-1134. Truck(s) are needed.

Keep those cards and prayers coming. If you want to visit, Mora is in room 224 of Drayton Community Hospital.
-C Fischer
END.

*   *   *

After dinner on Saturday, Karla came into the room with another nurse, Shelly, and announced, "We have a weekend home-work assignment for you from doctor Anwar. How would you like to stand up and take a few steps?"

"Now?" Mora asked, incredulous.

"Sure. We're ready if you are," Shelly answered.

Mora thought about it for a moment. "I guess I could try," she said faintly.

"Great. Karla, you raise the head of the bed while I hold onto Mora," Shelly said.

"Just go slow," Mora warned the two nurses as the bed began to move.

"Don't worry, we've got this down to a science. Okay Mora, first let's put your sneakers on, then we'll sit you up," Shelly said. In a few seconds the sneakers were on Mora's feet. Then, with one hand on a front halo bar and the other on Mora's back, Shelly eased her into a sitting position and held steady. "Are you okay?" she asked.

"Hold it," Mora said. "What next?"

"Karla will turn your body while I lower your legs over the side of the bed. Ready?" Shelly asked.

"Okay," Mora answered.

In a few seconds the two nurses had followed through, and stood on either side of Mora.

"We're going to lift you under your arms and hold you up, so don't worry about us letting go. Ready?"

Mora took two deep breaths and whispered, "Okay. I'm ready."

"Good. Here we go up," Karla said. She and Shelly lifted Mora just enough so that her feet landed gently on the floor, then raised her into an upright position.

After a moment's hesitation, Mora said hoarsly, "Hey! I'm an upstanding citizen!"

"Can you move one foot foward, Mora? We've got you."

"Wait. I feel a little dizzy." Mora sighed heavily, then said, "Okay, here goes." She carefully slid her right foot two inches forward, then her left, and the nurses stepped forward with her.

"Great!" Karla said.

"Look at you. You're walking. Want to try another one?" Shelly said.

"Okay," Mora whispered. Smiling faintly she repeated the steps, this time sliding each foot three inches forward.

"I'm walking," Mora whispered, looking at the floor ahead. "I'm walking. Let's keep going," she said, and took two more steps.

"Are you holding up? Ready to turn around?" Karla asked.

"Okay."

Karla and Shelly guided Mora into a turn, and in less time than it took to step forward, they stepped back to her bed.

"Mission accomplished. Good for you, Mora, Are you okay?" Karla asked.

"Yeah. Whew. . . that wiped me out. But it was worth it." Mora smiled and closed her eyes.

- 10 -

It was Sunday morning, a few days before the rehab move. The substitution of bedpan for catheter added urgency to Mora's basic needs and was cheered on by her newly developed ability to roll her body onto the nurse call button.

"Yes?"

"I've got to pee really bad." It often took a while for help to arrive so Mora vocalized urgency ahead of time.

"Okay. Be right there."

This time, Karla arrived within a few seconds and set the bedpan under her. "As soon as you finish, I'll do your pin care and bathe you, okay?"

"Wonderful." Mora had awakened feeling more cheerful than she had in days. "It's amazing how being able to eliminate without contraptions can pick up your spirits. Life's simple pleasures."

Hope arrived after the bath, just in time to feed Mora her breakfast.

"I talked to your mother last night," Hope said. "She and Louise will be here soon. The move went as smooth as glass and lots of folks showed up. I must say we did a stupendous job, very organized and upbeat. Your mother said something about Carl and a toaster oven but I didn't quite get it. She also said the insurance company paid full price on your car."

"Good," Mora said. "Now I can pay you back for all the expenses you've piled up over me."

"Forget it. I never did anything expecting repayment. You're going to need that money once you're out of here."

"Well, I'll think about it. Except for Kathleen's present. No way are you going to pay for that. Did you get the necklace?"

"I certainly did. Do you want to see it?" Hope breathed the same air of anticipation.

"Of course."

"It's lapis. There were earrings to match so I figured what the hell, go for it. I bought the set." Hope held the rich deep-sea blue stone necklace in one hand, the blue and pearl drop earrings in the other.

"They're beautiful! They'll match her eyes perfectly. Oh, I can't wait to see her face!"

"I have something for you, too."

"You're always giving me something. You already do too much for me." Mora's eyes filled with the day's first batch of tears.

"This is a little good-luck-in-rehab present." Hope turned her back and dug into the shopping bag. "Actually, I have two things for you." She put one package on the bed tray and held the other. "I'll open this one first." She unwrapped it and raised a turquoise cotton cardigan sweater with the words "Oh no! Not another learning experience!" printed on the pocket.

"Hope!" Mora feigned a whine. "What a scream. I suppose you'll expect me to wear it."

"Naturally. I got it oversized to fit over the halo vest. And since you get tired of the same old johnnies I figured. . ."

The two women shared a good laugh.

"Now I'll open this one for you." Hope removed a coffee mug from its wrapper and held it close so Mora could read the words.

"'I'd rather be in charge'. Hey! What's that supposed to mean?" Mora lowered her voice to a growl. "What are you trying to tell me?"

"Isn't it obvious?"

"If anybody sees this they're liable to get an accurate impression of me. What else is on the mug? It's a whip! You know, a more genteel woman would not be flattered."

"Am I missing anything?" Ellen Donovan called cheerfully as she entered.

"Ma, look at this! Hope is treading on thin ice here."

Ellen read the words on both gifts and laughed. "Your candor is refreshing, Hope."

"Speaking of candor, what were you telling Hope about Carl and the toaster oven, Ma?"

"Oh, gee." Ellen instinctively grimaced. "I don't want to upset you." She glanced questioningly from Mora to Hope and back to Mora.

"Whoops." Hope interrupted, lowered her head and raised her eyes. "I guess I wasn't supposed to mention it. Sorry."

Mora laughed. "Welcome to the Donovan family, Hope. We have an old family tradition that goes like this: 'Don't tell Louise or Claire I told you this, but. . .' Okay Ma, spill it."

"It's not really a big deal. Just that yesterday, when your friends came to help move your furniture, and I was packing and directing everybody where to put things, Carl came over. He said 'As long as Mora won't be needing the toaster oven for a while, I might as well get some use out of it.' I couldn't believe it! That beat-up old toaster oven."

Mora laughed. "That's Carl."

"It infuriated me." Ellen said in a flat voice, then lowered it to a whisper. "And I hated staying in that old dark house. . . I never liked it. I doubt he's vacuumed since you moved out nine months ago. I just packed up and left. I'm going to a hotel."

Hope turned to face Ellen. "There's a spare room at my house that you're welcome to use if you wish. My daughter Lisa and I would be happy to have you and I vacuumed a couple of days ago. Do you like obedient, well-mannered, short-haired dogs, beagles to be exact?"

"That's extremely generous of you, Hope. Thank you. I do indeed love dogs and I just might take you up on your offer. You've been so generous but I don't want to be a burden."

"No trouble at all. It would simplify things for everybody. Besides, Frankie's staying there too. She'd probably feel more secure around family."

"Oh, you've got the cat, too?" Ellen looked at Mora. "You're taking care of our entire family."

"I'd be lost without her, Ma."

Mora and Ellen looked at Hope in silence. Words were small

next to her actions. The gaps she had already bridged were big enough to have filled a year of normal life.

"I don't know how to thank you for everything you do, for all you've done," Ellen said.

"I told Mora and I'll tell you: I want Mora to have every chance to recover. If I have any positive affect on her, it's a huge reward for me. You have no idea." Hope's voice cracked on her last words.

"You're one of a kind, Hope." Tears filled Mora's eyes. "I don't know why you do so much for me but I am very grateful to you for it."

Silence marked the risk, like a rock on a ledge. Hope dropped her head and closed her eyes. How far was the drop, she wondered, and would she land on her feet? Mora and Ellen heard her call something from the edge of memory and waited, ready to catch her.

"I'll tell you something," Hope began tentatively. "I watched my husband die from alcoholism. Slowly, for years, life seeped out of his spirit until. . ." Hope's voice quavered as she struggled to keep the words coming. "I'd sit at his hospital bedside waiting, begging him to hang onto life, praying he would. But he just didn't want to. He just gave up." Her tears began to fall.

"It was awful, watching and waiting. There was nothing I could do." She wiped her tears with the back of her hand and cleared her throat. "But Mora, you're not like that. You're a fighter and you're determined to live, no matter how hard life is. And I want to help you stand again."

The Donovan women listened, silently making room for Hope's strong, vulnerable heart to open.

"Oh, Hope. If I could hug you I would," Mora cried.

"Let me give you a hug." Ellen Donovan opened her arms and wrapped them like graceful wings around Hope. "You're the kind-est-hearted woman we'd ever want to know. And you're welcome into this crazy family."

Sunny Sunday was renewed. The open windows welcomed warm breezes whispering of the future.

"Good morning, everyone. I hope all is well." Louise entered, bearing two shopping bags. Her green eyes and auburn hair deli-cately accented her handmade, soft aqua and peach dress.

"You always look so beautiful, Louise," Mora said. "I can't wait to get dressed again."

"In lieu of high fashion. . ." Louise put the bags on the extra bed and pulled out a cloth jumble of fuchsia, turquoise, and Chinese red. "Mommy and I decided to modify a few shirts as Mrs. Franklin suggested."

"Uhh, what a job!" Ellen shook her head and laughed. "Figuring out which flap fits over which piece of velcro. . . they better work."

"Do you want to try one on now?" Louise unfastened the flaps.
"Sure."

Louise lifted Mora's arm, holding her wrist and elbow while Ellen slid the shirt over the bulky vest.

Ellen fumbled with the velcro patches. "Tsss. . . what a silly thing." Her fingers yanked at the shirt.

"Ah yes, this reminds me of when I was four years old."

"Oh boy, here comes one of Mora's detailed childhood flashbacks!" Ellen laughed and tugged.

Relishing her introduction, Mora forged ahead. "We were in the bathroom at Bamburgers department store. I was wearing my favorite burgundy velveteen winter leggings with the black front zipper and I had to go to the bathroom. Being in a hurry, as always, Mommy went into the stall with me and when I got up from the toilet she yanked the zipper up and it caught my stomach. I screamed of course." Everyone laughed.

"Honestly," Ellen stood back and squinted at Mora's new shirt. "Is there anything you can't remember from childhood?"

Louise also stepped back to scrutinize. "I don't know. . . what do you think, Ma?"

Unable to contain her laughter, Ellen feebly covered her mouth. "I'm sorry, honey. I had a feeling this wasn't going to work."

"What?" Mora fretfully pulled her eyes from one fashion consultant to the other. "Does it look stupid?"

"It's not what you'd wear to the opera but it's definitely an improvement over the johnnies," Hope answered diplomatically.

"If you don't like them, I'll just buy some sweatshirt jackets and replace the zippers with velcro. You can wear easy pull-on pants. How does that sound?" Ellen offered.

"Sure, Ma. This'll be fine. Hopefully I won't be wearing them for the rest of my life. Which reminds me: I have a little surprise for everybody." Mora's eyes flashed a bright glint and everyone stood still.

"Watch this." Mora lowered her eyes to her legs. Slowly at first she shook her legs side to side, increased the speed gradually, then rested. With her eyes intently focused down below, she exhaled forcefully and slowly slid her right foot up the bed until the knee was bent. She repeated the motion with the left leg until two bony knees proudly leaned on each other. Mora grinned. "What do you think of that?"

"How wonderful!" Hope squealed and clapped.

"You're amazing." Ellen shook her head while tears slid down Louise's cheeks.

"It isn't much but. . ." Mora's apologetic words evoked unanimous objection.

"Honestly, Mora," Hope said. "I don't think you can see your progress as clearly as we can. Here you are, working at something over and over, hour after hour, day after day until you reach another point beyond where you'd just been. We don't see the painstaking progression you sweat through. We just see the result, which is radically different from what you could do yesterday. Do you understand that, Mora?" Hope looked at Ellen and Louise in search of agreement and they nodded.

"I never know what you'll be doing next." Ellen shook her head and smiled.

"I can tell I must have made progress by watching your drastic reactions to these little things," Mora admitted.

"Yeah, but they're not so little, I'm here to tell you," Hope pointed out.

"For my next act, I'll need an assistant." Mora grinned proudly. "Hope, if you get on one side of me and either Mommy or Louise get on the other, help me to the edge of the bed, bring my lower legs over the side and very slowly, stand me up."

"Oh gee, Mora," Ellen said nervously, "are you sure it's safe?"

"Of course!" Mora laughed confidently, the hesitation of the previous day completely gone. "If I can do it, then I should. That's how I'm going to get out of here. All I need is two strong people holding me up. Last night two nurses helped me do it and it worked fine. Ready?"

"I'll help," Louise offered as she moved in closer.

"I'll bring the head of the bed all the way up." Hope pressed the foot pedal and when the bed was upright, she positioned herself opposite Louise. "I'm ready."

"Okay. Hope, you bring my legs over the side. Louise, you balance my torso by holding me underneath my left armpit with one hand, and hold onto the front bar of the halo with your other hand."

"Do you want me to do anything?" Ellen asked.

Louise answered. "Ma, why don't you come around my side just in case I can't hold Mora up. . . if you don't need her over there, Hope."

Ellen rushed to Louise's side.

"Okay, now *slowly and gently* pull me up."

A jubilant smile slid across Mora's face as the two women raised her to her feet. "Hey, look at me! I'm up!" Her words plucked rusty vocal cords not accustomed to being stretched out. "Whoa! I'm dizzy. Wait one second." Closing her eyes she took a few deep breaths. "Okay. It's gone."

"Yippee! Hey, hey, hey! This is fabulous!" Hope cheered, bobbing up and down.

"This is truly amazing, just truly amazing." Ellen shook her head, her eyes as big as silver dollars.

"Want to try walking me a little? We did six whole steps last night."

"I'm ready if you are." Hope made eye contact with Louise.

"You must have lost weight," Louise chuckled. "I never thought you'd be this easy to hold up."

"Okay, I'm going to try to slide my leg foward, but you guys move with me. Keep holding me up, okay?"

"Okay." Hope's eyes alternated between Mora's feet and her face.

Breathing almost aerobically, Mora worked at push-dragging her left foot an inch forward, then let the new position settle into place. With eyes fiercely focused on the floor ahead, she successfully repeated the sequence with her right foot. "Keep going. I'm fine."

As Mora, Louise, and Hope completed another pair of steps, Ellen shook her head. "I almost can't believe what I'm seeing."

"Thanks, Ma." As if Mora's engine had just been recharged by acknowledgment, she refocused her attention further ahead. "Let's go out into the hallway. I think I can, I think I can. God, I really want to!"

After the third pair of steps her knees collapsed. "Aghh! That's it. Oh well. Can you guys drag me back?" Mora's eyes welled up with tears. Like two tugboats escorting a wounded ship to safe harbor, Hope and Loise glided Mora back to bedside.

"Ohhhh honey. . . what is it?" Ellen asked.

"It's so damn frustrating! Just when I think I can do it, my body gives out!"

"Mora," Louise said softly, "I look at you and I am amazed by your persistence, your drive, your will to forge ahead. I keep wondering what I would do if it had been me. I don't think I could do it."

"Really?" Mora soaked up the comfort in her sister's eyes and rebounded. "Pretty dramatic, ain't I? Look at all this attention I'm finally getting."

"I'm glad you said it and not me," Ellen teased.

"Oh, this reminds me of a TV movie I saw the other night. Susan Hayward's legs didn't work and she started to cry in her hospital bed. Her nurse got furious with her for crying and *yelled* at her for being weak! Can you imagine? Then the foolish nurse leaves the room and cries like a baby out in the hall where Susan Hayward can't see! 'You stupid nurse!' I yelled at the TV, 'Don't you know you're supposed to cry when you feel sad? Where's your compassion? What the hell do you think emotions are for?' Just as I said that, a nurse walking down the hall stuck her head in my room and looked around to see who I was yelling at. I said 'Not you. I'm talking to the TV'. I'd die if I couldn't cry regularly."

Louise said to Mora, "I went into Hartford on Friday for the official tour of MacKenzie Rehab Hospital. Do you want to hear about it now?"

"Oh." Mora's levity flattened like a blown tire. "I guess so. I'm kind of scared to leave here so soon."

"They've got everything you could possibly need. I was quite impressed with their level of care."

"Really?" Mora raised hopeful eyes to her big sister.

"Well for one thing, it's very clean. And as we all know, you can never be too clean." Louise grinned at Ellen. "And for another, each patient receives a totally individualized program. You're assigned a staff psychologist, a physical therapist, an occupational therapist, a team of doctors, and your weekdays are fully packed with supportive therapies. Another good thing is that they only admit one new patient per day because they focus a lot of attention on orienting the patients, helping them get comfortable in their new home, so to speak. You meet with each of your staff advocates individually on the first day."

"They should give you a commission," Mora joked. "It sounds more like a high-tech health spa than a rehab hospital."

"I even spoke to the head nurse on the spinal cord injury unit, where you'll be. She's a rather frumpy, heavy-set, middle-aged woman named Jane who seems very professional. She spoke in glowing terms about how the nursing and medical staff make you feel at home, encouraging you to do your best. It looks very good."

"Did you see any of the patients?" Mora asked

.   "Yes. But I didn't talk to any of them to find out how they like it, if that's what you mean. Everybody was very quiet, you know, minding their own business. It wasn't noisy or anything like that."

"Yeah, you wouldn't want patients making any noise." Mora caught and held onto Hope's eyes. "I hope we're going to be okay in this new place."

Hope smiled at her inclusion. "Yes indeed. And if they mess up, they'll have you, I mean me to reckon with."

"But what if I can't handle it? I don't know if I'm ready for this. Maybe I should just stay here for a while." Mora searched the three women's faces.

"I went to two other rehabs and this one really impressed me," Louise said. "They seem to be very good at customizing your program and not leaving any gaps in it. They fill every minute with therapies, activities, encouragement. Actually, they led me to believe you'll have quite a demanding schedule."

"I really appreciate all the effort you put into this, Louise, but what if it's too much?" Mora's voice rose. "What if I can't keep up? What do I do then, with you and Mommy back at home in New Jersey and Florida?"

"You won't be alone," Hope answered. "I'll be there."

"But you'll be working all day, you have other obligations. You can't drive over an hour each way after a full day's work."

"Hey, aren't you always telling other people they have no right to tell you what you can and cannot do?" Hope shoved her chin forward.

A long silence held everyone suspended until Mora moaned, "I want to stay here."

"Well, you can't and there really isn't much choice." Louise delivered the verdict flatly. "It's the best option we have. At this point it's really your only option for round-the-clock care."

A wave of despair swept over Mora. She closed her eyes and cried.

- 11 -

The sounds of eggbeater buzz and aerobic breathing greeted Ellen and Hope when they entered Mora's room on the morning of moving day. Mora lay in bed cycling on what appeared to be only the pedals of a bicycle. Her eyes focused intently on the ceiling as she panted rhythmically.

"Look at me! Whh, whh, whh. . . . Sherrie found it buried in the physical therapy closet this morning. . . whh, whh, whh. . . . She said nobody's ever used it! Whh, whh, whh. . . ha, ha, isn't this great?"

"I don't believe it," said Hope. She and Ellen stared with gaping mouths.

"Hope, could you take it away now? I've got something else to show you before I poop out."

Hope rushed over, released Mora's sneakered feet from the pedals, and removed the compact aparatus.

"Hope, you know how aerobics instructors are always trying to come up with new ways of torturing abdominal muscles?"

"Yeah?"

"When Sandy, my replacement instructor, comes in to visit me next I'm going to show her this." Panting, Mora bent one leg and lifted the other straight leg several inches off the bed then slid it from side to side. "Whh. . . whh. . . . I'm going to tell her to say 'Mora said if she can do this with a broken neck in a hospital bed, whh. . . whh. . . whh. . . you can do it now!' Whh. . . whh. . . whh. . . what do you think?" She closed her eyes and let her legs collapse.

"Should you be doing that Mora? I mean, is it dangerous?" Ellen clutched her purse nervously.

"Oh, it feels so good Ma, I feel alive again. My body's coming back more and more. How can it be bad for me?"

"Did doctor Anwar say it was okay?" Ellen persisted.

"He hasn't seen it yet." Mora brushed the caution aside, annoyed. "Don't you think I'm the best judge of what I can do?"

"I don't know, but I'd rather you get doctor Anwar's approval." Ellen looked directly into Mora's eyes. "Just in case. I'm concerned you may be putting yourself at risk. Would you just ask him?"

Mora studied her mother's face. "Okay. He's coming in to tighten my screws before I go. God. . ." She closed her eyes and sighed heavily. "I hate it when he tightens the screws. It's so painful and depressing."

"Good morning ladies, may I come in?" Doctor Anwar's soft voice preceded him into the room like a stream of smoke from exotic incense.

"Speak of the devil," Mora mumbled.

"Are you prepared for your voyage to the rehab this afternoon?" He wore a mauve silk bow tie with a lavender linen shirt and a maroon silk jacket.

"Doctor, Mora was just showing us something she's been doing and we were wondering, I was wondering, if it's safe." Ellen turned from the doctor to Mora. "Mora, show doctor Anwar, would you?"

"Okay." Mora demonstrated the leg lifts.

"You appear to be using your neck to support you. Are you?" he asked.

"Oh, I guess I am," Mora answered, and stopped moving.

Doctor Anwar shook his head. "You should not be doing that just now."

"I guess you're right."

"Now for the business at hand." He removed the wrench from his jacket pocket and pressed the nurse call button.

"Yes?"

"This is doctor Anwar. Please, I require the assistance of a nurse in Mora Donovan's room."

"Right away, doctor."

"We'll wait outside." Ellen said. She and Hope left.

Kathleen came in and held Mora's hand. Mora sucked in a deep breath before diving under. She closed her eyes and prayed silently. *Please God, help me get through this. Hold me?* As the wrench locked into position, the vibration of moving metal rocked every bone in her skeleton. The pressure on her skull increased, and increased further, crushing her spirit, wringing out tears. In a few seconds the dull clanging stopped, leaving in its trail duller, heavier, throbbing pressure. Mora sobbed out loud and Kathleen gently touched her shoulder until she stopped.

"I will examine the sensitivity of your dermatones now, Mora." Doctor Anwar proceeded to pin-prick Mora's right foot.

"Ow. Ow. OWW!" Mora squeeled behind closed eyes.

The doctor pricked a trail up her right leg. "Can you feel this?"

"What?"

"And this?" Switching to her left leg, he repeated the procedure and observed her facial reactions.

"I can't feel anything. Now that's *really* annoying."

Graduating to her arm, he pricked again.

Many seconds passed before Mora asked, "Are you doing anything?"

"Yes," he answered matter-of-factly, and moved to prick her fingers.

"Ohhh. . . will this ever change?" Mora sighed heavily. "OWW!"

The doctor returned his pin to the tray and stood with his hands clasped in front of him. "There is definitely increased sensation on more dermatones than just a few days ago, while others remain non-responsive. You *are* changing, and although it may not seem so, pain and hypersensitivity are improvements. I feel confident that you will progress well in the rehab hospital. Is there anything you wish to discuss with me before you leave here today?"

"I'm frightened, that's the main thing." Mora searched the doctor's strong, gentle face.

"They'll take good care of you. It's the finest, best-equipped rehabilitation facility in the Northeast."

"Okay, if you say so." Ignoring her pain, Mora absorbed the

familiar security of doctor Anwar's green eyes. "I know that being a neurosurgeon is your profession, but I want you to know your spirit has helped me so much. Thank you for everything you've done for me, doctor."

Doctor Anwar smiled and gently nodded. "It has been my pleasure to have you as my patient. I shall see you soon." He left the room and Hope and Ellen returned.

"How was it?" Hope instantly caught Mora's frayed threads.

Mora's eyelids dropped. "It's so depressing. . . having my skull screwed tighter."

"Maybe you ought to rest a while, before it's time to go," Kathleen offered.

"Okay, but first I have a present for you." Mora pulled her eyes open and turned them toward the nurse.

"Are you talking to me?" Kathleen caught sight of Hope's grin.

"I guess that's my cue." Hope rummaged through the shopping bag and handed Kathleen the giftwrapped box. "For you from Mora."

"Oh no. What's this?" Kathleen's face lit up.

"Open it and find out." Mora pulled herself back to life. "But stand in front of me so my eyeballs can rest."

Kathleen stepped forward and opened the present. "Ohhh. . . Mora, this is beautiful!" She held up the necklace, then lifted the cotton and removed the earrings. "They're gorgeous!"

"The gift is to remind you how much I appreciate you," Mora said. "I wanted it to match your eyes."

Kathleen put the box on the bed tray, opened her arms and leaned over to embrace Mora. "You're a special woman. It's been a joy knowing you." Standing upright, she straightened her uniform. "And thank you for the letter you wrote to my supervisor. She told me about it this morning. Hope, you must've written it."

"The words were madame's, the labor mine." Hope bowed with a sweep of her arm and everyone laughed.

"I've applied for a supervisory position, so your letter was quite a timely boost," Kathleen said.

"You bring honor to the nursing profession. I hope you get it and whatever happens, I'll never forget you."

"Excuse me, is this Mora Donovan's room?" A female EMT asked from the doorway.

"Time to go," Kathleen whispered. "Yes ma'am, you're in the right place. Come on in."

Hope and Ellen stepped aside as the EMT and her male partner wheeled in the gurney.

"Can my mother and friend ride with us?" Panic bled through Mora's words.

"No, I'm sorry. They can follow the ambulance if they want." The two EMTs quickly transferred Mora onto the narrow gurney.

"Oh goodie! I've always wondered what it would be like to be an ambulance chaser," Hope joked.

"Dear Hope, always finding the pony in a roomful of shit. Have we got everything?" Mora nervously asked as they rolled her toward the door. She said "WAIT! I want to say goodbye to my home."

The EMTs stopped.

"Bye, room. Bye, Kathleen."

"Bye, honey. See you someday."

*   *   *

The intermittent screech of the siren paved a path for the hour-long drive into Hartford.

"My last trip in one of these wasn't so easy. Do you use the siren for everybody, even a non-emergency like me?" Mora tried distracting herself from the distressing noise.

"In this case, we're only using it when we run into traffic. Do you mind if I ask what happened to you?" The EMT's badge said Dorothy and Dorothy had questions of her own.

Mora told her the whole story, including her near-death experience and absorption in God's love.

"I hope you don't mind me asking."

"Oh, no. I like telling people about it because it brings me right back into it. Like now. . . I want to remember."

Dorothy looked out the tiny window. "Looks like we're here."

"Are Hope and my mother still behind us?"

"In a blue van?"

"That's them."

Dorothy wheeled Mora's stretcher through the emergency entrance.

"Could we wait for my family?"

"I have to transport you directly to your room on the spinal cord injury unit. Sorry. It'll probably take them a while to park anyway. The information desk will tell them where you are."

Mora let her eyes slide over walls, ceilings, and upper bodies of passing people. As her nostrils unwillingly filled with the sour odor of illness and antiseptic, she resolved to block its frightening effect on her psyche. They rolled onto elevators and through building wings in various degrees of repair. As the last elevator door opened, Mora silently struggled to grasp a lifeline to the real world. Now, far away from anything familiar, still unable to stand up or use her arms and hands without assistance, her confidence drained out and was replaced by helpless terror. *Will I be safe here?*

"I have a patient here by the name of Mora Donovan." Dorothy halted the gurney at the clean, quiet nurses' station.

"She'll be in Room 602. Halfway down the hall on the left."

"My mother and friend will be coming up in a minute looking for me," Mora informed the unseen nurse.

"We'll send them down."

"Is there someone who can help me move the patient to the bed?" Dorothy asked the nurse.

"We're short-staffed today. I'll send someone down just as soon as I can," the nurse answered flatly.

Dorothy rolled the gurney down the hall and steered it into a light-drenched room.

"Ah, it's a private room, isn't it?" Mora's eyes strained to the limits of her peripheral vision. "What a relief."

Dorothy positioned the gurney parallel to the bed, then sat down in the single chair to wait. Minutes passed in silence while Mora closed her eyes, breathing deep and slow.

"We made it." Ellen entered and scanned the room, heading straight for the windows facing a a highrise across the street. "Plenty of light, curtains. . . good. Do you want some fresh air, honey?"

"Oh yes, that sounds wonderful. Where's Hope?"

"Here I am. I made a pit stop. This place is a huge maze!"

"It seemed big to me too." Mora's heart pounded. "What floor are we on?"

"Sixth." Hope peeked in the bathroom and closet. "You know, Room 602. But there's more than one hospital in this hospital. We're deep in the bowels of allopathic medicine, honey."

"A dream come true." Mora closed her eyes and sighed heavily. "Where is somebody to move me onto the bed so Dorothy can go?"

"I don't know, but my driver's waiting for me. I wish they'd hurry up." Dorothy glanced at her watch and cast a frown out the window.

"Want me to help lift?" Hope asked.

"Sure, if you don't mind." Dorothy stood up. "You get on the other side of the gurney and we'll pull the sheet over. Ready? Pull."

In one smooth move Mora lay on her new hospital bed. "There's no place like home." Her attempt to make herself laugh landed as hard as the mattress underneath.

"Well, I'll be on my way." Dorothy walked to the door and raised her hand. "Good luck, Mora."

"Thanks." Mora's eyelids dropped and her mouth fell open in exhaustion.

"I'll just put these things away while we're waiting," Ellen whispered to Hope. "Why don't you sit down and relax?"

"I can't. Not yet." Hope returned the whisper and nodded toward the door. "Where is the greeting committee we heard so much about?"

Ellen shrugged and rolled dubious eyes before returning to unpacking.

Hope paced the room, then leaned back against the hip-height windowsill. With arms crossed on her chest she watched Mora sleep. "I don't think I've seen her this still in weeks," she whispered to Ellen. "We'd better get a good look. I'm sure it won't last."

"True." Ellen sat down in the room's only chair, leaned back and closed her eyes.

Hope loyally guarded the two sleeping women for nearly an hour. The absence of staff gnawed at her insides.

A voice over the P.A. system woke Ellen. "Oh gee, I fell asleep." She sat up. "Has anyone been in yet?"

"Nope. And I'm about ready to look into it. Patience is one thing but this is ridiculous."

"I'll go." Ellen arose from the chair and strode purposefully out into the hall. In a few minutes she returned with a nurse.

"Sorry. We're so busy today. Have you been here long?" The nurse inquired pleasantly and Mora woke up.

"Over an hour!" Hope snapped. "Where's the greeting committee who's supposed to orient the patient?"

"Excuse me?" The nurse asked.

"Great." Hope shook her head and turned to look out the window.

"All I know is she's supposed to have X-rays."

"My name is Mora. You can call me by my name and I am really, really hungry. I haven't had any food since early this morning. What time is it now?"

"3:30." Hope threw the words out at the nurse and looked away.

"Dinner comes up around 5:30. You'll have to wait 'til then."

"But I'm starving! Can't you give me something to hold me over until dinner?"

"I'll see if somebody else can get you something. I'm not assigned to you and I'm really busy right now. You'll just have to wait. Anyway, they ordered transport to take you down to X-ray. They should be here soon." The nurse scurried out.

Ellen quietly walked over to Mora's bedside. "Honey, I hate to do this now but I have a 4:30 flight. Hope is going to take me to the airport. Do you think you'll be okay by yourself?"

Mora's breathing quickened and her eyes filled with tears. "Oh Ma, I'm scared."

"I know, honey, I hate to leave you like this." Ellen picked up her daughter's limp hand and held it in both of hers. "But you won't be alone for long. For heaven's sake, you're in a hospital, surrounded by nurses and doctors. This is just a sour start. Don't let it get you down."

Mora looked into her mother's eyes and drew comfort there.

"I'll come back as soon as I can, Mora." Hope joined Ellen at Mora's bedside. "We'll get you settled in and I'll massage you. Okay?"

"That's right." Relieved, Ellen looked from Hope to Mora. "Hope is so good. She'll take care of you and I'll come back soon. Louise and Claire are going to take turns visiting you."

"I know." Mora cried harder. "Mommy?"

"What, honey?" Ellen kept her hold on Mora's hand.

"I hope I'll be okay without you." Mora's throat tightened. "I love you and I really need you." She let herself cry unrestrained.

"I know you do. I love you too, sweetheart. I'll be back soon. In the meantime, I'll talk to Hope on the phone every day. She'll be with you, won't you, Hope?"

"Rain or shine."

"Okay." Mora's crying subsided. "I'll be all right."

"I don't doubt it for a second." Ellen's smile was bittersweet. She leaned over to kiss the top of Mora's head but banged her chin on the halo. "Oh gee! Did I hurt you?"

"No."

She touched Mora's cheek. "Goodbye, honey. See you soon. I love you."

When they had left, Mora strained her eyes to hold what waning amber daylight remained. September's first week had already come and gone and all she could do was lie and wait.

A large, lumbering young man pushed a gurney through the wide doorway. "You Mora Donovan?" he asked dully, his eyes barely open.

"Yes?" The man's dim, dense energy set off Mora's internal alarm system.

"Transport." He looked down at the paper in his hand and jerked his head back up, mouth open. "Says you go to X-ray."

"Okay. . ." Mora answered reluctantly, and noticed the name *Lucas* on his ID badge.

In one sweep he effortlessly push-pulled her body onto the gurney and the wheels began rolling. "Uhh. Forgot the brake." He grabbed the side handle and Mora's heart raced hard. *Please protect me God. I'm frightened. Please stay with me and keep me safe!* She prayed to herself as Lucas rolled her down the hallway past a clock that read 4:00.

An internal battle was underway. *I HAVE to trust him,* she thought. *This is a hospital. Of course you're safe in a hospital.* Back and forth, down the halls, into an empty elevator where he loomed dully over her. She forced a diplomatic smile at him to ease her own mind but his glazed eyes never saw it. When they exited the elevator he said "Gotta go to the bathroom," pushed the gurney against the wall, kicked on the brake and left. He was gone for a long, agonizing time and when he returned, the distinct residue of marijuana smoke wafted over Mora's nostrils. Her heart pounded against her throat. Closing her eyes, she tried to calm herself by praying.

Down more hallways. Once again, he pushed the gurney against a deserted, dark and dirty hallway wall, locked the brake, and disappeared, this time without a word. Her chest and throat throbbed and she prayed. When he returned his marijuana breath was unmistakable. He pushed her faster down the hall, into another elevator and down a hallway whose walls she distinctly recognized from before. He was taking her for a ride! She panted out loud. *Please God. No matter what happens, I can't defend myself. He could do anything. He's stoned and these halls are deserted. I'M FRIGHTENED! Please God, keep me safe!*

Finally, Lucas locked the brake and left Mora under an X-ray sign and a clock that read 4:30. She closed her eyes and breathed deeply, comforting her heart to still itself. Silently thanking God for keeping her safe, she opened her eyes and waited.

And she waited. And she waited some more. If she strained her eyes beyond her feet, she could see two uniformed X-ray technicians, one of them casually leaning on a desk while the other relaxed in a chair. There were no patients, just the two technicians, chatting, with Mora fully visible to them.

As jittery fear mixed with anger rose up from her gut, Mora

called to them. "Is anyone going to help me?"

"Just a minute," one of the technicians said blandly, before returning to his conversation.

Mora waited a few minutes more until the anger rising from her belly grew hotter. "Hello! Could you take care of me, please?" She spoke louder.

"In a minute," the technician snapped.

Mora lay still, mulling over the situation before deciding to use the power she had.

"WILL SOMEONE COME AND TAKE CARE OF ME NOW! I'VE WAITED LONG ENOUGH AND I CAN SEE YOU HAVE NO PATIENTS IN THERE!" she yelled.

Instantly one of the technicians ran to her. "Shhh, okay, okay. Keep your voice down!" He looked around at the increased human traffic stopping to look.

"DON'T YOU DARE FUCKING TELL ME TO KEEP MY VOICE DOWN! TAKE MY X-RAYS NOW OR I'LL SCREAM UNTIL YOU DO!"

"Okay, okay." He rolled Mora in and she burst into tears.

*   *   *

"I've called transport to come get you." The technician stated belligerently when he was finished.

"I will not allow that guy Lucas to transport me back. He was stoned. I want someone else." Mora looked straight ahead at the ceiling, rather than at the technician standing over her.

"I don't know who they'll send. Whoever's up next has to transport you."

"Oh yeah? Well if it's Lucas I'll just scream until I get somebody else." Mora set her jaw closed and held her focus on the ceiling.

A different transporter arrived and Mora instantly relaxed. Within minutes he had her back in her room.

"Excuse me," Mora stopped him before he left. "Would you please describe the route you took here? It's important to me."

The young man smiled. "Sure. We went to the elevator, took it up two flights, got out, and went down a hall to another elevator, went up, let's see, three flights, got out and presto, we're on the SCI unit."

"Then I need to report Lucas, the transporter who brought me down to X-ray. He was stoned on pot, I could smell it. He stopped twice to go off and smoke, once he forgot to put the gurney brake on, and he took a half an hour to make a trip that took you a few minutes. He's dangerous. Today is my first day here and I was terrified. I need to report him. How do I go about reporting him?"

"I don't know. Talk to the head of transport, I guess. Why don't you discuss it with your doctor or a nurse? I need to get you back into bed and report back now." He moved Mora back to bed and left.

Exhausted sleep skimmed the froth off Mora's frustration and sadness. The sounds and smells of dinner delivery brought back calmness and hopeful anticipation. A covered meal was placed on her bedtray and she inhaled the enticing aroma of chicken. She waited for a long time but no one came to feed her. No one had set her up with a nurse's call button either. So she called out.

"Hello! Is there anyone out there? Could someone feed me? I'm new and I'm in 602!" Anger and hunger returned together.

The same nurse from hours before poked her head in. "I'll get to you as soon as I can. We're short-staffed today."

"This sucks." Mora said outloud to herself and closed her eyes. Just as she took a deep breath of angry decision to yell for help, Hope walked in.

"Oh God, I'm so glad to see YOU! Wait 'til I tell you what happened. It was awful. But could you feed me first? I've been lying here just smelling that food." Mora's eyebrows were strings of woe and tears fell once again. "Have you eaten yet?"

"I grabbed a sub on the run. What kind of place is this anyway?" Hope quickly pushed the bedtray over the bed, removed the stainless steel plate cover, filled a fork with instant mashed potatoes and pale peas, and presented it to Mora's open mouth.

"It's cold. Shit." Mora lowered her eyes, chewed and swallowed. "If I weren't so fucking hungry I'd scream."

"Did they do the orientation yet?" Hope chopped off a piece of chicken loaf and presented it.

"No," snapped Mora, just before opening her mouth. She swallowed. "I'll tell you about it after I've eaten."

After dinner, Mora recounted the afternoon's events and lack thereof. "I've got a bad feeling about this place, Hope."

"Hm. . . you do, huh? So do I. Well. . . what do we do?"

"See what happens next and pray, I guess." Mora's eyes latched onto Hope's for assurance. "Did you ever hear of Norman Cousins?"

"Was he the terminally ill guy who watched funny movies and laughed himself into recovery?"

"That's him. He checked out of the hospital and into a hotel, hired a private nurse, and did his recovery there."

They sat in an unspoken agreement of silence for a long while, waiting for calmness to return. Hope had a sixth sense about when to say what and even more important, when not to. Neither one verbalized the contrast between Louise's promotional tour and the actual events of Mora's first day. The black cloud of disappointment permeated the air between them and cast a foreboding shadow over the future.

"Want me to close the curtains and turn on a light?"

"Sure. What time is it?"

Hope turned on the bathroom light and glanced at her watch. "8:15. I guess everybody's gone home for the day. Ha!"

"Tsss. . . oh well." Mora closed her eyes and took deep breaths. "Hope, I am so fucking angry and my neck and arms are in so much pain. Do you feel like working on me for a while?"

"Sure." Hope pulled her chair closer to the bed and got comfortable. "I almost forgot the music. Want to hear some?"

"Oh, that would be wonderful. Could you close the door while you're up?" Mora closed her eyes and let peace return.

The atmosphere was their own. Hope left the bathroom door open a few inches, allowing a soft stream of indirect light into the room. Air from an open window danced seductively with Nag Champa's incense spirit waving welcome to the other world. Seagulls and salt-crisp waves stroked the grand violin wings of Pachelbel's Canon. Hope's sure, smooth fingers softened Mora's knots and said "all is well. . . all is well."

"I can see my nerves calming down. Relaxing. They're remembering. Life is returning. Can you see my spinal cord, Hope, the strong and peaceful tree inside me?"

"What are you *doing* in here?" The shrill voice and fluorescent flash slashed serenity to shreds. "What's going on in here?"

"My friend Hope is massaging my neck," Mora said.

"Visiting hours were over at 9! You've got to *leave* immediately! What's that smoke?" The nurse ran to the windowsill, grabbed the incense, and extinguished it at the bathroom sink. "You can't have this in here! It's against fire regulations!" She scowled, planted both hands on her hips and shook her head. "I'm going to have to report all of this to Jane. We have specific regulations. No fires. No closed doors." She shook her head sharply and pursed her lips. "And *absolutely* no visitors are allowed after 9 P.M.!"

It happened so fast. Hope turned to Mora, who was equally stunned, and mumbled as she arose from her chair, "I've got a bad feeling. . ."

"Will I see you tomorrow?" Mora implored.

"Definitely. Maybe things'll look better after a good night's sleep." She leaned over to hug Mora, then left.

The nurse shook her head disapprovingly at Mora. "Well, it looks like you got started on the wrong foot here!"

"Look." Mora said behind closed eyes. "I'm tired and I don't want to get into an argument with you. You got a bedpan handy? I have to pee and I need my face washed, my pins cleaned, and my teeth brushed. Can you handle that?"

"Uhh!" The nurse's jaw fell open and she replaced her hands on her hips.

Mora closed her eyes. In a few seconds she heard the clanging of the metal bedpan in the bathroom.

- 12 -

Something of surrender must have seeped into Mora's good, deep sleep because she did not awaken until hallway bustling was well in progress.

"Good morning, Mora. Are you hungry?" A nurse named Priscilla set breakfast on the bedtray and stood ready to raise the bed.

"Good morning. Breakfast sounds good. What time is it?"

"A little after 7:30. After we get you fed we'll bathe you and get you ready for your first day." Priscilla lifted the cover to reveal oatmeal.

"This is my second day, and could you please mix the peaches in with the oatmeal? Just a little bit of the milk over it all if you would." Angry at the reminder of yesterday, Mora kept her eyes riveted on the mush.

"Your second day?" Priscilla fed Mora with easy swiftness.

"So what's supposed to happen around here?" Mora asked in between mouthfuls.

"Well, every day you'll be given a written schedule of what therapies you'll have and when: physical therapy, occupational therapy, psychologist appointments, tests, free time, staffings, whatever. But for your first day. . ."

"Second." Mora corrected as she zoned in on the approaching spoonful.

"Okay, second. The psychologist will be coming in for your initial profile interview. She'll fill you in on the rest of the day before you meet your other staff members."

"Before I do anything I need to report a hospital employee

named Lucas who transported me to X-ray yesterday stoned. Do you
know who I can file a formal complaint with?" Mora asked as another spoonful halted midair. "That's okay, I've had enough."

The nurse put the spoon down. "Really? Gee, that's awful.
You'd better tell Mrs. Veypoko."

"Who's that?"

"The psychologist." Priscilla got up and gracefully shoved the
chair with the backs of her legs. "I have to check on another patient,
then I'll come back to bathe you if one of the nursing students hasn't.
Are you okay for a few minutes?"

"Yes, but I need to go to the bathroom. I guess I can hold on a
few minutes."

"Good." Priscilla turned to leave and bumped into a nursing
student in a blue-and-white-striped uniform. "Sorry, Pam! She needs
bathing, okay?"

The red-haired, freckle-faced, blue-eyed young woman nodded
and smiled as she entered the room.

"Hi, I'm Pam." She rocked back and forth and clasped her
hands behind her. "I'm going to bathe you, okay?"

"Sure, if you can." Mora sensed the student nurse's self-doubt
and decided to address it. "Do you know what to do?"

"Uhh. . . " Pam's eyes darted around the room. "I *think* I do."
She laughed nervously. "This is my first week of practicum. Is there
anything special about your, about. . ." She brushed wiry stray hairs
off her forehead and they immediately bounced back down.

"I'll tell you what to do. But could you stand in front of me
where I can see you without straining my eyeballs? I can't turn my
head."

"Oh! I'm so sorry!" Pam jumped in front of Mora, her face
flushed red.

"So, let's get started before they steal you from me." Mora
extended comfort through a softened voice.

The redfaced greenhorn jumped again. "Okay. Yes. Uhhhhm. . . "
She scanned the room. "A wash basin. Let's see. Over here in the
closet?" She opened the cabinet. "Ah! And a washcloth. Oh. . . that's
down the hall." Pam's chest caved in and she dropped her head

guiltily. "Is it okay if I go get a towel and washcloth? I forgot to bring them. Sorry."

"Sure, but first may I use the bedpan?"

"Oh! Of course!" She jumped and nervously pushed persistent orange frizz off her forehead. She shook her head in self-reproach while rummaging noisily through the closet.

"I'll bet you a cookie it's in the bathroom."

"Oh, you're right!" She hopped into the bathroom and emerged grinning, holding up the stainless steel prize. "Ta da! Looks like I owe you a cookie."

Mora's laughter crept up slowly until she opened the gate and let it flood in.

"Did I say something funny?" Pam asked, wearing an innocent smile.

"Everything. You're a gift, easing my mind, reminding me to lighten up. You're a breath of fresh air, do you know that?"

"Really?" Pam flashed an impish smile. Her confidence regained, she set Mora up with the bedpan.

"Well, if you're ready to give me a bath, I'm ready. Do you know how to do pin care?"

"Pin care?" Pam stood back and looked at Mora. "If I do, I didn't know I could."

Mora laughed and playfully slipped into a Gaelic accent. "Ah, you're quite the one indeed and you don't even know it, do ya now? That curly red hair and freckles on ya sets me heart ta thinkin' on the dear auld sod. And why wouldn't it?"

"Hey, that's pretty good? Are you Irish too?" Pam's face lit up.

"Indeed, fifty one percent of meself." Mora matter-of-factly shifted to business. "Now, about these pins in my head. They need to be kept clean." Pam's bright blue eyes zeroed in on the subject at hand.

"So. They have to be cleaned. I've never seen anybody in one of those things before."

"At least three times a day. To avoid infection."

"Right." Pam stood upright and nodded in a very businesslike manner.

"Let's do that first, okay?" Mora could sense precious nursing time slipping away from her basic necessities. "There's a blue plastic basin we brought from the other hospital in the closet. It's got all the stuff in it."

"Oh. Okay. I'll get it."

"It's three steps: First, gently but thoroughly clean around them with hydrogen peroxide soaked sterile swabs. Oh, there's a box of latex gloves in the closet."

"Okay." Pam followed Mora's instructions.

"Next you apply more h.p. Then you apply some antiseptic ointment and you're finished. With that pin. You have to repeat the procedure with the other three."

Mora observed the young woman's smooth proficiency. "You're a very competent and thorough nurse, once you relax."

"Me? Really?" Pam stopped and looked at Mora, astonished.

"Yes. Really. You're just tripping over your own self-doubt a tiny bit. You remind me of myself at your age. You'll get over it. Clearly, you're very conscientious."

"Thanks. I like nursing. And I better finish you up. How about teeth brushing?"

"In that covered basin in the closet."

After teeth came the sponge bath. Pam prepared the basin, set it on the bedtray, and reached over to pull open the velcro flaps on the chest of the halo vest.

"What are you *doing*?" Mora's eyes almost jumped out of their sockets.

Pam quickly retracted her hands from Mora's body. "I'm opening the vest to wash under it." She waited to understand Mora's alarm.

"I thought it couldn't be opened."

"It looks like it's designed to be opened."

"I don't know. The nurses at Drayton never opened it because they thought it would destabilize my neck. Would you mind asking somebody who knows for sure?"

"Sure. Be right back." Pam left and returned within seconds. "I thought so. It's perfectly stable and opening it isn't hazardous to your health."

"Oh my God! My torso hasn't been washed since the shower I took the morning of my crash, over five weeks ago!"

Pam ripped open the super-charged patch of velcro. With great delicacy she dabbed the virgin flesh of Mora's chest and removed the washcloth. The two women stared at it.

"Ughhh. . ." Hypnotized with horror Mora looked at the layer of brown gunk on the washcloth. "There's my summer tan, not to mention layers of dead skin, dirty old sweat, and what are those tiny microscopic mites I've heard live on the surface of people's skin? I could grow potatoes in that."

Pam flinched, then instinctively dropped the soiled washcloth into the basin with a splash. "Ooops. . . Sorry." She looked apologetically at Mora. She straightened herself and pursed her lips while wringing out the washcloth.

"It *is* gross. The things you have to endure in nursing, huh?"

Pam replenished the washwater and adeptly finished bathing Mora.

"Ahhh, how lovely. A fresh new clean place on my body. I treasure the delicious results of a bath, although my flesh felt weird, hypersensitive. Thanks for doing it softly. The next major laundry item on my agenda is my hair, which hasn't been washed in over five weeks. Do you think you might be able to arrange a hair washing?"

"Good morning!" squealed a bizarrely theatrical woman's voice. "May I come in?" A very tall, slender woman stood before Mora holding a briefcase. The smooth curves of her short black hair dramatically framed her ivory face and accentuated the exotic lines of her eye makeup and bright, shiny red lips. When she spoke she managed to slide her voice up and down a full octave. "I'm Mrs. Veypoko, your psychologist," she said, and smiled broadly.

"Hi. I'd shake your hand but mine's paralyzed."

"I see our fine nursing student Pamela is taking good care of you this morning," Mrs. Veypoko lilted.

"Yes, she's very good."

"I just have to help Mora get dressed, then she'll be all ready."

"Well then, I'll come back when you're all finished." Mrs. Veypoko moved toward the door.

"Actually, if you could stay," Mora said, halting her exit, "there's an urgent matter I need to discuss with you. Maybe someone can help me get dressed later."

Mrs. Veypoko tilted her head and squinted slightly. "Oh? Yes. I believe it would be most efficient to proceed in that fashion. Pamela?"

"Oh. Sure." Pam grabbed the soiled towels and left.

"Now," sang the psychologist with a quick side-to-side flick of her head. She seated herself in the bedside chair, primly crossed her legs, and changed her expression to one of concern. "What is it you wish to discuss?"

Mora watched the psychologist's theatrical transfigurations in silent awe before proceeding. "Yesterday was my first day here and I had been told I would receive an orientation. I didn't get any. I was left alone like some slab of dead meat. I was frightened, very disoriented, and *then*. . ." Mora said, feeling the anger and terror of the previous day return, "I was transported to X-ray by a guy who was stoned, who drove me lying helpless on a gurney all over the damn hospital for a *half an hour!* He stopped *twice* to go into a broom closet to get high, and he forgot to put the brake on the gurney at least once because I started rolling away!" The frightful memory brought tears to her eyes. "I know what pot smells like and when he came out he *stank* of it! I *know* he took me up and down the same hallways more than once because I saw the same walls over and over! Here I am, physically helpless to move or protect my body from harm and my first experience in this place is a terrifying joyride at the mercy of some guy who's getting high — and my insurance is paying for it!" She shouted the last words before bursting into tears.

"You don't know for a fact that he was smoking marijuana, or as you say, getting high. This is quite improbable." Mrs. Veypoko shook her head. "I'm sure you're just overwrought with your difficult circumstances. Physical limitations can play peculiar games with one's mind." She leaned forward, tilted her head, smiled patronizingly, and touched Mora's arm lightly. "Would you like me to have doctor Jackson prescribe a nice sedative for you?"

"*What?*" Mora shouted. "Look lady, I *know* what happened and *I WANT TO FILE A COMPLAINT NOW!* Furthermore, I'm going to discuss this with my attorney. I'm willing to overlook the fact that I have not yet received the orientation which your sales and marketing departments conjured up to suck my insurance money into this dump. But I *will* file a formal complaint about the pothead transporter! Now, how do I file a complaint?" Mora set her jaw and narrowed the immovable arrowhead focus of her stormy dark eyes and brows.

Quickly recovering her composure, the psychologist jumped in with both feet. "I will look into this; however, before I do anything, it is necessary that I review our hospital policies with you *at this time.*" Mrs. Veypoko moved easily into the warm waters of regulations territory where she was most comfortable. She leaned back in her chair and put her hands together, her fingers pointing up. "I understand that on your very first day here you violated one of our most essential internal security regulations, which is that absolutely no visitors are permitted on hospital grounds after 9:00 P.M., *period.*" She shook her head disapprovingly.

"Let's see, where do I begin?" A blaze of anger caught fire in the pit of Mora's belly. "First, I do not at all appreciate your diverting from the subject of my safety. You are here for me. I'm the patient, and you haven't addressed my legitimate complaint yet." With fiery eyes and a clear voice forging straight ahead, Mora rode over Mrs. Veypoko's attempt to interrupt. "Second, had I been *informed* of *any* policy at all through an orientation, then the so-called *violation* might have some validity. In less than one day, this hospital was grossly negligent twice. Third, I do not appreciate your sloughing off my legitimate terror at being put in the care of a druggie employee by offering *me* drugs. Are you trying to put me in a silent stupor? Is that how you help patients adjust to problems? I am a recovering alcoholic and I do not consume narcotic substances, which brings me to point four: visitors. My friend Hope massages me. Her massages eliminate my pain and help my body heal. Without massage, I wouldn't be able to get a full night of drug-free sleep. Does this hospital provide massage therapy?" Furious, Mora glared at the psychologist.

"Miss Donovan." Mrs. Veypoko raised her chin high and sat up stiffly in the chair. "You are a patient in this hospital. I am here to introduce you to the rules and regulations of this institution, *not* to call our policies into question. You do not make hospital policy." She narrowed her eyes, leaned closer to Mora. "Every employee of this hospital is in total accord with these policies, which have been established for *your* protection and. . ."

"Including stoned orderlies?" Mora interrupted.

"And I will *not* sit here and take issue with an absurd accusation of negligence." Mrs. Veypoko flexed her jaw then leaned back in the chair with her fingertips together. "Now. I have a job to do. You are the patient and I am your psychologist and I am here to officially welcome you." She leaned forward, reached for her briefcase and without skipping a beat, produced a printed form. "As part of your intake profile, I need to ask you a few questions. Are you married?"

Mora sat in silent disbelief while her mind tried to make sense out of insanity. Looking through the walls of the room, she mentally exited. *Here I am up against another wall of authority. All my life. . . me versus a man-made institution obsessed with controlling people. Is that what this place is about too? Things are different now. I'm different. I don't want to do battle anymore. I know what really matters. How can I put aside the love I experienced in favor of attack? I just can't buy it anymore. It's meaningless.*

"Miss Donovan?" Mrs. Veypoko leaned forward and scrutinized Mora's face. "Are you all right?"

Mora returned to the present and looked at a different Mrs. Veypoko sitting before her. The mask of pretension had vanished.

"Am I all right?" Mora repeated the words in a daze. "Well, I'm here, that's for sure. What did you ask me?"

"Are you married?"

"I was. Up until about a month ago. Divorced."

"Any children?"

"No."

"Oh, no children." Mrs. Veypoko tilted her head and shook it. "That's too bad. Children are wonderful. I have a son. Now, I'm not biased, but he really is particularly adorable and smart. Would you like to see a picture of him?"

Mora considered responding with *Not really. I'd rather talk to my own therapist about how I feel than look at your stupid baby pictures.* But she didn't. Instead, she stepped back and observed herself engaging with a fellow human being. From behind a protective veil Mora silently comforted her own need. *Soon. But not now. You can't lean on this person right now.* She gave herself permission to listen. "Okay," she finally answered.

Mrs. Veypoko dug into her briefcase with unabashed fervor and pulled out a stack of photographs. "He just turned eighteen months last week and he's the light of my life." She raised the pile of photos for Mora to see. In an instant the psychologist's veil fell as genuine joy took its place. The real Mrs. Veypoko showed up.

"Where is he now?" Awed by the surprise twist, Mora was suddenly curious.

"Oh." Mrs. Veypoko looked down in her lap. "He's with a sitter." Then she raised her head and looked unguardedly into Mora's eyes. "I hate leaving him during the day. But my husband and I can't live on just his income so I have to keep working for now. The hospital provided excellent maternity benefits, don't get me wrong. I couldn't ask for more. But still. . ." Her eyes turned back to the pile of photographs. She lay them back in her lap, smiled and began to caption each one for Mora. "This one was taken a few weeks ago. Ohhhh. . . he's so sweet!" She kissed the photograph and quickly shrugged and giggled. "I just love my little baby boy so much."

Mora looked at the photo with greater interest. The baby was average looking, nothing outstanding, just a regular baby. "Yes, your son is beautiful. What does your husband do?" It was the best she could do to divert her own defensiveness.

"He's an accountant. He started his own business last year right after James came and it's been hard, you know, a new baby, a new business. He works very hard, even on weekends." Mrs. Veypoko looked at Mora hoping for encouragement. "Oh, I know I shouldn't complain. I just wish I could stay home with him. These early years of life are so precious, and before you know it they're gone. I don't want to look back when James is starting school and say 'where's my baby?'" She silently stared at her son's picture.

"There must be some way you could," Mora suggested. "I mean, where there's a will there's a way. If some kind of love means more to you than anything, there's got to be a way to have it, don't you think?"

"Uh oh," Mrs. Veypoko said, looking at her watch, "I've got a patient coming down to my office in three minutes. Mora, it's been a pleasure getting to know you. I've really enjoyed our little chat." She smiled genuinely, rose from the chair, and quickly stuffed the papers and photos into her briefcase. "I think I have enough information for now. Please, if I can be of *any* help to you, don't hesitate to call. Remember, I am here to help you. And I'm in my office Monday to Friday from 9 until 5, except between noon and 1. Bye now." She waved and left Mora alone.

"Whew. . . this place is a nuthouse."

*   *   *

"She told me she wants to file a complaint, doctor, something about being transported by an orderly high on drugs. I thought you should know," Mrs. Veypoko said.

"I'll look into it, Mrs. Veypoko. Thank you." Doctor Jackson rose from the chair behind his desk and walked her to the door. When the sound of her footsteps faded, he closed his office door behind him, and headed for patient room 602.

"May I come in?"

"Sure," Mora answered from her wheelchair facing the windows.

"Welcome to MacKenzie Rehabilitation Hospital, Mora. I'm doctor Jackson, the chief physician on the Spinal Cord Injury Unit. Do you mind if I pull up a chair?"

"No, go ahead." Mora watched as the gray-haired, round-bellied man, whom she guessed to be in his fifties, positioned the chair several feet in front of her and sat down.

"I'd like to get to know you a little, to help you feel at home here at MacKenzie. Would you tell me a little about yourself?" Doctor Jackson asked gently.

"Well, yes, but first, did Mrs. Veypoko tell what happened to me yesterday? About the stoned guy who transported me?"

"No, I haven't spoken to her yet. What happened?"

"It was awful. I was so frightened. In a strange environment where I don't know anybody, and he took me all over the place, over and over. I was lying on the gurney and I couldn't. . ." Mora began to cry, but continued anyway. "I couldn't get up! What if he'd hurt me? I was helpless!"

Doctor Jackson pulled his chair closer to Mora and touched her arm. "You've been dealt some awful blows lately, haven't you?"

Mora looked into his eyes and leaned on them. "It's been so hard," she cried.

"Don't worry yourself now. You've been under a tremendous strain and we're here to help you through." He leaned back in the chair and said, "I'll look into the matter for you, Mora, and see what I can find out. In the meantime, go easy on yourself."

Mora released a heavy sigh and said, "Okay. Thanks, doctor. I feel better now. I always feel better talking about what bothers me."

"Good," doctor Jackson said, nodding, as he rose from the chair. "Your physical therapist should be coming for you soon. I'll be checking in on you from time to time, making sure you're comfortable here. It's been a pleasure to have met you, Mora." He leaned over and touched her hand.

*   *   *

And on her first full day as a patient on the Spinal Cord Injury Unit at Mackenzie Rehab Hospital, Mora did . . . okay! That was the conclusion she and Hope came to later that evening.

"The physical therapist is great. Her name is Yvette. She's real tall, about six foot two from the looks of her."

"Maybe she just looks tall to you from down there." Hope jested as she filled the shelf space with clean laundry, audio tapes, and books.

"No, she's tall. She's thin, easy-moving, no quirky, obtrusive tensions to speak of, blue eyes, and very kind. She is so easy-going yet very focused, supportive of any any anything I can or cannot do. *And* next to that number one priority is her second greatest gift." Mora looked at Hope and waited for a response.

"Which is?"

"She's *in* the system but not *of* the system. Isn't that great?" Mora grinned broadly.

"Meaning?"

"She works in this hospital but she seems oblivious to politics. When she's with a patient, she's with the patient. She's soft and sweet, but strong and steady. I watched her respond to Jane and the doctors. She takes the information kindly enough but doesn't engage in power struggles. And let me tell you, Jane has a real power struggle going on inside *her*self. . . ooh-wee!" As soon as Mora had Hope's attention she rolled her eyes and Hope laughed.

"Imagine my surprise," Hope said.

"This afternoon I asked a custodian to close my door and it was as if the hinges are connected to a sonar sensing device in Jane's head because she appeared out of nowhere, shoved the door open, and hissed 'Doors opened at all times. Hospital regulations.' and zipped off. I shouted 'You must be Jane! Nice to make your acquaintance, too!' after her."

"Did she respond?" Hope asked, enthralled.

"I don't know if she heard me but it felt good to say it. Hey, see those multi-colored rubber bands over on the windowsill? Bring them over here and I'll tell you what they're for."

Hope jumped up from the chair and retrieved three thin, broad bands of rubber.

"Oh, I sure wish I could show you myself." Mora sighed longingly at the bands, "I'll explain and you can feel how they work, okay?"

"Okay."

"First, the green one is the weakest. Stretch it out."

Hope stretched it out. "Hey, this is cool!"

"Now do the orange one."

She did. "Hmmm. Harder."

"Yep. Now the yellow one."

"Wow! Quite a challenge." Hope put them down. "Are you able to do the green one at all?"

"No." Mora dropped her eyes. "Not really. Yvette mostly had to lift my arms. PT was pretty passive today." Mora's chest rose and fell with a heavy breath. "Hope?"

"Yes?"

Mora's eyes filled with tears. "What's going to happen here? I'm so discouraged." She began to sob.

Hope sat down in the chair and leaned forward to touch Mora's arm. "Aw, Mora. It's going to be okay." She gently patted her friend, then sat back and waited.

"I get so hopeful. I pray all day, talking to God. I try so hard to do the best I can. But my hands, my arms, my legs. . . I can't stand up by myself. I can't feed myself or go to the bathroom by myself. I just get so tired of being pulled back."

"I can only imagine what it would be like. Honestly." Hope shook her head sympathetically. "But I still have to remind you of how far you've come. Where's that foam ball Kathleen gave you before we left Drayton Hospital?" Hope scanned the room then went to the closet. In a moment she held out a baseball-sized soft foam ball. "Here." She placed it in Mora's right palm. "Go ahead. Squeeze it."

"Oh no," Mora sniffled, "I can't."

"Please? Just one squeeze." They both laughed at Hope's rhyme.

"Okay." Mora lowered her eyes to her hand, gripped her lips shut tight and tried desperately from the inside to move her hand, her fingers, any finger. The thumb and second finger moved in and pressed a slight indentation in the foam.

"See? Look, you're doing it!" Hope hopped up and down. "Can't you see?"

Mora cried again. "Well, but it's only a tiny bit."

"Sure, only a little bit, but I swear to you, just a few days ago you couldn't even do that. Today a squeeze on a foam ball, tomorrow mudwrestling with Jane!"

Laughing together, they settled back into conversation.

"So have you officially meet her?" Hope had a nose for drama.

"Who?"

"Jane, of course."

"Oh, yeah. First doctor Jackson came in and we had a talk. He's an older man with a puffy belly. He seemed kind enough, told me not to worry about the stoned orderly, he'll look into it. Then later, he came back to introduce me to Jane and doctor Weiss. Jane's about 50 I'd say, bottom-heavy, curly gray hair, and doctor Weiss is a 40-ish, blonde woman. It was very strange. . . ." Mora's voice trailed off with her eyes into space.

"What? Tell me." Hope reeled her friend's attention back.

"I got a chilling feeling from them, the way they play on each other. Jane's main objective is to please doctor Jackson and keep everything under control. She looks like she could wield a heavy sword down on anyone who doesn't do things the way she wants. And doctor Weiss just mimics everything doctor Jackson says. Doctor Jackson's kind demeanor toward me evaporated while he was around them. He seems to thrive on being the authority over people. The three of them feel uncomfortably familiar to me. I already know Jane doesn't particularly care for me." Mora's pensive face revealed genuine puzzlement.

"I can't think why," Hope jabbed sarcastically. "Your name has only appeared in big red letters on the nurses' and psychologist's reports eleven times in less than twenty-four hours, she's a control freak and you hate being controlled. Odd that she would regard you askance."

Mora laughed. "Hey, my function is *not* to ensure she's having a nice day. I am not one of her subordinates. She's here for *me* and I'm here to get *out* of here, not because I preferred this place to a vacation in the Yucatan." Mora's face shape-shifted into that of a charging bull who had just discovered he was chained to the wall, then just as quickly returned to normal.

"One thing's for sure, this place is a study in control forced upon human nature. Just when I had a defensive stance all set for battle with Mrs. Veypoko and it seemed as if she had me up against the wall, I saw what we were doing and let go. As soon as I did that,

I remembered how perfectly wonderful everything was in heaven and the next thing I knew, what was in front of me looked completely differrent. She's just a normal wife and mother who would rather be at home raising her son. I couldn't take her too seriously after that." Mora stopped, deep in thought. "There is a clearly unhealthy undercurrent going on here."

"Which is?"

"The hospital hires her to enforce rules and she agrees because she needs the money. If she had the number one goal of helping patients help themselves, they never would've hired her."

"Maybe an unintentional therapy here is standing up for yourself — literally and figuratively — by speaking up for what you need."

"Hmmm. You know, I've been thinking," Mora said. "The only reason I can see for me living here in the first place is because I'm under what they call medical supervision. And I'm sure the insurance company wouldn't cover the cost if I checked into a luxury suite at the Marriott, had fabulous room service and paid you a hefty salary to take care of me. You could drive me to outpatient PT and OT. We could visualize all day, sing, burn incense, have all kinds of health practitioners come and work on me under a howling full moon at midnight if we felt like it. I'm sure it would be cheaper, faster, and a whole lot more fun."

"True." Hope nodded.

"We'll just have to improvise." Mora's thoughts flew miles out to somewhere before she resurfaced fully focused.

"Do you want me to start working on you?" Hope had set up the room just as she had the night before, *sans* incense.

"Sure, I'd love it. But first I have kind of an unusual request, if there's enough time. You already do so much but. . ."

"Tell me, what do you need?"

"As you know, I have horrificly annoyingly painful and inexplicably uncomfortable. . . "

"You do a damn good job of explaining the inexplicable." Hope teased.

"Thank you. As I was saying, hypersensitivity on my legs. Now that I can move them, whenever one leg touches the other it's awful. It's so grating and irritating that I need to be scraped off the ceiling. The French part of my heritage has really thick, hairy legs and I haven't had my legs shaved in weeks. So. . ."

"You want me to shave your legs." Hope nodded.

"Could you?"

"Sure. Where's the shaver?"

"It's in my canvas bag." Mora released a dramatic sigh and closed her eyes. "This is going to put you in line for sainthood, I'll personally see to that."

"While I'm up, what will our musical entertainment be this evening? You've got several choices. Would you like to hear them?" Shaver in hand, Hope stood ready to read off music titles.

"Indubitably." Mora grinned in happy anticipation.

"There's always the ocean; there's Steve Halpern's 'Eastern Peace'; Akasha 'Lifesong: Music by Sri Chimoy'; 'Om Namaha Shivaya' the ancient Sanskrit chant by On Wings of Song; Patrick Bernhardt's 'Atlantis Angelis'; Walt Whitman and the Soul Children Choir of Chicago's 'We Are One'; or Santana 'Zebop!'"

"Zebop? How'd that one get in there?"

"I don't know. Maybe Carmella saw 'Chicago' and she thought 'Santana' would fit."

"Let's listen to Patrick Bernhardt. He always lifts my spirits." Mora closed her eyes and took a deep breath while Hope started the tape player and went into the little bathroom to fill the plastic tub with warm water. "Hope, have I told you lately how grateful I am for your tender loving care?"

"Yes, but I never seem to tire of repeats." Hope carried the full tub from the bathroom, a washcloth and towel draped over her forearm.

"You look so professional," Mora teased.

"At your service madame. We have hospital white or hospital white as your soap choices for this evening's plowing the back forty procedure."

"Such a hard choice. Go ahead, do what you must do, but may I make one request?" Mora frowned apologetically.

"I know that look. What is your one single only solitary minis-cule request?"

"Now here I am, a thirty-three year old woman who's absolute-ly accustomed to living life her own way, including the way she shaves. I just wanted to mention that if you skip a row, it'll feel absolutely terrible. So in conclusion and in summation and to make a long story short which, by now, it's too late, please be as thorough as possible. Okay?" Mora flashed a grin. "How am I doing?"

Hope laughed. "Ah, you're pushin' it girl, but sure, I'll do a thorough job. Jeeesh!" She shook her head, proceeded to soap-foam Mora's leg and pulled the shaver up a row.

"Aghhhh!" Mora shouted.

"What?!" Hope jumped, instantly retracting the shaver from her leg.

"Could you go a little lighter? It feels awful. I'm sorry. . . "

"It's okay. I'm new at this. You've got to give me a chance to get it right. I've never shaved anybody else's legs before." She tried to hold back a chuckle then a flood of laughter burst forth. "I'm sorry, Ms. Donovan, but this is too hysterical for words. What will you be having me do next?"

Mora sighed and closed her eyes. "Maybe someday I won't have to ask other people to do the very private personal care things that I always took for granted. The little things turn out to be so important."

Waves of restful calm washed over Mora's body and met the ocean waves' welcoming chants. Inhaling deeply, every cell in her body filled with the breath of life; exhaling completely, she released the residue of any tense thoughts, feelings, and energies, her body guided perfectly by her mind. Safe to let go, taking in life and letting it go, she always knew what to do from inside. Her heart opened with compassion, refreshed now from speaking her truth; her mind was at peace. Hope sat in the bedside chair, ready for the massage hour.

"Hope, could you hook me up again, one hand under my neck, the other under my sacrum?" Mora's eyes remained closed.

"Yes." Hope connected Mora's spinal circuit and held steady.

    Mora drifted, halfway between worlds.
    Fluid wandered her restful mind
    taken by a wild musical dive,
    deep down under where she remembered *I Am Alive!*

    Her right hand twitched. Hope caught the altered shadow from the corner of her eye. Holding steady, she stayed on line. Mora's left leg twitched, then her left foot. Hope watched, wide-eyed in wonder at the visible electrical surges. She stayed plugged in for a long time.

- 13 -

The first activity on the next day's agenda was occupational therapy. If Mora didn't know she was in a hospital, she would have guessed the OT room was a kindergarten. It's shelf-lined walls were packed full of rubber balls, puzzles, jacks, sewing and embroidery materials, multi-colored plastic stacking boxes, and elaborate eating utensils. All unusable, Mora reminded herself as she silently scanned the room.

"What's the difference between occupational therapy and physical thereapy?" She asked Corky in an effort to turn her attention toward something constructive.

Corky was a perky, petite woman in her late twenties with cropped black hair, hazel eyes, and a bouncy, steady-on manner. "Let's see. . ." she said as she prepared for the evaluation, "physical therapy deals primarily with mobilization and gross motor movements. Occupational therapy deals with fine muscle movement and their application to specific life tasks. Now, if Yvette heard me define her job in six words she'd have a fit."

"You mean she deals with the gross and you deal with the fine? She's gross, you're fine? That sounds a little biased, don't you think?" Mora teased.

"Hey wait a minute, are you a reporter for the *National Inquirer*?" Corky laughed and placed a stainless steel gripper and a felt sack on the table. "Let's find out where to begin."

"That should be easy. Where's the 'can't do' column? Just draw a line down the whole row." Tripping on her attempt at self-deprecating humor, Mora's eyes filled with tears.

"Oh. . . you may be surprised at what you can do. Besides,

you're just starting. Go easy on yourself, young lady." Corky lowered her head in search of Mora's averted eyes. "Are you okay?"

"Sure." Mora struggled to push back tears. It was too soon to fall.

Corky laid Mora's right hand in hers on the table. "When I say 'push,' you just do what you can to push this finger against me, okay?"

Mora sighed. "Okay. Here goes nothing."

Starting with Mora's pinky finger Corky positioned herself for resistance. "Push," she said. Nothing happened. "Are you doing it?"

Tears slid down Mora's cheeks. "Yes." A single word opened the floodgate. "I can't do this!" she sobbed.

Corky put her hand on Mora's shoulder. "This is very hard, I know." She patted softly. "Do you need a kleenex?"

"No." Mora's sobbing subsided. "This is so discouraging. I can't do the simplest things. My hands are useless. Is it ever going to change?"

Corky nodded. "You've got a right to be sad. Sometimes the best thing you can do is just let it out." She let Mora cry for a minute, then asked, "Would you rather I just do some passive rotations on your fingers? Or do you want to go back to your room and try again later?"

Mora pushed an exasperated breath off her chest. "No. Let's try again now. I might as well. It's the reason I'm here."

"That's the spirit! You're not a quitter, are you?" Corky took up Mora's right hand again.

"Sometimes. . ." Mora watched as Corky repositioned her hand.

"Okay. Ring finger. Push."

The two women focused intently as Mora pushed with all her might. Nothing happened.

"Next." Corky went on to the middle finger. "Push."

The middle finger moved a half-inch toward the palm.

"Hey! See? I told you we'd see some action today!"

Like a flicker of sun sparkling through showers, Mora's wounded courage leaked a smile.

"Next." Corky held Mora's index finger. "Push." It moved a tiny bit closer to her palm than her middle finger had.

"Jackpot! We're on a roll. Now for the thumb."

They watched as Mora's whole thumb, standing good, solid and strong, moved in toward her palm about a quarter of an inch. Mora laughed to see so much movement. Corky patted her shoulder. "I knew we'd find some buried treasure if we just looked hard enough. Now let's do the left hand."

The energy in the room shifted. In an instant it swirled up and around, sweeping *yes* into their task. Corky moved to a left-side chair and went through each finger. The only movement was a quarter-inch movement on the thumb, and a quarter-inch movement on the middle finger.

"I'm left-handed, too." Mora looked at Corky, her eyes expressing fear of the worst and hope for the best.

Corky said, "Well, why don't we approach this by taking what we have and using it for all it's got. Let's do something silly. . . putty." She retrieved a plastic tub from the shelf. "This is the softest one. Red. Each color indicates a particular level of strength required to squish it. We'll start at the beginning. Here you go." She placed a wad of soft shiny red rubber in the palm of Mora's hand. "Now, just use your imagination. And your hands, of course. Try to involve each finger, all fingers, different combinations of fingers, your palm, whatever, in any way you can imagine."

Mora did as she was asked. Tedious and slow, the labor brought little visible results. "I'm not getting much of anything out of this."

"That's perfect. Do whatever you can. It's how you improve. You'll see." Corky winked.

"My fingers are getting worse," Mora complained. "It seems like they're doing less and less with each attempt at squeezing."

"Oh, that's just muscle fatigue. It's normal."

"You call this normal? I've hardly done anything! How can I be fatigued?"

"Because I said so. Look sweetie, you can't compare yourself now to how you used to be. Now your body uses every ounce of energy to accomplish what seems like a tiny task, but really is a gigantic undertaking. It's part of healing. Not to worry. You're bouncing back. Let's do something different." Corky picked up the felt cloth bag. "I want to test your sensory recognition." She opened the bag and reached in. "Just close your eyes. I'm going to place an object in the palm of your hand and you try to identify it. Okay?"

Mora frowned. "Oh Jeez. I don't know if I can. I can't feel much with the skin on my hands." She hoped Corky's sympathy would rescue her from any more disappointing test results.

"Let's see anyway. Ready? Close your eyes."

Mora closed her eyes. She felt minimal pressure from the weight of Corky's hand vibrating through her bones.

"Can you tell me what this is?"

Tears spilled from beneath closed eyes. "No," Mora whispered.

Corky removed the little object and put another one in its place. "Try this."

Mora strained mentally, hoping she could grab a name. "A pebble?"

"No. . ." Corky removed the object and put another in its place.

"What was that?" Mora had to know.

"A penny. Now can you tell me what this one is?"

"A penny? You mean I couldn't even tell the difference between a coin and a rock?"

"That's all right. Can you tell me what this is?" Corky pressed a marble into Mora's palm.

"I can't feel anything." Mora opened her eyes to see Corky pressing a piece of heavy duty sandpaper into her hand. She closed her eyes and sobbed.

Corky reached over and gently touched Mora's shoulders. "Oh, honey, maybe this is too much in one day, hmmm? Some days are harder than others."

"I started off fine but now I feel like I just fell down. Oh, this is hopeless!" Mora cried.

Corky nodded. "I know it seems awful. And I wish I could fix it. But all we can do is take it one hour at a time, one task at a time, and hope for the best. I wish I could offer more." She tilted her head and waited until Mora calmed. "Anyway," she said, looking at her watch, "it's time for physical therapy. Maybe that'll be a little more encouraging. Yvette says you're getting some deltoid activity on the mats. Are you okay? Need a noseblow?"

"Yes, thanks."

Mora kept her swollen eyes lowered for the trip upstairs. It was too much, putting all her effort into tiny little tasks that availed mostly frustration. She wanted to crawl into a hole and abandon the entire struggle.

Yvette met them at the elevator and wheeled Mora to the spacious, sunfilled physical therapy room. "How was OT today?" She moved Mora to the ten-by-ten-foot, low, matted table.

"Terrible. I cried the whole time."

"Some days are like that and somehow, they just manage to pass. We're not giving up, nosiree." Yvette's blonde curls framed her bright smile like golden sunflower petals around a stamen. "Let's see if we can cheer you up. How about if we start with you lying on your back and I'll passively stretch muscles and rotate joints. Then we'll see what you can do on your own." Yvette laid Mora down and executed the first part of her plan with grace and secure strength. "Now, I'm going to assist you in each movement you can't do. We're going to bring each arm around in as full an arc as we can. I can feel when your strength is present as well as when it's absent. When it's present, I'll let you do it. When it's absent, I'll do it for you. Okay?"

"What's this technique called?"

"Proprioceptive neuromuscular facilitation, or p.n.f. for short."

"I'm ready when you are." Peripherally Mora noticed doctor Weiss, the blonde woman who was part of her medical team, enter the room and sit in a chair to observe.

Half kneeling and half squatting on the mat, Yvette effortlessly pushed and slid Mora's right arm away from her torso. "Whenever you can, try to do it with me."

Yvette stretched out Mora's arm and when her hand reached six inches distance from her body, Mora's shoulder muscles flexed alive and added slightly to the motion.

"Great! Keep going."

A few inches further and Mora's muscles collapsed. Yvette easily picked up the slack. "Good. Now we'll return." Without missing a beat Yvette changed the direction of the arm slide like a speed swimmer turning an underwater flip. Her peaceful expression fed Mora encouragement. "There's some good activity with your deltoids. You compensate extremely well. I can tell you're good at using whatever's available, aren't you?" She smiled. "Great. Now for the other side." In a single, lithe move Yvette was on Mora's left side, repeating the motions. A hint of strength appeared at the beginning of the left arm's arc, then, as on the right, the muscles collapsed. "Hmmm. . . there's a little bit more on this side."

"I used to be left-handed, but in OT my left hand didn't do as much as my right. Kind of a hodge-podge."

"A little here, a little there, and you're doing just fine. Had enough?"

"I guess so. Boy, it didn't take much to fatigue."

"You actually did quite a lot. I'm going to let you try some of these on your own while I go over and get Grace started. Just do whatever you can and I'll be back in a few minutes." Yvette walked to the other side of the room.

"Okay. Where do I begin?" Mora whispered out loud to herself. "I'll just do what I can. Okay." She closed her eyes and took deep, full breaths. With all her might she tried so hard, so very hard to push her left hand, her arm, anything out to the side. It moved ever so slightly on the outswing, about an inch, after a great deal of exertion. She felt a shadow cross over her. Opening her eyes she saw diminutive doctor Weiss looking down on her.

"Uh, you scared me." Mora stopped what she was doing and smiled up at her.

"You know, you may never walk again," doctor Weiss said.

"What?"

"You may never walk or use your hands or drive or do any of the things you used to do. And you'll have to get used to that fact." Looking down on Mora, she folded her arms across her chest.

For a split second of forever the doctor's words sank into Mora's awareness. Here she was, trying with all her might and will to move. . . anything. . . any way she could. And here was a physician supposedly dedicated to helping her. Anger rumbled inside:

This is not right! Mora spoke clearly. "How dare you tell me what I can't do! Who the hell do you think you are anyway?"

"I'm trying to help you face reality," doctor Weiss answered, raising her head higher.

Mora's jaw clenched as the anger arose from deep inside. "You call this help? How dare you try to impose limits on me! You don't know what this is about, do you?"

"It's for your own good that you face the fact that you'll never move again the way you used to." The doctor remained adamant, standing over Mora with her arms crossed.

"Get the fuck out of my face!" Mora yelled, loud enough for Yvette and her patient Grace to hear.

The doctor's chest collapsed as she absorbed the shock of Mora's words. "It's my job to make you face the facts." Standing erect again, she quickly left the room.

Mora burst into tears.

Yvette ran to her. "What happened?"

"That shit tried to tell me I'll never get my body back! Damnit! I'm not going to give up! I'm going to get my body back!" Mora's flesh ran with electricity. Blowing out fierce breaths, she closed her eyes and pushed both her arms out. . . out. . . putting three inches distance between her hands and her torso.

"All right!" Yvette caught the chill and clapped. "Yes!"

When Yvette wheeled Mora down to the spinal cord injury unit's group activity room, an air of elation surrounded them. "I'd like to prescribe an argument with a doctor at least once a day for you!" Yvette snaked her head around to read Mora's face as she wheeled.

"Yeah, I think I scared her though. I hope she's okay." Guilt leaked through the crevices of Mora's triumph.

"She's young. She'll survive. Maybe it'll help her put a little more thought into what she says to patients. Do you want me to leave you down here for lunch?"

"Sure." Mora's eyes darted from patient to patient. Most of them were male. Some were in electric wheelchairs; one very tall man in a wheelchair wore a halo vest; a young man with a burly muscular upper body and spindly thin legs sat smoking a cigarette in his souped-up racing chair. The only other woman besides Mora was Grace, the very attractive young woman she'd seen earlier in the physical therapy room.

Mora focused her energy sensors to perceive the prevailing mood of boredom, depression, and dull hopelessness. Most eyes seemed to be leaning aimlessly on a television soap opera and no one spoke to anyone else. Yvette had parked Mora close to the refrigerator which, rumor had it, was stocked with "goodies" for patients. Mora watched as a nurse carrying a tray of tiny white paper cups silently stepped around to each patient and helped each one swallow pills. Mora wondered what kind of pills everyone on the spinal cord injury unit but her seemed to need. Could it be a mid-day dose of vitamins, or food enzymes to help digestion? Another nurse opened the refrigerator door. Mora caught a glimpse of pre-packaged puddings and cakes, multi-colored gelatins, Cokes, 7-ups, candy bars, and a single serving container of fruit juice.

"Hey Mora," whispered Pam, the flame-haired student nurse now at Mora's side, "how would you like your hair washed before lunch?"

"You mean now? You're going to wash my hair now?" It was a dream come true.

"I corralled another nursing student to help. It's now or never."

"All right. Let's roll!"

Mora's unwashed scalp had started itching after the first couple of weeks. She imagined it would be unpleasant for anyone to touch. "How are we going to do this?"

Pam rolled Mora in swift gear down the hall. "We're going to get you on a gurney and do it over a big sink in the shower room. We have to be careful not to infect the pins or get the sheepskin lining of your vest wet. But we'll do it. I knew you'd love this so I took the liberty of getting your special shampoo out of your closet."

The two student nurses placed Mora face up on the rolling stretcher, wheeled her up to the big sink and maneuvered her haloed head as far over the sink as possible. Then the other student nurse held onto Mora while Pam washed.

Mora luxuriated behind closed eyes as warm wet splashes penetrated her hair and soothed her spirit. The pungent, revivifying aroma of rosemary and camomile shampoo danced alive all her senses. She imagined her worries being washed away and spilling down the drain, water and shampoo unburdening her of all woes.

"This is delicious!"

The two nursing students laughed.

Afterward, Pam carefully blotted Mora's head before they returned her to the wheelchair. "Just in time for lunch. Do you want to go back to the group room?"

"Sure. Isn't it amazing what water washing over the body can do for a person? I feel so much better, as if my head's clearer, calmer."

"Yeah, boy, I jump into that shower as soon as I get home. Pick out your table."

"Over by the windows, if you would."

Mora watched the early afternoon sun wash the buildings in clear light. Billowy white fluffs outlined in silver traveled faster than the speed of a New England summer across the baby blue sky. Brisk changes signaling autumn's approach invigorated her as she remembered her tan being washed away yesterday. Just as Mora recalled her encounter with doctor Weiss, she came into the room.

"Doctor Weiss, may I speak with you for a minute?"

Casting a suspicious glance, the doctor silently approached and stood with her arms crossed on her chest.

"I want to apologize for speaking so harshly to you this morning. And I'd like to explain what happened."

The doctor waited.

"I was having a bad day, frightened about my future, wondering if I'd ever walk again and basically fearing the exact things you said. Well, I had just done battle inside myself for the millionth time and thought I had beaten it. Then you came over and repeated it. Your words took me off guard. All of a sudden my greatest fears were right back in front of me again after I'd just kicked them out. So I reacted defensively. I apologize for cursing at you."

Doctor Weiss narrowed her eyes at Mora. "It's my responsibility as a physician to help you face reality, just as the other patients here do." She pivoted and swept an arm across the room.

"Okay, well. I can see we have a difference of opinion about what reality is." Mora set her jaw.

"You're not in charge here," the doctor whispered. "You'll see." She turned abruptly and left.

Mora's heart pounded so hard she needed to pant. She closed her eyes and breathed deeply until her heart stilled.

*   *   *

Lunch consisted of a hot dog, french fries, a piece of lettuce and a slice of tomato, jello topped with whipped white, and whatever her heart desired in the way of refrigerator beverages. "That's what I get for not asking Hope to fill out my food list," Mora mumbled to herself before asking the nurse, "May I please have some apple juice?"

"Oh, there's no more left. Would you like a Coke or some 7-up?"

"No, I'd like some juice. What other kind do you have?"

"There's no more juice."

"None? In the entire hospital?"

"Well. . ." The young woman looked around the room and thought about it. "I could see if there's some in the nurses' breakroom, but I'm not supposed to give it to patients."

"Yeah, why don't you do that," Mora snapped.

The nurse left and returned empty-handed. "There's none there either. How about some milk or coffee or water?"

"Okay, water." Mora waited while the nurse filled a glass at the nearby sink, stuck in a straw and put it to her mouth.

"Fffftt!" Mora spat out a short spray, fortunately missing the nurse. "What's in that?! It's disgusting!"

"Nothing. It's just water."

"That's not water! I've had water before and it doesn't taste anything like that." Mora sighed, exasperated. "Okay, milk."

"Milk is really good for building bones," the nurse said encouragingly while she opened the container.

"It would be if the dairy cows weren't injected with massive doses of growth hormones and antibiotics. On second thought, I'll have a 7-up."

The nurse shrugged. "Okay".

*   *   *

During OT that afternoon Mora accomplished one tiny milestone: she got more movement out of her left middle finger. That single digit opened new doors to freedom: now she could press the nurse call button and the television remote! Just as she was about to change the station, Carl strolled in.

"Uh oh. . . giving your brain a chewing gum fix again?"

"Hello to you too, Carl. What's happening?"

"I decided to leave work early and visit you." He looked around the room. "I thought your days were jam packed with therapy. What're you doing watching TV?"

"I'm waiting for physical therapy. Notice anything?" Mora asked expectantly.

"Uhh. . ." Carl squinted at her, then looked around the room. "You have more get-well cards than you had last week."

"No! Look at me." Mora pressed the channel-changing button several times and the TV picture flashed as many times.

"Oh. Hey, that's pretty good. When did that happen?"

"Today." Mora turned her eyes back to the TV and pressed the button several times until it landed on a religious station. A white-haired woman with her arms raised in the air stood crying beside a microphone-holding man. "I can hear the Lord speaking to me right now," the woman said. "He's saying something to me." The man smiled grandly and said, "You see, brothers and sisters, the Lord is speaking to her right now." The camera panned a huge audience. "Tell us sister, what is the Lord saying to you?" She lifted her head, her arms still raised, and said "He's saying. . ."

Mora changed the channel and a comic book picture of Superman, flying, appeared. "You have got to buy this special edition vintage Superman comic book now while supplies last." A woman's bejeweled manicured finger pointed to Superman as she spoke. "There's the number on your screen. Let's hear from you right now."

Mora chuckled and flicked the TV off. "Do you want to go to physical therapy with me?" she asked.

"I guess so. Do I need a special pass to get in?" Carl asked, smiling.

"If you wheel me down, you'll have an excuse."

Carl got behind the wheelchair and tried pushing it.

"The brakes are on," Mora said.

"Oh." Carl released the brakes and wheeled Mora out.

"I still have a few minutes before my appointment. I can show you around if you want," Mora offered. They entered the open therapy room and rolled past an apparently healthy young man sitting in a chair against the wall. He nodded and smiled warmly as they passed.

After Mora explained the equipment to Carl, she said, "Would you wheel me over to that guy we passed? I want to say hello to him."

"Do you know him?"

"I will in a minute," she answered, and Carl obliged her request.

"Hi, I'm Mora Donovan. I can't shake your hand. This is my ex-husband, Carl."

The man stood and shook Carl's hand. "Hi, I'm Roger Jenkins. Pleased to meet you." He sat down again and looked at Mora.

"You're not a patient here, are you?" Mora asked.

Roger shook his head, "No, I help a buddy of mine, Steven, with physical therapy twice a week. He's in the pool now."

"It's really kind of you to help a friend like that," Mora said.

"It doesn't even touch what he's done for me. It's the least I can do," Roger answered.

"Really?" Mora said, hoping he'd tell her more. After five seconds of waiting, she asked, "What did he do for you?"

Roger chuckled and nodded his head. "I thought you were a curious person. I don't mind telling you." He shifted in his chair, leaned forward on his knees, and said, looking from Mora to Carl, "I robbed and almost killed Steven, five years ago."

"Sounds like a strange friendship," Carl joked.

Roger laughed and nodded. "Man, you got that right. See, at that time, I was a heroin addict. I went into this convenience store where Steve was the night manager. I was high, I needed cash, and it wasn't the first time, you know, for this kind of activity in my life. I pulled a knife on him, told him to give me all his money, and when I saw him pedal the alarm, I stabbed him, over and over and over, must've been 12 or 13 times. Then I just booked outa there on foot, but the cops caught up with me a few blocks away. Luckily." Roger looked into Mora's eyes, then Carl's, and his face lit up when he caught sight of a man walking into the room. "Here he comes now."

Roger went over to his greet his friend, and talked to him as they strolled back toward Mora and Carl.

"Roger says he's been telling you about our unusual friendship. Hi, I'm Steven Almaro," the friend said.

"Carl Fischer." The two men shook hands.

"We've told the story quite a few times at recovering addicts meetings. What part are you up to?" Steven asked Roger, smiling calmly.

Mora and Carl shared a look of amazement.

"The cops picked me up. 'Luckily.' I said." Roger answered.

"Yeah, for both of us," Steven added.

"You tell 'em." Roger nodded and folded his arms across his chest.

"Do you two want to hear the rest?" Steven asked.

Carl laughed and said, "Are you kidding? The commercial break came right before the best part."

"All right," Steven said, "the next thing was. . . I was in bad shape. They took me to the hospital and started patching me up." Steven touched his head and said, "Here, and here," then touched his chest, "and here. While I was still in the hospital my family told me that the man who had stabbed me, Roger, was behind bars. I asked about him. . . who he was, stuff like that."

Roger picked up the story. "Yeah, here this dude was, almost dead from my hands, and he's worrying about me. Am I okay," he said, shaking his head.

"I thought about a lot of things, lying there in the hospital," Steven went on. "I knew that if I was hurting, the man who brought the hurt down on me had to be hurting. Anyway, I got out of the hospital, was on the mend and started physical therapy. Meanwhile, Roger got a fast conviction and was serving time."

Roger picked up the story. "About a year after it all happened, somebody came to the prison and told us about this amends program. You could volunteer to apologize to the people you committed the crime against. The victim doesn't have to accept, but you could at least offer it. So I did. And Steven agreed to come to the prison to hear my apology in person."

"If you don't mind my asking this, Steven, why were you willing to see him, after all he did to you?" Carl asked.

"Well, I found out that Roger had grown up poor, without a father, was a drug addict, and had suffered just about every hardship you can imagine. When I heard he wanted to apologize, I felt better. I was improving physically, and I didn't want to carry around a buden of resentment toward someone I didn't even know for the rest of my life. So I went to the prison to see him."

"He came to the prison one day," Roger said. "They brought me to the visitors' room. I was handcuffed and a guard was beside me. Steven was sitting in a chair at a table with another guard up against the wall behind him. I looked at Steven. . ." His voice quavered. "He looked me right in the eyes, he didn't look away or curse me. I sat down across the table from him and I said 'I'm sorry for almost takin' your life. It was wrong of me and I'm real sorry for it.'" Roger let his head drop to hide his tears, then raised it again and continued, "Here I was, facing the man I almost killed. All he said to me was 'It's okay now. The past is gone and I forgive you.'" Roger dropped his head again and wiped his hand across his cheek.

When Steven gently placed his hand on Roger's shoulder, Mora thought about how tables can turn, how a miracle can rise up from a wound. *We grow softly strong in the cracked places.*

Roger raised his head and looked at Steven. "That's not all Steven did for me. If you can believe it, this dude dropped the charges against me. He advocated for me before the judge. The judge said he had never seen anything like it in his courtroom before." Roger shook his head and laughed while still wiping tears from his cheeks.

"It didn't make any sense to me to punish a man for something he was sorry for," Steven said. "I knew his apology was sincere. I figured he'd done his time. He clearly wanted a chance to make something better of himself and I wanted to help him try."

Roger nodded. "That's right. He even helped me get a job and go back to school. He's done a lot for me, like I told you. Spotting for him on the exercise equipment is the least I can do for the man who saved my life."

"What happened to you, Mora?" Steven asked.

"I broke my neck in a car crash and was paralyzed, but I'm getting better. I died in the crash and. . . want to know what I found out in heaven?" Mora asked, her eyes filling with tears.

"Sure," Steven answered.

"The only thing in the world that matters is love. You and Roger are proof that it's true. Thanks for reminding me," Mora said.

"You're welcome. You're going to do just fine. I can tell. You keep the faith, you hear?" Steven leaned over and hugged her gently.

*   *   *

With Carl watching her do her mat stretches, Mora let the two men's story soak in. She wondered if forgiveness mattered as much to Carl as it did to her.

On the day she had told him about her extramarital love affair, Mora had been surprised by Carl's rare display of sorrow that matched her own. It had been a lonely marriage for her, and she tried to escape it by seeking comfort elsewhere. She thought about how they had so often misunderstood each other, reacting with defense and attack, when all along they had really done the best they could. There were also times they'd helped each other, one taking the first step toward the other.

But now they were divorced and he was involved with a new woman. He was traveling a path that no longer included her. Now was the time for her to forgive herself, whether it was on his mind or not.

"That was some story, wasn't it, Carl?"

"Uh huh. Leaving the past behind sure makes sense to me." Carl's words carried unspoken volumes.

And Mora held onto his few words, long after he had fed her dinner, including his most despised vegetable, broccoli, and didn't even ask to share her dessert. Long after he had left and the sun went down and Hope came in to massage her tree-roots neck and arms, Mora could still hear Carl's words.

That night she lay in bed, looking at the incandescent yellow glare of street lights reflected in the building windows across the street. She lay flat, her head never touching the pillow, and she cried. *Where will we go from here?* she wondered alone in shadowy darkness. *What will life be?*

Mora's arms lay resting at her sides. She decided to try again what she had accomplished earlier in the morning. Slowly she moved her arms out just a little, and this time, rocked her torso side to side enough to build momentum to push-pull them toward herself again. Then she decided to try and hook her own self up.

She rocked her body side to side just enough to drag her left hand, the familiar one, onto her body. There. She push-pulled her thighs open just enough. *Could I?* she thought. *Is it possible? What if it doesn't work?* With the middle finger of her left hand, she touched her precious self. She moved it around and around, for it could give exactly enough of what she wanted and no more. She closed her eyes and felt energy flowing through her pelvis, she imagined a man she might someday love was lying on top of her, inside her. She held it in her mind, and felt it real, and held it and felt it.

"Aghhhhh. . . ." She breathed out hard, expelling pent-up energy as heat flushed over the almost-forgotten part of herself. The release brought a wave of tears and she cried free, shaking off the past. She was alive and she was going to make it.

- 14 -

Michael Jones's "Pianoscapes" sounded the call to rejoice. A fresh day of Indian summer waved welcome through open windows and swirled the passionate essence of rose oil with it. More than one hundred get-well cards sent cheers from the wall while an expansive ocean poster encouraged Mora to think big. "I place the future in God's hands" filtered through her mind like a salt steam infusing early morning sunlight on the beach. "I am as innocent and free as I was the day God made me" greeted her eyes whenever she rested them on the open meditation book. *Fresh and new I am today. I am rejuvenated, full of hope. Thank you, God, for giving me my life.*

"Ohhhhh. . . it feels good in here!" Pam said, as she entered for bathtime. "What *is* it?"

"Why don't you tell me?" In the midst of an atmosphere she relished, Mora wanted to know what effect it had on another. Just as she had luxuriated in transforming her massage room into a haven of lightfilled comfort, she did her best to make the otherwise sterile hospital room cozy.

Pam's eyes dreamily drifted through the room like happy fish swimming in tropical home waters. "Oh. . . it feels peaceful, calm, bright, you know, happy." She sniffed and hunted the source. "I smell roses." She giggled. "Can I stay in here today?"

"Sure." Peaceful and still, Mora enjoyed just sitting silently in her wheelchair thinking about precious life and God's clear presence. As the pianist played an imaginary, private beach concert, she felt love inside herself, inside her cells. They literally felt joyful. She dared not tell this delicate secret to anyone but Hope, the one who carried out all the help she might give herself if she could move.

If she could move. But she could move. She corrected her thoughts: *if I could move more.* Then she thought about all that had returned to her body over the last few days. Just that morning at breakfast she successfully completed a trial run on self-feeding that endured for three entire spoonfuls! A nurse got her hand and arm engines revved by positioning her hands close to each other and strapping on the modified spoon. From there Mora used the little bit she had in her left hand to bolster the little bit she had in different places in her right hand. Thus she managed to maneuver the strange looking, lightweight spoon-on-a-strap to her mouth. Much joy was felt by nurse and patient. One small step for eating independence, one giant step for nursing staff workload!

"Earth calling Mora, Earth calling Mora, come in please." Pam stood beside Mora holding a fresh washcloth and towel.

"Oh, I guess I was still meditating." She smiled peacefully at Pam.

"Well, whatever you're doing must be good because now I feel better! I'll get the wash tub ready."

"Pam, before we start, could you please get me that card on the wall, the one with the hazy gold picture of the beach?"

"Sure." Pam retrieved the card and lay it on Mora's tray table.

"The music was reminding me of what happened the day I got this card."

"What happened?"

"It was a few days after surgery. They'd put me in a wheelchair and I couldn't move a thing. Sitting up in the chair was traumatic. I was in terrible pain and crying, completely depressed about my body, my life. Somebody brought me a pile of mail just as one of the aerobics instructors, Denise, came in to visit. Denise asked if I wanted her to open my mail. I said yes and this was in the first envelope she opened. Want me to read it to you?"

"Definitely." Pam pulled up the chair and sat beside Mora to listen.

"'Footprints: One night a man had a dream. He dreamed he was walking along the beach with God. Across the sky flashed scenes from his life. For each scene, he noticed two sets of footprints in the sand: one belonged to him, and the other to God.

"'When the last scene of his life flashed before him, he looked back at the footprints in the sand. He noticed that many times along the path of his life there was only one set of footprints. He also noticed that it happened at the very lowest and saddest times in his life.

"'This really bothered him and he questioned God about it. 'God, You said You'd walk with me all the way. But I've noticed that during the most troublesome times in my life, there is only one set of footprints. I don't understand why when I needed You most You would leave me.'

"'God answered him: 'My precious child, I love you and I would never leave you. During your times of trial and suffering, when you see only one set of footprints, it was then that I carried you.'"

Mora closed her eyes and let tears fall, touching the edges of a bittersweet smile. She opened her eyes and said, "That's me. God's been carrying me until I can carry myself."

Pam wiped tears from her own face, then touched Mora's arm gently. "Don't feel bad. It'll all work out."

"Oh, I'm not crying from feeling bad. I'm crying because I'm so grateful to still be alive. Life is so precious and I'm grateful for all that I have. The only thing that matters is love. Now I know the love of God is always inside me. . . forever. I've searched all my life to find love outside myself, maybe all my lives." Mora laughed lightly through the veil of tears.

"Wow. That's an amazing story." Pam swept tears from her cheeks again. "I can see why you want your door closed all the time. It's so different out there." She turned her head toward the wide open door. "You're not like the other patients. So many of them seem to give up. They just take their antidepressants, sedatives, and metabolic enhancers, and they buzz out because they don't want to face life. In all honesty, I don't blame them. Some of them have been paralyzed for years and years. Sometimes I don't know how they can keep going." Pam turned back to Mora, jerked her head back, cupped a hand over her mouth and just as quickly took it away. "Oops! I don't know if I'm supposed to talk to you like that. Is this improper protocol?"

Mora chuckled. "Ah Pamela, you're a marvel indeed. This is just two human beings talking together. It's okay. And I *am* just like the other patients. We're all made of the same stuff. Who am I to judge what 'getting better' or 'healing' looks like to an outsider? Lately I've been thinking a lot about the wheelchair racers in the Boston Marathon. Have you ever seen them?"

"No."

"They've always been my favorite part of the race. When they woosh by, you can just *feel* their strength, their courage, charge the air. It's better than church. I always saw them as proof that if something is taken away, the spirit is still capable of great triumph. Their misfortune challenged them to find their *real* strength inside." Mora sighed heavily.

"Okay, so my spinal cord wasn't cut but it was badly damaged. Even a cut though. . ." Mora narrowed her eyes and let them drift over Pam's shoulder. Pam turned around to see what Mora was looking at and found nothing.

"Why *can't* human spinal nerve cells regenerate once they've been cut?" Mora questioned an imaginary challenger in the room. "Why has medical science said 'Cells can regenerate but a severed spinal cord can't'? If cells have a basic behavior pattern, why can't spinal cord nerve cells have it too? Why are they banished from the neighborhood? There's something in me that rebels when someone tells me that what I saw in heaven is impossible. The Creator can do *anything!* Anything is possible. What human being has the full knowledge of God to be able to tell another human being she won't ever recover from something? I'm sorry, I just don't buy it. It's the same logic as 'The world is flat, don't sail to the edge or you'll fall off.' Is it a coverup for 'We'd rather tell you it's not possible than admit we don't actually understand the spinal cord'? Doctor Weiss thinks I live in a dream world but I'm beginning to believe that my own mind and heart are really the factories which produce the illusive product called 'my condition.'"

"I know one thing," Pam said.

"What's that?" Mora asked.

Pam leaned toward Mora and shielded her mouth to whisper,

"I get more out of our conversations than most of my nursing lectures." She stood erect and returned to a normal tone. "And I'd better bathe you before doctor Andrews comes in."

"Who's doctor Andrews?"

"Oh, she's the psychiatrist who's supposed to do your evaluation," Pam called out over the running water at the bathroom sink.

"I thought Mrs. Veypoko did that." Mora called back.

"No, this is big guns psychiatry, not just little old psychology."

"Oh?"

Pam returned carrying the plastic tub filled with water. "This is to find out if you're mentally disturbed."

Mora laughed out loud. "You're not serious, are you?"

"Of course I'm serious!" Pam pointed her orange eyebrows together. "I noticed you're not taking any meds except an occasional Tylenol. Around here they usually like patients to be properly diagnosed and have appropriate medications prescribed."

"What?" Mora demanded, incredulous. "I don't need any 'meds'. All I need is miracles, massage, meditation, 'magination, music, masturbation, and meals made of real food."

"You're different, Mora Donovan, I'll give you that much. Let's wash you."

*   *   *

At 9:30 A.M. a petite woman quietly stepped into the room.

"I'm doctor Andrews and I'll be conducting your psychiatric evaluation." So blandly dressed that she blended in with the two-toned beige and cream walls, the doctor did not look directly at Mora.

There were ink-blots to be interpreted. No eye contact from doctor A. There were questions of "If thus-and-so situation occurred, would you do (a) this, (b) this (c) this, or (d) none of these." Still no eye contact. Mora had always enjoyed being psychologically evaluated, examined, and questioned. But this was a first: being queried by someone who wasn't actually present. When the fifty-minute evaluation was complete, Mora marveled at how a human being could inquire into the deepest recesses of another's psyche without ever looking directly at that person.

"When will I know the results of the test?" she asked, eager to discover how psychiatry might rate her mind.

Without looking at Mora, the unsmiling doctor replied, "Definitely before you leave," and left.

"I think she's unhappy." Mora declared her diagnosis aloud to no one.

*   *   *

"Hooray, hooray, I'm kicking butt today!"

Yvette had lifted Mora onto the stationery bicycle in the physical therapy room and put Mora's sneakered feet into the bike clips. "Push or pull what you can. I have the tension down so it'll give you momentum up those hills. You're doing great!"

"Oh, this feels wonderful." Mora closed her eyes and glided easily and joyfully into aerobic panting. "My favorite sound: heavy breathing."

"Oh yeah, huh. Take it easy, you haven't done this for a while." Yvette had a soft and solid grip on Mora's upper body. "Tell me when you get tired."

Mora went around and around and around. Behind closed eyes she flew off into the sky on her bicycle with wings and it made her laugh. "Whoopee! Look at me! I'm flying!" She couldn't see the other patients in the room look at her, then look away. After ten minutes, her legs gave out.

"Had enough? Ready to get down now?"

"I guess. Whew! All of a sudden they just stopped. I used to be able to go for hours on a bike. . . hours and hours."

"It's like that. Remember, you're still rebuilding. Your body needs all that energy for recovery. I'm pleasantly surprised you pedaled as long as you did. Okay, down we go." Yvette dragged the braked wheelchair over with one foothold and gracefully lowered Mora's body into it.

"You are one strong, smooth-moving physical therapist. And you are very encouraging. I really appreciate the way you finagle me into doing more without using the 's' word, 'should'. You're very good at what you do."

Yvette knelt on the floor to loosen the footrest. She glanced up for a flash shine of her sunflower face. "Thank you," she replied, and returned to the footrest. "I want to try something."

"Oh goodie!" Mora was mentally ready to gallop forward.

Yvette removed the footrests, placed Mora's feet flat on the floor. "Let's see if you can move the wheelchair."

"You mean, like perambulate?" Mora's eyes opened wide.

"Yep." Yvette grinned broadly.

Mora slosh-pushed one foot an inch forward on the floor, then the other. "Ugh. I wish I could get my hands to help. Oh well." She push-slid again. This time each foot forged ahead two inches and the wheelchair moved forward. "I'm moving! I can move myself!" Mora shouted to a now empty room. "I CAN MOVE! YIPPEE!!"

Yvette watched, smiling. "Have you ever been an actress?"

"Burlesque. A former lifetime. Think of where I can go now, what I could do, what kinds of new trouble I can get myself into!" Mora contorted a devilish grin and cackled.

"Just don't get yourself into anything you can't get out of. Be careful. Remember, it's mostly your legs that are in gear. Your hands and arms aren't there yet."

"I know," Mora tossed back as she headed slowly for the wide open doors, one shoved foot-drag at a time. Yvette followed, releasing her newly independent charge into the world.

Not ten feet from the doorway, Jane and doctors Weiss and Jackson were huddled together in the visitors area. The instant Mora noticed them, her heart raced and she stopped perambulation. She waited, asking herself whether to proceed or go around the other way to her room. She chose to proceed forward.

The three buzzed and snickered, unaware of the quiet perambulator's approach. Mora halted to eavesdrop: ". . . an incense-burning, guru-chanting space alien. . ." They laughed. Doctor Weiss' voice was clearly discernable. "I don't know who she thinks she is, talking to me that way." Jane nodded and buzzed. "She keeps telling her friends to close her door. I gave strict instructions for the nurses to watch her. And that perverted masseuse left at ten past nine." Doctor Jackson nodded and listened. Just then, Jane looked around and spotted Mora. She "shhh'ed" the two doctors who instantly turned around and saw Mora. All three looked down, Jane and doctor Weiss barely suppressing their laughter, not bothering to pretend professional diplomacy.

Mora slowly perambulated forward. She commanded her breathing to remain steady and kept her eyes focused straight ahead, while the three silently watched. When Mora got close enough she said, "Pardon me but, are any of you trained in acupuncture? I'm in need of a treatment."

They sat stone silent and still until doctor Jackson answered "No, I'm afraid not."

"Oh well," Mora frowned. "At ease," she said as she rolled by.

*   *   *

It was with great relief that Mora was escorted, completely exhausted, down to OT. She told Corky about her close encounter on the way down.

"I couldn't believe it! These are *doctors?* People who have dedicated their lives to the hippocratic oath? Jeez." Mora enjoyed updating Corky and Yvette on the latest real life soap opera episodes unfolding in the 'hood, otherwise known as the spinal cord injury unit. "They're infuriating! How can you stand working for them?"

"Excuse me? Pfffft! I do *not* work for them." Corky turned the corner and wheeled Mora into the OT room. "I work for you and my boss, who is the director of occupational therapy. I just say 'yes doctor' and 'whatever you say doctor,' and I do what I do to help you so I can have a pleasant work day. That's all there is to it."

"I see." Mora's brain gears buzzed. "Boy, am I glad I can let off steam with a real human being like you."

"Thank you. . . I think. Anyway, let's see if you can put some round pegs in some round holes, or is it some round holes in some round pegs." Corky gave her pixie hair a quick shake and set Mora up at the table. She worked at that task for a little while, then switched to a table-top hand pedaler. "I'll give you a push and you can try with your arms what you did on the bicycle," Corky said. She placed Mora's hands on the handles and gave a gentle crank.

"Oww. . . this is stretching my arm muscles in ways I forgot about," Mora said.

As soon as Corky stopped helping, the wheel spun down. "Not working?"

"I can't get anything out of my arms on this. Have you got something in a blue silly putty, you know, for evening wear?"

Corky chuckled and shook her head. "You're nuts." She reached for the tub of putties. "Do you want to try the next level up from the other day?"

"Sure." Mora managed to get the outside heel of her right hand to fall a partial, undenting palm onto the putty. "Maybe I better stick with the easy red so I'll gain a sense of accomplishment for today."

"Oh yeah, huh?" Corky smirked and slapped the red onto the table.

"It smells good in here today, like pound cake." Mora inhaled and touched putty just enough to leave a light print here and there.

"Someone's baking." Corky answered nonchalantly.

"Really? How come?"

"We have a beautiful, new, modified kitchen. Do you want to see it?"

"Definitely. Especially if I can get some cake." Mora grinned.

Corky wheeled Mora around the corner into a large, open kitchen.

"Wow! This is great."

"Isn't it? Maybe next week we'll bake something."

"You mean, you think I could cook?" Mora looked at Corky in absolute disbelief.

"Sure! You've already fed yourself."

"Yeah, well, three mouthfuls." Mora frowned.

"So? With tonight's supper you'll do ten. And tomorrow you'll do the whole thing. You'll see. The kitchen is fully equipped with adaptive utensils, and I'll help."

"Okay." Mora wondered if she was destined to a future of cooking in a modified kitchen, but didn't dwell on it. There was too much change going on to worry about things not changing.

*   *   *

"Dinner!" called the voice from the hallway, identifying the source of the fish and potato aroma that had already alerted Mora's appetite. Startled awake from a dense nap in her wheelchair, she rolled a snail's scramble to the call button.

"Yes?" The P.A. voice answered.

"I'm going to feed myself. Could someone just set me up?" Mora felt encouraged by the day's acomplishments and didn't want to stop.

"Be right there."

In a few minutes Mora was feeding herself and wondering where Hope was. Lately Hope had been leaving work early and coming in to feed her dinner, making up the lost work time on weekends. Mora thought daily about her gratitude for Hope's loving care. She couldn't begin to imagine what life would be like without her.

Tray collected, windows closed against colder night air, Mora watched the amber-gold sun setting and wondered again where Hope was. All day long she'd anticipated massage as her finish line reward. *What if something happened to her?* Thoughts of being without Hope, her heart, her mind, her hands, shook fear into Mora's bones. She sat alone in the darkness.

"Yes?"

"Could someone just turn on my tape player?" She'd run out of steam hours ago and the pain in her neck and arms was building to an excruciating pitch. *Maybe meditating would help, but where's Hope?* Anxiety, fatigue, frustration and stabbing sharp neck and arm pain had set in.

"We're busy right now, nobody can come down. You'll just have to wait."

Mora sat still and waited for the pain to stop. When it grew along with her frustration, she perambulated through her doorway and down the hall to the empty nurses' station. She waited until a nurse appeared from behind the high counter.

"I am in a lot of pain," Mora told the nurse. "Could I please have a couple of Tylenol?"

"Doctor Jackson ordered a little something for you to relax your nerves. I'll give you that." The nurse smiled sweetly.

"You mean a sedative?"

"Yes."

Mora sighed heavily, too tired to argue. "Actually, I prefer something light, like a couple of Tylenol. It's really all I want." Closing her eyes she breathed deeply and tried to focus inner sight on her neck muscles. She breathed into them and thought of them relaxing, opening and moving through whatever needed to move. But there was just too much pain. When she opened her eyes, another nurse had appeared beside her colleague.

"Doreen, doctor Jackson ordered a sedative for Mora," the first nurse said. "All she wants is Tylenol. Do you think it's okay if we give her Tylenol?"

Grateful for fatigue, Mora listened to their discussion in amused disbelief. *All this just to get an over-the-counter pain pill.*

"Well, I suppose if she wants something lighter it's okay," the second nurse answered seriously. "Sure. I'll take responsibility for okaying the Tylenol."

Nurse number one shook two pills into a little paper cup and presented them, with a cup of water, to Mora.

"That's okay." Mora said. "I'll just take them back to my room. The pain in my neck is changing, so I'll just hold onto them in case I absolutely need them later."

The nurse shook her head. "I have to witness you taking the pills."

"Look, I'd rather go back to my room and see if meditating will get rid of the pain."

"Fine, but I can't let you take the Tylenol with you. Hospital rules," the nurse said as she crossed her arms on her chest.

The other nurse squinted suspiciously at Mora. "We need to document that you either took them or you didn't. You're not allowed to take them back to your room."

"I don't believe this." Mora sighed heavily and thought about it. "Okay, let's skip it altogether. I'll go do my thing and if I need Tylenol, I'll come back, okay?" She perambulated herself back toward her room.

The burning sensation in her neck had returned with anger. Noticing their simultaneous occurrence sparked a flash of excitement. She quickly shoved her door closed with her foot, then positioned herself in front of the windows and began breathing deeply. On each exhale, she intended her body drop its deeper defenses, while her inner eyes sought the core of the pain. "Ahhhhhhhhh. . ." she toned aloud, searching until she found the tone that fit. Increasing her volume slightly helped the sharp, hot jabs exit, and fizzle out her fingertips.

"What's going on in here?" Fluorescent lights flicked on, ripping her thoughts away. "Mora, you know it's against regulations to close your door," a different nurse reprimanded.

Mora sighed, exhausted. "I closed the door because I didn't want to disturb anyone while I released with sound."

"What?"

"Would you please turn off the flourescent light, put the bathroom light on and open the bathroom door slightly?"

"I came in to give you the sedative doctor Jackson ordered for you."

"I don't *want* a sedative so I'm not taking it. Would you please turn off that obnoxious flourescent light?" Mora let her eyelids drop closed.

"Are you refusing to take your medication?" the nurse demanded.

Mora opened just one eye to see the nurse standing in front of her with her arms folded across her belly. "It's not *my* medication. Just turn off the damn flourescent light and let me meditate and tone in peace!" The rising pain in her neck bit at her with firey teeth.

The nurse left without a word and Mora returned to her inner neck and arms thought. Flushing angry energy out her mind and down her neck, she fell asleep in her chair.

"Mora, are you awake?" Hope's voice called to her from a dream.

Mora opened her eyes. "Oh God, you're here!" she cried.

"I got out of work late, then Lisa needed to talk. I got here as soon as I could." Shadowy silence met Hope's words. "Are you okay?"

Mora burst into tears.

"Oh sweetie, what is it?" Hope touched Mora's shoulder.

"I had a terrible dream that you couldn't help me any more and I need your help so much." Mora pushed the truth out as fast as she could.

"I know you do. That's why I came in anyway, even though it was late. I thought, 'Screw Jane's rules'. So what if I stay past the damn curfew. Are they going to throw me in hospital jail?" Hope laughed and Mora joined in. Somehow, the image of a punishment dungeon in the basement of a hospital seemed absurdly comical.

"Hope, do you think you could take me out of here over the weekend? I can't take it anymore. Maybe I could get some acupuncture treatments lined up, some network or polarity or energy work done on me? I'm really desperate."

"I was just thinking the same thing myself. Sure."

It was after ten-thirty when Hope tip-toed out. Mora lay in bed on her side in the dark. It was a constant painful disturbance, never resting her head on the pillow but feeling instead the force of gravity pressing her head's weight into the pins. Always the pins, the ever-present bars in front of her, between her aching head and the seductive softness of the pillow. She looked out the windows and could see only the bars on the windows. Bars on her head, bars on the windows, bars everywhere. She was in prison. "LET ME OUT OF HERE!" she screamed from her bed, then fell into sobbing.

"What's wrong?" The nurse of her last encounter rushed in.

"I want to get out of here!" Desperation forced out truthful words. "I feel like I'm in a fucking prison instead of a hospital and *I hate it!*" She shouted the last furious words.

"Shhh! If you don't lower your voice I'll call doctor Jackson to make you take a sedative! You're disturbing other patients!" The nurse stood over her, hands on her hips, and waited.

Mora's sobs subsided to just crying. "I'll be quiet."

"Good. Now just go to sleep." Satisfied with the sign of submission, the nurse left with the door bolted open.

- 15 -

On Saturday morning the bath and breakfast nurse placed the ancient, black telephone on Mora's lowered bedtray. It rang and rang while Mora labored in her fastest slo-mo to get it. It rang and rang until she maneuvered both hands on top of the heavy receiver and, leaning both elbows on the tray for leverage, lifted it. As she watched her wrists and hands collapse, her grip gave out and the receiver fell to the floor, the telephone following behind.

"Shit."

"It's okay, I'll get it." The nurse hurriedly picked the receiver off the floor and overshot her aim, clanking it hard against Mora's metal frame.

"Hello?" Mora said behind closed eyes as her bones slowly recovered from the vibratory shock.

From a distance of a couple of inches, the voice sounded remotely like Hope's. "Mora, is that you?"

"Yes, I'm here." Mora's heart sank.

"It's Hope. Are you in the middle of anything?"

Impatient to hear the bad news — the only reason Hope would call so close to the scheduled weekend pick-up time — Mora answered quickly. "No. What's up?"

"Well, I hate to do this, but I can't bring you here for the weekend. Two major obstacles have come up. One is my project deadline and the other is Lisa, and I have to handle them now. I'm very sorry."

Mora sighed heavily and let her tired eyelids fall closed. Aware that the nurse was holding the receiver, she reopened them against the heavy pull of gravity from her heart. "That's okay. You've got to do what you've got to do."

"The fact is, I've got to do some major catching up over the weekend."

Mora desperately sought a hopeful thread. "Will you be able to come in at all, like in the evening?" What would she do without Hope for an entire weekend, alone in the hospital?

Hope cleared her throat. "Well, that's the Lisa part. I won't be able to come tonight. Lisa and I had a long talk last night and she feels I've been neglecting her since, well, for a while."

Mora's panicked heart pounded as the frightful prospect flooded her mind: *What if I lose Hope? What if I really am left totally alone from now on?*

"Mora, I have to get moving," the nurse said.

"Okay, just one second more," Mora said. "Hope, when can you come again?" She feared hearing the word *never* and her bitter throat tightened.

"Probably tomorrow evening. Now Mora, listen. Are you still there?"

Mora determined not to crack over the wires. Her eyes and throat burned. "Yes."

"You know it would have to take something unavoidable to stop me from coming in, don't you?" Hope waited.

"Yes."

"I feel terrible. I really want to come and help you. I'm sorry for letting you down but I want you to know my heart and mind are there with you, okay?"

"Thanks Hope. I don't want to cause problems for you." That did it. The tears broke.

"Oh Mora, you're not causing a problem for me. Helping you has been one of the most fulfilling things to happen in my life in a long time. Don't you dare go thinking you're a problem, understand?"

Hearing Hope's sincerity, Mora put the lid on her disappointment. "Okay."

"Just hang on 'til Sunday night. I promise I'll come in. You can count on me, okay?"

"Okay," Mora answered. "And you hang in there too. Don't worry about me. I'll see you Sunday night, buddy."

*   *   *

The weekend brought blocks of open time with no regular routine, a skeleton staff, and plenty of empty rooms, since most of the patients had gone home on leave. Mora's crew of visitors had dwindled drastically, leaving wide gaps in her life.

All her life Mora had run away from the aloneness of empty spaces. She filled the gaps with busy activities, goals, and relationships focused on the other person's needs rather than sitting with aloneness. It had been the great black shadow eternally looming over, threatening. Terrified that it would suck her down into its drain, she'd always negotiated with it: *Please, I'll do anything you ask! I'll trade anything, I'll give up what I want, just please, don't sit down with me!*

Mora felt a bitter contraction in her chest, a signal that a storm of sorrow was heading up. Like the vile taste of bile rising to warn of sick expulsion, she had to be ready for its impending release.

She perambulated toward her door. On the final stretch of emotional holding endurance, she engaged all her strength to push-pull the door from its grip. A nurse appeared, ready to resist.

"Oh, please." Mora's eyes filled with tears. "I know I'm not supposed to close my door, but I can't hold back crying." She cried through her words. "I need to be alone, so no one will hear me. . . it's private." Mora searched the nurse's face. "Do you ever cry when you're very sad and alone at home?"

The nurse's face softened. "Yes, I do."

"Well, this is home to me now and I need to cry." She looked into the nurse's eyes and waited for a verdict.

"Okay." The nurse touched Mora's shoulder gently, then helped move the door. "I'm the only one on this side today and I won't tell if you don't tell."

"Thank you." Mora's quiet words slipped out just before the door closed.

Instinctively, she rolled over to the windows. Voluminous charcoal thunderclouds that matched her feelings moved quickly overhead. She sat still, crying and watching, feeling the impending storm gather.

"God," she said aloud, "my head is so full. I can't figure it out.

How do I live alone? It's too much. Please help me!" She let the unfinished pain come. As if a bookmark on loneliness had been put in place since the crash, now she was faced with reading the rest of the chapter. Mora sobbed beneath the cover of thundering rain.

"This world is such a lonely place, God. Everybody thinks they're separate from everyone else. Divorce. Cut the ties forever. It's hard not to believe it here. . . it's nothing like it was when I was with You. I'm forgetting again, God. Please help me!" She surrendered to the pain and felt a direct-line window opened above her. "God, I desperately want to know love with a man. . . I came back for it, to learn it, to experience it. But now I'm so alone!" Crying, she dove deeper into the dark well, down, down, to the place she least wanted to be but had to go into.

Stuffed-up breathing brought her back to the surface for air. She shuffled the wheelchair over to the box of tissues, struggled with hands and arms, and pulled one out. The box fell to the floor beyond her reach. She pushed and pulled and lifted her elbows onto her knees, her hands trying to be ready to blow, but her efforts were in vain and she gave up, collapsing back into her well. Drained to exhaustion and held in place by her halo, she fell asleep in the wheelchair.

*   *   *

The autumn rain fell peacefully from dove-gray skies when Mora awakened. *This is how heaven's welcome looked that day on the highway. I want to remember.* The warm rain cleared the air inside and out, leaving relief in its wake.

The halo forces me to hold my head up. The thought made Mora smile. She flashed a contrasting memory, from seventh grade, of Mother Joseph Eleanor's verbal stoning. "Lower your head in shame, you disgusting slut!" The nun had publicly slapped and ridiculed 12-year-old Mora for sharing kisses with a boy. *Maybe the nuns had been abused themselves. Why else would they treat innocent children that way?*

Something inside Mora had changed. Was her cry for love answered in sleep? As she watched the sky break into clear blue she said out loud, "Only I am in charge of my life. I am the only one who thinks in my mind. As God is my witness, no one will ever over-power my mind again!" Jets of life coursed through Mora's sudden-ly vibrantly energized body. She shuffled to reopen her door with one sweeping leg-and-foot motion and thought, *This is great. The hospital's quiet, peaceful, plenty of room to do what I want. Funny how one minute the scene can look terrifying, and the next, it's positively hopeful.*

On this Saturday afternoon, with nothing much to do but let the sun warm her back, Mora perambulated up the hall in search of other life. Gratitude had returned to Mora Donovan, and she was ready to give it away.

She came upon a large room containing six beds. In the middle, beneath the elevated television, sat a handsome young man in a wheelchair. His eyes were closed peacefully as a tall, attractive woman stood behind him, gently combing his hair. The sight of the tender pair touched Mora. No one else was in the room so she decid-ed to shuffle in.

"Hello," the woman said, smiling warmly, and the man's sad eyes opened.

"Hi. My name is Mora. Would I disturb you with a visit?"

The woman's dark brown eyes lit her ivory face. "Oh no, that would be very nice." She spoke in a soft, Puerto Rican accent. "My name is Florinda and this is my husband, Carlos."

"*Con mucho gusto.*" Mora timidly responded in Spanish.

"*Oh, hablas espanol. Que bueno.*" Florinda nodded and smiled.

"*Un poquito.*"

Carlos dragged his heavy-lidded eyes toward Mora. The words fell laboriously from the left side of his mouth. "What happened to you?"

"I broke my neck and died in a car crash last month. At first I was completely paralyzed but I seem to be coming back."

"You really died?" Florinda asked.

"Yes, I did."

"How did you. . . what brought you back to life?" Florinda's searching eyes penetrated Mora's.

"I met God. I mean, God turned out to be more of an experi-ence than a man with a beard in the sky. What I experienced was total and complete, absolute, one hundred percent Love." Mora's eyes filled with tears to say it again and to see the truth touch Florinda. Carlos focused rapt attention on Mora as she continued. "I'm a miracle." The tears rolled down Mora's cheeks as she saw that Carlos and Florinda were crying as well.

Florinda looked down tenderly upon her husband's head and stroked his hair. "My husband had a stroke and it paralyzed the right side of his body. That's why we're here, because they didn't know where else to put us while we wait for a heart transplant. It caused great difficulties for his heart."

"*Lo siento*, Carlos." Mora's heart opened, wanting desperately to give something, to help, to feed him, them, compassion from the well of her own heart. *I could have helped him before. If only I could touch him I KNOW I could help. I KNOW IT!* Mora heard the call from inside. In doubt she questioned herself. Then it seemed her spirit stepped outside her body and stood before her imploring: *Come on, Mora! You can help. . . just ask. . . it's the power of love that heals, not muscle strength. . . Go on, ASK!* She sat in silence for a long minute, then spoke in Spanish. "Before my car crash, I was a massage therapist. For seven years I helped many people recover from injuries. Now, although my body's strength is gone, I still have the love of God moving through my hands. I know now that it's love that heals." Mora rested her tearful eyes on the puffy hands in her lap, then raised them to Carlos expectantly. "My heart thrives on extending care to others. These hands are connected to my heart and I would like to help yours. It would give me great honor and happiness if you would allow me to massage you." The healing had already begun.

"*Gracias*, Mora." Carlos answered.

Florinda came to Mora and leaned over. "Thank you. God bless you. May I hug you please?"

"Thank you, yes," Mora answered, grateful that exposing a piece of herself had been met with tenderness. "Would you like me to begin now? Or I could come back another time if you want."

"Now is good." Carlos blinked.

Mora perambulated her chair as close to Carlos' right side as she could. "Florinda, could you lock my wheels?"

"Of course." Florinda said, as she leaned down to engage the brakes. "Do you need anything else?"

"Yes." Mora managed to use some of one arm to help some of the other into position. "Now, could you please put my arms onto his chair arm, then place Carlos' right hand in his lap?"

"Certainly." Florinda followed the instructions and watched.

"I'm like a wire. Just by making contact we're sending loving energy to your body." Mora looked at Carlos' tired eyes. "Your mind and your body know what to do with it. Also, it helps for us to picture life moving throughout your right arm, the right side of your face, and everywhere." Mixing all she had in one hand with all she had in the other, Mora worked on her first "client" since the crash.

Now her eyes saw things as they never had before. Everything was outlined with thin layers of vibrant color and surrounded by a layer of white light. Mora felt as if she were floating just above the floor. She saw subtle rays of golden light streaming out her fingertips and penetrating directly into Carlos. Her hands felt very warm on his flesh; she watched them move with more grace and clarity than they had shown since the crash. For nearly half an hour Mora felt some strange and wonderful new energy using her as an instrument.

"Carlos, do you want me to do this again, maybe tomorrow?" she asked when she felt finished.

"*Si, por favor,*" He said, still wrestling with his tongue but with more life in his eyes than before. "I feel better. *Gracias por su cuidad.*"

"*Con mucho gusto. Hasta mañana.*" Rejuvenated and grateful, Mora perambulated back to her room.

Dinner and entertainment came and went easily enough. More spoonfuls made it to her mouth than ever before. When television held no nourishment for mind or spirit, she pressed it off and pressed on the tape player. In an instant the world switched from TV's pre-packaged, empty calories to limitless mind-sight through music. Brian Eno's "Music for Airports" softly soared her spirit up and away. With her eyes closed, Mora could imagine anything. This night she would focus on pictures of her body full of light. With eyes closed she welcomed the music's angelic voices and allowed them to lift her light-filled arms and turn them into wings. "I can't be held down," Mora whispered, feeling chills move gently and repeatedly along the circuit of her spine. "Only I think in my mind. My mind keeps only what I think with God. I feel light. . . I am light. . . I am light. . . I am light. . . I am light." As her spirit soared, her body felt freed from gravity and her arms were wings.

*   *   *

Amber-gold quiet spread calm over the world outside Mora's windows. The Sunday sunset spoke of bustling lives on the street below as city folks briskly shopped for the week ahead, or so she imagined. A favorite game, left over from childhood, was to pretend she knew what private worlds people occupied. Sipping tea at a street cafe or waiting in an airport, she made up their secret stories, needing only subtle glances to render imagination's fabric. Usually, as now, they were scenes of daily life shared between a man and a woman.

How Mora longed to be part of the fiber in such a world! Alone in her room she watched as the streets below emptied. The copper light of the setting sun kissed doors shut to shelter intimate lives from the cool indigo night. Above them, where they could not see her or even know she existed, she whispered, "I'm lonely, God. It comes upon me so suddenly. Will you remember our plan for me to find love with a man? Please take this longing I have. Please help me now."

"I'll help you now."

Mora pulled her eyes as far toward the door as she could and rolled herself around to see who had spoken. Her face flushed as she recognized his voice. Taking up a good portion of the doorway, her friend Eric stood tall, strong, muscular, and wide, his white-blonde hair and blue-eyes testifying to his Norwegian heritage. Ever so gently he hugged her.

"Eric! You're here!" Mora said, embarrassed.

"Of course I'm here. I even brought my hands."

"Yes!" Mora's green-brown eyes found their sparkle. "I've been picturing having a treatment all week. In fact, if I had gotten out of here this weekend, I would have called you."

"Well, I must've heard the message, because here I am. You've been on my mind all week too. So tell me," he said, pulling a chair up close to hers. "What's happening?"

Mora dropped her eyes and warmth flushed her face. "I was just talking to God."

"Yeah, I guess I came in on you. I hope I didn't come at a bad time."

"Oh no. It seems that every time I ask for help, some miraculous surprise arrives. People I've never met come in to meet me because 'something told them to come'. Dreams send me hopeful pictures, serendipitous events. Oh, the list is long. And now you're here." Mora's open face shone with happiness. "I even have a new client, right here on the spinal cord injury unit."

"A client? You have a *massage* client?"

"Yep. Actually to call it massage would be stretching the truth. I'd never pass the national exam with what I do. But it's a different kind of thing. It's more like passing on love than muscle wrestling. And the most amazing thing happened. It was the first time I've attempted to help someone else since my visit with God and I swear, I saw rays of light beaming out my fingertips. Everything appeared to be outlined in multi-colored light, kind of like when I did mushrooms in college, only better. I was absolutely in an altered state. It felt like a state of grace." Mora's eyes watered. "Has that ever happened to you?"

Eric listened intently. At the mention of the word "grace," the serious lines on his face disappeared. "Yes," he nodded. "It doesn't always happen that way for me, but when it does, I know my work is being done from love and not from ego."

They talked for a while. Then Eric said, "Let's get you lying down comfortably for a treatment." He helped Mora into bed. "Boy, you're almost walking. Let's see what happens. I bet we'll open up some more energy flow." First, he held her right wrist for several seconds and listened to the quality of her six pulses, then held the left to hear the other six pulses. He raised the bed to his hip level, scanned the field of her body and let his eyes land first on her forehead, and second on her solar plexus. Then he gently touched these places.

Mora closed her eyes and relaxed, going deep down inside to feel everything. She felt Eric's fingertips lightly touch the back of her neck and the small of her back, just as she had taught Hope to do.

He watched and waited, tuning all of his senses, including insight, into her rhythms. He waited for the two dissonant pulses to beat as one, so subtle but clearly perceptible to one who trusts what he feels: the neck beat "dup, dup, dup, dup," even and pale. The sacrum beat "ba-dum. . . ba-dum. . . ba-dum," heavy and dull. He held and waited, feeling for life that wants one single beat for a soul to hum.

Within seconds Mora's arms and hands fluttered, unconsciously flicking out little bits of static. Blockage flushed out, rushed away, and was gone. Just on the half-conscious rim of awake, the large, all-body sigh escaped, and she fell asleep.

"You can come back whenever you're ready, Mora." Eric's confident blue-eyed smile drew her awake.

"Your work always put me to sleep. How long was I out?"

"Oh, just a few minutes, ten or fifteen at the most. How do you feel?"

Mora checked inside. "I don't feel any more pain. Let's see." She closed her eyes and searched, then opened them again. "Nope. My neck was hurting, stinging, before. That lump in my left arm was screaming but now the pain's gone." She grinned joyfully.

"Now let's see how your movement is, if you get any more tread out of your tires." Eric stepped back slightly and watched.

Mora moved her legs around. "This feels great! They were exhausted before, probably from all the work I've been doing. Now they feel reenergized." Next, she was able to lift her hands off the bed, open and close them halfway, then slide her arms out in the largest arc yet. "Wow! This is great! Would you help me up so I can try a few more?"

"Sure." Eric had her sitting up in a few seconds and watched as she moved her forearms in substantial arcs.

"I've been having a hard time lifting my deltoids or using the triceps and biceps." She closed her eyes and concentrated, gaining greater forward motion from her upper arms. "Wow, look at this! I can get them forward but it's the pulling back that's been so hard." She focused sight through the ceiling and pulled her arms back with more ease than ever. She laughed, and her face lit up with joy. "How are you?"

"Actually," Eric said, "I feel pretty good myself. I'm glad I came in to see you."

"Do you have to leave already?" Mora didn't try to hide her disappointment.

"Nope." Eric playfully raised and lowered his bushy blonde eyebrows. "Is there anything else I can do for you?"

"Well, I don't think I'm ready for some things yet but. . ." Mora flushed and lowered her eyes shyly, "I would like you to help me walk. We've been working on it in physical therapy but I still need help with balancing and gait. It's weird being retrained to walk."

"If it's a walk you want it's a walk you'll have." Eric stood and easily assisted Mora to her feet. "Ready?"

"One second." Mora stood looking at the door, then closed her eyes. "There. I found it."

"What?"

"My center of gravity. I couldn't find it yesterday but now here it is, and it's right where it always used to be. Isn't that strange? Let's go." She lifted a foot and shuffled it forward as Eric helped. "I never would have thought I'd lose my center of gravity. That's something the walking lessons have been trying to reestablish. Now I'm going forward without having to find out where I'm walking *from*. Thank You, God. And thank you too, Eric."

Once out of the room, Mora tried to reach for the railing that lined both sides of the SCI unit's hallways. "Could you help me get my hand up on this, sweet man?"

He gently placed her hand on the railing.

"Hey, I've got an idea." Mora said. "Let's prop me with one foot crossed in front of the other, my arms folded in front, while I nonchalantly lean on the wall. Hope left her camera here last week. You can set my body up and take my picture. How does that sound?"

"Like you." Eric shook his head and smiled. "Can you hold steady while I go get it?"

"I think so. Just lean me against the wall."

He leaned her so that the rubber tipped pins at the back of her head served as wall bumpers. Then he ran for the camera.

"You okay?" he asked, camera in hand.

"Yep. Now fold my arms and I'll make a casually sophisticated but utterly bored face." Mora prepared her expression.

"Ready?" Eric said from behind the camera. "Say 'I love you.'"

Mora flushed crimson and lost her theatrics to laughter. Then, with Eric supporting her, she slowly walked down the hall. One foot. Grounding. Another foot. Grounding. Very slowly, her pace stepped up. Eric only stood close for safety, touching her elbow with tenderness. "Will you be my daddy?" she asked, keeping her eyes on the hallway up ahead.

"Actually, I had something better in mind, but we'll talk about that when you're out of here." He answered plainly and watched as Mora's face flushed again. "You sure embarrass easily." He laughed.

"Whew, this is tiring." She stopped and planted both feet flat. "Let me turn around and see how far I've come."

Eric helped her around and she looked far down the hallway. "Wow! Look at that. I walked all that way!" She stared at the long expanse in front of her and tears filled her eyes.

"Mora Donovan, you're a good gentlewoman, and I'm honored to know you." Eric opened his arms and embraced her.

Slowly they made their way back to her room. Sitting in the chair beside her, Eric tenderly stroked her hands.

*   *   *

Hope swirled in at seven, toting a wooden easel, a large drawing pad, and a box of pastel chalks. Before Mora and Eric could say a word of greeting, Hope had the new equipment set up at the foot of Mora's bed. She kicked the door closed with her foot and lifted the pad's cover page to reveal a finely etched green and brown tree loaded with branches and leaves. "Ta Da!" She said, and turned around to face Eric. "Imagine my surprise at seeing you here. Small world. How's the energy industry treating you? Any blowouts lately? Or maybe I shouldn't shock your circuits with loaded questions," she laughed.

"So you're the Hope Mora was talking about — the electronics industry's secret weapon! Or are you leaving your umpti-thousand-dollar-a-year niche in corporate eternity to follow the path of a struggling student of massage therapy?" Eric played back.

Hope halted in her tracks. "How did you know? I haven't even told Mora yet."

"Wait a minute. How do you two know each other? You're going to massage school, Hope? Really?" Mora's eyes darted from one to the other.

"You're surprised?" Hope asked Mora.

"Oh, no. It makes perfect sense to me, but how do you two know each other?"

"It seems like a natural transition to graduate from electrical engineering to body electricity, don't you think? We knew eachother at Teknet before I went through 'the change.'" Eric answered.

"Well, congratulations, Hope. I think you're a natural. Plus, after all the ornery picky instructions I give you, massage school's going to be a breeze," said Mora.

"I haven't actually applied yet. But I visited the school and it looks good."

"That's great, Hope." Eric offered Hope his right hand. "The world of bodyworkers needs compassionate people like you." As soon as she shook his hand he held it and turned it into a fierce grip.

"Ahah!" She gripped back and laughed. In a second the two were staging a fake hand-wrestling match. Eric dropped to his knees on the floor and grimaced. Hope released his hand and raised her fist in the air. "The winner once again!"

Eric stood up and went to Mora's side. "Now I have an idea."

"Shoot." Hope said.

"Before I leave you two ladies, Hope, why don't you and I lay hands on Mora and send her love."

"Definitely," said Hope.

And they each took a side of Mora, Hope seated, Eric standing.

"Do you have a preference on where you want my hands, Mora?" Eric asked innocently.

"Act professional." Hope rolled her eyes at him, Mora flushed, and everyone laughed. Then, as the two faithful guardians rested their hands on Mora, she said, "I'm picturing white light moving through your fingertips from God into me. My cells accept it completely, and use it all to regrow, regrow, regrow. They're all just hummin' with the lovin' you're feeding them. It feels wonderful."

*   *   *

"Oh. . . it's getting late. This is the part I hate." Mora sighed into the dark night. Her room was lit only by the pale-yellow reflection from street lights far below and the bright eyes of her friends.

"Yeah, the Hippocratic Cops are probably on the prowl," Hope said, and got up from her chair.

"Is it after 9?" Mora asked.

"Slightly closer to 10."

"Oh shit! They're really going to put little red skull-and-crossbones all over my patient records now. Hurry up and give me a little hug an' a kiss before you two criminals sneak down the rear freight elevator."

As Mora spoke, the door was flung open. A white-clad form stood there, her arms akimbo.

"What's going on in here? Who's in here with you?" Fluorescent lights flicked on to reveal a hostile nurse.

"Captain! Incoming phasers distorting energy field! Beam us up!" Eric dramatically thrashed his arms in front of his eyes, making Hope and Mora laugh.

"Get out of here now, both of you! Visiting hours were over long ago! I'm going to report you!" the nurse threatened.

"Shhh. . . keep your voice down. There are paying customers trying to sleep in this hospital." Mora scowled back. "Before you go, Hope or Eric, could one of you help me up to my potty seat over there?"

"Sure." Oblivious to hospital rules Eric helped Mora stand and waited for her to gather her center of gravity again before moving to the potty chair.

"Enough of that!" the nurse snapped, and gripped Mora's free arm.

"Uh, excuse me?" Mora said angrily to the nurse. "I feel very secure with Eric doing this, and I have to pee immediately. Could you please let him finish getting me over there and then you can have the honor of helping me back to bed."

The nurse waited for Mora to be seated on the potty. "I will handle this. If both of you don't leave now I'm calling security."

"We're outa here, Mora." Hope grabbed Eric's sleeve and yanked on it.

"Okay. I'll keep in touch, and I mean that literally." Eric winked at the indignant nurse as they left.

Accutely aware of the hostility oozing from the nurse's every pore, Mora was grateful it was bedtime.

"Honestly, you close your door against hospital security regulations, your visitors stay 'til all hours against security regulations, and you won't take the medications your personal physician has prescribed. I just don't know. . ." the nurse went on.

"Just get me over to the bed and skip the naughty-girl routine, will you? I'm tired."

"You realize I'm going to have to report your insubordination to Jane, don't you?"

Anger flared like a quick match. Mora did her best to jerk herself away from the nurse. "Get off my back!" she shouted, "I feel like I'm a fucking hostage here! How the hell do you expect me to recover from paralysis when you insist on paralyzing my every move toward independence?" Mora looked down at Hope's little massage stool. With all the leg strength she possessed, she shoved it and it fell over.

"Aaaaah!" The nurse gasped, jumped back and stared fearfully at the pin-headed patient towering over her.

"I *hate* this fucking place!" Mora shouted. Forgetting she had limits, she faced her bed and bent her knee, intending to flop on it as easily as in the old days. Instead, she collapsed and fell forward, her face and the front pins breaking her fall. She sobbed, unable to push herself away.

The nurse folded her arms and stood over Mora. "Now you've *really* done it! Jane is going to hear about *this!*"

"Help me up!" Mora cried in panic, her words muffled into the mattress. "I can't get up! HELP ME!"

Reluctantly, the angry nurse helped her sobbing patient into bed.

- 16 -

Monday morning's low-hanging, puffy, gray clouds rumored that they were in for a rainy spell. Mora sensed impending doom after last night's fall from grace, or fall on her face, depending on whether she wanted to laugh or dread the consequences. It revived an old shame pattern: if Mora followed her heart, the priests and nuns would inevitably punish her for defiance. Last night, when the nurse accused her of "insubordination," a wind of Mother Joseph Eleanor's long, craggy, wagging finger of accusation blew through Mora's memory. Yes indeed, Mora Donovan had been down this road many times.

At l6 she'd been fired from a waitressing job in Florida for fraternizing with the kitchen help, who happened to be a black man. The charge came down the line from her supervisor Lil, who possessed an eighth-grade education, while the "help," Chuck the cook, had a master's degree in music. During customer lulls, while Lil smoked and gossiped in the back corner, Mora would listen to Chuck's stories about the Manhattan music scene and about teaching music to Southern white high school students. Mora didn't appreciate Lil splashing prejudice all over her uniform; so with her first paying job came her first experience of being fired.

Then there was the temporary position as night receptionist in a Boston hospital emergency room. Mora watched as a drunk black man was brought in on a stretcher late one Saturday night after a car wreck. The flesh beneath his nose was so deeply cut that his nose separated from his lip when the nose was lifted. A white medical doctor tapped the man's nose and the man responded by snapping his teeth at the doctor. Mora watched as the doctor laughed and touched the man's nose again and the man snapped. The doctor laughingly repeated his taunting game and called out to a nurse, "Hey, come here and watch this!"

The nurse came, but so did Mora. She said, "Stop doing that. You're insulting this patient's dignity." The doctor glanced at her with a sneer and said "Just who do you think *you* are?" Mora answered matter-of-factly, "I'm a human being just like this patient. You're insulting his dignity, so I'm telling you to stop." The doctor glared and said, "I'm providing this nurse with medical instructions, and you're out of line." Mora answered, "I'm not moving until I'm sure this patient is safe." The doctor returned the eye-to-eye stare and said "Nurse, call this person's supervisor and have her replaced immediately for insubordinate behavior."

Now Mora smiled inwardly, thinking about her impressive record. "Sometimes a girl's gotta do what a girl's gotta do," she said out loud to no one. Helping people accept themselves was a primary goal in Mora's life, and massage therapy had been a perfect vehicle to achieve it. "Everybody has a God-given right to freedom of choice, and nobody's got the right to impose their agenda on a harmless person against their will." Saying the words gave Mora a renewed sense of peace.

During her morning meditation she asked for assistance in overriding the conflicts she felt brewing around her self-determined choices. The picture that came to her was a gentle violet flame rising just above her crown — the connection or entry point for God in the body. Mora pictured herself completely surrounded and protected by a violet flame. Then she pictured both doctors, Jane, and Mrs. Veypoko surrounded by the same violet flame.

Sure enough, right after bath and breakfast, Mora was given the chance to practice.

"Mrs. Veypoko. What a nice surprise to see you first thing on this lovely Monday morning. Did you have a good weekend with your family?"

"Mora, I have a very serious matter to discuss with you." Mrs. Veypoko sat down on the little massage stool.

"Indeed. And what might that be?"

"I have just been advised of your violent behavior directed at the night nurse yesterday and. . ."

"Excuse me, did you say *violet?*" Mora asked, delighted with Mrs. Veypoko's coincidental choice of words.

"No, I did not. I said *violent*. I must advise you that if you do not follow the rules and regulations of this hospital, we will have no choice but to release you before you are medically stable on the grounds that your violent behavior poses a threat to the safety of the staff and patients. Now, termination of care in this institution could cripple your efforts. . ."

"*Cripple?*"

". . .to obtain medical insurance coverage for the remainder of your pre-determined, medically prescribed treatment program." Mrs. Veypoko pursed her lips and waited for Mora's response.

"You know," Mora began, "if I were a psychologist and my incomplete quad patient suddenly had enough function to be able to stand unsupported for several seconds and enough strength to knock over a little footstool, I would put two gold stars on her chart." Surprised by her clear, calm expression of anger inside a protective violet flame, Mora went on. "The first star would be for the fact that she had enough strength to do it. I'd take it as a sign of rehabilitation success and after all, isn't that why patients are here? The second star would be for the fact that she didn't stuff normal anger at being treated like a hostage. I would understand her harmlessly venting her anger on an inanimate object, which, by the way, is barely large enough to hold you right now."

"Well!" Mrs. Veypoko jumped up from the stool; it fell over, and Mora laughed. Regaining her composure and stiffening her jaw, Mrs. Veypoko forged ahead. "It is my responsibility to inform you that any further insubordinate behavior from you will not be tolerated. Disregard for the nurses' orders will not be tolerated. Violation of visitors' curfew of 9:00 P.M. *will not be tolerated* and will immediately result in a further restriction placed upon your visitor privileges. I emphasize that visitation is a privilege, not a right. If your visitors leave one second past 9:00 P.M., they will be not be allowed on hospital grounds past 7:00 P.M. in the future. Is that absolutely understood?" Mrs. Veypoko's bright pink face glistened with sweat. She reached into the briefcase under her arm, withdrew a white lace handkerchief, and mopped her forehead with it.

Mora calmly observed and thought, *This violet flame really works. Mrs. Veypoko must be under a lot of pressure to be sweating. . . hmm.*

"Well, Mora? What do you have to say?"

"Huh. Very interesting," Mora answered, enjoying her growing calmness.

"Well, good. I see you understand what I've said. Now, that brings me to the second item on my agenda this morning: the matter of your refusal to take medications."

Mora had noticed that drugs seemed to be an "in" topic among hospital staff and was curious about how Mrs. Veypoko would try to sell them to her. "Yes?"

"Doctor Jackson is your personal primary physician legally entrusted with the responsibility of your health care and he has pre-scribed a sedative for you to take in the evenings to help you deal with your depression."

"But I'm not depressed."

"Well, I wouldn't exactly call your outburst last night not being depressed." Mrs. Veypoko narrowed her eyes.

"Oh, that's not depression. Depression is when you stuff your emotions back into yourself. I didn't do that at all. I released my anger, just as I cry when I'm sad. But even if I were depressed, which is highly possible in an emotionally constipated environment like this, I certainly wouldn't want to take drugs and bury my emotions deeper. If you want to see real depression, watch doctor Andrews the psychiatrist. Now *she's* depressed. In fact I'm glad we're talking about this because I've been concerned about her. How is she any-way? I've been trying to get a hold of her for days."

Mrs. Veypoko lowered her head and pointed her eyes straight at Mora. "This discussion is about you, and I would advise you to keep your unqualified remarks about the hospital staff to yourself!"

"Mrs. Veypoko, what's the matter? You seem so upset. Did something happen over the weekend?" But before Mrs. Veypoko could position herself to reply, Mora's large intestine began emitting clear signs of having entered its pre-elimination cycle. She farted, loud and clear. "Uh. . . pardon me, Mrs. Veypoko. I knew that was coming. Go on, I'm listening."

Speechless, Mrs. Veypoko was suddenly disarmed by the distinctly unpleasant odor which now engulfed her olfactory senses.

"Excuse me Mrs. Veypoko, but you have no idea how happy I am to announce that nature is calling me to the potty. . . now. Could you please hurry and help me get over there to it? Ohhh. . . do you realize what this means?" Mora's facial expression resembled the utter absorption of a recently potty-trained child.

"I'll just call a nurse." Mrs. Veypoko moved toward the door.

"No, please! I can't wait. Quick, help me over there. . . it's coming out!"

In a distasteful panic Mrs. Veypoko helped Mora to the high-seated potty in the middle of the room. Fortunately Mora was still dressed in her bare-bottomed, open-backed hospital johnny.

"Would you close the curtains before you leave, Mrs. Veypoko? Just in case somebody out there sees me pooping." Mora's eyes pleaded playfully with the psychologist.

But Mrs. Veypoko had no intention of sticking around. "No need. We're on the sixth floor. I'll be outside." She began to close the door behind her.

"Uh, uh, uh Mrs. Veypoko. Hospital rules. Keep that door open!"

Mora closed her eyes and relaxed as she enjoyed the utter bliss of her own beautiful body's simple functions, which meant no more enemas. "Ah, it's the little things in life that mean so much," she said. Then, just as she opened her eyes and attempted her first-ever wipe, something moved in her strong peripheral vision. Turning her torso, she looked directly into the face of a man washing her windows.

"I don't believe it!" Mora cried gleefully, "my first totally self-sufficient poop and I have a witness, six stories up!" She laughed, turned beet-red, and smiled at the window washer. "Hi. How ya doin'?" She mouthed the words, he smiled back, flushed red, and returned to his work.

"Okay Mrs. Veypoko, the coast is clear. You can come in now!" Mora called out, her spirit renewed from a lighter body.

Corky entered along with Mrs. Veypoko. The psychologist halted in her tracks when she saw the window washer.

Corky shook her head and smiled, as she pointed at the window washer. "Congratulations on taking care of yourself, but don't you think your penchant for audiences has gone a little bit too far?"

"Another milestone, my dear occupational therapist. Mrs. Veypoko, I hate to say I told you so but. . ." Mora grinned devilishly and laughed.

"That's one less thing we'll have to practice together! Now, let's get you dressed for OT," Corky said as she opened the closet.

"If all goes well I'll be seeing you later in the week, Mora. Remember our little talk," Mrs. Veypoko said, and left.

"A lot's happened since Friday, Corky." Mora was referring to her body's successes.

"I heard. You're a hot topic down at the nurse's station. What happened? On second thought, why don't you tell me all about it downstairs. We've got a schedule to keep."

"You mean you're not afraid I'll attack you in a fit of violets?" Mora played with the new colorful image.

"Afraid of *you*? Pfffft. . . yeah, right." Corky rolled her eyes at Mora then asked, "Red shirt, blue pants okay?"

"Have you got anything in a low-cut, winter white organza with a puffed sleeve and a naughty, Chinese-red crinoline? Grab my matching red stiletto sling-backs while you're in there."

"Coming right up," Corky answered and returned with the red and blue sweats. "Actually, why don't you try dressing yourself today?" She raised her eyebrows and smiled.

"Sure. I'm feeling so confident, I don't think *anything* could go wrong today."

"Watch what you say," Corky answered in a sing-song voice as she helped Mora remove the johnny. "Don't go invitin' trouble, cause trouble just might take up on you." She slid Mora's arms through the velcro-modifed shirt sleeves. "Let's see if you can close the velcro flaps."

"I'll try." Mora slowly moved her hands, almost matching the soft side to the scratchy side. When she got up to the third patch, at solar plexus level, her arms collapsed. "Whew, this is hard."

"Yeah, but look how far you got. Wow, you're moving fast. You'll be out of here a lot sooner than anybody expected. Now let's do your pants." Corky squatted down and started pulling up the undies. "Do you want to see if you can pull them up?"

"Sure. Let's give it a shot." Mora let her arms drop down. "Could you bring them up a little more and hold onto one of my bars so I don't fall over?"

Corky helped and Mora pulled up about an inch. "Pushing is somewhat possible, It's pulling that's still not happening." Discouragement began to creep across Mora's face.

"You're making tremendous strides. Quite honestly, I'm amazed you're doing this today, after such a short time. How long ago was your accident?"

"My *crash* was . . . oh, I think about 6 or 7 weeks ago. August 18th."

"Your recovery has been amazing. I don't think I've seen a case move as fast as yours. In fact, I was talking to my boss about the training video we're doing and I wanted to ask if you ever had a desire to be in the movies."

"Are you kidding? I'm convinced that I'm destined to be a silver screen star. Of course I'll have to discuss it with my agent. How much are we talking here?" Mora grinned.

"Dream on." Corky pulled Mora's sweatpants up halfway. "Here, try these. I don't mean to reduce your dreams to dust but do you really think you'll make the big time pulling up your pants in front of a camera operated by an occupational therapy student?"

Mora managed a light hold of the blue sweatpants and labored through pulling them up a couple of inches. "That's all I can do. You mean you want me to get dressed on camera? Like from naked?"

Corky gently but firmly pulled the long pants way, way up.

"Wedgie alert," Mora warned.

"Whoops, sorry." Corky pulled the crotch down a little. "Well, not from naked, more like the velcro closing, stuff like that. And we'll have some other tasks too. We're doing a 'before' and 'after' on each patient, but you're progressing so fast we'd better hurry up on the before part. We'll film you say, tomorrow, then maybe next week, to show progress." Corky reached for Mora's socks and velcroed running shoes. "Want me to put your socks on?"

"Please do."

She pulled them up and slipped on the shoes. "Want to try closing the shoes?"

"I'll have to put my feet up higher."

Corky looked around and grabbed the famous stool, holding it steady in front of Mora. "Okay, can you get your feet up?"

Mora focused her eyes on the stool and tried, with all her might, to throw her leg up onto it. She missed. "Maybe you better put my feet up, then I'll try closing the shoes once they're up."

Corky did as Mora asked.

"Hold my bars?"

"Sure." Corky held a front and a back bar as Mora leaned forward.

With all her concentration Mora's stiff and puffy fingers fumbled soft up against scratchy.

"All right!" Corky lowered Mora's feet down, moved the stool and stood up. "Ready to roll?"

"Sure, but do we have any time left?"

Corky glanced at her wristwatch. "Only a half-hour's gone. At the rate you're going, you'll probably sew a new dress in the second half-hour." She stepped to the back of Mora's wheelchair, gripped the handle bars and released the brake. "Oh, I forgot, you don't need me to wheel you anymore." Corky stepped away and headed for the door.

In the elevator, Mora gave Corky her dramatic interpretation of recent spine-tingling, true-life soap opera events. The elevator doors opened and they reentered the happy kindergarten.

"I have an idea." Corky took a large box down from a shelf and set it on the table in front of Mora. "Here's a box of crafts."

"You mean like normal people crafts?"

Corky nodded and began removing one bag at a time. "Bead work. Embroidery. Macrame, if you are so inclined."

"Maybe I could!" Mora's mind instantly called up the image of a thank-you gift for Hope: an oak tree embroidered on a piece of cloth. Knowing she worked well under the pressure of an approaching deadline, Mora imagined embroidering with feverish excitement. Of course she'd be out sooner than anyone had expected. And what a miracle it would be, to have an embroidery piece as a part and a product of her healing! Imagining Hope's surprised glee sent chills of joy through her body.

"Mora, are you okay?" Corky leaned over with her hand on Mora's shoulder.

"Oh, I'm great. I just ran the mental pictures on giving Hope a completed embroidery project as a gift and it felt wonderful! That's what I'm going to do. I know I can do it. If I can wipe my ass, I can embroider!"

"Well, I don't think I've ever heard that logic before, but hey!" Corky chuckled. "Do you want to try first, I mean to see if you can even do it?"

Mora stared through the embroidery materials and straight through the table. "I already know I can. I pictured it so clearly, it's as if it's already done. Now all I have to do is the sweaty, gravity-bound, finger-pricking labor. That'll be a breeze, I'm sure. I'll let you help me get started, of course."

"Well gee, thanks." Corky pretended to grimace. "I have to do something to earn my paycheck. Getting started is about all we have time for now. What does the finished product look like? I mean, since you already finished it mentally, we don't have to waste time trying to decide which materials to use." Corky chuckled and shook her head.

They chose a piece of blue cotton fabric with a medium weave. Corky cut the threads per Mora's instructions, threaded the needle and stretched the fabric into the round frame. With Corky holding the fabric ring, Mora used all her fingers' unified ability, made her first stitch, and cried.

*   *   *

Everything is changing so fast, she thought on the way back to her room. She felt a deep, quiet power that nothing and no one could remove.

"Mora Donovan." The voice called from behind, sending shivers up Mora's spine. "I'd like to see you in my office now."

Mora slowly turned her chair around to see Jane's hazel eyes attempting to bore a hole in her. "Don't I have physical therapy now?" Mora grabbed the first escape hatch she thought of.

"Not for another half-hour," Jane said, "and this won't take long." She flashed a quick, false smile, then turned, pointing her finger down the hall. "This way, please."

Mora felt a strange sensation, as if a cold November wind were biting her neck. There was something ominously familiar about Jane, something Mora couldn't pinpoint. She shuffled after the nurse in her wheelchair and prayed.

Jane entered her tiny office and sat behind the disproportionately large desk. "Come in please."

Mora had no intention of going all the way in. Instead, she parked herself directly on the threshold. "I'm fine here, thanks. So, what do you want to talk about?"

"I'm moving you out of your private room tomorrow, into the women's ward," Jane answered, without looking up from the papers she shuffled on her desk.

Mora's heart raced and she kept praying.

Jane continued. "There's no medical reason for you to be in your own room. I want the space for a more needy patient than you."

"Wait a minute. I don't want to be in the women's ward. I'm as needy as any patient here. My privacy has contributed greatly to the speed of my recovery. In fact, I can't do without it." Mora's pounding heart was beginning to slip into her voice.

Jane leaned forward and pointed directly at Mora. "You are a selfish woman. You think everyone is here just for you."

"Actually, I. . ." Mora meant to discuss the point.

" Well, I'm moving you." Jane interrupted with a smile. "I have a lot of other patients to think about and I can't waste my valuable time discussing administrative decisions with you. Besides, since there's no medical reason for you to be in a private room, your insurance doesn't cover it." Jane sat back in her swivel chair and rocked, her fingertips together.

From where Mora sat she could peripherally see Grace moving up the hallway in her wheelchair. "Look," Mora began, "the women in the group ward watch soap operas and smoke. They're very nice people, but I hate soap operas. Besides," she continued, knowing Grace was listening just a few feet away, "I am very allergic to smoke and I doubt that doctor Anwar, my neurosurgeon, would support such a move."

"I am not interested in what kinds of television programs you prefer." Jane flamed her eyes open. "You think you're someone special, don't you? Well, I've got news for you. You're treading on thin ice in this hospital. I'm in charge of this unit and if you don't shape up, I'll have you and your visitors thrown out."

"Look, if it's money you're worried about, you can bill me personally for the difference it costs to stay in a private room. I've also noticed there are several empty rooms. Can't you give them to incoming patients?"

Jane blandly returned to paper shuffling. "Those rooms have been previously committed and my administrative decisions are not up for discussion."

"But they've been empty since I got here and they still are. Maybe it would be best if I talked this over with my attorney and doctor Anwar, to see if they think it's wise for me to risk smoke damage to my spinal nerves or other such complications by moving into the group ward. Would you like me to let you know what they say, or would you prefer to speak to them directly?" Relieved to have located the right bureaurcratic nerve in the nick of time, Mora silently heaved a sigh and waited.

Jane glared at her. "That won't be necessary. You can *keep* you private room. . . for the time being. But as soon as I need that room, you're out. That's all. You can go." Jane swiveled her chair and turned her back to Mora.

As soon as Mora backed out of the doorway, Jane got up and shoved the door shut.

"She seems upset," Mora said to Grace, and smiled.

Grace glared angrily at Mora and said, "I heard how you talked to the bitch. You've got guts. I wish I had the nerve to stand up for myself." Suddenly hearing the literal meaning of her own words, Grace looked down at her lap and burst into tears, covering her beautifully made-up eyes with her hands.

Mora's heart opened. "Oh Grace, do you want to come down to my office for a few minutes?"

Happy to be entertaining a guest, Mora shuffled in ahead of Grace, pressed "play" on her tape player, and clumsily reached for the violet essential oil on her bedside table. "Welcome to my humble chapel slash healing laboratory," she said.

Grace looked around and soaked up the atmosphere: the easel with a picture of the tree-that-she-was proudly displayed Mora's projected goal; the music was the deeply insightful wandering bass of David Darling's "Eight String Religion"; the cheerful, handmade quilt decorated the bed; the aromatic air soothed her spirit.

"Would you like to be uplifted with some delicate violet essential oil strategically placed behind an ear or wherever you please?" Mora offered.

Grace nodded. "Yes." She took the tiny vial from Mora, opened it and, inhaling deeply with her eyes closed said, "Oh, it smells like spring." She opened her eyes and looked around again.

"No wonder you want your door closed. It's so nice and peaceful in here. It fucking sucks out there." She looked at Mora with a hopeless expression. "I heard you tell Jane you're allergic to smoke. You're not, are you? You've come over and talked to me when I was smoking and you never said anything or seemed bothered. The reason I'm asking isn't to give you a hard time. I don't blame you," she said, lowering her eyes to her lap. "I've been trying to quit for years." Looking back up at Mora she continued. "I've tried to quit a lot of things a lot of times, but I don't seem to have the will power. But *you* sure do." She scanned Mora's body up and down through a thin veil of resentment, then closed her eyes and sighed. "I hate my fucking body. I hate it."

Mora waited and listened.

"Knock knock," Yvette called from the doorway. "Sorry I'm late, I was unavoidably detained." She smiled brightly.

"Hi Yvette. And as perfect timing would have it, Grace and I are having an important talk. Would it be okay with you if I skipped PT right now? I'll stay after and clean the erasers later."

"Sure, if you don't mind, I don't mind. Be back this afta. Bye, Grace." Yvette waved and left.

"Don't let me be the reason for you not to go to therapy." Grace said.

"I'd much rather talk with you. Where did we leave off?" Mora answered.

"I said I hate this body I'm stuck with," Grace said. "What happened to you? How come you're getting better and nobody else on the floor is?" She demanded angrily.

"I don't know what's different about me, Grace. I'd be making it up if I tried to answer." Mora studied her own thoughts. "I have a pretty wild imagination. You might think that some of my thoughts on the subject are totally outrageous and don't hold up scientifically. So I don't know if there's anything I could say that you'd find. . . well. . . agreeable with what you already think." Mora waited patiently for her words to register.

This wasn't what Grace had expected. "Well, like what for instance? Are you one of those people who believes you can recover from anything if you really want to?" She posed the question as if it were proof of insanity.

"After what I experienced in heaven I believe it's possible, but whether or not it's likely or probable depends on the person, on her deepest intentions."

Grace looked into Mora's eyes with accusation. "So you think I'm still paralyzed from the waist down because I *want to be?*" She shouted, "That's a bunch of fucking crap!" She looked away and when she received no response, she looked back at Mora. "Well? Why the hell are you walking and I'm paralyzed?" Grace closed her eyes and sobbed.

"Grace, do you want to know what happened with me? Maybe you'll hear something in my experience that calls out to you with help."

Grace raised her head and wiped her tears. "Okay. Yeah." She nodded with a hint of reluctance. "I'd like you to tell me what happened to you. Really, I would. I'm sorry for getting angry. It's not your fault I'm still paralyzed. I know you're just trying to help me. I just get so angry and frustrated sometimes being locked in this prison!"

"I know. Even though I'm moving now, I still know. I was paralyzed too. And I still get angry and cry at feeling like I'm in prison. But I'd be happy to tell you."

Mora proceeded to relay the events of her life before the day of her crash: the self-blame, guilt, and shame that burdened her until she encountered the absolute love of God. How, in the instant of death, the burdens vanished into nothingness and she chose to return to her totally paralyzed body with that love carrying her. She told Grace about seeing her paralyzed body as a small inconvenience in the sight of heaven, and that to God, it could be healed. Then she told Grace about the flying dream, the prayers being answered, laying on of hands, her constant visualizing, her refusal to turn the power to think in her own mind over to anyone else, especially those she didn't trust. Only she knew what was true and best for herself, she told her neighbor.

"Just like you Grace. I'm just like you."

Grace cried throughout the entire story. Then she asked The Question.

"Mora, was your spinal cord cut?"

"No. It was badly damaged but not severed." Mora watched as Grace's mind block went up.

"That's *it* then. That's why you're getting better and I'm not. My spinal cord was cut!" Grace looked away in a cloud of hopeless rage.

"This is what I meant at the beginning of our conversation, when I said I have a wild, as in free as a bird, imagination and some of my ideas might sound insane to you. I haven't even gotten to telling you that part yet. All I told you was the regular part."

Grace laughed. "Yeah? Okay, tell me."

"First I'll tell you about a magazine article my friend Hope found last week. Apparently, there's a team of medical doctors that is researching a cure for paralysis. They predict a cure within ten years. Some millionaire is paying for the project, which costs something like six or seven million dollars a year, because he was recently para-lyzed. What the doctors are researching is the possibility of injecting live cells from one part of the body into the spinal cord. They hope that will stimulate the spinal cord to produce new cells."

"So are you saying there's a possibility I might be able to move in another ten years, after these guys finish their research?" Grace asked, her angry edges softened by the possibility.

"Not necessarily. Okay, now I want to tell you a great story. Want to hear it?" Energized with fiery enthusiasm, Mora was doing what she really loved best: planting seeds in a mind fertile for expansion.

"Sure." Grace sat back in her wheelchair and listened.

"I was taught polarity in massage school by a man, Henry, who had witnessed and participated in a most amazing healing miracle. First, I'll explain that polarity is a kind of energy work based on the fact that the physical body is affected by changes in our energy fields. When certain energy pockets or centers are touched and moved by an intuitive individual, the body's circuitry opens and healing can take place on the inside. If it's happening inside, it will definitely show up outside. That's an oversimplification of it, but basically, this kind of healing is an inside job, so to speak. Do you fol-low me so far?"

"I think so."

"There are many kinds of energy work out there, besides polar-ity and massage therapy, like acupuncture, body electronics, network chiropractic, reiki, psychic healing, cranio-sacral therapy; they go by lots of names. But back to my massage teacher, Henry.

"Henry was there with doctor Randolph Stone, the founder of polarity therapy, years ago, on the very day doctor Stone did a most amazing thing."

"So *tell* me already!"

"Okay." Mora chuckled, glad to see Grace generating extra-cur-ricular energy. "One day, doctor Stone, who was a genuinely com-passionate man, received a patient into his large classroom treatment room. Henry remembered clearly that the woman was regarded as a hopeless case. She had to be carried onto the massage table by sever-al strong people because she'd been paralyzed three years earlier.

After all that time of inactivity she weighed around 280 pounds. Henry told us the patient was absolutely dark and seemed barely alive. What little life she put out into the room was angry, sad and very black. As doctor Stone spoke with her, the patient began to reveal that she saw life as hardly worth living. Henry and the other students felt repulsed by the paralyzed woman. But not doctor Stone. He had a presence that touched people with tenderness, and it was this, rather than specific techniques, that his healing work was about. Anyway, doctor Stone hummed while he placed his broad hands on the young paralyzed woman with complete comfort and presence. He looked directly into the young woman's eyes with the compassion of Christ. That's exactly the way Henry described it. Doctor Stone saw the sorrow and rage within those eyes, but he didn't let that keep him from looking deeper into the core of the woman that was still purely good and innocent and divine. That little ray of light was what doctor Stone communicated with and the young woman knew it. Assisted by the students under his direction, doctor Stone gently manipulated the woman with absolute acceptance of life's presence in every cell of her being. Everyone was touched by the loving energy present in the room.

"While all this was going on, very slowly but visibly, the patient began to change. There appeared a soft vulnerability in her whole being, like an innocent little girl finding the love she'd always needed right there in her kind father's eyes. She and doctor Stone were connected and it was love that ran the circuits between them." Mora paused to give Grace a chance to catch up. . . or at least to blow her nose from crying. Beautiful Grace knew exactly how the young woman must have felt!

"All of a sudden," Mora continued, her eyes lit like flames, "doctor Stone told the young woman to raise her arms. The assisting students looked at doctor Stone as if he had made a mistake. But naturally, he hadn't. They all looked back to the patient and, when doctor Stone repeated his command, the young woman moved! First her fingers twitched, then her hand slowly opened and closed, then she actually moved her whole arm!" Mora paused briefly to absorb the trance of delight which enveloped Grace at that very moment, then she continued. "It's important to move once an energy blockage has been opened. Henry saw the whole thing. And he never stretched a truth as long as I knew him. He said doctor Stone could see past the dark clouds of the symptoms, the paralysis, right on down to the core of his patient's spirit. So simple. . . that's what Henry said. And so cheap! That's what I said!"

Grace narrowed her eyes. "Do the doctors here know about this?"

"Yeah right, do you really think the doctors here . . ." Mora broke off in mid-sentence.

"Yeah? Do I really think the doctors here, what?" Grace persisted.

"This is amazing, Grace. I was just going to say, 'Sure, do you really think if I told them this story they'd decide they could quit being medical doctors and do energy work instead?' I was just about to decide their thinking outcome *for* them, and that's the same thing I've been accusing them of doing with me! Wow, I prayed for help, and look what I got." Mora laughed.

"Look, I don't know what you're talking about now, but I want to get back to what you said before." Grace wheeled herself closer to Mora.

"Okay, so what do you think about those two stories?"

"Well, I don't know." Grace shifted her upper body. "I don't really want to wait ten years to watch the medical doctors learn how to remove cells from one place and inject them into another and have an insurance bill of a million dollars and that's only if the insurance companies don't all go bankrupt first from my pumped-up medical bills."

"Okay." Mora grinned.

"So where can I find this doctor Randolph Stone so he can fix me?"

"He's dead."

"How about Henry? Where's he?" Grace asked.

"He died an old man a few years ago too. But that's not the point." Mora baited.

"What do you *mean*, 'that's not the point'?" Grace shouted, biting the bait. "What *is* the point if it isn't about how I get my body back?"

"I'm glad you asked that." Mora fluttered her eyelashes. "Okay, now I'm going to tell you one more teensie-weensie story. Ready?"

Grace rolled her eyes. "I'll never get out of this room if I don't. Go ahead, I'm listening."

"Once upon a time, oh, I think it was in 1490 or 1491, something like that, in a far away country across the sea — Italy, let's say — everybody who lived by the seashore would look out at the horizon, which means 'as far as you can see from where you are now.' They would look at this horizon and say to each other, 'Oooooh. . . don't ever go too close to the edge. Because if you do, you might reach the place where the clingons live and fall into the black hole forever.' Everybody believed it was absolutely positively God's will that the earth was flat. Well, I bet you know what's coming next." Mora paused for dramatic effect. "Anyway, one day this Italian sailor got really bored because he was a type A personality, and he said, 'I know. I'll sail right up to the edge of the horizon to see what's there. All's I need is Queenie Isabella's bucks and a boat and I'm all set for the vacation adventure of a lifetime.' So he got Queenie's goodies and went for the edge, but it stayed ahead of him the whole time. He kept going, and going, and going, but it always stayed ahead of him. He looked back and saw that the place he'd lived all his life was just a tiny speck on the horizon. The next minute, it disappeared completely. So he scratched his head and said 'Huh. Maybe the world isn't really flat after all. Maybe it's a tetrahedron. No, maybe it's a triple isosceles triangle or, I don't know, but I don't think it's flat. I better go back and tell everybody!' As the story goes, this humble sailor went home and changed the entire world's understanding of the horizon *as well* as expanding our concept of vacation travel to what we know today. End of story."

Grace's mouth formed a perfectly straight line. "So what's that supposed to mean?"

"I was hoping you'd ask me that. What it means is, on one hand," Mora clumsily held out her puffy right hand, "here we have a monumental institution dedicated to the belief that it will take ten years and $70 million to hypodermically transport cells from one spot on a body to another in order to cure paralysis. Then, on the other hand," Mora clumsily held out her puffy left hand, "we have a nice guy who touches people and gets them to move, probably for free or $50 tops. And he already *did* it so we don't have to wait ten years. Which hand do you pick?" Mora opened her wild eyes and mouth as wide as they would go. "Here's a hint: the world is round, the world is round, the world is round. . ." Mora smiled. Then she laughed and said, "I can't say for sure, but maybe you *do* have the nerve to stand up for yourself. Maybe it just needs to get hooked up!"

- 17 -

That afternoon, physical therapy consisted of Mora's first out-door walk. She longed to feel real earth beneath her, so Yvette wheeled her toward a patch of grass behind the hospital.

A dove-gray sky hovered over the passing pedestrians. Mora gratefully noticed it and breathed in the aromas of a world she had chosen, for better or for worse. Soon she would have to make another choice.

Following the medical staff's recommendation, Mrs. Veypoko had scheduled an appointment to discuss a change of career for Mora. Mora had agreed, partly because she was curious about Mrs. Veypoko's counseling methods, and partly because Fitness & More was not an option. Mora's first career love was massage therapy and it was a sad prospect to consider never being able to massage again.

Mora's "staffing" was also scheduled for later in the week, when each of her staff members would present a brief progress report to her and her family. Ellen and Louise were scheduled to fly in the day before and Mora planned to include Hope, whose presence would be essential. "It'll be entertaining, that's for sure." she mumbled.

"Did you say something, Mora?" Yvette asked as she wheeled Mora around the corner.

"Oh, I was just planning my staffing on Thursday. How much time do they allow for the whole thing, and how much of it is taken up by the patient's agenda?"

"Generally they take about twenty minutes, even though they're scheduled to last an hour. It's hard to hold the doctors' attention for longer than that, so when they think it's over, it's over. The staffing actually has more to do with the therapists communicating progress to the patient's family. Most patients just listen and don't say much." Yvette engaged the brakes and stood ready to help Mora stand. "Here we are. Ready to boogie?"

"Oh boy, the grass looks so sumptuous," Mora said, as she shared the labor of standing up. "I'd sure like to sit on it."

"Okay." Yvette lowered Mora down.

"Ohhhh. . . you have no idea what this does for me."

Yvette lent Mora back support with one hand, and squinted toward the peeking sun. "I bet I do. I go hiking and plant my butt on terra firma just about every weekend. Isn't this the most secure feeling in the world?"

"Indeed." Mora carefully slid her hands onto the grass. "My hands still have big numb patches. In some places the tissue inside feels so itchy that only my teeth can scratch them hard enough, but even that doesn't relieve the itch and my hand just bleeds. Other places are just plain hyper-annoying or nothing at all. I wonder if the feeling will ever come back."

"It takes time. Do you want to walk some now?"

"Okay."

Yvette gracefully shifted and helped Mora stand.

"Wow, this feels so weird. I can't look right down at what's under me and I can't feel it." Mora turned her torso toward Yvette and waited.

"This uneven terrain takes a little bit more effort to negotiate than a smooth hospital floor. Why don't you bend over a little so you can see the ground ahead of you, then stand up again and try a step or two? I'll hold you."

Mora did as Yvette suggested and succeeded in taking several steps. "Yvette, you and Corky are always so encouraging. I don't know what I'd do in this nuthouse without you. Right now I feel like an infant learning to walk." After several bend-look-stand-step cycles, Mora reached the edge of the curb. "What do I do now?"

"Do you want to try negotiating it?"

"You mean step down?" Mora's heart pushed hard against her

chest. "Will you catch me if I fall?"

Still holding onto Mora's hand, Yvette stepped down and said, "Okay, I'm right here."

Mora plunked a flat foot down onto the asphalt and it sent a mild jolt through her bones. "Ughh, that wasn't very smooth."

"Let's take a few steps, then turn around and go back up the curb." Yvette patiently steered the turn and helped Mora step back up. "That was great," she said. "Now let's do it again."

After their third up and down cycle, Yvette led Mora back to the uneven grass patch. "Look at how quickly you're improving," she said. Suddenly, Mora lost her balance and Yvette quickly caught her.

"Very interesting," Mora said. "As soon as I stopped thinking about what I was doing and shifted to worrying about my appointment with Mrs. Veypoko, I lost my balance."

"Well, maybe it's a good indicator of what's good to think about. And don't forget one very important fact."

"What's that?" Mora asked anxiously. Yvette spoke little, but when she did her wisdom was not lost on Mora.

Yvette faced Mora with her bright, shining face. "You're just passin' through here. It won't be long before you're home again."

For a moment Mora felt as if an angel disguised as a physical therapist had reminded her of her real home, which was not of this earth.

"Oh yeah," Mora said as she returned Yvette's smile, "I keep forgetting. I think I'm ready to go back now. I have a client to see."

"You mean Carlos?"

"How did you know?"

"I read the weekend nurse's log. Pretty impressive if I do say so myself. And you're worried about whether or not you'll be able to help people again?" Yvette helped Mora into her wheelchair. "You've got too much spunk. Want me to push? I bet you're tired."

"I am pretty wiped out. Maybe I'd better take a nap. Starting now." Mora closed her eyes and Yvette pushed.

Back in her room, Mora let Yvette help her into bed. Before she could focus on the sudden appearance of excruciating neck and arm pain, she was fast asleep.

*   *   *

"Mora, are you awake?" Corky stood over Mora and waited for signs of alertness. "I hate to wake you up but you said you wanted to work on your embroidery project. I hope it's okay."

Mora opened her eyes. "Uhhh. . . no that's fine. How much time do we have left today?"

"Same as usual. Let's help you up."

Fumbling through every stitch, Mora had to push the embroidery hoop on top of the needle to pass it through the fabric. The hoop frequently popped off and required Corky's hands, which were also busy with two other patients, to replace it. It was slow and frustrating work.

"Damn!" Mora clumsily threw the hoop on the table. "I can't do this. It's too hard. What made me think I could?" Tears of frustration fell.

Corky sat down and calmly examined Mora's progress. "Do you think it might be too discouraging to keep trying? Should we drop this for now?" She looked at Mora and waited.

Mora clenched her jaw. "No."

Corky leaned back and laughed. "I set you up on that one, Mora Donovan."

Mora laughed too. "I just needed to throw in the hoop for a minute. I'll keep plugging away." She sighed and picked up where she had left off. With each small movement, all her available upper body strength was used up and fresh pain arrived, but Mora was determined to push through it. The burning drive to make Hope's gift was stronger than the burning pain. By the time her OT hour was up she'd finished outlining one side of the brown tree trunk. She let her arms finally drop and looked proudly at what she was creating. *An oak is solid, endures all seasons and to the Druids, it represented the doorway to the world of spiritual healing, protection and strength. Just like Hope.*

After a brief rest, Mora's neck and arm pain subsided and she decided she could massage Carlos. She found him alone, gazing out the windows of the group room. His tired eyes rested their welcome on her. She silently asked God to help her give Carlos what he needed and gently stroked his neck and arm. "I can see your arm and your hand receiving life," she whispered, just loud enough for Carlos to hear. "Love is moving through your arm and into your fingertips."

At the opposite end of the room, where Carlos and Mora could not see them, doctor Jackson and Jane watched the two patients and laughed. Doctor Jackson mumbled and Jane playfully tapped his arm and rocked with amusement. Then Pam stepped up behind them.

"What are you guys laughing at? Can I see?" Pam smiled and looked, her bright blue eyes finding the only other people in the room. Bewildered, she looked at the laughing doctor and nurse who seemed oblivious to her presence.

"You're laughing at them?" Pam said, scowling. "I think it's wonderful that Mora wants to help other patients. I think the hospital should be providing massage."

"Excuse me?" Jane snapped, glaring at the nursing student. Doctor Jackson folded his arms on his chest and laughed at the fresh source of entertainment.

"I know Mora and she's a fine person. Honestly, I'm shocked at your behavior!" Looking from one to the other, Pam's face reflected both fear and anger.

Jane raised her head and said, "Young lady, I will see you in my office now." Pivoting on her heels, she pointed down the hall.

Pam searched the eyes of the doctor whom she'd respected and admired. He said blandly, "You better do what you're told."

Pam slumped her shoulders and dropped her head as tears fell. She dragged herself down the hall toward doom, with Jane following behind.

* * *

Mora devoured dinner while watching Miss Jane devour Jethro with her bedroom eyes out by the "SEE-ment pond" on "The Beverly Hillbillies." She laughed as Jethro bragged about his sixth-grade education and his plan to become a brain surgeon.

"Howdy, howdy." Hope's cheery voice entered before her.

"Hey girl. Come on in. I was just watching the educational channel." Mora turned back to the television just in time to see Granny force some possum gizzard stew down Mr. Drysdale's sore throat. "It's a fascinating program about folk medicine." Mora laughed and clicked off the television.

"Oh, don't tell anybody, but I love that show. And after the day I've just had, I could use a little of Granny's medicine. How are you today?"

Mora was bursting with pride over her embroidery project but wanted to keep it a secret until it was finished. "Good. Let's see. . . OT was good, nothing remarkable," she lied, "but in PT, Yvette and I took a walk outside, and I sat on the ground and walked all over an uneven patch of grass. It was great!"

"Hey, hey, hey!" Hope extended her hand tentatively. "Can ya gimme five?"

Mora accepted the challenge by pushing her right arm out with her left forearm and opening her right palm.

Hope gently clapped it. "That's great. Any late-breaking news on the hot political front? Any new wars broken out? I got a really dirty look from two of the nurses when I passed the nurses' station."

"Really? How ridiculous." Mora sighed, flustered. "Yvette reminded me today I won't be in here forever. It's so easy to forget I'm actually going to have a life after this place. Even though I don't know where I'm going to live."

"Now, don't worry about that. I told you that I want you to move into my house, into the spare room, until we know how you're going to be, until you can. . . until you're healed enough to be on your own. Everybody thinks you'd be better off staying at my house than anywhere."

"Oh really? And just who does 'everybody' consist of?"

"Ellen, me, David, me, Louise, me, Claire, me. . . you know, the whole crowd." They laughed.

"I guess you are the whole crowd." Mora's energy and spirit were slipping fast.

"You're tired aren't you? Do you want to finish your dinner?" Hope glanced at the remains of lumpy mashed potatoes, shriveled, peas, dried up, too-pungent whitefish, and the unopened carton of milk. "Gee, it doesn't look very appetizing. Want me to go down and get you something slightly-more-palatable-because-it's-for-sale from the normal people's cafeteria?"

"No thanks," Mora's voice drooped. "Maybe I'd better go to bed early, after such a packed day. But first, before we do massage, we have to talk about the staffing. And first before that first, how was your day?"

Hope sighed heavily and shook her head. "I think I had a mental argument with everybody who came within ten feet of me today. It was the kind of day where nothing made any sense. I wanted to be here helping you. Am I crazy or what?"

"Both. Do you think you're changing inside, and maybe the outside hasn't shown up yet?"

"Maybe. We'll see what happens next. I just kept thinking about how much I wanted to be here."

"I thank you from the bottom of my heart for all the tender loving care you give me."

"Okay, dues paid." Hope laughed. "Want me to tell you what I found out?"

"Definitely. Did you get into the kitchen?" Mora whispered, her energy suddenly perked up.

"Yes! And have I got some good poop on them. I'm speaking figuratively of course." Hope grabbed the chair, pulled it closer to Mora and sat down.

"Oh, that reminds me of a good story but I'll tell you later. Have you talked to Louise and Ellen about the staffing?"

"Yes. I'm picking up your mother the night before. Your sister's going to rent a car and get here that morning. I think I got everything you wanted. Oh boy, this is going to be good!" Hope rubbed her hands together and grinned.

"Are you sure you want to go to the staffing?"

"Are you kidding? This'll be the most fun I've had kicking butt since I coached high school soccer!"

"Okay, tell me what you found out."

*   *   *

Mora waited outside Mrs. Veypoko's office the following morning, her stomach turning sumersaults. She gazed despondently out the foggy waiting room windows onto another rainy New England day. *What could I ever want to do that even mildly compares to massage?*

God, it would be awful if I could never. . .

"Good morning, Mora. Sorry to keep you waiting." Mrs. Veypoko appeared, unlocked her door, and pushed it open. Her small office was crammed with sagging bookshelves, framed pictures, a small desk covered with a large computer, and two ancient file cabinets. A pale hanging plant vied for whatever light might come in through the window and partially obstructed the view of a highrise across the street.

"Come in," Mrs. Veypoko said as she seated herself behind the desk, "it's crowded but there's just enough room for your wheelchair. We do it all the time."

Mora negotiated a spot in front of the desk and waited.

"As you know," Mrs. Veypoko began, folding her hands on the desk, "we're here to discuss a career change in view of your. . . current condition."

I hate this, God. What's going to become of me? Tears slid down Mora's cheeks.

"Now Mora dear, I know it's hard for you to think about getting out of hairdressing but. . ."

"I'm a massage therapist, an aerobics instructor, and a fitness trainer," Mora snapped.

"Yes, well, I'm sure they're all very legitimate occupations. And they require a great deal of physical strength and function, do they not?"

"Yes," Mora sighed, reluctantly facing the truth.

"Now dear," Mrs. Veypoko leaned forward, "if we're going to proceed, you must trust me. I'm here to help you find a more appropriate occupation." Mrs. Veypoko put on her reading glasses, opened a file on her desk, and removed a pre-printed form. "I'd like to ask you a few questions to get a better idea of what you're qualified to do in that big world out there, as well as what actual, marketable skills you have. Let's begin. How would you describe yourself as an employee?"

"I wouldn't."

"Pardon me?" Mrs. Veypoko raised her eyes over the rims of her glasses.

"I prefer self-employment. I like to be my own boss, make my own hours, you know, the job fits the person rather than the person fitting the job." Mora's eyes roamed the room. *How can she STAND being cooped up in this little box? Eight hours a day, five days a week . . .*

"P r e f e r s   s e l f - e m p l o y m e n t. Okay, next question: What kinds of tasks motivate you to perform at your maximum? In other words, in what skills would you confidently say you excel?"

"Good question. Let's see. . . I am good at intuitively reading human energy fields. I listen while a person's body speaks to my hands, then I respond by using just the right touch to walk the line between pleasure and pain. Or I might simply touch the connected contractions, thereby helping to release the energy blockages stored in the body." Pleased with her own response, Mora paused, then added, "Oh, when my touch contacts my client's emotional memory and they release their feelings, they couldn't be supported by a more compassionate person than myself." Satisfied, Mora smiled and awaited the next question.

Mrs. Veypoko raised her eyes. "I don't have a category for those particular skills listed on our questionairre." She sat up. "Do you have any legitimate job skills?"

Mora gazed out the window. "I love motivating people, helping them see the value in where they are no matter how hopeless it seems to be and encouraging them to reach into their own hearts. And I love to make people laugh, especially at me. Ever since I was a kid. . . . There were eight people at the dinner table every night. If I wanted attention, I imitated the nuns and made fun of myself so my family would say, 'Look at Mora! Isn't she clever.' I guess I loved teaching aerobics because it was the next best thing to being on stage." Mora sighed. "I just love to encourage people. When I offer encouragement to someone else, it goes through me first and we both get it."

"M o t i v a t i n g   p e o p l e," Mrs. Veypoko said as she wrote. "Do you have any sales experience? Have you considered a career in, say, selling cars or large appliances? There must be a great deal of money to be made in those occupations."

"You mean keeping up with somebody else's quotas, performance pressure, manipulating customers, putting on a false image, and doing almost anything to get a commission? Not really." Mora smiled.

Mrs. Veypoko sighed. "Mora, you're making it very difficult for me to help you. Do you have any skills through which you could earn a living?"

Mora looked out the window again, letting her mouth fall open in a half-daze.

"Mora. . ."

"Oh. Sorry. I was thinking. I like to write, and I think I'm pretty good."

"W r i t i n g. Okay, what have you written?"

"Oh, satirical poems, haiku. Once I wrote a birthday poem for my ex-mother-in-law. It went 'Lanelle, Lanelle, you're really swell, I mean, well! You'll more than do. I find you're kind, and won't stand behind anyone you can outdo.' It was my way of acknowledging her, uh, spunkiness, if you know what I mean." Mora winked.

"Yes, well, I'm sure that was lovely. But Mora," Mrs. Veypoko shook her head, "we haven't much to go on here. Is there anything, anything at all you can do that could support you?"

"I know!" Mora's face lit up. "Cookies!"

"Cookies. What about cookies?" Mrs. Veypoko asked wearily.

"I bake the best cookies in the universe. In fact, oh, this is another shining ability of mine. I love giving the cookies away. Every time we have a staff meeting I begin by offering my homemade oat-meal-coconut-raisin-walnut-chocolate chip cookies to everybody. It's amazing how a little diplomacy relaxes people. Like one time I was stranded at Logan airport. I took out my cookies, went over to the ticket agent and . . ."

"Mora, Mora, Mora." Mrs. Veypoko shook her head, "we need to follow the form here. You can't make a living by giving away homemade cookies. Okay, let's start at the beginnning. In what area did you receive your education?"

"You mean what's my B.A. in, before I got my degree in mas-sage therapy?"

"Yes." Mrs. Veypoko sighed impatiently.

"That's a very interesting question. . ."

Mrs. Veypoko rolled her eyes. "Just the answer please."

"Well, it's an involved answer. First I wanted to be a lawyer so I got into political science. The professor's only required reading was the book he wrote, which I read and I totally disagreed with. When the final essay exam was given I put my all into answering his questions. To be quite frank, I expected an A. But when I got a D- . . . well, goodbye political science. Then one day. . ."

"Mora, I don't have a lot of time here." Mrs. Veypoko shook her head and viewed Mora over the rims of her spectacles.

"I'm getting to it. One day I was walking across campus and ran into a friend who said she'd just changed her major to sociology. I said, 'What's sociology?' She said, 'the study of groups of people'. 'Hey,' I thought, 'I love studying groups of people. I do it all the time. I think I'll change my major.' So that's what my B.A. is in. Sociology." Mora smiled.

Mrs. Veypoko's eyelids drooped and she asked in a monotone, "Did you work in the field at all?"

"Yes. I was a counselor for delinquent teenaged boys living in foster homes. Whew! That was rough. Mostly because they didn't want my help. They'd been so abused and neglected and they naturally tried to take it out on anyone around them, including me. I just wasn't cut out to handle such harshness. The few who weren't openly hostile wanted me to fix things for them so they wouldn't have to. It was a hopelessly codependent system and I lasted a year. It ended one day when one of my boys, a 17-year-old, got his foster sister pregnant and the foster family dumped him. My boss called me in and demanded I take the boy home with me or I'd be out of a job. Naturally I said, 'You can't fire me because I quit.'"

"Naturally." Mrs. Veypoko narrowed her eyes. "You don't seem to have a particularly good work history, do you?"

"Well, it depends on how you look at it. I just quit trying to force insane ideas of helping onto real human beings who have their own individual needs. Then I got into massage therapy. You see, you can't make people take off their clothes, lie on a table, properly draped of course, and force them to relax. They have to want to. So

only people who really want the help get so-called alternative body
work. Why else would they pay out of their own pockets for help
that most insurance doesn't cover? Sometimes that's what it takes for
people to take back their lives. They need to make their own choices
about what helps them." Surprisingly comforted by her own words,
Mora relaxed in her wheelchair.

Mora's words had apparently registered with Mrs. Veypoko
too. She sat in silence for a long moment.

"Mrs. Veypoko. Are you okay?"

"Mora, would you consider going back to school to earn your
master's degree in social work?"

"To what end, may I ask?"

"Well, I was just thinking. Maybe you could become a counselor and work, say, in a hospital."

"You mean get a job like yours?" Mora squinted.

"That's precisely what I mean!" Mrs. Veypoko hopped in her
chair. "It would be a good, steady job, two weeks vacation per year,
unpaid for the first five years of course, working for highly prestigious
professionals, not to mention the fabulous hospitalization benefits."

Mora gnawed on her lip before responding. "You know Mrs.
Veypoko, I'm not sure I could do your job. I mean, I've been watching you."

"Yes." Mrs. Veypoko smiled and nodded. "I must say it is a
demanding profession. But the rewards are. . . well. . ." She scanned
the crammed office with a hand, "they're obvious."

"Yes, but. . ." Mora searched her imagination for diplomatic
words, "I'm not sure I posess the. . .uh. . . how can I put it. . . special
qualities you have that enable you to. . ." Mora cleared her throat.

"I know, I know." Mrs. Veypoko nodded. "That's what you'd
learn in a master's program."

"Well," Mora cleared her throat again, "I think what you do,
Mrs. Veypoko, you never learned in school." Mora smiled, satisfied.

"You may be right." Mrs. Veypoko relaxed back in her chair. "It
is possible you lack the, shall we say, affinity for this type of position."

"Right."

"But I'd like to recommend a return to graduate school for you, and with your actual work experience and present financial situation I'm sure you could earn money in an internship say, working in a hospital like this."

Mora took a moment to consider before responding. "Mrs. Veypoko, our discussion has been quite an eye-opener. And you know what I'd like to do?"

"What?"

"I'd like to let all this simmer and see what happens. If you need to have some career objective written down on your form, if there's a space for 'other' you can just put 'self-healer' and quote me on it. That way you won't get into trouble with the doctors and Jane. In the meantime I'll guarantee you one thing: the minute I need your help in choosing a new career, I'll ask you. Okay?" Mora smiled.

"All right then." Mrs. Veypoko got up and moved toward the door. "I'll see you at the staffing, if not sooner."

Mora wheeled herself out.

*   *   *

On the way back to her room, Mora decided to visit Tony, the man in the room next to hers. "Knock, knock, may I come in?"

"Hi Mora. Come in," Tony's soft voice answered.

Mora perambulated into position next to Tony's bed. "How are you doing today?" she asked.

"Oh, not so bad. I've seen better days but I've seen worse," he answered gently.

Mora's heart ached for Tony, and she marveled at his ability to endure quadraplegia with apparent serenity. Just as she was about to ask him if he wanted his hand held, Tony contracted with a full-body spasm.

"Damn spasticity." He laughed, embarrassed.

"You moved!" Mora's flesh chilled with excitement.

"Spasms aren't movement. They're involuntary reflexes and they're humiliating."

"But Tony, you moved! I saw you. Your whole body moved. How can you say it's not movement?" Mora insisted.

"Doctor Jackson said spasticity is not movement, and he should know because he's a spinal cord injury specialist. I still can't feel anything, I have no control over spasticity, so I wasn't the one who moved." A slight edge of anger began to seep through Tony's words.

Mora dropped the subject as her attention ran ahead. "I have to talk to someone. I'll see you later Tony, okay?" Without waiting for an answer, she rolled out and up the hall.

Samuel Jackson was sitting at his desk, rubbing his tired eyes behind his glasses, when he heard a thump on his door.

"Doctor Jackson?"

"Just a moment." He got up and opened the door to Mora.

"I know you're busy, doctor, but do you have a minute?"

"Yes, come in."

As Mora rolled in, she caught sight of a photograph on the wall. Five men wearing long black robes stood together on the steps of a very old, stone church. Doctor Jackson was among them. He noticed her interest.

"Salem Church is the oldest congregation in Massachusetts. My mother's family were founding members and I'm an elder."

A copy of *The Salem Tribune* lay on his desk. When Mora saw it, her flesh crawled and her heart began to pound.

"What's on your mind?" the doctor asked.

Intuition told her she was about to enter dangerous waters, but at that moment, her drive toward truth was stronger than the familiar nagging fear. "It's about Tony Sanders. He said you told him spasticity isn't movement. Why did you tell him that?"

Doctor Jackson squinted behind his steel-rimmed glasses, leaned back in his chair, and folded his hands on his belly. "I don't think that's any of your concern, young lady. I am his doctor, in case you haven't noticed, and you're hardly qualified to question my medical authority."

"But that's just it. Maybe I'm as qualified as anyone can get because I've been where he is. Tony and I both had the same injury -- a C5 fracture, damaged spinal cord and paralysis -- but he believes your word is God. When you tell him he's permanently paralyzed, he believes it. Why do you tell him his movement doesn't count, banishing it to the trash by labelling it 'involuntary'? You rob him of seeing it as a true sign of hope, an indication that his body is still hooked up!"

Doctor Jackson stood up and leaned on his desk. "Ms. Donovan, the other patients in this hospital are none of your concern. In fact, I strongly disapprove of your touching them because of the damage you may be inflicting. Your behavior is highly disruptive. Take warning here; don't make me put my foot down. If you wish to delude yourself about the medical complexities of paralysis, that's your choice. But if you don't keep your absurd, unfounded opinions to yourself, you may find yourself in a regrettable position. Now, if you'll excuse me, I have work to do."

Mora's tightened neck screamed with pain. When the clenched-fist sensation in her solar plexus caught her attention, she let it relax, and nausea took its place. Then she heard the voice speak from inside, saying "just let go." Without a word, she pedaled her wheelchair around and left.

- 18 -

By the time Mora returned to her room, a gathering swell of funk had swept her in. The end product of the day's activities was a heap of confusion piled on the floor. She rolled over it to get to the window, wishing she could stand up by herself and walk out, or at least do something more than kick a footstool. She was physically exhausted and her emotions were a jumble of disturbed sediment. *Which way do I go, God? I'm so tired. Maybe it's futile to take a stand for myself here. . . maybe I should just let it all slide.* She felt the frightened, hostile undertow leaking through her determined veneer. Anger that needed to be let out of her ribcage fizzled. She gazed dully upon the lost gray day like a misplaced soul. None of the options she tried on felt right, except sleep. She turned her chair around, parked herself on the threshold facing the hallway, and waited. When a nurse finally strayed by, Mora enlisted her help getting into bed.

Deep sleep softened the blows to her falling ego, whisking her away from the world of judging eyes and into the open arms of comfort.

She dreamed. . .
of being upstairs. . . in a second story room. . .
She is helping people sent to her by three doctors. . . hopeless people, coming to her last of all.

Bright white light streams down through the pointed ceiling, penetrating her crown, filling her, overflowing, forming a solid energy field around her. . . radiating beams of laser light out her hands and into each person's body. She wordlessly says to God, "Please use me. Let me help this person any way You see fit." The patient knows he is in good hands and his face fills with renewed hope.

Upstairs. . . in a second story room. . .

Then she's in a bustling, expansive airport. . .
walking briskly, effortlessly carrying a suitcase in each hand. She's
traveling overseas, to a place she's never been but always wanted to
go, and she's delighted!

"Mora."

She awakened to Eric's blue eyes. "Oh, what time is it?"

"About 4."

Coming out of sleep with a full-body spastic stretch, Mora
decided not to worry about whether or not she'd missed her afternoon schedule. She didn't care. "What are you doing here?"

"I came in to see if you wanted an acupuncture treatment." He
smiled placidly.

"Do I! I hit a wall today. All of a sudden. Zap."

Eric gently lifted both her wrists and lowered his eyes into
nowhere to hear her pulses. After several seconds he rested her
hands on the bed. "Let me see your tongue."

Mora stuck out her tongue and he studied it.

"Can we raise your pant legs up past your knees comfortably,
or would you prefer we take them off and cover you?"

"Let's take them off."

Together they removed the sweatpants and Eric covered all but
her legs with the sheet.

"Hurt?" He asked as he tapped a fiber-thin needle into a point
on her right thigh.

"No. Tell me as you go, okay?" Mora derived great comfort
from hearing the intuitive reasoning process that guided an energy
worker's choices.

"Have you been feeling angry, or like you're compressing
anger inward?" Eric asked without taking his eyes off the shin and
foot needle points.

"Bingo," she said without enthusiasm.

"Have you been feeling listless?"

"Double bingo."

"Blocked liver and gall bladder, yang deficiency. This will increase blood circulation and increase the flow of yang energy. Your new sobriety could be contributing to it." He was duplicating many but not all of the same needle points on the other leg.

She opened her eyes to answer. "Yes. Liver filters anger and slow yang can be depression and apathy, right?"

"Bingo." Eric glanced at Mora long enough to smile, then tapped a needle lightly over her manubrium to open her heart energy.

She inhaled deeply and exhaled with sounding fire. "Huhhhh!" She repeated it several times and with each cycle. "I feel like I have to pant. My chest is stretching open." Again, she inhaled and released a heavy vocal exhale.

"Good. Open up and move it out." Eric pulled the chair up beside her bed and made himself comfortable. "Now just relax and let your body do the rest."

Mora's instinctive need to exhale with sound soon subsided and her breathing calmed by itself. After forty minutes she began to feel energized and calm. Eric removed the needles, helped her back into her wheelchair, kissed the crown of her head, and left.

"Boy," Mora whispered to herself, "I feel like I just had a whole night's restful sleep." Partly because she now had a job to do, and partly because she interpreted her dream as a premonition, Mora perambulated to her client's room with renewed encouragement.

*   *   *

The morning of Mora's staffing, Hope arrived with Ellen at 10. Renewed by acupuncture, massage, a good night's sleep, and a deeply delicious morning meditation, Mora was overjoyed to see them. Hope left mother and daughter alone while she returned to her car to retrieve the day's materials.

Ellen stepped back to take in Mora's costume, laughed and shook her head. "I don't know, Mora. Don't you think you're being a little overly dramatic? Why are you wearing *that?*"

"Me? Dramatic?" Mora said, proudly sporting the sleeveless fire-engine-red Superwoman shirt that she'd made in college. Hope had modified it to fit over the halo vest. The "S" was made of royal-blue satin on a canary-yellow naugahyde background. In conjunction with her wheelchair and halo, Mora's get-up was guaranteed to grab attention.

"I'm wearing this because Corky asked me to be in her training video today. It has nothing whatsoever to do with the 'S' for stand-up-for-myself-staffing." Mora fluttered her eyelashes. "Corky and a bunch of OT students are making a movie and I'm going to be a star doing an exercise routine. . . sort of. Besides, Ma, if anyone knows you have to dress to fit the occasion, you would. You taught me all I know about fashion."

Ellen shook her head. "You take it to a place I wouldn't even think of going."

"Hello!" Louise's lilty voice announced her arrival. She set her stuffed shopping bag down to hug Mora, then stepped back to get a good look. "You look one thousand percent better. I can't believe it. Well, actually I can. I think you're the kid with the guts in the family." Squinting, she added, "Are you going to change your shirt first?"

"Hi everybody, I'm back!" Hope returned in a flurry and set her briefcase down."Corky says they're ready for us."

"You got the *stuff*?" Mora asked Hope.

"Yep. I'm ready to roll. . . heads. . . if you are." Hope couldn't resist.

The four women proceeded to the conference room at the end of the hall just as Corky and Yvette approached from the opposite direction. After exchanging greetings, everyone went in and sat down at the long oval conference table. It was precisely 11 o'clock.

At ten past the hour, Mrs. Veypoko came in. At 11:15, Jane and doctors Jackson and Weiss entered and sat as far from Mora and her family as they could.

Jane opened the folder in front of her. "We don't have quite as much time as we had hoped to have for this staffing, so let's begin."

"Uh, excuse me, Jane, but there are a few things I need to discuss today and I want to be sure you allow time for me, too." Mora smiled nervously above her "S" shield.

Jane glared at Mora. "Well," she said, "we'll start by asking the immediate family members to introduce themselves to the medical staff, if you would."

Ellen introduced herself, followed by Louise, who smiled graciously at Jane. "You may recall I met you on my tour of the hospital before Mora was admitted."

"Yes, of course. Good to have you." Jane said brusquely, and turned thinly veiled hostility on Hope. "This meeting is for immediate family only."

Mora nervously intervened. "I wanted Hope here because she's like family to me. Also, since she's played a major therapeutic role in my healing program by massaging me every day, it seemed appropriate that she participate."

Jane turned her attention toward the doctors. "Let's get started. The sooner we get this over with, the sooner we can all go to lunch." She smiled and received a nod of approval from doctor Jackson. "Physical therapy, let's hear from you first."

"Sure." Yvette sailed into her report "Mora's been doing great, making progress in every area. She's walking on uneven terrain outside and instead of her old stomping ground weight-training, she's excelling in assisted, indoor gait-training. She was also up to twelve minutes on the stationary bicycle until it broke. Her legs are growing in strength. You've probably seen her rolling around the halls at quite a clip lately." Yvette offered Mora a smile. "Mora's arms are not quite up to the same pace as her lower extremeties but we're working successfully with proprioceptive neuromuscular facilitation to increase her range of motion as well as muscle flexibility. Personally, I find Mora a pleasure to work with." Yvette looked at Mora's family. "She's not a quitter and she'll try anything until she gets it right. I've had no problems at all with motivating her. She's got a big supply of her own. In fact, she's spreading it around the unit to some of the other patients." Yvette sat back in her chair and nodded graciously.

"Occupational therapy, you're next," Jane said, glancing at her watch.

"Well, I'd say the same thing about Mora's motivation and effort,"Corky said energetically. "She tries everything and even if she gets frustrated and cries, it doesn't take long for her to bounce back. The progress she's made just in the last week on her fine finger muscle movement has been tremendous. She's feeding herself and we're working on self-dressing along with other personal care activities. I've really enjoyed working with her, too." Corky winked at Mora and sat back in her chair.

"I really appreciate both of you, too." Mora wanted to acknowledge her two therapists in the presence of everyone. "Your support has been the most valuable aspect of my stay here."

"Well, thank you," said Yvette.

"Thanks, Mora," came from Corky.

"Mrs. Veypoko." Jane glanced at her watch again and began clicking her ballpoint pen over and over, her eyes planted firmly on her papers.

"Thank you, Jane." Mrs. Veypoko put on her reading glasses and repositioned herself demurely. "The psychology department received the psychiatrist's evaluation results and. . ."

"Really?" Mora interrupted excitedly, "what were the results?"

"Mora, I don't think. . ." Mrs. Veypoko turned to Jane for direction.

"You may say a brief word about the results Mrs. Veypoko, but this is not the proper time to discuss them in depth. The patient will have to consult with the evaluating psychiatrist directly for complete results."

"But I've been trying to reach doctor Andrews for over a week and she doesn't respond," Mora answered.

"Mrs. Veypoko," Jane said, nodding to the psychologist, "continue please."

"Well, let's see. I can say that you scored quite high in creative problem-solving." Glancing at Jane, who was fiercely drawing hard, fast lines on her paper margins, Mrs. Veypoko continued. "Mora and I have discussed her need to find another more suitable occupation. With her physical limitations she will obviously not be able to continue her career as a weight lifter."

"Massage therapist," Mora and Hope said simultaneously, then laughed. "And fitness trainer and aerobics instructor," Mora added. "But Mrs. Veypoko, don't you remember I said I'd think about it?"

Avoiding looking directly at Mora, Mrs. Veypoko addressed

Ellen and Louise. "The recommendation to choose another career was made unanimously by Mora's entire medical team who of course are better qualified to determine the extent of Mora's future recovery than anyone in this room, don't you agree?" Mrs. Veypoko turned to the two silent doctors for approval, and doctor Jackson looked at his watch.

"Well I don't agree and I'm the one who decides," Mora stated clearly, feeling anger rising from her chest to her throat.

"Doctor Jackson, perhaps you'd like to comment at this point," Jane said.

"Yes." Doctor Jackson leaned forward and folded his arms on the table. "As Mrs. Veypoko said, I do believe it would be advisable for Mora to seriously consider another career. We'd hate to see her waste valuable time hoping for something beyond her reach." He sat back and turned to doctor Weiss, who nodded silent agreement. "Beyond that, I don't believe I have anything more to add, except to continue her program as per previously made recommendations."

"Very good. If there are no further questions, I believe we can bring this meeting to a close." Jane gave her pen one final snap on the table, glanced quickly at everyone but Mora, and pushed her chair back to leave.

"Jane," Mora said, her shaking vocal cords throwing off frightened sparks, "as I said, there are a few things I need to say. I understand that part of the staffing time is to be devoted to hearing from the patient. First, I'd like Hope to give *her* progress report as my massage therapist. Hope?"

Hope began nervously. "Mora responds very well to massage. Each evening when I come in to work on her neck, arms and hands, I can actually feel her tight muscles softening and letting go. We also do a lot of visualizing, to help the pain go away and to regrow nerves."

"This is ridiculous," doctor Weiss said, "I beg your pardon, madam, but this meeting is for Mackenzie Rehabilitation Hospital staff to discuss the patient's progress, not for your . . ."

Mora broke in. "Doctor, Hope has been helping me just as much as Corky and Yvette and I wanted everyone to be aware of my progress through massage. Thanks, Hope. Now, for the second item on my agenda."

Hope jumped up from her chair, opened her briefcase, removed a stack of papers, and distributed them around the room. Mora continued before anyone had a chance to object. "On behalf of myself and the other patients on the spinal cord injury unit, I've taken the liberty of compiling a list of suggested changes. There are things I've experienced here that have been counterproductive to my recovery. That is what I'd like to address now." Vibrating with fear and daring, Mora quickly scanned the room.

Jane whippped her head toward doctor Jackson who smiled sarcastically, leaned toward doctor Weiss, and whispered loud enough for everyone to hear: "Nothing like a little entertainment to work up a good appetite." Doctor Weiss chuckled. Jane was not amused.

Mora rushed ahead. "The top page includes a list of the foods and beverages served to us patients, and their proven links to cancer and other health problems. The most toxic substance is tap water. Hope brought two separate water samples to an independent laboratory for analysis. Their results are on page two and are, in my opinion, shocking. Lead, arsenic, chlorine, aluminum, mercury, and copper, to name just a few, have proven to be poisonous to humans in much lower levels than what is coming out of the taps here. . . far beyond what the EPA labels a qualified health risk. Patients recovering from surgery, and any kind of cell damage need a lot of fresh water for cell repair. As I'm sure you know, kidney infection is a common complication resulting from paralysis, and the kidneys *must* have plenty of pure water to function. Hope's been bringing me purified water since I got here, but I think all the patients would benefit from drinking clean water. Minimally, I think the hospital could discontinue giving patients poisoned water. Ideally, patients should only be fed purified water." Anxious for a response, Mora scanned the room and held her breath.

Doctor Jackson whispered in a disinterested huddle with doctor Weiss; Behind a locked jaw, Jane glared at the ceiling and clicked her pen; Ellen's pointed, paralegal brow was in concentrated courtroom mode; Louise remained completely composed; Hope leaned back with serious arms crossed on her chest; and Corky and Yvette listened, fascinated.

"About the food," Mora said, moving headlong into the winds of resistance. "With Hope's assistance, we were able to find out what's actually in a lot of the processed food fed to patients. Labels from kitchen cans list more toxins: hydrolyzed wood resin, MSG, disodium phosphate, inosinate and guanylate, so-called 'flavor enhancers,' color protectors, shelf-life increasers, sugar, and caffeine, as well as antibiotics and growth hormones that are fed to, and remain in the tissue of agri-farmed beef and chicken. Many of these chemicals cause cell damage and alter mental and emotional states. What starts out as food is so heavily processed that is has virtually no remaining nutritional value. Most of the additives even deplete what nutrients the body already had available. How can we regenerate nerve cells on this crap?"

Without waiting for an answer, Mora went on. "I've asked other conscious patients for their opinions and they want real food and pure water, too. They unanimously want massage therapy and some would also like to learn how to meditate. Which brings me to the subject of my last item: emotional support." Mora paused long enough to take a deep breath, then continued.

"With the exception of Pam, Yvette, and Corky, I've found a real lack of compassion for patients' emotions among staff. I doubt that any of you here, except Corky and Yvette, really have any idea what it's like to be paralyzed, unable to do the simplest things in life that give one a sense dignity and independence. If you knew the sorrow, the absolute terror and the rage that arise, you might understand how your patients feel. We *need* to be free to feel. . . to cry when we're desperately sad, to express anger without being judged. Okay, maybe it isn't appropriate to kick a stool and scare a nurse, but there's got to be some compassionate middle ground. Is there an old broom closet that can be padded and turned into an emotional release room, for instance?

"As for me, I feel safe crying in private, not with my door wide open. We need to be allowed to feel our normal emotions, not be fed drugs to keep our seams from ripping, not be reprimanded as if we were bad children or convicted felons. I *know* that feeling my emotions has been helping my body, my mind and my spirit to heal. They're all linked together. You can't separate them. We patients need you to stop trying to control us, and start putting your effort into *supporting* us." Mora leaned back in her wheelchair and sighed.

A blanket of silence enveloped the room until doctor Jackson pushed his chair back and stood up, stretched into an exaggerated yawn, and drawled, "Well, I don't know about anyone else but this bull is enough to take my appetite away. I believe we can call this meeting adjourned. Jane, doctor Weiss? Join me for lunch?"

"Doctor Jackson, I believe there's something we've neglected to discuss." Ellen Donovan's sharp voice instantly snatched his attention. "Are you aware that on my daughter's first day in this hospital she was left in the care of an employee who was under the influence of a class B narcotic substance?"

The room fell silent again.

"Mora's attorneys are fully aware of the details and are waiting for us to advise them." Ellen sat back in her chair, raised her head, and waited.

Doctor Jackson's jaw tightened and his face flushed crimson. "You think you've got something, don't you?" he said to Ellen. Then, pointing at Mora, he seethed. "You're right! You *do* belong in a padded cell. And I am personally going to see to it that your permanent medical record carries the medical opinion from two medical doctors that you are violent as well as mentally and emotionally unstable. You can guarantee I'll see you out of here, you witch!" He turned and made a quick exit, his two colleagues following on his tail.

Sparkling fibers of life spread out around Mora's throat and ears and back around through her cervical vertebrae. Highly charged energy tingled every cell at her occipital ridge and sent pulsating currents into her head. The power surge was so great that it flooded her conscious awareness.

"Bravo! What a team!" Hope's energetic cheer broke the silence. She got up, patted Mora's shoulder, veered around Ellen, then shook Corky's and Yvette's hands before the two therapists left for lunch.

"Ohhhh. . . you haven't heard the last of this!" Still fuming, Ellen shook her fist at the empty doorway.

"Maybe I should go up and make sure they deliver your lunch, Mora," Louise suggested, hoping for a quick exit.

"Thanks, Louise." Mora answered, emerging from her trance. "Ma, Hope, the most amazing thing happened!"

"How infuriating!" Ellen stood up and slapped her hand on the table.

"Ma, there's no need to fight with them."

"What do you mean? You're not going to let them get away with it, are you?" Ellen asked incredulously.

"Get away with what? They have nothing I want."

"Mora, this is not. . ." Ellen shook her head impatiently.

"Ma, listen to me." Mora waited until she had her mother's attention before continuing. "The most amazing thing happened inside me when doctor Jackson called me a witch. May I tell you?"

Hope pulled up a chair in front of Mora. "I want to hear."

"This fear of standing up for the truth is really old in me, and I believe that somehow, it's related to my neck. I mean, jeez! Breaking my neck on Breakneck Hill Road tells me I'm on a marked path. When doctor Jackson spoke, something really wonderful happened and now I know I can let go."

"But they can't keep treating people like dirt under their shoes! And what if that stoned orderly really *does* harm a helpless patient? Somebody has to fight them!" Ellen cried out.

"Ma, I love you, but I see something here that you might not agree with. Are you going to listen or not?" Mora set her jaw, then relaxed and laughed. "I can see right now how this is an old example of standing up for myself with *you*, Ma. Hear me out, will you?"

"All right."

"It has everything to do with this situation. Okay, mechanically, my neck is responsible for pivoting my head or my mind. When it's well-adjusted, literally and figuratively, I'm able to see things from all points of view or directions. When I'm afraid to see multiple points of view, my neck becomes rigid. The moment before my death, I saw only one thing, which was that I had failed. When I visited with God, I saw that I was perfect and that there's nothing to fear, not even death. There *is* no death. The real me kept going, and going, and going, and here I am.

"When I came back into my body, I knew I had to finish finding my blocks to love. Doctor Jackson, doctor Weiss, and Jane have done me a great service. They've gone out of their way to show me some of my greatest blocks to love, and I'm grateful for their willingness to play major roles in this movie called 'Mora's Life.' The happy-ever-after part is that I found out I'm intact. I've lost nothing; in fact, I'm really beginning to see the unlimited power of love within me. That's what's been healing me, and I'm going to keep on healing."

"But Mora, if you don't fight them, how are you going to make them change? They're accountable for the harm they've done."

Mora answered calmly. "Ma. You can't make tight muscles relax by forcing them, and it's the same way with human nature. Resistance creates more resistance. Who says they've harmed me, anyway? Have they taken anything valuable away from me? I have everything I really need inside me. I say, let nature take her course. Everything works out. If there's a need for change in their system, it will happen. I say 'God bless 'em' for helping me learn to lay down my arms. It's my arms that seem to be so greatly affected by my broken neck. I need to lay down my old defensiveness and let love heal my arms so I can extend love to others through my arms. I don't want to use my valuable energy to engage in fighting with them."

Ellen listened, sighed, and shook her head.

"Ma, have you ever seen a big, wide, open, grassy field get turned into an asphalt parking lot?"

"Mora. . ."

"Come on, Ma, humor me. You've seen it, haven't you?"

"Of course I have."

"Okay. And haven't you seen the asphalt crack and blades of grass somehow manage to burst through?"

"Yes? So?"

"Well, I'm a blade of grass. Every patient in this hospital is a blade of grass and a hospital bureaucracy can't alter that fact. Real live people need the same things blades of grass need to thrive: sunlight of hope and love, waters of their emotions, and open-minded winds of inspiration. They'll push through the asphalt to get them because you can't stop Mother Nature."

"If it were me, I'd fight back," Ellen insisted.

Mora smiled. "I know. That's why you're an excellent paralegal and I'm an excellent massage therapist. I hope. See how things work out?" Mora grinned, then added, "When doctor Jackson spoke, I focused on my power inside and decided not to react defensively. Instead, I went right into the sensations in my body, in my neck, and watched the thoughts roll across my mind. It was wild! As soon as I sat with myself and didn't resist, the fear vanished and turned into something wonderful. I imagined the outward situation was just like getting a massage and it worked! I'm not in pain anymore!" Mora's eyes flashed with a rare, deep, green light.

Sensing Mora's genuine calm, Ellen relaxed and said, "If I were the patient after a scene like that, I think I'd want to scream or collapse."

"Well, I feel great." Mora turned toward Hope. "How are you holding up, my friend?"

Hope squirmed excitedly. "This is the most fun I've had all year!"

"If you two are ready, I think I'd better go up and eat lunch before my film debut. I'd like to walk. Anyone want a ride in my wheelchair?" Mora asked, grinning.

Hope helped her stand.

"Ma, Hope, may I have a hug first?"

As the three women embraced, Mora said, "Thanks for loving me so much."

*   *   *

Louise was waiting in Mora's room when Jane appeared in the doorway.

"Mora's on her way up," Louise said quickly. Whatever trust she'd had in Jane was now gone.

Jane stepped into the room. "Oh, I'm not here to talk to Mora. I'm here to talk to *you*. You seem like an intelligent woman and I'm sure you have your sister's welfare as a priority. Therefore I am telling you now." She shook a pointed finger a few inches from

Louise's face. "If your sister doesn't shape up, she's out of this hospital and onto the street!"

"I don't think so." Ellen's voice surprised the charge nurse from behind. "Why don't you just go dip your nose into somebody else's soap opera?"

*   *   *

"One, two, three, you're on!"

"Hi. My name is Mora and I'm recovering from four-and-a-half spine-tingling weeks of life in this hospital and complete physical paralysis. Corky, my fabulous occupational therapist, asked me to show you my progress in this training video.

"After spending so much time with Corky, I discovered her work is a lot like an aerobics instructor's because she focuses on what you *can* do rather than what you can't do, even if the only thing you can do is blink. If your patients cry or get angry because they don't have the function they wish they had, just do what Corky does: love 'em and let 'em cry. They'll stop eventually. I say, be courageous and show them what's in your heart. Show them you're a real person. Corky's compassion has been more helpful to me than any technique.

"Before I cracked up. . . my car that is. . . I taught aerobics. So it's natural for me to call out counts and verbal encouragement to people in a roomful of loud music. There's something about upbeat music that makes me want to move. Rhythm lures my bones into motion, saying 'come on, get up and move it'.

"Sing along if you want." Mora turned her torso and motioned toward the student holding a pointer over the easel. "The song is by Prince and it's called 'Baby, I'm A Star.'" Mora touched her chest and the camera slowly followed. "This 'S' stands for Star or maybe it's S-for-Selfish-about-what-I-need-to-recover, or S-for-Still-free." Mora pulled her eyes up to Corky, who stood above her wheelchair. "Ready to roll?"

The camera operator moved out of Mora's close-up into a maximum angle, encompassing the entire room. Against the back wall stood a wide, double-ended ramp. "You can press 'play' now," Mora called out.

Drums led the way. Still sitting in the wheelchair, Mora clumsi-ly touched one foot forward, then back, then the other foot forward, then back, in perfect rhythm with the drumbeat. When the music started, Corky helped her stand. Beginning with the most movable part of her body, Mora swiveled her hips. Back and forth half time, side to side half-time. She sang along with the words.

She began to step forward in half-time rhythm, right on target, slow but tootie-shakin'. Her dramatic exhales took on the vocal syn-copation specific to her former occupation. Corky laughed and occa-sionally sang along while supporting Mora's ramp approach. Although her movement was clumsy, Mora performed with her old impeccable rhythm.

With Corky's hands guarding her hips, Mora arrived at the bot-tom of the ramp, and turned to face the camera. The focus shifted to arm action as Mora rhythmically moved her arms around in small, awkward, bilaterally uneven motions. She panted loudly to the music's beat as a good aerobics instructor would.

Dropping tired arms and still panting, Mora began her inele-gant climb up the ramp, while Corky laughed and guarded. The lyrics-pointing student began to boogie and sing.

Mora reached the top of the ramp and turned to face the cam-era. "Okay, here come the hands!" she called out and the camera focused on her hands. With all her concentration and never missing a single beat, she exhibited whatever motion she had in both hands, then isolated each finger of each hand. At the song's end, applause greeted the Star, and she bowed her thank-yous before the camera.

*   *   *

At 9:30 that night, Hope sat beside Mora's bed and massaged her arm.

"What a day!" Mora sighed behind closed eyes. "I feel like I ran the Boston Marathon. I'm wiped."

Hope held down a hard lumpy spot on Mora's upper arm. "With a day like today, what could possibly happen to outdo it?"

"Watch what you say," Mora sing-songed. "Anyway, I bet you're exhausted after all your research and legwork in addition to your unerring physical, mental, emotional, and moral support. I never could have done it without you."

"It's been my pleasure. And thank you for thanking me." Hope sighed heavily.

"Okay, that's my cue. I have to let you go now."

"Yes, I've got work tomorrow. It won't be long now. Just two more weeks and I'll be in massage school." Hope got up, gathered her things, and leaned over to kiss Mora on the crown of her head. "Good night. See you tomorrow." She turned off the bathroom light and left Mora asleep.

All was quiet as Hope padded softly down the hall at 9:45. She held her breath, hoping to make it unnoticed past the empty nurses' station and into the elevator. She pushed the elevator 'down' button and waited, bobbing up and down, silently coaching it, *come on!* The elevator finally arrived and the doors opened. In a flash she jumped in, quickly turned around and pushed the 'down' button. Just as the doors began to close, the night charge nurse appeared.

"Hey! What are you doing here?" The nurse shouted and ran for the elevator control panel. But the doors closed in her face before she could halt the escape.

Hope prayed all six floors down that there were no security guards at the front entrance.

*   *   *

Safe in her bed upstairs Mora dreamed. . .

All is the color of midnight ocean. . .

deep indigo blue. . .

Inside a candlelit, high-steepled church, a middle-aged woman in severe gray-and-white Puritan dress steps up to a lectern. Seated behind her are an angry man, elder Thomas, dressed in a long black robe, and his wife. The angry congregation stirs.

She speaks, her steely cold eyes issuing forth controlled rage: "I have seen them! She, the devilwoman Abigail Fenn. . . laid her hands upon the Robertson boy. . .with the witch Hortense Coopersmith." Her cold green fire eyes pierce the eyes of the dreamer now. . . cold green flames of

accusation. . . "Burn the witches!" The eyes of death. . .
eyes of death. . .

"Josephine. . ." Mora twitched in half-sleep, the deeply buried memory pushing its way up from beneath her consciousness.

"J a n e ! Doctor Jackson!" Mora screamed, fully awake. Chills raced her spinal circuits as the ancient fright waited for this moment to recognize those eyes. "I CAN SEE NOW! I'M NOT AFRAID ANYMORE!" The door to sight flung open as old terror flew out, gone forever.

- 19 -

A deeper, truer blue than Mora had ever seen in a Northeastern sky greeted her the next morning. She recognized peace and gratitude in all life outside her windows and felt autumn's cool hints of forward movement deep in her bones. She thanked God for giving her the dream, a vision so real that it seemed to unlock a door in her soul. *Give me your troubles and I will give you miracles in return,* she heard the voice inside say, and she smiled. Early morning oatmeal waited patiently for her, but Mora felt no physical hunger, so satiated was she in spirit and thought.

"Mora?" The quivering voice called. "May I talk to you?" Pam peered from behind the door, her eyes red and puffy from crying.

"What happened?" Mora asked, as she motioned a clumsy welcome.

"Jane gave me a six-month suspension from rotations!" Pam burst into tears, then tried to muffle the sound by pressing her hands over her mouth.

"So you won't get into trouble if we close the door. Close it and come over here."

Pam did as she was told. "I don't know if I should tell you what happened." Her head dropped while she sobbed. "Because I'm afraid it would hurt your feelings."

Mora's smile was soft. "No matter what you tell me, I already know who *you* are, Pam. Look at you! You just got canned and you're worried about hurting my feelings. Now that's compassion. But before you tell me, could you help me into my wheelchair?"

Pam jumped into action and within seconds she had Mora mobile.

"So tell me."

Pam recounted her discovery of doctor Jackson and Jane laughing at Mora while she massaged Carlos. "I just couldn't keep my mouth shut! Their outright hostility toward you as a patient, as a person caring for another person. . . it was worse than unprofessional. It was positively degrading! And it made me so damn mad!" Pam's release of emotion cleared the way for her anger to surface. "They're such hypocrites! That word always reminds me of the Hippocratic oath doctors supposedly live by. Huh! Not on this floor!" Pam strode around the room and let off angry steam before taking a seat in front of Mora.

"We studied medical ethics last term," she said in a clear voice. "The Hippocratic oath is tatooed on my brain forever, especially the part that says 'I will follow that system of regimen which, according to my ability and judgment, I consider for the benefit of my patients, and abstain from whatever is deleterious and mischievous.'" She sighed angrily. "Well, I would definitely call their attitudes deleterious and mischievous. I *had* to say something!"

"Maybe it's perfect that this happened," Mora said, calmly placing one swollen hand on the other on her lap.

Pam looked at Mora questioningly.

"One door closes, another one opens, and you're safe throughout because it's just change. What if it's all part of a perfect plan choreographed by the One Who Knows?" Mora pronounced these last three words in a soft deep voice. "What if Someone up there's been listening to your frustrations about rules invented by insecure egos who forgot what really matters. What if God's whispering, 'Hey! Pam! Let it go. You've done your part here. I've got plans for you elsewhere. I have a really important purpose for you and your flaming red hair and voluminous enthusiasm to fulfill, and it's a job nobody but you can do. You've been in training here. This isn't where I need you the most right now. So relax. Now I'm going to open a few new doors to lead you where you'll be the happiest.'" Mora's brightness easily enveloped Pam.

"Do you really think so?" Pam searched Mora's clear eyes. "You mean you think I'm not supposed to be a nurse?"

"I don't know. Do you want to be a nurse?"

"Oh, yes. It's just the butt-kissing I can't stand." Pam's face had calmed from bright red to a flushed pink.

"Is there another form of patient care that focuses more on helping people and less on politics?" Mora asked, searching Pam's face for a clue. "Maybe this suspension might give you a chance to open up to new ideas, to look into other possibilities."

"Yeah. . . maybe so." Pam looked out the window. "Maybe physical therapy, or hospice care, or maybe what you do, I mean what you used to do. Massage."

"Oh, don't give up on me yet. These hands are far from finished." Mora sat relaxed for a moment and a final thought surfaced. "You know, we humans are so resistant to change. We think we have control over life. Then, something different comes along; we're shocked, we panic, we think it means we're going to fall off the edge into death. If only we could let go of our grip just a teensie bit. . ." Mora's eyes dreamily wandered over Pam's shoulder and beyond. "What if we could say 'Oh boy, this is fantastic! Here comes a totally different set-up from what I felt comfortable with!' Or probably it would be more accurate to say 'from what I felt *un*comfortable with!'" Mora considered her own words before continuing. "My advice, which you did not request of course, is to let go and let God show you what He or She has up her sleeve, see what kind of voyage into the unknown you're on. You can always come visit me. I'll be home real soon."

"You're leaving?" Pam's face perked up. "When?"

"I don't know. But for some reason this morning I feel as if I'm already out of here."

"Well. . ." Pam looked around the room and noticed Mora's cold oatmeal. "Hey! Nobody's fed you!" Embarrassed, she added,"I was supposed to. I came in all ready for a full day's work but got suspended first thing."

"I would be honored if you would set me up." Mora glided over Pam's guilt. "I can feed myself now."

Pam pulled the breakfast tray over and opened the milk container, pouring a little on Mora's cold oatmeal.

"Hello!" Ellen Donovan came in, smiling brightly. "How's my poor little helpless waif this morning?"

"Hi, Ma. I'd like you to meet Pam, a newly suspended student nurse who deserves commendation for her courage. Pam, this is my equally courageous mother, Ellen."

The two women shook hands.

"So, you question authority too." Ellen's blue eyes gleamed encouragingly. "Welcome to Systems Busters International. I'm the Southeastern regional director and my daughter here is working undercover."

"Oh, I wasn't aware of your organization but I'm happy to meet you."

Mora laughed. "She's joking, Pam. My mother's favorite hobby, next to whipping up double-breasted tailor-made suits, is whipping out class action suits against discriminating institutions."

"Ohhh. . ." Pam nodded. Just as a tentative smile crept across her face, Jane marched in with doctors Jackson and Weiss in tow.

"I have to go Mora. Bye!" Pam ran out the door in a single bound.

The two doctors positioned themselves against the wall, their arms folded on their chests, while Jane stepped up to Mora and said, "We have something to discuss with you privately." She glared at Ellen.

"I beg your pardon!" Ellen took her position beside Mora. "Anything you have to say to my disabled daughter you can say while I'm a witness!"

Mora turned toward Ellen. "It's okay, Ma. I'll be all right."

"Are you sure? I can stay if you want me to."

"No. It's okay."

Ellen left the room and Jane stepped forward. "Hospital security has informed us that your visitor left after visiting hours last night. As a result of this security violation, we have drawn up a contract. If you refuse to sign this contract, you will be removed from this hospital immediately. I will now read the contract aloud."

The doctors remained silent. Mora sensed the depth of their fear of her, and knew it was this fear that motivated them now. Chills rushed her spine's circuits as she recalled last night's dream.

Jane read: "I, Mora Donovan, agree to have my visitors leave the premesis of Mackenzie Rehabilitation Hospital by 7 P.M. of each day for the remainder of my hospitalization. If I fail to keep this agreement, I will be released immediately." Stepping forward, Jane shoved Mora's uneaten breakfast aside and slapped the contract and a pen on the tray.

Mora earnestly searched the faces of the nurse and doctors now glaring down upon her. "Why do I frighten you so?"

"Sign it!" Jane's eyes narrowed, increasing the concentration of her focused anger.

"I really want to know. Are you afraid I'm trying to take something important away from you?" Mora asked as she studied their faces frozen in angry fear. "If that's what you think, you're mistaken. The fact is, there's enough for everybody."

"You've said plenty already." Doctor Jackson shifted his weight and narrowed his eyes. "Just sign it. Jane, help her write an 'X.'"

Mora looked down at the paper and said, "I haven't tried to write since last week. I couldn't then, but maybe I can now!" She picked up the pen with her right hand, fumbling for a full grasp. The pen slipped out of her hand and onto the tray. She picked it up again, this time determined to hold it in a lighter grasp. "I used to be left handed," she said. "So I don't know how this will come out."

Readying her pen hand into position, she began a large scribble. "M O R . . . whoops!" She raised excited eyes as a first grade child might look up to her teachers and said, "I messed up, but I think I can do it! Let me try again." Returning to her paper she laboriously etched all four letters of her name.

"I *did* it! I can write!" She looked from one angry face to another. "May I have another piece of paper?"

Jane stepped forward and yanked the paper from Mora's hands. "That'll do." She hissed, and marched out the door with doctors in tow.

Mora burst into tears just as Ellen rushed in. "What did they do to you?"

"I can write, Ma!" Mora rested into her first earthly home: her mother's eyes. "Do you have a piece of paper and a pen?"

Ellen rummaged through her purse and quickly produced pen and paper.

Through tearful eyes, Mora tried grasping the pen in her left hand. Holding the paper still with her right hand she began to write her name for the second time. "M O R A . . ." She spelled outloud, crying to see her familiar signature seeping through ever so slightly, reconnecting her heart to her left hand. "D O N O V A N . . ." Some letters were big and squiggly while others tiny and squished. But it was her name, her signature, and she could write!

*   *   *

Ellen and Louise went into the city to shop for Mora's post-hospital attire, while Mora embroidered Hope's tree in her room and watched "The Wizard of Oz" on TV. She threaded and stitched her labor of love into the land of Oz, just in time to see gorgeous, glitzy Glinda reveal herself as the good witch of the North.

"Yep, we're back, Dorothy, and there's nothing you can do about it!" Mora snickered at the TV.

"I'm back," Louise called out as she entered the room.

Mora laughed. "Just in time to see the wizard," she said, and clicked off the television. "Where's Ma?"

"She decided to do a little more shopping herself before coming back." Louise set her full shopping bag on the bed.

"Get any good booty?" Mora asked.

"I hope you like sweat pants and zip-up sweat jackets. It's really all we could find." Louise began removing articles one by one. "Honestly, it's not easy finding fashionable halo vest attire." She laughed and held the royal-blue, hooded jacket up to Mora's chest plate.

"Is this okay?" Louise asked apologetically.

"Oh, sure it's okay. It won't be forever." Mora shivered at her own words. "Jeez! Even the *thought* of being stuck with this cage for the rest of my life gives me the creeps!"

"Mora? May I come in?" A soft voice called out.

"Ruth! What a wonderful surprise!" Mora opened her arms as best she could, and Ruth embraced her. "You remember my sister Louise don't you?"

The two women exchanged greetings. Then Ruth explained her

visit: "I came in to make you an offer."

"What?" Mora caught the whiff of good fortune.

"You know the two-bedroom apartment attached to my house in Duffin?"

"It's hard to forget," Mora answered, recalling the beautiful, light-filled, 200-year-old colonial home surrounded by trees.

"Well, I got this idea. I'd been thinking, 'What's Mora going to do once she's out of the hospital? How is she going to manage living alone in an apartment when she's not able to do things for herself?' So I decided I would explain the situation to Jack and Margo, the couple living there now. I'd tell them that you need special care, that I could be available in emergencies almost 24 hours a day because my home and office are right there." She paused. "Then, you know what happened?" She looked from Mora to Louise, then back to Mora again.

"What?" Mora asked, joyriding the wave of anticipation.

"Two days after I got the idea, Jack, who's been living in that apartment for over four years, knocked on my door and told me he and Margo just bought a house and they're moving!" She laughed. "Isn't that amazing?" Ruth looked excitedly from one to the other and laughed again.

Mora saw the whole idyllic scene collapse into a pit before her eyes. "Ruth, I don't think I can afford your apartment. I can't work yet and I don't know about my future financial situation."

"I know. That's why for the first six months I'd be willing to let you have it for the same amount you paid for your last apartment. Then, I'll raise it a little, then every six months after that until the rent is what I normally charge. That'll give you some time to get your feet back on the ground. What do you say?" Ruth's genuine pleasure in making her offer touched Mora deeply.

"Yes! Of course I want it." Mora's eyes filled with tears. "This is a miracle. Thank you!" She reached for Ruth's hand. "I never could have imagined such a turn of events. I can walk, you know."

"Really?" Ruth's warm brown eyes opened wide. "Gee, a lot's happened in a couple of weeks!"

"You know what else?"

"What?"

"I haven't been in a car yet, not since the crash. I've been wondering if I'd be afraid. I was just thinking. Do you have time to take
me for a ride in your car?"

"You mean now?"

"Do you think you should, Mora?" Louise asked her sister
doubtfully.

"I have to face getting into a car again so I might as well do it
now. I'm ready if you are," Mora answered.

Ruth chuckled. "That's our Mora. What should I do?" She
stood ready next to Mora in the wheelchair.

"Just give me a lift up and we'll walk."

They walked slowly down the hall, past the empty nurses' station, and out to the street. Autumn sunshine broke through fast-
moving clouds that refused to be taken seriously. Carefully, the two
women crossed the street to the parking lot and approached Ruth's
fire-engine-red Audi. Ruth unlocked the passenger side door and,
with meticulous maneuvering, helped Mora climb in.

Once buckled into the driver's seat, Ruth asked, "How are you
doing?"

"I'm going to be just fine," Mora answered, pulling her tearful
eyes over. "Engage."

Just as the two pulled away, Ellen walked toward the hospital's
front entrance and spotted her daughter in the car. She stopped in her
tracks, shook her head, and said out loud, "That girl's a survivor."

*   *   *

By the time dinner arrived, Mora was approaching the final
stitches of her embroidered tree. Her gift-giving anticipation was
growing, generating juice to her healing nerves.

Mora ate dinner alone, absorbed in peaceful thought. That
afternoon Florinda had come to say goodbye. Carlos was being
transferred to another hospital where he would receive the medical
care he needed. Florinda thanked Mora and gave her a hand-made
gift: a sleek, mid-calf length skirt she had designed. "Carlos and I
will never forget you," she said with warm sincerity as they hugged
their goodbyes.

Mora recalled their brief union and treasured it.

Hope came in for massage soon after dinner, and was thrilled about Ruth's offer. They spoke of the way things seemed to be falling rapidly into place. By the time Mora remembered to tell Hope about the contract, her "righteous indignation" energy charge was down to almost zero and approaching joy. The two women joined minds for healing massage in a roomful of gratitude and by 6:45, a full quarter-hour before the new turn-into-a-pumpkin-deadline, Hope was gone.

*　　*　　*

Mora lay on her bed in the dark watching "M.A.S.H." on TV. Just that evening she'd figured out how to push-roll herself onto her side, drop her lower legs over the edge of the bed and, using her strong leg and abdominal muscles to grip the bedside, push-rock-and-roll herself with sufficient momentum to sit up. She took it as a home stretch sign of independence, along with being able to use her strong Sagittarian thighs to lower herself onto the toilet seat. She still took small, cautious steps and couldn't walk a great distance, but she knew she was well on the way.

An aggressive knock on her illegally closed door whipped up her attention at 7:05. Mora decided to have a little fun.

"Who is it?" She sang out while push-rolling herself into a sitting position on the bed. Then she slid her feet to the floor and for the first time, stood up on her own!

"SECURITY!" The male voice boomed ominously through the closed door. "We're coming in to inspect your room!"

"Just a minute," she sing-songed. Then, she pretended in a loud whisper: "Hope! Quick! Hide in the bathroom! Security's here!"

"We're coming in now!" The angry voice threatened just as the door opened. There stood two security guards, one black, one white. "Have you got a visitor in here?" the white guard demanded.

"Oh no, officer, I wouldn't do that! But whatever you do, please don't go in the bathroom. Uh . . . it's a mess!" Mora feigned an exaggerated face of terror.

The serious white guard commanded the bored black guard: "Go look in the bathroom!"

The black guard narrowed disbelieving eyes at his co-worker, then went to the bathroom, turned on the light, and looked around. "Nobody in here."

Recalling silent film scenes of an approaching villain, Mora opened her eyes and mouth wide, backed up toward the bed, and said, "Whatever you do, *please* don't look under the bed!"

The angry white guard commanded the black guard: "Go look under the bed!" The black guard shook his head, sighed, and got down on hands and knees to look. "Nobody under here."

Wondering how far they would go, Mora looked around the room and walked over to the windows. Backing up to them and flaring her arms, she said, "Whatever you do, please don't go out on the ledge! There's nobody out there!"

The white guard looked at Mora, shocked. Then he looked at his bored assistant. When his eyes returned to Mora, he got it.

"Made ya look," Mora chuckled.

The black guard smiled, shook his head and left, his embarrassed boss following behind.

*   *   *

"Ready for a walk?" Yvette of the sunflower face appeared at 10 A.M. sharp the next morning.

"Absolutely. Watch this." Mora said as she performed her getting-out-of-bed routine.

"Whoa. . . that's great! When did you teach yourself that?"

Mora whispered, "I'll tell you aaaaall about it and more once we're outside the building," then winked.

When they reached the sidewalk Mora began telling her rambunctious tale. "You should've seen the look on the white guard's face when he finally got it. What comedy!"

"Yup. There's going to be a lot less excitement around here when you leave." Yvette stopped still at the corner. "But first, I have a special task for you."

Mora grinned, feeling as if she could do anything.

"We're going to fall down on purpose so you can practice getting up."

Mora laughed. "How perfectly wonderful! Nobody can tell me life isn't full of metaphors!" Holding onto both of Yvette's hands

Mora delicately bobbed up and down in place.

They returned to the tiny patch of grass behind the hospital. Following Yvette's expert instructions, Mora bent her knees, lowered herself three-quarters of the way down to the ground, then let herself fall the rest of the way. Her arms and hands were prepared of course, to break her fall. But in the end she landed on her side on the ground, laughing. "How wonderful it feels to have this much power!" Mora push-rolled herself to sitting, then shifted into an awkward, wobbly kneel, and called out for Yvette. Yvette touched Mora's hand, more for reassurance than anything else, and Mora reestablished her center of gravity. Carefully planting one foot flat on the ground, she rebalanced and in one swift motion, threw the other foot down and pushed herself up to stand. Yvette caught her just in time.

"What's left for me to do now?" Mora asked, wondering if there was a hidden answer.

Yvette shrugged. "More of the same, but I'd call you graduated."

Mora smiled and sighed. "Ahhh. . . as Nelson Mandela said when they released him: 'My body was in prison but my mind was free'."

The two women headed back to the pen.

*   *   *

The next day, exactly two months after the crash, Mora went home.

Hope and Ellen arrived after breakfast to pack up. Mora had insisted that Hope not come in on her last night, saying she wanted to spend it alone in contemplation. The truth was, she wanted to finish her embroidery. The brown trunk and branches now gave rich green life to a profusion of specks that were lush leaves. The words "Thank You Hope" arced over the tree in purple thread, and Mora had added "Love Mora" beneath the tree's ground. She even managed to stitch in a few yellow rays of sunlight shining over all.

Hope cried when Mora gave her the gift and vowed to treasure it forever.

As soon as everthing was packed and ready to go, Mora took a final look around the room of her transformative tribulations. "Goodbye, old womb," she said to the empty bed and open space.

"Thank you for holding me."

All hospital patients were required to be released on a conveyance, so Ellen and Hope wheeled Mora out in her trusty perambulator. Silently, as they passed occupied patient rooms, Mora said goodbye and thought, *I'll remember each one of you. No matter what, hold onto your hope.* Mora thought how strange it was that other hospital lives would proceed as usual, while hers was suddenly wide open, new, and free.

Ellen pushed the elevator button for the last time and they waited. Just then, Jane came out of the nurses' break room to stand behind the nurses' station counter. She looked at Mora with indifferent eyes that had already forgotten her.

"Thanks for everything, Jane," Mora said, honestly grateful.

Jane nodded and returned to her paperwork. When the elevator arrived and the doors opened, she raised her head and said blandly, "Good luck in your future life."

"Thanks, but I'm not finished with this one yet," Mora answered.

Hope laughed and the three women quickly piled in. With great relief they watched the doors close on another day in Mackenzie Rehabilitation Hospital's Spinal Cord Injury Unit.

- 20 -

Mora drank in the aromatic autumn winds sweeping out the dead and boldly tempting the new to enter. Gazing out the window of Hope's car on the way to Duffin, she imagined herself as an innocent prisoner finally released to freedom's unknown future. The necessary dependency on the hospital was suddenly gone, along with the expected payment of submission. She pictured herself now living a life of delicious, private silence blended with chosen companionship, at any time of day or night, and for any reason. The joy of freedom outweighed any fears about her needs being met.

As if hearing her daughter's thoughts, Ellen spoke up from the back seat. "The visiting nurse is scheduled to start tomorrow morning. I wonder if we can get her to do any cleaning, although we did a pretty good job of it yesterday. Oh, I can't wait to see how all your things will look in the new apartment."

"Did the moving crew deliver everything?"

"I'm sure. Ruth said she let them in at 9 this morning and it's 1 now. Besides, you really didn't have much." Ellen sat back, soaking in New England's vibrant, colorful foliage. "This is the one time of year I really miss the North."

Louise had said her goodbyes-for-now at the hospital and driven directly to the airport. Claire would be next to fill the sister-care shift. Later in the week, she was expected to arrive from Florida to help close the doors of Fitness & More.

Ellen and Claire had full-time jobs from which they were taking leaves of absence, and Louise's family didn't like having her away too long. These familial feats of compassion were not lost on their recipient. Mora's trauma had revived family ties that had seemingly lain dormant for years.

The unexpected gifts of support helped ease the sorrowful burden Mora had yet to face. Fitness & More was fast slipping through fingers still too weak to hold it. Sometimes she believed she could surrender to the financial facts and just let go. But mostly she mourned her creation's impending death. Louise's husband Donald, the financial wizard in the family, suggested she sell it.

"Sell what," she'd asked him, "a reputation?" What was the market value of all the labor, thought, heart and spirit she had poured into her dream-child for five years? It had been a service of love to the community and the community's choice to participate wasn't for sale. Now Mora either had to invest more money and effort toward a remotely possible profit, or walk away empty-handed. She'd already turned the corporate contracts over to a go-getter employee. If she sold what little equipment remained there would be enough money for final paychecks and customer refunds. Without her physical involvement there was no way F&M could survive beyond another payroll.

"You're not running a business," her brother-in-law had answered, as if accusing her of the worst crime in America. "You're running a damn charity."

Although Mora knew he was right, she had defended herself anyway. "Look, I majored in sociology. My favorite system is a mix of social-capitalism and that's what I tried to create. I just didn't get the capitalism part right."

"How are you doing, Mora?" Solid and stable behind the wheel, Hope seemed to have heard Mora's thoughts, too.

"I was just thinking about the club and what I'm going to have to do." Mora sighed, relieved to say the truth.

Hope shot a glance at her friend to read her face. "One thing's for sure. Whatever it is you're going to do, you're not doing it today. Today is a day of celebration for your new life, in a beautiful new place, surrounded by people who love you."

"That's right, honey." Ellen leaned forward and touched Mora's shoulder. "Everything's going to work out fine. To borrow one of your phrases, I can just feel it. This is a happy day, don't you think?"

"And here we are." Hope turned down the long gravel road protected by overhanging rows of bright, broad, yellow-leafed oak trees. "Home sweet home."

"What are all these cars doing here?" Mora asked.

"Hmmm. . . I wonder." Hope helped Mora out of the car and walked her to the back door while Ellen carried her belongings. They opened the door and stepped into an energetically loaded living room.

"SURPRISE!" shouted twenty or thirty souls as they jumped out of closets, the bedroom, and the kitchen. "WELCOME HOME!"

Mora stood still, her mouth dropped open, and she burst into tears. "Thank you for caring about me," she said.

Katie, an aerobics instructor, stepped forward. "We knew you could do it, Mora, and we were rooting for you all the way. We wanted to show you how glad we are that you're home."

Hope emerged from the kitchen carrying a huge cake covered with lighted candles and topped with the words "Happy Homecoming" in green icing. Everyone joined in singing one revised verse of the birthday tune. "Do you want to blow out your candles?" Hope asked.

Mora wiped her tears and looked around the room into each caring face. "You'll never know how much your prayers and loving thoughts have meant to me, that you didn't forget me." Lowering her eyes, she cried again.

Never one to encourage sadness at a party, Ellen gently pressed a tissue into Mora's hand. Mora understood her mother's nudge and honked her nose loudly, to make everyone laugh. Then she asked, "Did you all move my things today?"

Out from the sea of nodding heads someone said "Yep, and we're hungry! Blow out them candles and let's chow down!"

Mora took a few building breaths and, with all her respiratory might, blew out half the candles. Inhaling deeply, she finished them off.

While trays of food were passed among the happily buzzing crowd, Mora took her time answering questions and receiving hugs. As fatigue began to creep over her, she stepped carefully into her new bedroom and answered the beckoning call of the colonial window's uneven glass. She soaked in all that Mother Nature presented.

The lush green lawn lay comfort at her feet. Great, healthy old trees burst with yellow, red, and orange leaves. She pictured herself walking, sitting, and lying on the secure ground, inhaling the pungent green grass and fresh clean autumn air. She imagined herself watching fast-moving clouds dance with birds above her and saying good-bye to geese on their way south. Everywhere life was rich.

"Want some company, sweetie?"

It was her long-time friend Lenore, standing in the bedroom threshold. "Sure," Mora answered, and walked over to the edge of the bed. "But I think I'm pooping out. I need to sit down."

"Need help?"

"No, it just takes me a minute." Mora slowly lowered herself down.

"You're pretty amazing." Lenore shook her head. "Nobody I know could do what you've done."

"I don't know about that." Mora raised her eyes calmly. "Strength you never knew you had suddenly appears. I don't think I'm really any different from anyone else. . . maybe a teeeeenie bit more dramatic."

The two friends laughed over a favorite topic. Both Sagittarians, they shared a penchant for the theater of life.

"You have to admit it though," Lenore said, "not everybody would be such a fighter."

"If you mean deciding to live, then maybe you're right. I had a choice, you know. If you mean fight with somebody about whether or not I can live in my own way, I guess I had to tell a few people they couldn't dominate my spirit."

Lenore burst out laughing. Pressing her hand to her chest, she rocked back and forth. "That day I came in to see you. . ."

Mora flushed crimson. "Oh, yeah."

"It was the first time I saw you in your metallic support system. There you were, lying motionless in your bed. Ugh! What a shock you were to behold. And as soon as you saw me, you cried out 'Lenore, what if I can't ever play with myself again.' I didn't know whether to laugh or cry. I really wanted to laugh but you looked so. . . so. . ."

"Pitiful," Mora suggested.

"Yes!" Lenore clapped her hands together.

"Imposing."

"Of course."

"Like the Statue of Liberty." Mora was on a roll.

"Yes! And here you are now, still playing with yourself."

Laughter cast an instant spell over them and just as quickly, Mora shook it off. "I don't know how things will go, what I'll do, if I'll ever do massage again. . ." Her eyes flew out the window and rested upon the emerald carpet.

"Don't worry, sweetie. Everything's going to work out fine. You'll see. I just know it." Lenore touched Mora's arm. "You've been so far down already, where else is there to go but up?"

Mora smiled, even as tears filled her eyes. "Thanks for being my friend all these years."

"I love you, too," Lenore said and she put her arms around Mora. "Do you want to get some rest?"

"I'm okay, I can sleep later. It isn't every day a girl gets to be homecoming queen. Only this crown doesn't come off." Mora laughed at her own joke.

"How long are you supposed to keep it on?"

"Doctor Anwar said at least three months. Three months will be my birthday, November 25th. Getting rid of it would be the best birthday present ever."

Lenore looked around the room. "How about if I start unpacking some of your clothes and you tell me where you want them?"

"Okay, but only if I can lie down."

One beloved article of clothing at a time, Mora saw her old life's story waltz by. Since Lenore had always been a deep-secret-telling buddy, Mora shared her reminiscing. They laughed, recalling playful times as well as shadow times.

Mora's friend George stuck his head into the room. "We're leaving you in peace now, Mora. Is there anything else you need?"

"Have you got a million dollars and a videotape of my life in five years?"

"Well, I just hope there's enough room in that big head of yours to remember how happy everybody is to see you. Your mother has my number if you need anything. I'll come by next week to visit."

"Thanks for everything, George."

Guests said their goodbyes and by mid-afternoon Mora and Ellen were alone in the house.

"Want me to help you get under your covers?" Ellen wore her mommy-is-concerned expression that never failed to comfort.

"I think I could sleep for a whole day. I don't know why I'm so tired. I slept like a log last night."

"Are you kidding? All this excitement, the anticipation, the acitivity, being a hostess. . . that doesn't even include the energy your body needs for recovery." Ellen smiled and gently removed Mora's shoes, then cozied her between soft flannel sheets. The familiar pillows called Mora's heavy head to rest. *And now I'm closer to my own pillow. Thank you, God, for giving me my life.* She greeted the solid, friendly ceiling and fell asleep instantly.

When Mora awakened, the early evening amber sun serenely passed her on its way west. She lay still, inhaling every peaceful breath, then push-rolled herself into sitting up, dropped her feet to the floor, mobilized strong thighs, and stood up. On her way to the kitchen, she stepped high, just in case she encountered anything unexpected. The space and floors of the "real world" appeared risky enough to tread cautiously. She walked into the kitchen like Frankenstein's monster, purposefully resting all her weight first on one foot, then the other.

Ellen was there, beaverishly emptying boxes and stocking cabinets. "Did you have a good nap, honey?" She pulled a chair out from the small kitchen table. "Here, why don't you sit down for a while."

"Okay." Slowly Mora sat down.

"Can I get you a nice cup of tea?"

"I love the Irish way you always offer 'a nice cup of tea' to make anything better, Ma. Yes, I would love a cup of tea."

Ellen put the kettle on, removed two mugs from the old-fashioned, glass-fronted cabinet, and returned to her task. "Ah. . ." She lifted Mora's bathroom curtains out of the box. "I was looking for these. I wonder if they'll match in your new bathroom."

Home decorating held a magical power of rejuvenation for the Donovan women. "Let's go see," Mora answered, and she slowly followed her mother into the bathroom. As Ellen held the burgundy and beige fleur-de-lis patterned curtains against the windows, chills shot up and down Mora's spine. The curtains exactly matched the wallpaper, except that the colors were reversed.

"Oh my God!"

"What?" The frog of panic jumped out Ellen's throat.

"It matches exactly!" Mora's wide-open eyes searched Ellen's for recognition. "I made these curtains for my other apartment, months ago, when I'd never even seen this bathroom! Do you know what this *means*, Ma?"

"It means I won't need to make new curtains."

"No, it means I'm *meant* to live here! It's a sign!"

"Well, that's good because. . . here you are," Ellen teased. She didn't regard synchronicity as highly as her daughter did.

Ellen laid the curtains on the bathroom counter when the teakettle whistled. By the time Mora moseyed behind, her tea was set. They sipped while chatting about how they would fix up the new nest.

The spacious kitchen, a 1920s addition to the old farmhouse, still held the memorable essence of thousands of meals prepared for large families. Mora visualized herself, haloless of course, wearing an apron and waltzing about the kitchen. She would bake scrumptous apple pies while rays of sunlight poured through her bright, peaceful home. And the trees! Surrounded by these luscious, strong, healthy trees, she knew she would grow well and have a fruitful and happy life, no matter what was in store for her body's future.

Ellen dug into the box again, this time retrieving the blue flower-patterned slipcover she'd made for Mora's curvacious Victorian couch. They took it into the living room, where Ellen began to fit it over the couch.

"Oh my God!" Mora shouted once more.

"Mora! You're making me nervous. What's the matter now?"

"*Look!* The wallpaper matches the colors in the slipcover better than if you and I had gone to the fabric store and gone through 300 bolts of material until we came to this one!"

Ellen held the fabric up to the wallpaper. "I guess you're right. It is a beautiful match."

"You made this for me while I was in my other apartment. And it looked awful there, you said so yourself. Remember?" Mora tried to extract excitement from Ellen. "You have to admit Ma, these are signs that I'm meant to live here."

Ellen resumed expertly fitting the slipcover on the couch. When it was finished she stepped back and said, "You're right. Now that it's on, I can see how perfect it really is." She smiled tenderly at her daughter.

Mora sat down in the kitchen to rest while Ellen ran on a second wind. Or was it her third or fourth? Mora's weary eyes watched her mother scurry upstairs and down, back and forth. "MA! Stop!"

Ellen halted in her tracks. "What?"

"You're wiping me out watching you do so much. Give yourself a rest, will ya, before I collapse from your exhaustion." Mora laughed, letting her mother know she was joking but meant it.

"Oh, I'm just going to do a little more, then I'll stop and make us some dinner. Are you hungry?"

"A little. We can have leftover pizza if you want. I wish I could cook. Maybe I can do something." Mora looked sadly around the kitchen.

"You will. Just be patient."

"You mean like you?" Mora teased.

"Do you want to see how I set up the upstairs room?" Ellen asked.

Mora looked at the winding staircase. "I guess I can try holding onto the railings. They look sturdier than my arms."

Slowly, one foot shoved up to the wooden wall of each next step, Mora climbed the winding staircase while her mother spotted from behind. At the top, Ellen opened the French door and they entered the spacious room. Mora stood beneath the small steeple in the center and absorbed the evening light coming through two wood-framed windows.

"Oh Ma!"

"What now?"

"Remember the dream I had about doing massage in an upstairs room? And working on people who felt hopeless who were sent to me by three doctors? Remember?"

"Yes, I remember."

"This is the room! Now I *know* I'm going to do massage again! I can feel it here as if it's already happened!" Mora raised her eyes to the ceiling's steeple. "My table's going right where I'm standing. I *know* it!" Mora's face lit up with joy. "I know it," she whispered and tears slid down her cheeks. "God wouldn't have brought me this far if I couldn't give back what I have."

Ellen watched her daughter's strength of spirit shine. "I'm so proud of you, Mora."

Mora opened her arms. "I really love you, Mommy," she said, and with their embrace, mother and daughter blessed the space.

*   *   *

A week later, Ellen and Claire switched places. The task that lay ahead now filled Mora with dread. This was the day Fitness & More would die.

So far Mora had stayed close to home, going out only for walks away from the public eye. But the account had to be closed in person; so Claire dropped her off at the front entrance of the bank. She entered with lowered eyes and stepped up to a teller. "I need to close my business acount."

Tears filled Mora's eyes as she wrote the final check. Feeling the teller's intrusive stare she raised her eyes and demanded, "What are you looking at?"

Without taking her awe-filled eyes off Mora's head, the teller grimaced and said "What are those things in your head?"

Mora's tears broke. She considered fleeing but another thought pushed its way through.

"Miss, it really hurts my feelings that you're staring at me. Do you mind?"

A woman seated at a desk several feet behind the teller stepped up to the window. "Is there a problem here?" she asked.

The teller answered apologetically, "I've just never seen any-thing like that before."

"It's called a halo. I broke my neck in a car crash and it's hold-ing my neck in place." Her tears subsided, Mora slid the check under the window.

The supervisor glanced first at the check, then kindly at Mora. "Ms. Donovan, I'll have a talk with Diane but please accept my apol-ogy if she's offended you in any way."

Mora raised her eyes and saw one who understood and one who was learning. "It's okay," she fibbed, swallowing her sorrow. She took the last twenty-seven dollars, shuffled toward the door, and let the tears fall.

Claire jumped out of the car and ran to help her sister climb in. Helpless to stop the flood, Mora covered her face with her hands for the ride home. Back at the house, she collapsed into bed and poured her grief into her pillow. "God, I did everything I could, and still I couldn't make it work. I'm so tired." She sobbed, allowing the old feeling of fail-ure to rise up. It was too great a burden to carry another step, so she dropped all that was left into her pillow and onto the lap of God.

*   *   *

Days passed, weeks came and went, without much disturbance from the outer world. Daily living functions gradually returned, family returned to their homes, and Mora's life settled into a routine. Early each morning before the rest of the world awakened she read and meditated, sitting in the kitchen where she could watch as rosy dawn silently brought hope. Alone in her peaceful home, she talked to God openly. Right then, she knew it was the most worthy occupa-tion she could have. *The rest will come. All that I need will be provided. I'm safe in God's care now. I've come home.*

Compassion for all she had been through blossomed. Mora rec-ognized that surrendering to solitude filled an ancient need shared by her soul and God. It was a time of gratitude for her life, and unex-pected gifts kept coming.

Ruth and other neighbors helped Mora with grocery shopping. For the first few weeks, a nurse came every day for bathing, dress-ing, meals, and basic housekeeping. A physical therapist helped with exercises until she could do them independently. Hope loaned her a stationary bicycle and, before massage school grew too demanding, continued her attentive massages. At just about the same time Rose, a former Fitness & More customer who had just graduated from massage school, offered to massage Mora regularly free of charge. When Mora asked her why, Rose answered, "Because I want to." Mora watched in awe as each need was miraculously met.

The life of her body was growing too. "If I can walk, I can dance!" was how Mora saw things, and little by little she tried light dance steps in her living room. Strong hips and thighs led the show while the rest of her still-weak upper body followed along.

Mora's 34th birthday arrived. She pictured the day as she wanted it: prayer and meditation, exercise, breakfast and nap. Then Hope would take her to doctor Anwar's office, where he would release her from the halo's prison forever! She reran the unlocking scene over and over in her mind. Afterward, she would change into a lovely dress and go out to a birthday dinner with Hope.

But that wasn't all. That night she would take her first purely naked shower alone, and put on the feminine, pale blue-and-white flannel and satin nightgown Nana Donovan had sent. Then, at last, she would lay her head on the pillow and sleep, nothing between her body and the natural world.

Hope arrived at the appointed time and gathered up Mora's dress-up clothes. The two women gleefully headed out for "Operation Halo Removal." As they sat in doctor Anwar's hospital waiting room, Mora sensed a palpable atmosphere of trust, hope, gratitude, and good will among the waiting patients. Striking up a conversation with the patient beside her, Mora shared her story while another patient joined in with his. It was the most uplifting experience she'd ever had in a doctor's waiting room.

"Mora, you can go in now."

"Good luck," Hope said as Mora went into the examining room.

Doctor Anwar's familiar green eyes greeted her. "How have you been, Mora?"

"Great, considering the circumstances," she answered, wiggling while she waited for him to proceed.

He removed the screwdriver from his pocket and applied it to her front left pin. Mora closed her eyes. . . and felt the pin's pressure on her skull increase. Her shocked eyes flashed open. "What are you *doing?*"

"I'm tightening the pins, of course."

"But you said you'd remove the halo after three months!" Mora cried.

"No, I said you would wear the halo for a minimum of three months."

"Today is three months," Mora wailed, "and it's my birthday. Please doctor, take the halo off for my birthday!"

"But Mora, we need to be sure your neck is stable, that it has fused properly before we can remove it."

"But I *am* stable! Watch!" Desperately, Mora let her body slide off the table until her feet reached the floor. Once standing, she began humming and dancing around the room, using every bit of body she had that was awake.

Doctor Anwar's mouth fell open. "Wait one minute please! I will return in a moment. Don't move!" he said with uncharacteristic surprise. He rushed from the room and within seconds, returned with doctor Jacobs, the orthopedic surgeon who had assisted Mora's surgery with a hip bone graft. "Mora, please demonstrate for doctor Jacobs what you just showed me!"

The two doctors watched in amazement as Mora repeated her performance with extra enthusiasm for a larger audience. She hummed and danced around the room. Pretending she had wings, she spread her arms as far as they would go, gliding past the astounded physicians and out into the waiting room. She swirled around smiling patients and Hope's laughter before coming to a smooth halt before the doctors. When doctor Jacobs left, doctor Anwar removed Mora's halo.

"We're going to give you a collar to wear during the day. It will still provide neck support, in fact, even more specific neck support than before. You must remove it for bed at night." He laid her cage, her home away from home, on the examining table next to Mora. She scrutinized it.

"Gee. . .it looks so small out there away from me. To think that's what held me together." Her eyes filled with tears as she saw the vulnerable self she had been, living inside the protective metal, plastic and lambswool monster.

"Do you want it as a souvenir?" The doctor joked.

"No thanks! When you're through with one of those, you're *through*. Bye-bye, trusty old halo." Mora closed her eyes and let doctor Anwar clean the empty pin holes. He pressed a bandage strip over the two front indentations and left the back two to scab under her hair. "My head feels like it's expanding, settling, like the fissures are falling into place. Oh, this is wonderful!" Carrying five pounds less in weight made her feel almost gravityless.

Wearing her much less imposing collar, Mora presented her new self to Hope. Elation accompanied them as they stepped lightly through dressing up, going out to birthday dinner, and finally home where the shower called out to her.

Still unable to lift her arms, Mora required Hope's assistance in preparation, then was left alone. Stepping gently into the steamy spray, she stood beneath the warm splash. . . refreshing, cleansing, clearing water, water, water. . . sweeping clean every inch of her flesh, her hair, her face, her bare chest and back, her free and unencumbered body. Now she was one single unified body, rejoined under the flow of clean, clear water.

"Thank you God, for giving me this life," she said out loud. "Thank you God, for giving me this life!" Each time she said it, subtle, electrifying surges generated more life inside her, more water flushed down, down, down and over her thirsty, grateful flesh. Then she sang it, composing the tune on the spot. For the rest of her life, she would always remember that moment, whenever she sang it again: "Thank you God, for giving me this life, Thank you God, for giving me this life!"

After the shower, Mora stood in front of the mirror for a long time, absorbing the beautiful sight of her freed head and neck. Compassionate tears fell for all that she saw, for the strong, gentle woman standing before her who had the will to survive. Femininity wanting desperately to be expressed through her body was tenderly reassured. "You must be patient. Your hair will grow. The wounds will heal. You will come back into your womanhood again. But you must be patient." Stepping into the long nightgown that reminded her of Snow White, she managed to drag it up over her body. Soft flannel ruffles and white satin ribbons graced its tiny white flowers on a blue background.

Mora's bed had been made up that morning in freshly laundered floral sheets. Now, she approached it ceremoniously and, using all the effort in both hands as well as her legs, push-pulled down the covers. She sat down on the edge of the bed, positioned her legs to hold steady, and slowly lowered her free self down. Her head touched the soft pillow and finally rested there with nothing between herself and soft comfort. Her body's time of alienation was over. "I'm back together again God. Thank you for my life."

- 21 -

Autumn swept the active world away to cozy up to winter fires. All around her, Mora watched other lives moving in full involvement while she healed. The white, quiet world of winter brought cold bright sunlight into her nest, guiding a slow ascent up the stairs of recovery. One nerve fiber at a time, one sensation at a time, Mora moved forward. Still, some threads remained asleep for a long, long time. The days formed a steady pattern of prayer and meditation, nurturing body and soul, and visiting with friends new and old.

When spring came, doctor Anwar promoted Mora to a soft collar. She didn't last too long in that one, abandoning it for the increasing security of gradual movement. And along with the budding spring came an opportunity of a most unexpected nature.

Still physically unable to seek employment, and living frugally on the single insurance payment, Mora had plenty of time on her hands. Her daily walks grew longer and she began to rebuild endurance. One day she learned of a neighbor, Mark, who had broken his neck in a rock climbing fall. One inspiration snapped onto another; within two months, Mora borrowed money to buy a used car. She decided she didn't need doctor Anwar's permission to drive, primarily because she didn't want to risk snagging her already-made-up mind with his disapproval. Since she lacked sufficient function to operate a stick shift, the car had an automatic transmission and plenty of wide window views, which minimized the need to turn her head. Another healing milestone was reached the instant Mora got into the driver's seat. Although it took all the effort in both arms to push-pull the shifter into drive, she was mobile again, and unstoppable. Driving slightly under the speed limit for the first time in her life, she cautiously set out on her maiden voyage to the Boston rehab hospital where Mark was a patient.

He gladly accepted her offer of twice weekly massages. Still recovering herself, the work didn't really amount to "massage" any more than what she'd done for Carlos had. But besides lending comfort to a struggling soul, Mora was convinced that having a helping goal accelerated her own healing. Lying awake in bed at night, after she had massaged her only client, she felt surges of gratitude flush every cell in her body. How could such an important piece of life, this giving to another what had once been lost and then found, not help her to heal?

One day six months after she got out of the hospital, Mora carefully chopped her first fresh vegetable salad and wondered how life would present an opportunity for her to earn a living. As if the heavens had watched and heard her readiness, they sent a reply in the form of a telephone call.

"Mora, you may not remember me, but I used to be in Jody's aerobics classes." The woman's voice carried urgency over the wires. "I saw her in the grocery store yesterday and she told me how miraculously you've recovered. Something told me to give you a call and find out if you were doing massages again."

Mora expressed her surprised thoughts out loud. "Well, I haven't given a real massage for payment yet. I don't have all my hand and finger function back, but I've been modifying movements so I compensate with other parts of my body like elbows, soft fists, things like that. I could certainly try. It would be different from the heavy massages I gave before but. . . sure! I could give you a massage." Mora felt the blessed door open again, but wider this time. Something broader was in store, she could just feel it.

"I'm sure whatever you could do would help me," The woman answered without hesitation. "If you could recover from all that and be doing as well as you are, I want you to work on me. It's kind of a mix of physical and emotional, if you know what I mean."

"Indeed I do!" Mora laughed and silently thanked God for bringing her back.

Over the next few months, abundance flowed miraculously into Mora's life. Calls for her help came in as word spread and clients old and new made appointments. People with a vast array of emotional, mental, physical, and spiritual injuries asked for help. Her days were filled with focused self-care, plenty of rest, and extending hope and healing to others. In the helping, she grew in strength of spirit as well as finances.

That summer Mora planted a glorious garden of flowers alongside bountiful basil and tender tomatoes. A year after she left the hospital she was completely self-supporting. Her new, simpler life was rooted in a proven true reliance on spirit. She went to recovering alcoholics meetings, made new friends, shared her miraculous story with those who asked, and prospered in peace beyond any she had ever known.

Mora received referrals from four doctors, not the three of her foretelling dream: One was a medical doctor, two were doctors of chiropractic, and the fourth was her friend and minister client, doctor Howard. He resumed his weekly massages, confidentially unburdening himself of stress as the bond between them deepened. Mora described her work to him one day: "I love nurturing the nurturer. I feel I'm actively fulfilling my part of the plan that I prayed for while I was paralyzed."

"I feel very privileged to be one of your clients, my dear," doctor Howard said, "and I want to refer one of my parishoners to you. Would you like me to tell you about her?"

"Definitely." Mora pulled out her kitchen chair for him while she sat listening intently.

"Her name is Teresa. She sixteen years old and she's dying of a brain tumor. Her neurologist has already told her that she has just a few months to live. Her brain function appears to be deteriorating, and she's rapidly losing speech and movement coordination. It's heartwrenching to watch this once-beautifully vibrant, blossoming girl. . . young woman I should say . . . approach death. Just last year she was an honor student and a star basketball player." Doctor Howard sighed heavily. "I thought that in her last few months of life, it would be good for her to have whatever pleasurable, comforting experiences with her body she can. And I thought massage would be perfect. May I refer her to you?"

"I'd be glad to help any way I can," Mora answered without hesitation.

"I knew you would. I've already discussed it with her doctors, her parents and of course with Teresa herself. She seemed excited about it, so we all think it's a good idea." Doctor Howard arose from his chair and smiled warmly. "I'll have her mother call you to set up the appointment. Same time next week for me?"

"Sure," Mora answered as they shared a hug.

The following week, Teresa's mother escorted her up Mora's front walk. Mora watched the beautiful young woman lean on her mother like a crutch while she labored through every step. Mora welcomed them, extended her hands to Teresa's, and helped her into the massage room.

"Have you ever had a massage before?"

"Uh. . . ayeee. . . uh. . . nooo. . ." Teresa's verbal struggle evoked tears.

Mora's bright, compassionate eyes filled too, but they were seeded with joy. Some strong fervor rising within her told her not to be preoccupied with Teresa's death but rather, to recognize her life in the present moment. Mora gently touched Teresa's arm. "May I comfort you? I'm very honored that you're allowing me to help you. I just know you'll feel better with massage."

Teresa lifted her head unsteadily and struggled to focus her eyes on Mora's. Mora allowed her time to find what she needed there, and after a long moment, Teresa blinked.

Mora's hands extended comfort with long, smooth, tender strokes while her deepest mind offered safe nurturance. *I am with you now, child. . . . All is well. . . you are safe. I will care for you as long as you need me.* The surprising words fit Mora's intention exactly. As she cradled the young woman's head in her hands, Mora's sight moved from her body's eyes to etheric vision. Patterns of light in Teresa's energy field swerved until a steady pattern emerged, and remained still. As in a trance, the fields of light guided Mora's hands, and she intuitively touched the young woman's heart and crown. With each place she touched Teresa, Mora knew she was being guided to reach the bottom of the well.

When Mora finally took her eyes off Teresa and noticed their surroundings, she saw the room outlined in thin layers of multi-colored light and unified by an overlying field of white light. Everything, including Teresa and herself, appeared slightly elevated off the floor. Mora knew she was on target.

Each week Teresa arrived escorted, seemingly unchanged except for the enthusiastic smile she wore as she greeted Mora. Her speech seemed to come and go. When it was present, the two women shared humor about life, a keen body awareness, and an uncanny familiarity that hinted at a tender bond that had always been there.

Mora began each session on Teresa's head as she lay supine, contacting that miraculous spot, the information center below the occipital ridge. Mora sat on her stool and held Teresa's head, picturing the opening of Teresa's internal communication system. She shared her vision with Teresa.

"Teresa, as I'm holding your head right now, I see light coming in through the top of my head, filtering down through me as if I were a wire, traveling through my arms and hands, through your skull and directly into your brain. The light is nourishing your brain, feeding you what you need to thrive. I see light going into every one of your brain cells and every cell of your body." Mora opened her eyes and looked down at Teresa. She saw bright, white light radiate from Teresa's head and tears slide into her ears.

*   *   *

One luscious summer morning Mora was weeding her garden. She dug her bare hands into the rich, moist soil, inhaling the pungent blend of dirt, floral bouquet, and her own sweat. Surrounded by a profusion of purple-pink cosmos that stood proudly over all, she could almost hear them say "Look at me! Look at me!" Carnations, zinnias, marigolds, and asters opened their promising, cheerful faces to the sun.

Suddenly, a picture in Mora's mind sent enough energy through her body to jolt her into standing upright. She saw herself crowning Teresa with a bountiful floral wreath, saying, "I crown you

Teresa, ruler of your own destiny." When she tried out the grand declaration on the garden population, a cool breeze swept across the flowers and lush carpeted lawn, as if applauding. Ruth's dog Daisy ran around the side of the house barking and wagging her tail.

"Yes!" Mora shouted, and began picking perfect flowers for Teresa's afternoon coronation. She asked each plant's permission before picking, leaving behind those that resisted. She ran into the house, where she dextrously fashioned the crown with flowers and leaves, and tied long, streaming satin ribbons onto the back. *How did this skill came to me so easily, God, even though I've never made one of these before? See how perfect it is!* When she finished, she presented it to the sky for blessing.

It took every ounce of patience for Mora to contain her excitement until afternoon. And just moments before Teresa was to arrive, Hope appeared.

"Hey girl, I thought you had massage clinic this afternoon?" Pleasantly surprised to see her dearest friend, Mora welcomed Hope inside.

"Cancelled. On my way home, I got a loud hint to come by and see you." Hope caught sight of the flower hair wreath. "Wow. . . where did you get that?"

"I just made it. My first one. Isn't it beautiful?"

"You're kidding! It looks professional."

The doorbell rang. They looked out the window to see Teresa standing at the door with her mother.

Hope focused intently on Teresa. "Who's *that*?" she asked.

"My client, Teresa," Mora answered. Noticing Hope's odd behavior, she added, "What's wrong?"

"Whew!" Hope shook her head and shoulders, as if trying to wake herself from a dream. "I don't know. . ." she said, still staring at Teresa through the window.

"Well, I have to help Teresa in. Would you mind putting the wreath upstairs on top of the shelf? It's a surprise for her. Then I'll introduce you."

"Sure."

While Mora slowly escorted Teresa into the kitchen, Hope ran upstairs and returned.

"Teresa, I'd like you to meet my dearest friend, Hope. Hope, this is Teresa." Mora's smile faded when she saw Teresa and Hope lock eyes. They appeared to recognize each other.

"In the name of God, as I am called Faith, I shall live to witness thy reunion. . ." The clear words penetrated Mora's mind. She closed her eyes and willed the memory to awaken. When she opened her eyes, Hope and Teresa were looking at her. Chills spread throughout Mora's neck, throat and around her ears, shooting up the back of her head and out her crown. Instinctively, she extended her free hand to Hope, who took it and offered her other hand to Teresa. For a single, electrifying moment, the three women were joined.

"I guess I'd better let you two get started." Hope said, releasing her hands. She shook her head and shoulders again, this time wearing a radiant smile. "It was a pleasure to meet you, Teresa. You're in good hands now." Hope nodded and winked at Mora. "Later, sister Mora," she said, and left.

"Teresa, I have a present for you up in the massage room."

Teresa tried to focus on Mora's bright, clear face to comprehend. "Wuh? You shun do tha." She shook her head unsteadily.

"Let's go see." Mora helped Teresa up the stairs. In the room, she reached on top of the shelf. "I made this for you from the flowers in my garden," she said, and showed Teresa the floral crown. "You can put it on if you want to."

Teresa's eyes focused wide open as she touched it. "Oh. . . iss boouful," she said and looked up at Mora through tearful eyes.

"Just like you." Mora smiled and her own eyes filled with tears. "Would you like to stand in front of the mirror over there and see how you look in it?"

Leaning on Mora, Teresa slowly approached the full-length mirror. She looked into it and turned away as soon as she saw herself — just as Mora had when she first glimpsed herself in the hospital mirror!

Mora stood beside Teresa, holding the wreath. "May I put it on you?" she asked.

"Ya." Teresa nodded unsteadily.

Mora lifted the wreath over Teresa's head and said: "You are a beautiful, blossoming young woman. You're just like a flower with a strong, growing, green, life-filled stem. And you are wise because you know best which way to grow. This wreath is filled with love from the flowers, the earth, from God, from the sun, and from me." Mora's voice cracked and she continued. "I crown you Teresa, Ruler of your own Life." She rested the wreath upon Teresa's head.

Teresa beheld her own reflection, her head adorned with nature's priceless jewels. She recognized herself after a long time away and tears spilled from eyes that could *see* herself once more. She turned to Mora, sobbed, and let herself receive the loving embrace.

Mora cried too. She inhaled the flowers' deep fragrance and easily let the voice take her back. . .

to the memory of a place long ago. . .

"child, I shall always be with thee. . . . My love goes with thee wherever thou goest. Know this for all time."

Inhaling the ancient aromatic memory of hair and flowers, Mora knew that no matter what happened now, her love would accompany the child's voyages forever.

Mora released her gentle hold and stood upright. "How about a massage, young woman?"

Teresa nodded awkwardly and Mora helped her prepare.

Seated on her stool at the head of the table, Mora cradled Teresa's head and felt a stronger current of energy than she ever had before. "Teresa," Mora said from behind closed eyes, "if you want to, you can picture with me, so that we join our minds together and send love into every cell of your being."

Teresa nodded and closed her eyes.

"We don't need to be concerned about doing it right because we *are* doing it right. Love knows where to go. From all around us it's being absorbed right now, especially into your willing brain." As Mora said the words, chills shot up and down her spine, over and over until they held a steady, constant, thrilling circuit. All she could think was *Thank you, God. . . Thank you, God.* When Mora opened her eyes, she saw the unified circle of blue Light encased in gold surround them.

*   *   *

Several weeks passed, during which Teresa was unable to come for massage. One day, doctor Howard called.

"Mora, I spoke with Teresa's neurologist this morning and he gave me some rather startling news. Do you have a minute to chat?" The uncharacteristic tentativeness in his voice alarmed Mora.

"Oh yes, of course!"

"It seems that her most recent CAT scan, of last week in fact, indicates that the tumor has shrunk in size to less than half of what it was just a month ago."

Stone silence reverberated across the miles.

"Oh! Did he say what he thinks happened? Did anything change?" Mora asked, already knowing the truth.

"No, nothing in her treatments or therapies seems to have changed. Nothing changed, yet the tumor is rapidly disappearing! Her coordination is returning, her speech is back completely. At this rate, he expects it'll be completely gone within a couple of weeks!"

In the silent space over the wires, Mora gathered her thoughts into a single idea. "Doctor Howard, I think I know what changed."

"What?"

"Her mind. She changed her mind."

*   *   *

Three weeks later Teresa arrived at Mora's for her last massage. As Mora sat at the kitchen table looking out the window, she watched Teresa, unattended, bound up the walk singing and swinging her arms gleefully.

Mora knew then that they had, each in her own way and for her own needs, resealed the endless circle of love they shared. Teresa was free to live the rest of her life as she chose, and Mora would hold the treasure dear to her heart forever.

- 22 -

Mora's life leaped forward over the next few years. What had seemed like a death for Fitness & More burst forth into new buds of prosperity in her private massage practice. She adapted techniques to fit her body's ability, and anything her physical strength lacked was provided by her spiritual strength.

Her friendship with Eric deepened, but knowing there was work for her to do before she could honestly share love with a man, Mora focused on rebuilding her foundation. It was during a rolfing session that she brought forth the memories of two teenage rapes that had been stored away in the deep, contracted caverns of her hips.

In both instances, her gut feelings had warned Mora she was in danger. But she had been too frightened of the potential violence to fight off her agressors. Instead, she "checked out," dissociating herself from her body during the rapes. Only now was she able to experience the emotional pain that had been patiently stored in her body for years. Only now could she begin to feel compassion for the innocent teenager who still lived inside her. Heaven's love had shown her she was never judged. At last she was ready to let her own forgiveness enter.

In her peers she found hopeful support. "Go through to get out" was the philosophy of the day among advocates of self-healing. Over and over again, Mora saw it proved true with courageous clients as she watched their physical contractions relax and transform into original form beneath her touch.

On their final session together, the rolfer asked Mora to stand and put her feet as close together as she could. Her knees knocked and her feet were five inches apart. The rolfer scanned Mora's body, saw that her hips were out of joint, and had her get back on the table. Working only on Mora's jaw, she brought forth intense emotions and complete realignment of the hips. When Mora got off the table, she could put her feet together! Looking down at her newly aligned body Mora told the rolfer, "You worked a miracle on me." To which the rolfer replied, "Hey, I just work here."

That humble response inspired Mora to write a poem about body workers:

"I JUST WORK HERE"
Hands of Light cross fields of brain
Pass the prayer through blocks of pain.

This they knew as evermore:
"Breathe, let go" the words explain,
"If you walk with fear an open door,
only dust from fear remains".

Eyes see tangible color and flow
the River of Life runs free and sure;
Flesh feels pain to comfort grow,
these hands: truthful tools of peace secure.

And when at last is each at rest
accepting of time and place,
the prayer is passed then safely nests
in Hands of Light, whose gift is Grace.

The grace that had enfolded Mora in near-death was the same Light she saw in doctor Anwar's eyes and hands, in her rolfer's hands, in Hope's hands, in Eric's, and in her own. Mora felt honored to be part of the hands-on profession. A professional journal published the poem and she hung it in a gold frame in her massage room.

The dream she had had in the hospital, about carrying two suitcases through a busy airport destined for a faraway land, was also realized. A year before the Soviet Union was dissolved, Mora and Ellen visited Russia and the Ukraine with a U.S. peace group. Mora attended a recovering alcoholics meeting in Moscow. No one spoke English and Mora spoke no Russian, but the language of the heart was unmistakable. During the meeting, Mora flashed on a mental picture of a day in 1960 when she was in grade school. The school alarm had called the children to file out into the hallway, crouch down on the floor, and cover their heads. It was air raid practice, and "the enemy" she had been taught to fear now surrounded her in the Moscow recovering alcoholics meeting room. She saw with the eyes of her own heart that the Russian people had been her brothers and sisters all along.

On the last day of their trip, Mora and Ellen were in the Ukranian capital of Kiev, staying in a hotel across the street from the Ukranian Legislative building. Awakened by the sounds of loud-speaker voices and a cheering crowd, they quickly threw on their clothes and ran down to the street to see what the excitement was about. Several hundred people, many carrying blue and yellow Ukranian flags, were gathered in the courtyard, listening intently to the loudspeaker voice. Just as Mora and Ellen began searching for someone who spoke English, a tremendous wave of cheers broke forth from the crowd. Old men in soldiers uniforms cried and embraced each other; women cried and laughed and embraced everyone; children ran through the crowds gleefully waving the bright, proud flags; young soldiers originally installed as guards smiled and clapped and shook hands with anyone and everyone, including Ellen and Mora.

Finally finding a man who spoke English, Mora shouted above the jubilant din. "What happened?"

"The Ukranian Legislature has just unanimously voted to secede from the Soviet Union!" The man shouted back as he wiped his tears. "We are now the Independent State of Ukraine!"

Mora and Ellen were thrilled to be right in the middle of the realization of a bright historical beginning.

*   *   *

The following year Mora and Ellen traveled to Ireland, a land

where a unified freedom was still a distant dream. Mora loved the
people, her people. . . their sense of humor, the creativity they
expressed in poetry, song, music and theater, and their mystical bond
with the land. On their last day, she lay down to rest in a remote field
off the coast of the Irish Sea. Her arms spread wide, resting on a
thick patch of clover, she watched the clouds dance overhead and
absorbed the strength from the auld sod. "I'm home again" she said
as she lay resting on her Mother's green lap. "My family had to
leave your rocky soil in order to survive. But you're in our blood and
we'll be at peace when you're unified and free again."

*   *   *

Back in Massachusetts, Mora scanned the agenda for the 1994
National Massage Therapists Convention in Boston.

"I can't miss this when it's practically in my own backyard,"
she said to Hope over the phone. "You've never been to a National.
It's so powerful, so energizing, to be in a room with thousands of
intuitive massage therapists from all over the country. . . whew! You
have to experience it to get the charge."

"I just got the brochure in the mail and it looks really exciting,"
Hope answered. "Did you see the keynote speaker's blurb?"

"I did, and it's strange," Mora hesitated as she looked over the
brochure in her hand. "Every time I look at her photograph I get
chills. I *know* that I know her but I also know I've never met her
before. Do you know what I mean?"

Hope chuckled and said, "Odd as it may seem, I actually *do*
know what you mean and the reason is I think I've met her before
too, even though I know I never have."

"Hmmm. . . ." Mora's mind gears cranked.

"'hmmm' is right."

*   *   *

At the opening ceremonies of the convention, Hope and Mora
sat in the full auditorium abuzz with soft chatter. Everyone quieted
down when the group's president appeared on the stage.

"Welcome to the 1994 National Convention of Massage
Therapists. We are 25 thousand strong, in the United States alone,
and growing stronger every day!" Applause greeted his words.

"And since we're so well know for being on time for appointments," the audience laughed and clapped, "without any further delay, it's time for me to introduce our keynote speaker, doctor Annie Boone." A tremendous swell of applause filled the auditorium and he waited for it to subside. "Doctor Boone carries a briefcase full of academic and experential credentials which would ordinarily belong to several individuals. In 1985 she earned her doctoral degree in physics while serving as a nurse practitioner at the St. Louis Franciscan rehabilitation hospital. Then in 1990 her career and entire life took a drastic turn. While attending a conference right here in Boston, she was involved in a car crash in which she had what's commonly referred to as an NDE or 'near-death experience.' She returned from the other side with a broken neck."

Mora and Hope looked at each other, their eyes opening wide. Mora's body shot through with chills at the same moment Hope pointed to her own gooseflesh.

"Without surgical intervention, doctor Boone made use of various healing modalities and completely repaired her neck. She became a massage therapist and polarity practitioner, received her doctoral degree in Network chiropractic this year, and is currently pursuing her doctoral degree in Neurological Intuitive Cognition Energetics. . .whew!" The audience laughed as the speaker paused to facetiously wipe perspiration from his forehead. "She is with us today on a cross-country tour to promote her recently published book, 'Happily Ever After: the Healing Power of Forgiveness.' It is with great pleasure that I bring you doctor Annie Boone!"

The audience stood and applauded as a strikingly beautiful, tall, slender woman with long silver hair and bright blue eyes walked onstage. Her warm, calm smile spoke of familiarity with audiences of equals. She raised her hands and joined in the applause, saying into the microphone, "We all deserve praise. Thank you for your caring hands and hearts." She nodded and smiled until everyone was seated.

"For those of you familiar with the ancient enneagram system of soul-path typology, I'll say that whenever I'm introduced through my credentials I always want to pipe in with 'It's because I'm a seven

that I want more of everything!' I just have a lot to do before I'm finished!" She laughed along with the audience.

"I have a question for you." Annie removed the microphone
from its stand and gracefully moved to the edge of the stage, her
long, violet silk dress flowing gently around her. "How old are you?"
She smiled and looked around the auditorium. "I don't mean how
old is your body, I mean how old are *you?*" She scanned the auditorium for recognition and as the audience answered with chuckles and
nods, she chuckled and nodded too. "We understand each other
then. I believe it's because the truth is, we share only one mind. I am
no different from you. We all contain the same original light information. And would you say that our hands-on work is not so much
about *doing* but rather, *undoing?*" Many nods answered her question.

"I'd like to invite you to join me on a little trip into your deepest mind right now." The house lights dimmed and were replaced by
a flood of deep indigo blue light. The sound of ocean waves gradually swept over the rows. "If you'll gently close your eyes. . . gently
close your eyes. . . just breathe and *r e l a x. . . .*"

Mora followed her intrinsic connectedness with the speaker
and began to feel she was riding the crest of a tremendous wave.

"Imagine right now that we're traveling low and deep, into the
deepest darkest recesses of your ancient mind. Except now, you
occupy a different physical form. Now you are a tree. A very, very,
very old tree. Whatever kind of tree you are suits you perfectly."

Mora's thoughts bubbled. *I can't believe this! One idea after another. She's had the same thoughts I have!* Every once in a while she opened
her eyes to watch Annie.

"You're an ancient tree with many, many age rings. They go
around and around, and they speak of your resonance with perfection in every way as you follow cycles of growth and dormancy,
growth and dormancy, always adapting to life."

After two or three slowly delivered thoughts, she'd pause to
ride out a deep breath in rhythm with the sound of a crashing ocean
wave.

"And now look. Can you see? On your outer bark you have a
knot, a funny shaped lump that, when you use your intuitive eyes to

see underneath it, you find another similarly shaped knot in the next-innermost age ring. And then look! At the same place, in the next innermost age ring, there's a similar impression of the same knot.

"Now you begin to look at all your age rings and you find that each one shows the original knot's impression with slightly different variations upon each ring cycle. Can you see that? Okay. Now, hold onto my dress tail and follow me down. We're going to swim deeper into the ocean of 'what if.'"

The sound of a crashing wave escorted Annie's light steps from one side of the stage to the center. "What if you, as a tree, understood that each of your age rings represented a full cycle of growth and dormancy. In other words, a lifetime. Each age ring represents the records of a round-trip voyage in the vehicle called your body." She paused and breathed along with the sound of a gathering swell. "Now, what if that knot were merely a contraction against love in that lifetime. Nothing really serious in the big picture. Just a defense reaction. You might call it a wound to your will or a mistake, a hurt to your heart. Whatever you call it, it's a contraction against love.

"What if, in each lifetime, as shown by each of your age rings, your wise soul brought forth similar circumstances and events around your knot, around your contraction against love, for the purpose of giving you another chance at *going through it*?" She paused to let her words soak into the atmosphere. "And what if, by going through it, by providing the good nourishments you need, by feeling the previously unexpressed feelings and re-sealing the fibers with the nutrient of forgiveness. . .what if the knot were to miraculously soften? Might there no longer be a knot but a smooth continuity in the newest age ring?"

Mora marveled at the similarity of her own thoughts.

"You are a tree. And a tree is a part of nature. Nature dwells in circles. What goes around, comes around. What you give, you receive. Cells are round, your age rings are round, the earth is round, muscles wrap around bones. Around and around we go, where will we stop? Does anyone know?" She breathed in tandem with a cresting, crashing wave and continued.

"Is death merely a transitional phase? Does who we really are go on and on? And do we bring our knots with us until we free ourselves of the bondage of our own contractions against love? The word 'knot'. It also means 'no', does it not? When it appears in us trees, maybe what we're doing is saying 'no' to love. And maybe the cure lies in undoing the contraction by saying 'yes' to love.

"Now we're going to slowly bring you back to awareness of the present moment. Slowly, become aware of yourself returning to the room. Take your time. And whenever you're ready, you can open your eyes."

Replacing the microphone in its stand, Annie stepped out to the edge of the stage. In a strong and clear voice she spoke: "I'd like to close with a poem I wrote not long after I got back on my feet four years ago. I'll accompany the poem with a hand-dance interpretation in American Sign Language." In a strong, clear, melodic voice she recited, signing with her entire being.

"WELCOME EVERYONE, ESPECIALLY MYSELF

Tree that I am with worth rooted strong
in spring sheds old wood while budding new growth.
This season of rebirth in a world where I belong
shows me there's room for both.

As each leaf and limb welcomes water and sun
the tree that I am hums a hymn of perfection.
So it is I recall we are ALL part of the ONE
my branches spread love in every direction.

Thank You!"

Cheering applause resounded throughout the auditorium as virtually everyone arose from their seats. Annie returned the applause and spoke into the microphone: "Thank you! We're all in this together!"

*   *   *

"Wow," Mora said. "I think I just blew a fuse." She turned to face Hope beside her.

"Pretty powerful." Hope looked into Mora's big eyes. "Now I *know* that I know that woman. But I still don't know from whence or wherefore."

Mora nodded. "It'll come." She looked around the almost-empty auditorium, then turned back to face Hope. "I've got to talk to her. I've got to find out." Her eyes seared through Hope. "I have to talk to her now." She jumped out of her seat, grabbed her purse, and headed down the aisle. "I'll meet you at the hospitality booth at noon."

*   *   *

"Hello, is this doctor Boone?" Mora called from a house phone in the lobby.

"Yes?"

"I hope I'm not disturbing you but I was in the audience just now and I just *have* to talk to you." Mora spoke fast. "My name's Mora Donovan and I broke my neck and was paralyzed in a car crash outside of Boston the same year you were, and. . .oh, there's so much I want to ask you. And tell you if you want to know. I think we have some connection together and I *really* want to meet you. Is there any way we can meet?"

"Sounds pretty interesting." Annie spoke evenly. "Maybe we *should* get together. Tell you what. Where are you staying?"

"I live an hour's drive outside Boston." Mora's heart raced with excitement.

"My husband and I are staying with friends in Lexington over the weekend. Maybe you can meet me out there."

"How's Saturday evening?"

"Perfect! I'll give you directions and we'll meet. What did you say your name was again?"

"Mora. Mora Donovan."

"Your voice feels extremely familiar. There's something. . ." Annie picked up the intriguing thread of fate. "Have we spoken before?"

"I guess we'll find out tomorrow!" Mora got her pen and paper ready. "Okay, I'm ready for directions."

*   *   *

Although thoroughly energized by events of the day, by the time Mora's head hit the pillow at midnight, she instantly conked out. Enthusiasm awakened her just before sunrise and she vibrated during her meditation. The only cure for her immense supply of spirit fire came through a run.

Panting to the rhythm, panting to the rhythm of legs leaping high. Through the empty streets, soars a memory bittersweet. Dear Annie Boone in a time gone by. . .

Thirteen women gathered in a circle. . .

"Blessed Be, Blessed Be, Blessed Be". . .

The sound of horses' hooves pounds the earth beneath them.

"Abby! Hattie, they come for thee now!"

Riding fiercely against dark night's wind and rain. . .their long capes slapping wet behind them. . . Hattie falls. . .

"GO ABBY! Leave me! I accept my end here. Save thine own precious life!" The clear bright blue eyes look into the deep well of eternal bond seen in her companion's green-brown eyes.

"NO! I stay with thee my beloved friend! We shall accept our fate together. . .

> *accept our fate together. . .*
>
> > *together. . . ."*

Energy so strong, fierce bolts of electrical confirmation surged up and down Mora's spinal circuits, so strong and forceful it could not be contained. . .

"AGGGHHHH!!" Mora shouted as she ran. "HATTIE! I FOUND YOU!"

*   *   *

On Saturday, Mora drove up to a secluded, hilltop home nestled on the edge of a wildlife sanctuary in Lexington. Glorious, billowy, charcoal and silver storm clouds were fast moving in on the warm August evening.

Every year since her crash Mora noted a high energy charge in the air several days before the August 18th anniversary. And it was so on this day.

She walked up the long path leading to the sprawling, contemporary home. Through the large glass panels on the front and back walls of the house, Mora could see the panoramic sky build power. Her body trembled with excitement as she rang the doorbell. Booming thunder rumbled nearby.

The doorknob turned from the inside and the door opened to Annie Boone. Caught in a single, silent split-second between time, the soul in the bright blue eyes looked straight into the soul in the bright green-brown eyes.

"HATTIE! It's me, ABBY! Do you remember me?" Mora said.

A bolt of clear, bright, silver-blue lightening flash-split the sky far above Annie's head, and just as quickly, thunder's crash rumbled the unshakable earth beneath them.

Opening her arms wide, Annie embraced Mora as tears streamed down her cheeks. "I've waited so long, hoping we would meet again. At last."

The two forever-friends held fast.

*   *   *

They talked long into the night. After everyone else in the world had gone to bed, they forged ahead, filling in blank spaces. There were ways of understanding which needed no explaining, as if their friendship had never ceased. They followed threads of common interest throughout their lives, and found uncannily similar motivations and choices. Their natural abilities in healing arts and expanded sight added credence to the possibility they had entered this life with some of the knowledge already intact.

Mora and Annie discovered that they had crossed paths more than once in their current lives. They had attended the same professional seminars across the country. But the most strikingly serendipitous crossing was in 1959. It seemed they had both lived in the same small town in New Jersey, attended the same Catholic kindergarten, and had even been in the same class. Later, when Mora showed Annie her kindergarten class picture, Annie pointed to the girl seated behind Mora and said, "That's me."

As dawn approached, Annie asked,"What about the other women? Have you known them this time?"

Mora nodded. "Yes, some. . .maybe all. I'm not exactly sure. How about you?"

Annie shook her head thoughtfully. "Not yet. I feel in my bones that everyone will meet here." Annie smiled and sighed. "This place, this land holds a part of my spirit that I can't break. I keep coming back to Salem, and driving up the Old Postal Road into Duffin, and stopping at the Cross Junction. I park at Breakneck Hill Road and I just sit in the grass and stare at the granite road marker: Boston 100 miles East. Whitelaw 15 miles West."

Mora nodded. "Every time I drive by I feel magnetized to it. I pray all the way through the intersection, but like you, the charge is still there, unfinished." After a moment's thought, Mora added, "My best friend Hope. She was there, I'm sure of it, even though she's uncertain about the idea of reincarnation. Maybe that doesn't really matter. Maybe making peace in our soul is where we're headed no matter what beliefs we profess."

Annie nodded. "If there is really just one continuous life, as you and I both experienced, then each one of us being able to forgive and remember love must be possible, no matter how long it takes to get there."

*   *   *

Annie and Mora agreed: the voice of fate was steering them to follow the divinely set path before them.

Weeks earlier Mora had decided to hold a "Celebration of Life" gathering at her home for a group of her women friends who, she felt, just had to meet each other. The day set for the gathering of sisters was the day after Mora and Annie's reunion.

It was a blessed time of coming together for many things, healing many rings in the circle of trees. The morning was soft, light, and sweetly annointed with the essence of late summer wildflowers. The dewy, green grass upon which they stood brought the fertile aroma of earth's soulful soil to their spirits. Thirteen women formed a circle in the broad private space of Mora's treebound yard. Carrying a woven basket filled with strands of different colored satin ribbons, Mora took her place in the circle and spoke.

"Thank you for coming together today. If you all agree, I'd like to set our intention now upon love, for the greater good of all." Scanning the circle, Mora accepted the nods as unanimous agreement. "I have a basket of ribbons and what I'd like to do is this: each of us in turn will take a ribbon from the basket and tell the others who we are and what we are about in the world. Then if you wish, speak your prayer for yourself, your family, the community or the world, and pass the basket onto the woman to your left, tying your ribbon to your sister's on your right. Our prayers will be growing in strength of purpose as we go around. Finally, when all our ribbons are joined, we'll hold the circle up to the heavens with One Mind. How does that sound?" Mora looked around the circle and received every woman's pleased consent.

Choosing a raspberry red ribbon, Mora began. "I'm Mora Donovan, I'm a massage therapist and I thank God for my renewed life, and for all the lives I touch with love. I pray that belief in defense and attack will dissolve, in favor of free will and forgiveness." Mora passed the ribbon basket to Annie.

Choosing a violet ribbon, Annie said, "I'm Annie Boone, I'm a wife, a mother, and an assistant to God in healing people's lives. I pray that every soul is instilled with the courage to walk through their wounds, ancient and recent, until they know they've already been forgiven." She handed the basket leftward.

"My name is Teresa. I'm a teenager." Everyone laughed and she continued. "I'm so happy to be alive and I thank you, Mora, for helping me. I pray that I'll live to be an old lady." Taking a navy-blue ribbon, Teresa tied it to Annie's ribbon.

"I'm Hope and this feels very familiar to me. I used to be an electronics design engineer but now I'm a massage therapist and my prayer is that all people will find strength in their own defenselessness."

"I'm Vivian and I'm a midwife and a nurse, and this feels very familiar to me too. I pray that each person find the peace of God they seek inside their own heart."

Mary was next, a wife, mother, and psychotherapist, followed by Debra, a wife, cook and psychic healer; Laura, an occupational therapist, massage therapist and wife; Lynne, a wife and an accountant; Cathy, a wife and mother, geologist, musician and massage therapist; followed by the rest, until the last woman.

"My name is Bridgit McGrath and I'm an engineer for Teknet in Dublin, Ireland." She spoke with a melodic brogue. "I'm here temporarily only but I feel a very strong kinship with each of you. I would like to ask God or the Goddess or however you so choose to name the source of life, to return the people of Ireland to the sovereign unity we had centuries ago. And I'd like to recite an ancient Druid prayer if I might, in Gaelic. It was a prayer oft used by women of the Isle centuries ago, when they gathered just as we are today, to pray for the repair of their community. It's been quietly passed down from mother to daughter for generations in my family. I guess the truth never dies, don't y'think." Bridgit scanned the circle of nodding heads and smiling faces before continuing."This is the prayer:

Go bhfaighimid neart an cruthu o brollach ar mhathair
thorthuil agus go mbeimid cosuil leis an cailis
an soitheach a d'iomparodh cumhacht do gra cneasu.

"What it means is this:
May we draw from the bosom of our fruitful Mother,
the life force of creation, that we may be as the chalice,
a vessel to carry the power of thy healing love."

Bridgit connected the last tie of emerald green onto the chain of ribbons. The thirteen women stood silent and still for a long moment. Then, as they raised the rainbow cord, high up to the heavens, they saw the swirling surge of pink light rising from the ground, lifting the strong and gentle arms that held their prayers together. All watched as the ribbon was enclosed in a cord of blue light and the sky reached down and bestowed its golden blessing on The BLUE CORD.

*   *   *

The last link in the chain. . . .

When Mora shared her idea with Annie, they laughed in gleeful agreement to carry it out the next day.

Mora baked a big batch of oatmeal-coconut-raisin-walnut-chocolate chip cookies and ironed her favorite, flair-skirted, pink-and-white checked dress. She called the Duffin fire chief to make the arrangements, and all was ready.

Annie and Mora walked across the field. Soft golden light fil-tered through the tall grass surrounding Cedar Pond where the twelve firemen, good and true, practiced underwater rescue. Steam arose from warm bodies sealed in scuba skins as they re-entered the earth's atmosphere from the deep. Thick summer morning air was already crossing the cool-to-hot-and-humid threshold familiar to these Massachusetts men of many generations. Some stood on shore, their arms crossed, curious to know the women's intentions.

"Chief Arnold?" Annie smiled and extended her right hand.

"Yes. You must be Anne Boone." He shook her hand, then looked to Mora. "And I remember you, Mora." Releasing Annie's hand he extended his hand for Mora to shake. "I haven't told the men, just as you asked. Are you ready now?"

"Are we ever!" Annie answered as she and Mora nodded with energetic pleasure.

Chief Arnold stepped to the edge of the pond. "Men, I'd like your attention please. Those of you in the water, if you'd come out for just a moment. We have a couple of visitors you might be very interested in meeting." He waited until all twelve men were out of the water.

"These two ladies here, if you remember, were each involved in car wrecks out here at Breakneck Hill Road back in 1990. All you men were on the team then, so they have something to tell you." He turned to Annie and Mora and nodded. "Okay ladies, they're all yours."

Annie began. "I broke my neck in that crash and you, the Duffin, Massachusetts fire department EMTs, rescued me. Without damaging my body further, you carefully took me home, even though you disapproved. What I wanted was different from what you were accustomed to doing, and you honored my choice. With the help of many friends and through the power of Love, I'm now completely free of any physical limitation. I came here today for many reasons, but the most important one is. . ." Annie's voice cracked and she cleared her throat, "I want to thank you for saving my life." Annie joined her hands together in front of her heart and bowed to the men. Mora stepped forward.

"I want to thank you for saving my life, too." Mora laid out her clear petal voice like a magic carpet set with gifts. "If it weren't for your conscientious care in moving my body, I might not have recovered as well as I have. I'm a massage therapist again. I help people with these hands, and I wouldn't be able to if you hadn't helped me as you did."

She opened the bag of cookies. "I made these cookies for you with my own two hands. My hands are connected to my heart and I wanted to give you a gift from my heart. They're made with a lot of love. I want to give each of you a cookie and shake your hand. We both want to shake your hands."

"Nobody's ever come forward to us like this before." Chief Arnold said shyly. "My men and I really appreciate it."

One by one, each man received a cookie from Mora and shook the women's hands. And when all was complete, the cord of bright blue Light encased in gold descended from above, encircling and rejoining them with the heavens.

Afterword

Mora Donovan's death on Breakneck Hill Road and her return to a paralyzed body and broken neck, as portrayed in Chapter 1, are completely true experiences taken from my life. The character of Mora resembles me, yet she is more. In Gaelic, Mora means Mary, and I see Mary as the universal feminine living inside every human being.

The members of the Donovan family, doctor Anwar, Hope Lester, Kathleen, Yvette and Corky, Carlos and Florinda, Eric, Teresa, and Annie Boone are fictionalized characters based loosely on real people. In order to ensure their privacy, their names, circumstances, and other identifying details have been changed. All other characters, events, and locations are products of my imagination, and any resemblance to actual persons, living or dead, events, or locales is entirely coincidental.

At the moment of my death I rediscovered many truths, the main one being that God and Love are identical. Love is unlimited; it has already forgiven all things; and there is actually nothing to forgive. Many of our cherished beliefs, such as punishment for "sins" through withdrawal of Love, fear of God, and death as a final ending, are actually irrelevant to God. I believe that we all carry God's truth inside but many of us, myself included, forget what it is from time to time.

I (my conscious mind/spirit) was present for the transition phase called death, and completely free to choose to proceed or return. I thought, "Hey, now that I see Love's unlimited power, overcoming a paralyzed body is easy. Okay, I'll go back to my life. I still have a lot to accomplish as Laurel. I'll simply bring this knowledge back with me and apply it to everything on earth."

Life has been far from easy, yet I know my life was blessed with a miraculous book mark that contained the simple seed for all the enduring value I find in this strange, gravity-bound world. And though that experience lasted for only a moment, as time goes by I find it is the single moment to which I compare everything that happens to me. Those experiences that resemble it, I treasure. Those that don't, I endeavor to release.

What ensued upon my return to life turned out to be a very "big deal" after all; terrifying, dramatic, and miraculous. During my recovery, I created many projections of resistance to Love, engaged in inner battles, and put a lot of energy into releasing the accompanying static or emotions. Now I am convinced that prayer and meditation, emotional release, hopeful visualization, and loving touch play major roles in my soul's ongoing recovery, while my body seems to follow along. I believe that anything is possible and there truly is no order of difficulty in miracles. I also believe it is up to each of us to decide how deep and how far we take our personal healing. This is a private matter between the individual soul and Love's Source within.

Modern physics provides us with abundant evidence that *what* we observe is affected by our observation. Collections of matter in all forms, including physical dysfunction and personal relationships, have the capacity to change according to how we choose to observe them. For example, walls of resistance reflected outside me may appear very real, yet when I imagine them as projected images of my own blocks to love, it's easier to trace their threads down to a core contraction remembered in my soul. If I stay with it and experience the energy attached to the contraction, it eventually breaks up, and I am free to love again. I see emotion as energy and motion, or moving energy. Over and over again, I have seen an individual's collections of energy (matter) literally move when the emotion is experienced. This was an essential part of Mora Donovan's healing process.

Regarding Mora's past-life flashback as a Salem healer accused of witchcraft, I pose two questions: Is reincarnation fact or fiction? Do we really live more than one lifetime? I believe that I am much more than the plastic projection of pluffy plasma called my body. In death/heaven, I knew everything. The real me is my eternal soul, which merely takes up temporary residence in various vehicles. Maybe my body is like a car; when my engine burns out, I can either trade it in for a newer model or use the valuable parts to rebuild my engine, as Mora did. Maybe that's the real meaning of "car-ma."

Whatever your beliefs, I hope that you will feel supported and encouraged by The BLUE CORD. In the worst of times as well as the best of times, it's Love that will carry you if you will let it.

My name is Laurel and I'm a recovering human being.

-LD, Summer 1995

About the Author

Laurel Duran grew up in New York, New Jersey, Florida, and Massachusetts, and is still growing up in New Mexico. After surviving a Catholic school education, she graduated from the University of Florida and the Bancroft School of Massage Therapy, in Worcester, Massachusetts. Laurel has practiced therapeutic massage in Massachusetts and New Mexico since 1979. She also conducts and performs in audience-interactive lectures. For more information, please contact DuirSoul Books, P.O. Box 22596, Santa Fe, NM 87502-2596.

ORDER FORM

* Fax orders: (505) GET-1-VEG or (505)438-1834
* Telephone orders: Call Toll Free: 1 (800) OAK-SOUL or
    1-800-625-7685. Please have your MasterCard / VISA ready.
    Locally, call (505) 438-1834
* Postal Orders: DuirSoul Books, P.O. Box 22596, Santa Fe, NM
    87502-2596, USA   Tel: (505) 438-1834 or (505) GET-1-VEG

PLEASE SEND _____copies of The BLUE CORD @ $13.95 per copy to:

Name: _____

Address: _____

City: _____ State: _____ Zip: _____

Telephone: (_____)_____

Sales tax:
Please add 6.24% for books shipped to New Mexico addresses.

Shipping:
Book Rate: $2.00 for the first book and 75 cents for each additional book
(Surface shipping may take three to four weeks)
Air Mail: $3.50 per book

Payment:
( ) Check enclosed
( ) Credit Card: ( ) MasterCard   ( ) VISA

Card number: _____

Name on card: _____ exp. date:_____

Call *toll free* and order *NOW!*